"Sexual attra... mediate..."

"It's about a man and... ...ng his fingers along the line of Hailey's jaw. "The feel of her skin, the way she smells." His voice dropped to a near whisper. "The way she tastes."

And he closed the short distance between them and put his mouth on hers.

Nothing could have prepared Hailey for the lust that punched through her system. A light, teasing kiss turned hungry and hot in a nanosecond. She made a little moaning sound in the back of her throat as she reached for him, wanting to feel the solid outline of his chest. His tongue teased and tormented her. She'd never been kissed like this. Never imagined anything close to this.

He kissed her for seven eternities, taking his time, not trying to rip off her clothes or talk her into his bed, but kissing her as though his whole existence depended on nothing but this moment.

Getting involved with Rob wasn't on her agenda, but she knew that she'd been seriously compromised.

When he pulled slowly away from her, he grinned at her wryly.

"You can't get *that* on the internet..."

Dear Reader,

I confess, I love those real estate shows on television. I love the ones where we follow a couple as they try to pick the perfect home, I love the ones where decorators turn disasters into showplaces. I even love looking at real estate listings in cities where I know I will never live.

I suspect I'm not alone, given the popularity of real estate shows on TV, the constant talk about where the market is and where it's going. I think the fun is in the fantasy that that home could be yours. That couple squabbling over an extra bedroom versus a bigger yard could be you. So I set out to write a book where a Realtor falls in love, not only with the home she's listed, but most inconveniently, with the guy who is selling it. And in particular with one big, beautiful four-poster bed in the master bedroom.

I hope you enjoy Hailey and Rob's story, and get a little vicarious pleasure out of the story of how the wrong man in the wrong bed turns out to be exactly the right man in the right bed.

I love hearing from readers. Visit me on the web at www.nancywarren.net.

Happy reading,

Nancy Warren

JUST ONE NIGHT

BY
NANCY WARREN

First published in Great Britain 2012
by Mills & Boon, an imprint of Harlequin (UK) Limited,
Eton House, 18-24 Paradise Road, Richmond, Surrey TW9 1SR

© Nancy Warren 2012

ISBN: 978 0 263 89391 5
ebook ISBN: 978 1 408 96942 7

14-1112

Harlequin (UK) policy is to use papers that are natural, renewable and recyclable products and made from wood grown in sustainable forests. The logging and manufacturing processes conform to the legal environmental regulations of the country of origin.

Printed and bound in Spain
by Blackprint CPI, Barcelona

USA TODAY bestselling author **Nancy Warren** lives in the Pacific Northwest where her hobbies include skiing, hiking and snowshoeing. She's an author of more than thirty novels and novellas for Mills & Boon and has won numerous awards. Visit her website at www.nancywarren.net.

To Sally, the best stager I know!

1

"SICK LEAVE?" Rob Klassen yelled, unable to believe what he was hearing from the editor of *World Week,* the international current affairs magazine he'd worked for as a photojournalist for twelve years. "I'm not sick!"

Gary Wallanger pulled off his glasses and tossed them onto his desktop cluttered with Rob's proof sheets documenting a skirmish in a small town near the Ras Ajdir border between Tunisia and Libya. "What do you suggest I call it? Shot-in-the-ass leave? You damned near got yourself killed. Again."

Gary didn't like his people getting too close to the action they were reporting on and his glare was fierce.

Rob put all his weight on his good leg, but even so, the throbbing in his left thigh was hard to ignore. "I was running away as fast as I could."

"I saw the hospital report. You were running toward the shooter. Bad luck for you. They can tell those things from the entry and exit wounds." In the uncomfortable silence that followed Rob heard the roar of traffic, honking cabs and sirens on the Manhattan streets far below. He hadn't counted on Gary finding out the details he'd have rather kept to himself.

"You want to be a war hero," his editor snapped, "join the forces. We report news. We don't make it."

Another beat ticked by.

"There were bullets flying everywhere. I got disoriented."

"Bull. You were playing hero again, weren't you?"

Rob could still picture the toddler cowering behind an oil drum. Yeah, his boss would have been happier if he'd left her scared and crying in the line of gunfire. But he was the one who had to wake up every morning and look himself in the mirror. Truth was he hadn't thought at all. He'd merely dashed over to the girl and hauled her to safety. Getting shot hadn't been in his plan.

Would he have acted any differently if he'd known what the outcome would be? He sure as hell hoped not.

He knew better than to tell Gary any of that. "You don't win Pulitzers with a telephoto lens. I needed to get close enough to capture the real story."

"Close enough to take a bullet in the leg."

"That was unfortunate," Rob admitted. "I can still handle a camera though. I can still walk." He made a big show of stalking across the carpeted office, scooting around the obstacle course of stacked back issues, piled newspapers and a leaning tower of reference books. If he concentrated he could manage to stride without a limp or a wince though he could feel sweat begin to break out from the effort.

"No." The single word stopped him in his tracks.

He turned. "I'm the best you've got. You *have* to send me back out on assignment."

"I will. As soon as you can run a mile in six."

"A mile in six minutes? Why so fast?"

Gary's voice was as dry as the North African desert. "So the next time you have to run for your life you can make it."

Rob paused for breath and grabbed a chair back for support. He and Gary had been friends for a long time and he knew the guy was making the right decision even if it did piss him off. "It was pure bad luck. If I'd dodged right instead of left…"

"You know most people would be pretty happy to be alive if they were you. And they'd be thrilled to get a paid vacation." Gary picked up his glasses and settled himself behind his desk.

"They patched me up at the closest military hospital. It was nothing but a flesh wound."

"The bullet nicked your femur. I do know how to read a hospital report."

Damn.

"Go home. Rest up. The world will continue to be full of trouble when you get back." Rob knew Gary was still aggravated by the fact that he didn't compliment him on his photos, which they both knew to be superb. Instead of getting the praise he deserved, he was being sent home like a kid who'd screwed up.

He scowled.

Home.

He'd been on the road so much in the past few years that home was usually wherever he stashed his backpack.

If he'd ever had a home, it was in Fremont, Washington, a suburb of Seattle that prided itself on celebrating counterculture, considering itself the center of the universe and officially endorsing the right to be peculiar. Fremont seemed a fitting destination for him right now that he was feeling both self-centered and peculiar. Besides, it was the only place he could think of to go even though everything that had made the place home was now gone.

"All right. But I heal fast. I'll be running six-minute miles in a couple weeks. Tops."

"You'll be under a doctor's care and I'll be needing the physician's report before I can reinstate you for any assignments in the field."

"Oh, come on, Gary. Give me a freakin' break."

Once more the glasses came off and he was regarded by tired hazel eyes. "I *am* giving you a break. I could assign you to a desk right here in New York. That's your other option."

He shook his head. No way he was being trapped in a small space. He didn't like feeling trapped. Not ever. "See you in a couple of weeks."

Once he was out of Gary's office and in the hallway Rob gave up the manly act and tried to put as little weight on his injured leg as possible.

"Rob, you should be on crutches," a female voice called out.

He turned, recognizing the voice and mustering a happy-to-see-you smile. "Romona, hi."

A print business reporter making the transition to television, Romona had the looks of a South American runway model and the brains of Hillary Clinton. They got together whenever they were both in New York. Neither had any interest in commitment but enjoyed each other's company and bodies. "I heard you were hurt. How are you doing?" she asked.

He shrugged. "Okay."

Even though they'd never do anything as obvious as hug in public, the glance she sent him from tilted green eyes steamed around the edges. She dropped her voice. "Why don't you come over later and I'll kiss you all better?"

"I'm filthy. Haven't shaved in days, had a haircut in weeks, my—"

"I like you scruffy. You look like a sunburned pirate."

He knew he'd hit rock bottom when he realized he had no desire to spend the night with a passionate woman. His leg was burning, he had a vicious case of jet lag and he'd been pulled out of the field. He felt too worn-out tired even to get laid. All he wanted to do was hide out for a while and heal.

He shook his head attempting to appear more disappointed than he was. "Sorry. I have a plane to catch."

She knew as well as he did that plane tickets could be changed and it was a measure of his exhaustion that this was the best excuse he could come up with.

She didn't call him on it though, merely patted his arm and said, "Maybe next time."

That was the great thing about Romona. She was a lot like him. He'd enjoyed any number of women over the years, loved sex, but had no interest in settling down. Career came first. Maybe it was shallow, and maybe there was a part of him that longed for a woman to comfort him, to listen to his stories, share his pain. The only woman who'd ever been like that, though, had been his grandmother. Ruefully, he suspected she'd been the love of his life.

And now she was gone.

He had so many frequent flyer miles that upgrading was no problem when he got to LaGuardia. He even scored an aisle seat so he could stretch his bad leg out a little.

Once airborne, he recalled that the family attorney

had tried to talk to him about the Fremont house. What with getting shot and all, he hadn't got around to calling back. He'd call him as soon as he got into Seattle.

It was something to do with Bellamy House, the old family place where he'd spent so much time with his grandmother.

He couldn't imagine the place without her. As a stab of pain hit, he took out the paperback he'd brought and forced himself to read.

HAILEY FLEMING WAS a woman with an agenda. Two in fact. The electronic one that she relied on so heavily that she'd recently started keeping a backup paper day planner because the thought of somehow losing her electronic schedule made her feel too close to losing her mind for comfort.

She was nothing if not organized.

And both agendas told her that she was exactly on time for the best appointment of the day. An after-work glass of wine with a colleague who'd become a close friend, Julia Atkinson.

As she made her way into the bistro off North Phinney Avenue, a former record store turned trendy bar, she scanned the tables and was not surprised to find she was the first to arrive. She was always early.

And Julia was always late.

She settled at a table and ordered a glass of white wine then spent ten minutes going through tomorrow's appointments and writing some notes on improvements she wanted to make on her website.

"Am I late?" a breezy, breathless voice said as Julia swished into her chair, a loose black garment that resembled a combination sweater, poncho and cloak settling in around her.

"Of course you are. You're always late."

Julia's red hair was newly cut into a curly bob and her full lips curved in a smile. "I was at the opening of a new furniture gallery which has brought in several fantastic new lines from Milan. I got chatting, and there were these delicious cookies. I left after three. It was the only way I could stop myself. I don't feel guilty. I bet you did a day's work while you waited."

"Half a day's anyway."

A waiter arrived and Julia ordered a vodka tonic. Which meant she was on another of her diets. Which meant…

"I think I've met someone." She sounded so excited that Hailey leaned forward.

"Tell me everything."

Julia unbuttoned the cloak thing and draped it over the back of her chair, revealing a black-and-red dress enlivened by one of the hundreds of chunky, glitzy vintage necklaces she owned.

"He's an engineer who lives downtown. He was married, but his wife left him and broke his heart."

"Wow. That was fast. I just saw you last week. Where did you meet him?"

Julia's drink came and she took a quick sip. "I haven't actually met him yet."

"Huh?"

She shrugged, and the slight movement made all the rhinestones in her jewelry glitter under the bar's chandeliers. "I met him on LoveMatch.com."

"Oh. Online dating."

"I'd never tried it before, but lots of women meet great guys online. So I figured, why not? It's not like you meet men if you're a home stager." She thought for a second. "At least not straight men."

"How do you already know so much about him?"

"We've been talking on the phone. He's away on business in the Philippines, but I'll be meeting him next Tuesday." Her eyes were bright with excitement. "Do you want to see a picture?"

"Of course."

Julia hauled her computer tablet out of her bag and within a few moments passed over the electronic device complete with a grinning blond guy. Not Hailey's type at all. Too pretty for her tastes, but Julia liked her men pretty. "Wow."

"My big fear is that he's too good-looking for me. Oh, and he has the cutest accent. He was born in Manchester, but he's lived all over the world. An army brat like you."

Hailey regarded the electronic image once more. He was wearing shorts and a loose cotton shirt. Despite the square jaw, he seemed somehow lacking in character. She'd never say so to her friend. Besides, even she knew that her own taste was notoriously picky.

"He's not too good-looking for you. You are beautiful."

"Do you think I can lose ten pounds by Tuesday?"

"Stop it," Hailey said, trying not to laugh. "He's seen your photo, right? He obviously liked what he saw."

Julia nibbled her lower lip. "I used one from after I took that fitness boot camp last year. When I was thinner."

For a smart, self-confident woman, Julia had body-image issues and Hailey knew there was no point arguing. Instead she went with a reassuring "It will be fine."

"I guess. I just have such terrible luck with men." Julia took a last, longing glance at the picture and then put the tablet away. "How are you?"

Hailey let the excitement she'd been feeling all day bubble out. "I have news, too."

Julia's eyes bugged out. "You met a guy?"

"No. I don't have time for men. I'm building a business. Once I feel more successful, then maybe in a couple of years…"

"I know. You and your agendas."

"Lists keep me on track." She sometimes thought she'd had so much chaos in her life that relying on lists gave her a sense of control and stability that she'd never had growing up. Moving twelve times in thirteen years when she was a kid had given her a need for order. Her poor mother had quit even trying to decorate their homes. What was the point? So home had always been temporary and she'd grown to hate the sight of a moving box.

She didn't need psychoanalysis to understand why she'd chosen a career in real estate. She loved helping clients buy permanent homes. The kinds of places where you could plant a sapling and know you'd be around to enjoy the shade of the tree.

"Don't you miss having a man in your life?" Julia lowered her voice. "Don't you miss sex?"

"I have lots of men in my life. Realtors, clients, friends."

One of Julia's eyebrows went up. "And sex?"

"I have sex." Even to her ears she sounded defensive. "Okay, not a lot of sex. It's been a while, but sex for me means commitment. I can't do casual." She shrugged. "Ever since my engagement ended…" She'd believed Drake, who was a lawyer, was perfect for her. They'd worked together on a few closings. They were both hard-working and ambitious. It wasn't until they were talking wedding dates that they'd realized how little their agendas meshed. He wanted to move to New York to a bigger firm. She was building a business in Seattle. He wanted children right away. She felt they should wait a couple of years until the marriage had strong roots. A year ago he'd gone to New York without her. Since then she'd thrown herself into work and hadn't missed Drake as much as she would have imagined.

"He was a moron to pick New York over you."

"Thank you. I agree!"

"So, your big news?"

"I got an amazing listing today. It's my big break. Uncle Ned, an old friend of my father's, called me out of the blue and offered me the Bellamy House."

Julia's eyes widened once more. "That beautiful old place on the hill?"

"Yeah. The woman who owned it died a couple of months ago. Uncle Ned is her executor. There's a grandson and he okayed the sale."

"That's terrific."

"I know." She turned mock serious. "There's just one problem."

Julia grabbed her hand. "It needs staging?"

"Yes! The problem is I need it staged right away. I think I have the perfect buyers. I hate to ask you, but do you think you could stage it tomorrow? I'd love to show them the place Thursday morning."

"Miracles are what I do." Julia morphed from love-addicted friend into professional home stager, tapping at her tablet, then nodding. "Do you have the key to the place?"

"Yes."

"If you can show me the home tonight, I'll figure

out what I need and by tomorrow night, you'll have your miracle."

"I can't wait to show you. This house is going to change everything for us."

2

ROB'S BACKPACK WEIGHED a thousand tons as he hauled it out of the back of the cab. His eyes were dry and gritty and his leg hurt like a son of a bitch. Fog had grounded the plane in Chicago turning a relatively straightforward eight-hour trip into a two-day ordeal. He'd never yet figured out how to sleep on airplanes. Not a real plus for somebody whose job required constant travel.

But he was finally home. Or as close to a home as anything he'd ever known.

As he stood gazing at the big old house, a pang of sadness hit him that was as vicious and intense as his bullet wound.

His grandmother was gone.

He hadn't even made it home for her funeral, her death had occurred so quickly. Not that she'd have wanted him there, but he'd have liked to have been for his own sake. They'd seen each other a few months back when he'd come to visit between assignments. Had she seemed more frail?

Worse, had she known her end was near and not told him?

He shook his head. No.

At eighty-eight his grandmother had impressed him as being mentally as sharp as ever. She'd even chided him to hurry up and get married and give her some great-grandbabies before she got to a hundred. Naturally he'd told her the truth. That he'd never settle until he found somebody like her. Hadn't happened in thirty-five years. He doubted it ever would.

She'd laughed and told him he'd have to set his sights lower. He grinned at the memory. No. His grandmother definitely hadn't planned on dying.

Damn it. He was going to miss that woman.

There were affairs to settle and likely some papers to sign. Right now though all he could think about was a huge glass of Pacific Northwest water, the kind you could drink straight from the tap, a long, hot shower, and sleep.

Long, uninterrupted sleep in a real bed.

As Rob hefted his pack and limped up the path he noted that somebody had swept the front steps recently and even planted blooming bushes in the brick planters.

For early September the night was cool, but to a man who'd spent the past few weeks in the African desert, almost everywhere seemed cool.

He couldn't imagine who would have planted bushes, or why. His brain was way too tired to puzzle out such minor mysteries. Tomorrow. He'd think tomorrow.

As a Realtor, Hailey liked to think of herself as a matchmaker putting the right house together with the right buyer. As of today she had a new unattached single waiting for the right person to fall in love with it—a loft condo downtown that she'd listed this morning, thanks to a referral from a satisfied client. She was new enough to the business that every referral, every listing and especially every sale filled her with pride.

Now she was ready to make another match.

She had a gut instinct that the Bellamy House she was about to show Samantha and Luke MacDonald was going to be a fit. A real-estate marriage made not in heaven but in the offices of Dalbello and Company, where she worked fiendish hours to make her mark in a competitive business.

Like any good matchmaker, she'd prepped carefully, hiring Julia to stage the faded but solid turn-of-the-century Craftsman and bringing in cleaners and a window washer. Hailey had planted cheerfully blooming winter kale and pansies at the entranceway in an effort to keep the buyers' eyes from going immediately to the neglected garden. She wished she had the time and resources to do more, but this was an estate sale.

Everything was as perfect as she could make it. The sun shining on the gleaming diamond-paned windows showed the gracious contours of the home that must have been a real showpiece in its day.

The young couple scheduled to see the place arrived at eleven as scheduled. "I think you're really going to like this one," Hailey said, passing them a feature sheet. "It's just come on the market and I immediately thought of you."

She unlocked the shiny black front door and light spilled into the foyer bringing out the gleam on the newly waxed oak floors. It was amazing what a good cleaning could do to a house. Not that the previous owner hadn't been a good housekeeper; Hailey could tell from the order in the home that she had. Still, in the months since Agnes Neeson had died, the house had been shut up and grown dusty. Today the air smelled not of must as it had the first time she'd viewed it, but of the lilies and roses that Julia had placed in a glass vase on the entranceway table.

Her heels clacked on the original hardwood floors as she pointed out the spacious dimensions of the dining and living areas, the original heritage features such as the hand-carved fireplace mantel and the built-in glass-fronted cabinets. Julia had indeed worked a miracle, hauling clutter and the dated furniture to a storage facility and replacing it all with modern pieces and splashes of designer color in cushions and throws.

She could tell Samantha and Luke were excited and she shared a little of the thrill. Who wouldn't want a great house like this? It was barely in their price range but she knew they could do it. She glanced over at the couple, arguing good-naturedly about where they'd put his wine fridge and how hard it would be to baby-proof the place.

"You could put in a new kitchen, the space is here," she said as she walked them through it. Personally she liked the big old cupboards and the cheerful yellow walls. She suspected though that the MacDonalds would probably prefer stainless appliances and granite countertops. When Samantha reminded her husband that they'd have to build renovation costs into their budget she knew she'd guessed right. He groaned theatrically, but his grin indicated he was excited about the home, too.

Hailey loved being single in the city. All the same there were times, like now, when she got a glimpse of another life. A man at her side, a baby on the way—and a home.

She loved the way Julia had artfully tossed a purple

woolen throw over a gray couch to give the impression
that someone with great taste and no clutter lived here.

"Four bedrooms?" Samantha asked.

"That's right. One's ideal for the baby's room, there's
a nice-sized room for a guest bedroom, a home office,
and the master is a treat. Come on, I'll show you."

They reached the top landing. She first showed them
the two smaller rooms and the main bathroom, fine but
nothing special. Then she opened the door to the master. "This is my favorite room in the house. There's a
vintage four-poster that you might be able to buy with
the house if you're interested. It's a large room with
wonderful dimensions, a window seat, a fireplace and
a full en suite." She flipped on the overhead light. She
knew the room by heart but wanted to watch their faces
when they saw the blissful space.

Hailey ushered them into the room. "What do you
think?"

She was so ready for squeals of delight that Sam's
reaction was puzzling. The woman's eyes opened wide.
She blinked, looking over at her equally stupefied husband.

Hailey turned around and saw that the white bed-
cover she'd so carefully smoothed to rid it of any
wrinkles was marred, not by a wrinkle, but by a big
unshaven man in a blue-and-green checked work shirt,
worn jeans and socks that didn't match.

He was sound asleep.

Two grubby sneakers sat on the Aubusson rug where
he'd obviously kicked them off prior to napping.

Silence reigned for a moment.

"Does *he* come with the place?" Samantha asked.

Sleepy blue eyes blinked at them out of a lean, weathered, stubbly face. The stranger's overgrown brown

hair was more tangle than style. He regarded them, seeming to consider the question, and cracked a smile. "Everything's negotiable." His voice was low, a little husky from sleep.

Sam giggled, thank heaven, though Hailey didn't find anything amusing about finding a homeless guy with a whacked sense of humor snoozing in the house she was trying to sell.

His gaze then focused only on her and she felt the strangest sense of connection with this utter stranger. For a second their gazes held, her heart sped up and she felt as though something that had been out of place suddenly had clicked back in. She closed her eyes against the strange sensation.

She tried to ask "Who are you?" and "What are you doing here?" but in the rush to get it all out her brain short-circuited and instead she asked, "Who are you doing here?"

The twinkle in his blue eyes deepened and when he smiled she noted he had Bradley Cooper–white teeth. No homeless guy she'd ever seen had teeth that gleaming. "I'm not doing anybody here."

Sam giggled again as if they were at an impromptu comedy club.

"I meant what are you doing here?"

He yawned and settled himself onto his back. "Until you showed up I was sleeping."

You didn't get to be a top Realtor—okay, an up-and-coming Realtor—without a lot of tact, so she didn't take off her shoe and throw it at his head, as much as she was tempted. "Okay, let's try the other question. Who are you?" she asked, in a calm, clear voice.

"Robert Klassen. And you are?"

"My name is Hailey Fleming. I'm a Realtor and this house is for sale."

He put up two hands with nails that could use a scrub and rubbed his eyes. "Is that why the place looks like a furniture store? I barely recognized it. My grandmother sure never had such modern taste. The only thing I recognize is this bed." He glanced at the MacDonalds. "She died in it."

Sam made a startled sound, and took a step back, glancing around as though a ghost might be hovering in the room.

Hailey's sale fell through in that moment. She knew it as well as she knew that if she had her way that bed would see another casualty very soon.

"She didn't die here in the house," Hailey said through gritted teeth. "She passed away peacefully in hospital." She doubted the MacDonalds would believe her. For some reason they believed this guy. Was he really Mrs. Neeson's grandson? If he was, she had to tread carefully.

The house bore no signs of a break-in and the scruffy backpack leaning against the wall shouted Drifter. However, a pretty fancy camera bag leaned beside it. Hadn't she heard the grandson was some kind of photographer?

Her unwanted visitor didn't leap off the bed and race for the door, rather he simply grabbed hold of the two green silk accent pillows behind him and propped himself up. Even wearing mismatched socks, he was imposing, undeniably gorgeous in that annoying unkempt way that only certain men can pull off.

She had absolutely no idea how to proceed. Not that she had years of experience under her belt, but she doubted a scenario like this happened very often to any agent, no matter how experienced. And she really,

really needed to keep this listing. It was her biggest break yet in an industry that was tough to crack. The estate lawyer was an old family friend giving her a chance. For some shaggy backpacker to come in here and take it away from her was too much.

However, until she got this mess sorted out there wasn't much she could do, so she pulled herself together and turned to the MacDonalds. "I am so sorry. There is obviously some kind of a mix-up that I will have to sort out before we go any further."

"We understand," said Luke. He stepped back out into the hall. "It's too bad though. It's a great house. Perfect for our needs."

"I know." At least she had the satisfaction of knowing she'd been correct about the match. Thanks to tall, dark and shaggy, it wouldn't fatten her bank account, but at least she knew she was on the right track. "I promise to get things figured out, and when I do, you'll be the first people I call. In the meantime I'll put together some more houses that will work for you."

As they went down the stairs, Sam glanced back over her shoulder. "Did the previous owner really die in this house?"

"Of course not. If she had I'd tell you. Agnes Neeson died in hospital. She was almost ninety and lived here happily until a few days before she passed on. It was a stroke. She died peacefully without ever regaining consciousness. We should all be so lucky."

She kept her bright smile intact until she'd seen the MacDonalds out and then she dropped the happy act and turned back to confront the complete stranger who was doing his best to upset all her careful plans.

Hailey had no intention of letting that happen and tall, dark and disheveled was about to find that out.

3

ROB YAWNED AND STRETCHED, wanting to close his eyes and finish that long sleep he so desperately needed. He heard the front door slam and groaned; clearly he wasn't alone in the house.

With ominous certainty he knew the woman who had so rudely woken him was on her way back to the bedroom. And he didn't think she was going anywhere anytime soon.

He listened as she marched up the stairs, striking the creaky section in the middle of the sixth step. There was another creaky spot on step eleven and she struck that one, too.

This house had no secrets from him.

When she appeared in the doorway of the bedroom he was ready for her. Not at so much of a disadvantage.

Of course, his grandmother would have been horrified to see him lounging on the bed, leaning against stacked pillows he didn't recognize any more than anything else in this room.

He felt almost as though he were in a dream where things were familiar but weren't. The woman currently surveying him was real though. No question there.

She was also hot, he realized, surveying her. She looked pissed off yet confused and unsure of herself all at once. An interesting combination.

He liked the neat way she'd put herself together. She had long blond hair and eyes that couldn't make up their mind between gray and blue and so made you keep noticing them, to wonder.

She wore a black skirt and white blouse with chunky black jewelry. She had nice legs. She might have a nice smile; however, at the moment her lips were so tight together they could be sewed shut.

Then she opened them. Not to smile unfortunately. To speak.

"We have to talk."

He let his head fall back, and if it weren't for all the fancy pillows on the bed he'd have hit the walnut headboard. "Four most frightening words in the English language."

He almost got a glimpse of her smile, but to his consternation she managed to suppress it. "I think there's been some kind of mistake."

"Yeah. I think so, too." He glanced around the room once more. "Did you move in here or something?"

"Of course not. I told you, I'm a Realtor. I've listed this house for sale."

"Well, unless my grandmother spent the last months of her life redecorating her house in condo-modern, somebody else's stuff is in here."

She looked at him as though he was missing half his marbles. He was tired, but he couldn't be that tired.

"I had this home professionally staged."

When it was clear he didn't have a clue what she was talking about, she continued.

"We clear out the clutter and bring in pieces and accessories to showcase the home in the best way possible. I think the improvement is amazing."

"It doesn't look like my grandmother's house anymore." Except for the big bed which he'd instinctively been drawn to last night. It had reminded him of home, tradition, his grandmother.

As he stared up at her, suddenly the four-poster filled him with other thoughts. Adult thoughts. Her slim hands wrapped around the bedposts while she writhed in passion. He blinked, glancing away before she could catch the lust in his eyes.

"It's not supposed to. The concept of staging is to inspire the buyer to see the possibilities and leave them space to imagine their own furniture and personal items in the home."

There were all sorts of things he could reply, such as, he wanted his grandmother's stuff brought back. Even as tired as he was, still he knew that what he really wanted was his grandmother back and that wasn't going to happen. So he went on the offensive. "You need to move all this crap out of here."

Her eyes shifted more to gray when she got huffy. She crossed her arms in front of her. "I have a listing agreement."

"Not with me."

"My agreement is with Mrs. Neeson's attorney."

"That's a funny thing, because the house was left to me." He had to be honest though. "I do remember some weird-ass conversation with her lawyer. I was in Libya with a camp of rebels. It was a bad connection. Maybe he thought I said yes to listing the house when I didn't." He scrubbed his hands across his eyes. He'd kill for a cup of coffee. "I'll probably sell, but I haven't figured out what I'm going to do yet."

"This puts me in a very difficult position." She seemed not to know what to do. He got the impression that she was as staged as the house she was attempting to sell. All at once it occurred to him that she was pretty new at this biz. Probably hadn't come across any difficult situations yet.

Well, she was in one now.

A frown marred her pretty face. "I don't want to be rude but I have no proof you are Mrs. Neeson's grandson."

He figured she had a point, and he already sensed she was stubborn enough that she wouldn't leave until she was satisfied he was who he said he was. So he shifted until he could reach his wallet, took it out, seeing it through her eyes as a grubby, falling-apart-at-the-seams excuse for a wallet. He opened the Velcro flap that was only half stuck down and offered her his driver's license.

She took a look. Stared at him and back at the picture as if she was a bouncer wondering if his ID was fake. "You don't have the same last name."

"That's right. It's a maternal/paternal thing."

"I think maybe you should leave and we'll sort this out tomorrow."

He was no more going to leave this house than he was going to put up with being bossed around by an uppity blond in too-high heels. "That's not going to happen." Enough already. He wanted to get back to his nap. In peace. "Let's call Edward Barnes. He knows me."

"He's on a wine-tasting trip in California. And if you actually know him, you'll know he—"

"Doesn't carry a cell phone," he finished for her, feeling increasingly irritated. He prided himself on keeping cool in a crisis but this was getting ridiculous. "How did I get in?"

She looked at him, puzzled.

"I opened the door, which was locked. How did I get in if I'm not her grandson?"

"The key hidden under the planter. Probably the second place anyone would look, after checking under the mat."

"I am not leaving here. I am the legal owner of this home."

"All I'm asking you to do is prove it."

He jumped up as the obvious solution struck him. "Photo albums with pictures of me and my grandmother."

She looked guilty. "Remember what I told you about decluttering?"

"Where are the photo albums?"

"In storage."

This was turning into a bad farce. You might as well try and milk a rhinoceros as reason with this woman. Some of the old neighbors might have recognized him but most had moved on. Or died.

It was difficult to think when he was in a bedroom, in a bed, and a very attractive woman was alone with him. In heels. Now he pictured her in nothing but those black heels stretched out on the white expanse of the bed.

He had to get out of here. And soon, before he was as hard as one of the bedposts. He shifted and sat up. "Follow me."

She was instantly suspicious. "Follow you where?"

"My first choice would be to the front door—" he was lying, it was his second choice "—but if that's not going to happen, then I want to show you something in my old bedroom down the hall." He scowled as he maneuvered his legs off the bed, trying not to wince, and headed for the door. "I mean, what used to be my old bedroom. Before you turned it into a nursery." Which was why he'd had to crash in his grandmother's bed instead of his own.

His progress was halting at best. She followed slowly, then said, "Oh, my gosh. We moved a black cane into storage. I assumed it was Mrs. Neeson's. Was it yours?"

"No. It was my grandmother's." He didn't feel like explaining. Especially since she supposedly didn't even believe he was Mrs. Neeson's grandson.

"Oh, good."

She wisely refrained from further comment and simply followed his slow progress to the room that had been his for what seemed like his entire life. His grandmother had let him redecorate it after his parents got divorced and maybe that had helped him feel like there'd always be somewhere in his life that was permanent.

The daylight filtered through the dormer window and he remembered all the mornings he'd lain in bed, gazing at the sky, dreaming of travel, of adventure, of a future where he set his own rules.

Under the dormer was a window seat. He noted that the stager had placed a fancy cushion on top of the spot where he'd folded himself into the space between the walls and read comic books hour after hour.

He removed the designer cushion, tossed it onto the faux-leather chair neither he nor his grandmother would ever have chosen. He pulled up on the wooden top of the box and it gave slightly.

"That doesn't open," she said in a smug tone. "We tried it."

"Yeah it does." He'd worked ages on the project figuring out an intricate puzzle opening to keep his stash

of treasures secret. The cool thing about his grandmother was that she'd never asked him how to get into
the thing. Never asked him what he kept in there. She
was the kind of woman who respected a man's privacy
and trusted him with his secrets. He wished there were
more women like that in the world.

When Hailey moved closer to check out what he was
doing he caught her scent. Elusive, feminine, sexy as a
woman in nothing but stilettos. And maybe a wisp or
two of lingerie.

He slid his index finger into the familiar groove.
His fingers were thicker now he'd grown up but he
could still maneuver the latch that raised the top another inch, allowing him access to the second mecha-
nism. It took him another minute and then he lifted the
lid all the way, staring down into the hollow box for the
first time in years.

There wasn't much there. A few old comics he'd
never part with. He pushed his first baseball glove out
of the way, a dog-eared *National Geographic,* and there,
underneath a wooden knife he'd carved himself in his
Samurai phase, was the leather folder. He took it out,
brushed a dead moth off, and handed it to her. He rose
from his crouched position and looked over her shoulder as she opened it.

Once more he caught her scent. Not flowery. Citrus
with underlying tones of heat.

The photograph and accompanying citation were
among his few treasures. "You won a city-wide pho-
tography contest," she said. "You were in high school."
When she turned to him he was struck again by the
blue-gray eyes. Like her scent, the first impression was
coolness, and then you caught the heat behind the cool
facade.

"Yes, but that's not the point. Check out the picture. And read the caption."

An absurdly young version of himself in a sports jacket—one of half a dozen times in his life he'd ever worn anything formal—his grandmother and his mom stood in a little trio, him holding his winning photograph—a bear cub sitting on top of a Dumpster eating an apple. It wasn't much of a big event in a person's life but to him that award had signaled the beginning of a career. Becoming a photojournalist had given him freedom, adventure, life on the road and a reasonable salary.

She read aloud. "'Robert Klassen, fifteen, wins for his photograph, An Apple a Day, while his mother, Emily Klassen, and his grandmother, Agnes Neeson, look on."

He pointed to his young self. "That's me and that's my grandmother."

Her expression softened in a smile. "It's a great photograph. And you were a very cute teenager." She closed the folder and handed it back to him.

"Are you satisfied now that I am who I say I am?"

She turned her head and he was struck once more by the impact of those in-between-blue-and-gray eyes. "You pretty much had me when you opened the Chinese-puzzle-box window seat."

"I'm sorry about the misunderstanding." He was, too. Apart from being a little high-strung, she seemed like a nice woman. "Thing is, I haven't decided yet whether I'm going to sell the place. And if I do I'll want to choose my own Realtor."

Her nostrils flared at that. "Do you have a relationship with a Realtor in Seattle?"

"Not exactly."

"Well, let me tell you, I am an extremely competent Realtor with excellent references. I think the MacDonalds were a real possibility."

"They seemed freaked out that my grandmother died in her bed."

She slammed her hands to her hips. Perfectly manicured hands, no wedding ring. "She didn't. Your grandmother, as I'm sure you know, passed away in hospital."

A shaft of pain stabbed him. Grief, he supposed. He tried to ignore it. "Not the point. If you'd known my grandmother you'd have wanted her spirit to stay in the house." Maybe that was why he had such a heavy feeling when he thought of other people occupying this place. To him she was still here. "People who are scared of ghosts, they wouldn't be my kind of people or my grandmother's." He knew he was overtired and would soon feel more like his old self; until then though he really had to get a grip. And probably stop talking before he made a fool of himself.

The woman smiled at him. "It's hard to let go when we've loved someone," she said softly.

"Yeah." As trite as her words sound, they were sincere.

"Were you close?"

"Oh, yeah. She pretty much raised me." He couldn't imagine what would have happened to him if he'd been left with his mother. His grandmother had not only raised him; she'd saved him. Given him a chance to make something of his life.

When Hailey looked at him, he felt as though she could see inside him. It was the weirdest feeling and he knew she felt it, too, from how she took an instinctive step back toward the door. It was as if they both became aware at the same moment that they were alone together in a bedroom—even if the spread was covered in little yellow duckies. He could have sworn the temperature zoomed up a few degrees.

"Would you like a cup of coffee?" she asked.

That's when he became convinced she really could read his mind. "I would get on my knees and beg for a cup."

A genuine smile tilted her lips. Finally. "No need to beg. I'll meet you downstairs."

He thought about asking her to bring the coffee up but knew she'd get the wrong impression. Thing was, stairs were the hardest for him to navigate. For some reason, which he could not identify, he didn't want this woman to see him limping. "It's okay," he said. "I'll make some later."

"I'd like a cup anyway. And besides, I do want to talk to you."

HAILEY GAVE HERSELF a pep talk as she prepared coffee. *Stay confident,* she reminded herself as she poured freshly ground beans into a French press. *Be positive.* Luckily she'd stocked up on coffee the day before, even had fresh milk in the refrigerator, so it wasn't long before her favorite scent in the world filled the bright kitchen.

She heard a noise behind her and turned to find Robert Klassen in the kitchen. He was taller than she'd first imagined and upright he was more commanding and definitely more sexy.

"Have a seat," she said brightly, pointing to the oak chairs at the kitchen table that she and Julia had decided to keep.

"Thanks." He seemed to hesitate, then moved forward. Slowly. Stiffly. When he went to sit down, he leaned on the table and lowered himself slowly into a chair.

She turned away, busying herself with coffee so he wouldn't think she was staring.

"Do you take milk and sugar?"

"No. Black."

She brought coffees to the table and sat opposite him. According to her electronic planner she had thirty-five minutes until she had to be at the office for the weekly meeting and pep talk. She was determined to use the time to save her listing.

He sipped coffee. Seemed to savor every drop.

"You like your coffee," she said, somewhat amused.

"When you live the way I do, you don't take things like coffee or a good meal for granted. Even clean water is a luxury." He sipped again, caught her gaze and then said, "I got shot. That's why I'm limping. It's no big deal, but I need to rest up for a few weeks."

"Shot? I thought you were a photographer." She wished she'd listened more closely.

"I'm a photojournalist. I work for *World Week*."

World Week was one of the top news magazines in the country, covering international affairs, finance, politics and the arts. "Wow. That must be fascinating."

"It is. Obviously the nature of my job requires me to cover war zones, famines, devastation both natural and human made. As you can imagine there isn't a Starbucks on every corner."

She sipped her own coffee, for once stopping to enjoy the flavor. How often did she even really taste her morning brew? But, with only thirty-four minutes left, she couldn't waste time savoring coffee. She had work to do.

"Do you have a wife and family?"

The question obviously startled him. He nearly choked on his coffee. "No."

"Are you planning to live in this house?"

She asked it innocently, but he had to know where this was going.

A crease formed between his eyebrows. She could see that he was actually thinking about her question. She decided to help him along. "A house this size might not fit with your lifestyle. I imagine you're not home very much."

"See the thing is—"

He stopped talking when they both heard the front door open and a female voice called, "Can I come in?"

Julia. "Sure. In the kitchen," she called back.

"So the coast is clear." And then Julia walked in, a swish of red cashmere coat and black pants, saw the man sitting there and said, "Oh."

His lips twitched, which made her feel once more that strange sense of connection with him. "Julia, this is Robert Klassen."

"I go by Rob," he said as they shook hands.

"Hi, Rob," she said, and flicked Hailey a glance. "Are you interested in buying Bellamy House?"

"I might be, if I didn't already own it."

In a few seconds Hailey had filled her friend in on the situation. Julia poured herself a coffee and sat down. "It's great that you're here to see Hailey at work. She's fantastic. This place will sell in no time." She turned to Hailey. "How did the MacDonalds like it? I think we were genius to stage the small bedroom as a nursery."

"I think they're interested," Hailey said, keeping her tone carefully neutral.

"They're not the right people for this house," Robert Klassen, call-me-Rob, announced.

Hailey and Julia exchanged glances. The unspoken message being *trouble ahead.*

There was an awkward silence, then Julia broke it. "I dropped by to see if you want me to finish the staging on Tuesday night. I had to rush on the upstairs."

"Don't you have a date Tuesday night?" Hailey had been so excited about the blond guy that she had added a notation to her agenda just so she'd remember to phone and ask how the date had gone.

"No. He had to postpone. His business trip has been extended. He's got to go to Nigeria next week. I'll meet him the week after."

"Oh, too bad."

"Gives me time to lose a couple more pounds before we meet." She turned to Rob. "We connected through LoveMatch.com."

"What kind of work does he do?" Rob asked.

"He's a civil engineer."

Hailey said, "I'm not sure about Tuesday. Can I let you know?"

"Sure." Julia took another quick sip of coffee, and then rose. "Sorry to run, but I've got to write up a staging proposal and head to an old friend's baby shower. And I'm already running late. Nice to meet you, Rob."

"You, too."

"I'll call you," Hailey said.

When her friend had gone, she only had twenty minutes to convince this man to let her keep the listing. She opened her mouth to get back to business when he surprised her.

"So your friend hasn't met that guy?"

"What guy?"

"The one she has the date with?"

"No. Not yet. Why?" He was messing with her careful arguments on why she should keep this listing. And besides, what business was it of his if two people he didn't know had a date?

"Tell her he's probably a scammer."

"What?"

"Nigeria is the scam capital of the world. And something about 'civil engineer' sounds fishy to me."

"How can you be so judgmental? She's talked to him on the phone. I'm sure it's fine."

"Maybe. You spend long enough in the news business, you get an instinct." Between telling prospective buyers ghost stories and trying to kill her friend's happy buzz, she wasn't too sure about his supposed instincts. Apparently he didn't have much of an instinct for dodging bullets. "Just tell her, whatever she does, not to send the guy money."

"All right. Fine." She shifted and glanced at her watch. "Can we talk about us?"

He had the sexiest way of looking at her. She'd known the man all of about an hour and every time he looked at her thoughts she had no business thinking flitted through her mind.

"Us?"

As their gazes connected, she thought maybe Julia had a point. It had been way too long since she had sex if a shaggy drifter who was trying to mess with her career could make her overheated with a mere glance. She crossed her legs. "You know what I meant. The listing."

He leaned back in his chair, savored another sip of coffee. Then he said, "Okay. Here's what I propose. You can keep the listing. I'll be living here so you have to work around me. I don't want open houses. Appointment only. We'll see how it goes."

She was so relieved not to find herself fired before

she'd started that she nodded. "Okay." However, she wasn't a complete fool or a pushover. "I have a condition of my own." And she drilled him with her serious-business-woman look. "No more stories about your grandmother dying in that bed. As I'm sure Mrs. Neeson taught you, if you can't say something nice, don't say anything at all."

4

AFTER THE HOT REALTOR LEFT, Rob drained the rest of the coffee into his mug and began to wander through the house.

She was right, of course. It didn't make any sense for him to keep the place. It was too big, with maintenance issues always cropping up. It was a house meant for a family, and now that his grandmother was gone, he didn't have one anymore.

Maybe he hadn't been able to say goodbye formally at her funeral, but he could for damn sure make certain that the next people who lived in this house were a family his grandmother would have approved of.

He suddenly realized that was what had brought him back to Seattle.

He needed to hand on the house to the right people. Then maybe he could let his memories go and get back to his regular life.

If he owed anything to Agnes Neeson's memory it was not to let weenies who were scared of their own shadows live in her place.

He didn't have much of an idea what he was going to do with himself for the next several weeks, apart from get his strength back, so he called Dr. Greene's office and wasn't remotely surprised to get an appointment that very afternoon.

HAILEY BARELY MADE the weekly office meeting at Dalbello and Company, sliding in as the office manager was in the midst of his weekly speech. Normally she worked from home, not interested in renting an overpriced desk. She dropped by to use the photocopy machine and to visit with her mentor and friend, Hal Wilson, who'd been in the business for thirty years.

She saw Hal standing near the water cooler and went over to him. "Did I miss anything?" she whispered.

"Ted says listings are up overall in the city and the house prices are starting to creep up."

"Good news." There were about thirty Realtors in the open area where they held the weekly meetings. Rows of desks stretched out behind her all currently empty. Two high-end printers and photocopiers sat to the side underneath a line of windows. A big whiteboard dominated this end of the room.

Ted told a couple of jokes, gave them a weekly sales tip, and then moved on to the reason she had raced to get here.

"Let's look at the new listings."

He boomed out the listings like an auctioneer. The standard mix of houses, condos, a couple of commercial properties. "And Bellamy House. Listed by Hailey Fleming. Her biggest listing yet and the biggest listing for our office this week." He turned to her with a big two-thumbs-up. "Way to go, Hailey!" He started clapping and all the assembled Realtors joined in.

Sure it was cheesy, but the clapping and cheering worked to make her feel more confident.

Naturally she didn't bother sharing with a group of sharks, all of whom would love to list and sell Bellamy House, that her listing was hanging by a thread.

When the meeting was over, a stylish redhead walked over to Hailey and Hal. "Congratulations again." Her name was Diane and her congrats were as fake as her smile. She was a successful Realtor with a reputation for ruthlessness. "When's the agents' open?"

She shook her head. "The client's very clear. He doesn't want any opens. I've got photos on my website. Give me a call if you've got clients who might be interested. We'll arrange a private showing."

"Will do." Diane asked a couple of questions about the kitchen and made a few notes, then walked off when her cell phone buzzed.

When Diane was out of earshot, Hal said, "I heard she tried to get that listing. She has a contact in the hospital. If a property owner dies, she hears about it before next of kin."

"No!"

He shrugged. "I wouldn't put it past her."

Good thing the lawyer was a family friend. "Hal, I've got a problem. I need some advice."

"Okay."

She told Hal about Rob and the tentative agreement they had that she could keep the listing as long as she didn't disturb him. "I'm sure the MacDonalds would have made an offer if he hadn't scared them off with stories of his grandmother dying upstairs in the bedroom."

Hal took his time answering her, finally, saying, "This is a great opportunity for you. I don't want you to lose it."

"Me neither."

"Some clients don't even know what they want. Sounds like he's one. You're going to have to manage him."

"Manage him? How?"

"Hailey, my dear. Use one of your greatest assets. Your charm."

DR. GREENE'S OFFICE smelled the same as it had for the thirty years he'd been dragged here, Rob thought, as he sat leafing through an ancient golf magazine. And the decor hadn't changed since he was a kid either, he realized as he shifted on the cracked vinyl seat in the waiting room. He tossed the magazine aside. He didn't even like golf. He took out his phone and checked his email. Nothing interesting.

He hated waiting rooms. Hated anything with the word *waiting* in it. He checked the time on his phone. He'd been here fifteen minutes. It wasn't even his idea to be under a doctor's care. Damn Gary and his officious dictates. So his leg hurt. It would heal.

A mom and her kid emerged from the treatment room. The kid hunch-shouldered and coughing. This family doctor was so old-fashioned he only had one room. As soon as the outer door closed behind the cougher and his mom, the receptionist, Carol, who'd been sitting behind that old oak counter since before Rob was born nodded toward him. "You can go on in."

Horace Greene had to be closing in on seventy. His hair, what was left of it, was salt-and-pepper, his beard was Santa Claus–white and his pale blue eyes focused as keenly as ever from behind bifocal lenses. Doc Greene had been his grandmother's family doctor longer than he'd been alive, and if he had a family doctor, he supposed it was this one. Doc rose to his feet as Rob limped into his office and held out a hand.

"Rob, how you doing?"

"Been better, Doc."

The physician gestured to the oak chair in front of his scarred oak desk and took his own seat on the other side. "Haven't seen you in a long time. How long's it been?"

"Must be five years."

He nodded. He might be chitchatting, but Rob wasn't fooled. Those old eyes didn't miss a thing. "Sorry about your grandmother passing. It was a big loss for you."

"Yeah."

"And what's this? You're limping. What happened?"

"I got shot."

If Doc was surprised by the news he didn't show it. "Mmm-hmm, so when was this? Who's looked at it?" He pulled out a notepad and began scribbling.

"About a week ago. On assignment in Libya. My boss pulled some strings and got me in to a military surgeon. He took some X-rays, said there were no remaining fragments. Gave me a few stitches and told me I was good to go."

Doc glanced at him over his glasses and said, "I bet he or she also told you to use crutches."

The military surgeon had said that and a few other less complimentary things. He shrugged. "You know what a fast healer I am. You've always said I've got a head like a rock."

"But you're not bullet-proof. I should take a look at the wound."

"I'm going to need a report from you that says I'm cleared to go back to work."

Doc Greene rose and headed for his treatment room

adjoining the office. "Drop your duds and let's have a look."

Rob followed him, trying his hardest not to limp, and soon found himself sitting on the exam table, his pants folded over a chair, his leg bared to the doctor's prying gaze. And fingers. "Ow."

"No discharge on the bandage and the wound is healing nicely." Doc nodded, tossing the old bandage into the trash. "You said it's been a week since the injury. We'll redress that for you and it should be okay."

The older man fussed around in a cabinet, taking out the things he'd need. "I'm putting on a dry dressing," he said as he began. "Dry gauze and tape. As soon as the wound stops weeping you can leave it open to the air to speed healing. That should happen in the next few days. Pat dry after showers."

"Great, thanks," Rob said after the new dressing was taped to his leg. He was happy he'd got off without a lecture on being careful or some other impertinence from the man who'd been doctoring him for three decades.

But he didn't get off that easy.

"Put your pants back on and come on back to my office. There's a few things I'd like to talk to you about."

Reluctantly, Rob returned to the chair in front of the desk and slumped down.

Doc Greene pushed the pad aside and looked at him intently. "How are you coping?"

"Fine."

A beat of silence passed but Rob wasn't going to break it. Doc continued. "You've been through an emotionally exhausting time. You've lost someone special and you've got a significant enough injury that it's brought you home. All that combined is going to take a toll."

"I'm fine," he repeated, sounding less than fine even to his own ears. This was the man who had treated his grandmother through her few illnesses and had looked after her at the end. He licked his lips. "My grandmother—she seemed fine when I was home six months ago…" He let the unspoken question hover.

Doc sat back. No wonder patients were always kept waiting. He never rushed.

"Agnes Neeson lived a life anyone would be proud of. She kept her independence to the end." Doc smiled. "And you know how important that was to her. She was getting frail. She had a massive stroke and died in hospital without ever regaining consciousness." He didn't need to consult a file. He knew all his patients and he and Agnes had been friends as well as doctor and patient.

"Would she have suffered?"

Doc shook his head. "There are no nerve endings in your brain. There wouldn't be pain."

"Good," Rob said, relieved and somehow comforted. "I wish I'd been there."

Doc nodded. "I know. Reading every issue of *World Week* cover to cover made your grandmother feel close to you. Nobody could have been prouder of you than she was."

The prickling of tears horrified Rob. He cleared his throat and changed the subject fast. "There's a Realtor who messed up the house." He rubbed his sore leg. "She took out my grandmother's furniture and staged the place. Everything's different since I was here."

"It is. I heard the place was for sale. It's that nice young gal from Dalbello who has the listing. She'll do a good job for you."

Rob didn't have the energy to talk about his confused

feelings so he mumbled his thanks and struggled to his feet. Limping to the door, he realized that the doc was right. He wasn't as okay as he tried to pretend he was.

JULIA RAN INTO BEANANZA, her favorite coffee shop. "Hey, Julia. How's it going?" Bruno, her favorite barista, called over the hiss of the espresso machine.

"It's a beautiful day," she called back.

Bruno sent her a disbelieving look out of his big brown Italian eyes. "It's raining," he said. He wore a bill cap, one from his huge collection. She was pretty sure he was sensitive about the thinning patch of hair at the crown of his head, though maybe it was a fashion statement. Who knew?

He had a gold hoop in one ear and wore a T-shirt that said Decaf Is for Sissies.

When he'd served a hot chocolate and a chai latte to the customers in front of her, he started her drink. There was no need to ask, she ordered the same thing every day. A tall skinny latte. As though drinking enough of it might rub off and she'd awaken one day to find herself tall and skinny.

She lived in hope.

While preparing her drink, he said, "Brownies are fresh out of the oven." As though she needed reminding, as though the smell weren't enticing her to sin, leading her down the calorie path of doom. She could see them behind the glass case, the chocolate glistening on top, the cakey part dense and rich. "I can't," she moaned. "I'm on a diet."

"Really? Who is he?"

"Why do you think I'm only on a diet because of a man?"

"Because you've been coming into Beananza nearly

every day for three years. That's like a thousand days in a row. And every time you tell me you're on a diet there's a guy."

"Okay, there's a guy."

He smiled as he passed her latte over. She glanced down at the surface, as she did every morning. And laughed. He'd drawn a heart into the froth on the top of her latte.

She settled into one of the small tables to enjoy her coffee. Bruno always served coffee in china mugs unless a customer specifically asked for a to-go cup. Customers only made that mistake once. Bruno made it very clear he strongly disapproved of people carrying coffees around. He served his brew the way he believed it was meant to be drunk, sitting down and savoring it, and if you didn't like drinking coffee his way, you could go elsewhere.

His café was always packed.

Julia had learned to appreciate Bruno's point of view. She looked forward to settling into one of the small tables or the long bar by the windows. She would sip her coffee and read the paper or a magazine, or, as now, open her tablet computer to savor the latest email from her LoveMatch.

Hi sweetie,

She absolutely loved that he called her *sweetie*. It seemed so casually intimate. As though they'd been a couple for years.

The weather is hot and sticky here. I have to catch a plane soon. We'll be looking at large pipes for a construction project. I miss you so much. I have

never felt so close to someone before. I long to see
you next week.
Love, Gregory

Not only coffee was meant to be savored, she thought
as she read the message again, slowly. Love was meant
to be savored, too. She only hoped Gregory wasn't disappointed when they met in person.

She sent a worried glance down at her latte. Should
she switch to green tea?

ROB LEFT THE DOCTOR'S OFFICE with an aching thigh from
where the good doc had prodded and poked at him. He
didn't like doctors mostly because he didn't like being
sick or incapacitated.

As he limped along the sidewalk, clutching a
scrawled prescription for painkillers he knew he'd never
fill, he got caught in a downpour of rain. He loved the
rain. After the heat and dry dustiness of the desert, the
cooling water dripping from gray skies should have
made him happy. Instead he felt as though the sky was
suffering a massive outpouring of grief. Irritable, achy
and at a loss for something to do, he just stood getting wet.

He didn't want to go back to Bellamy House with all
that designer stuff he didn't recognize, and he didn't
want to visit the few friends he still had in the area. He
wanted to get on a plane and get back to work. That
wasn't about to happen, though, until he could run a
mile in six. He set his jaw, knowing he'd have to walk
before he could run and not for the first time cursed the
trigger-happy rebel who'd fired on him. He squinted
up and down the street and saw the sign for a coffee
shop a couple of blocks away. He figured that would

do for a destination. He'd walk a few blocks today, a few more tomorrow, and in a couple of weeks he'd be up to running.

Crutches. As if.

He took a step toward the coffee shop and another one. Two women chattering away beneath umbrellas passed him. As he stepped around them, he stepped into a puddle and felt the cold wetness soak his sock. Yup, he was home.

By the time he'd gone one block he felt as though someone were jabbing hot pokers into his thigh. The remaining block seemed like such a long way he contemplated stopping where he was, sagging onto a bus stop bench and calling a cab. Turning his head toward the road ensured he no longer saw the tempting bus bench. He squinted at the coffee shop and pushed his foot forward. He liked the name of the café. Beananza. He vaguely remembered driving past it last time he'd been home but he'd never been inside.

He imagined how good that coffee was going to taste when he got past the next block, assuming he could get there before the place closed for the night. One foot in front of the other, he reminded himself. It was only pain, he could get through it.

A car slowed beside him and he paid no attention until the window closest to him slid down and a voice said, "Rob, I found you."

He turned to see Hailey behind the wheel of a small gray SUV, looking as perky as ever in a blue raincoat. "Why were you looking for me?"

She pulled over and parked because it was that kind of a neighborhood—parking spaces were plentiful. She got out, popped a blue umbrella and then reached into the back of her car and took out his grandmother's walking cane.

For a second Rob experienced a pang of grief so sharp it numbed the pain in his leg. That cane had been supporting his grandmother for years. Of course she'd resisted the thing like crazy and then had come to rely on it in her later years.

Hailey came around the back of the car and offered him the worn black handle. "Here."

He wrapped his hand around the handle and tried out the cane. It was a little on the short side but he wasn't going to complain. Strangely, clutching the spot where his grandmother's hand had gripped made him feel better, connected to her in some sentimental fashion that still comforted. "How did you know?"

"Doc called me. He said you could use your grandmother's cane." She seemed a lot warmer than last time he'd seen her. As though she genuinely cared.

"My doctor called you?" His shock must have shown because she laughed. "So much for doctor-patient privilege."

"Your grandmother had quite a network. They all know each other and their business. And their friends' business, and their friends' grandsons' business."

"He told me to go get crutches."

"I know. And he told me you wouldn't. He said to tell you to use the cane on the opposite side to your bad leg."

He switched the cane to the other hand. "Huh."

"Where are you going?" she asked him. "Do you want a ride?"

He shook his head. Under the blue glow from her umbrella, her eyes were as blue as the sky would be if you could see it. "Only tourists use umbrellas," he informed her.

"And people who actually care about their appearance."

"I'm heading for that coffee shop over there," he said, hoping he sounded casual, as though he'd be there in a couple of minutes, no biggie.

"Bruno's place?" she asked.

"Beananza," he said, since he had no idea who Bruno might be.

"Right. That's Bruno's place. I'll come with you." A crease appeared between her perfectly shaped brows. "Or I could drive you."

"It's a block."

"You have a bullet in your leg."

"Do not."

She let out a sigh of frustration. "Whatever."

They started off and he thought he made a pretty respectable showing, thanks to the cane. He hoped his companion couldn't tell how heavily he was leaning on the thing. It was a little awkward, her with her umbrella, him with his cane, as they made their slow way toward the cheerful yellow sign.

To take his mind off the ache in his thigh he checked out her legs, slim and toned and sexy as hell in those heels.

5

AT THE ENTRANCE TO BEANANZA, Hailey shut her umbrella and stepped in front of Rob, pushing the door open so he could limp in without making a big deal of it.

"Since you're a client it's my treat," she said, and he somehow knew she was saving him the hassle of navigating the small tables and trying to balance coffees and the cane. He liked the simple way she helped him without making an issue of it.

"Thanks. An Americano."

"Hi, Hailey," a familiar voice called out.

"Julia." Hailey checked her watch. "I should have known you'd be here." She slipped off her coat and slid it over the back of a wooden chair at Julia's table, pulling out a second chair and angling it so he could slip into it without a lot of maneuvering. "Can I get you another?" She gestured to her friend's half-empty cup.

"No, thanks. I'm counting calories."

While Hailey clacked up to the front, her heels hitting the reclaimed fir floors, he looked around. The place was packed. Two old men at a corner table talked politics; one wore a blazer, as though he'd spent so many years dressing for the office that he couldn't stop even in retirement.

A trio of young mothers gossiped while their offspring dozed in strollers or gummed some kind of food from a reusable plastic container. A young guy with earphones on typed frantically into a computer. Two Asian women sat in a corner with textbooks and open notebooks.

Change the faces, the clothing and the language, and you could be in any public meeting place in the world, he thought.

"It's funky, isn't it?"

He turned back to Julia. "Yeah. Lots of character. I like it."

"Wait until you taste the coffee. It's so much better than anything you can get in a chain."

He nodded, thinking how people always seem to say that whether it's true or not. "You working?"

"No. Taking an email break." She blushed. "I'm like a teenager. It's ridiculous. He calls me *sweetie.* Isn't that romantic?"

A guy calling a woman *sweetie* might have trouble remembering names, but he kept that thought to himself.

"Have you done much online dating?"

"No. This is my first time. I can't believe I lucked out first time."

Hailey arrived with two steaming china mugs, and placed one down in front of him.

"Thanks."

Hers was some frothy drink. "I got an umbrella," she said to Julia.

He glanced over half expecting that the baristas had taken to putting paper parasols into coffees now.

It would hardly surprise him. Every time he came back to the States there seemed to be some new and crazier innovation—Earl Grey lattes or raspberry flavoring or some damn thing. It turned out though that they were talking latte art. The barista had decorated the foam with the outline of an umbrella. He checked the surface of his own coffee before taking a sip but found it blessedly manly, black and decoration-free.

He drank and found the brew gratifyingly strong.

"I was just telling Rob that my engineer calls me *sweetie* in his emails."

"Oh, that's so cute."

Julia shifted forward in her seat. "I've already lost two pounds. I think I can lose another one before we meet. Do you think I should go for jeans and a sweater for our date? Or do I put on a dress? I can fit into that red one I wore to your birthday last year."

Hailey seemed to ponder the choices the way a judge might consider a felon before a sentencing. "Where are you going on your date?"

"I'm not sure. He asked me which are my favorite restaurants so I assume he wants to go for dinner. He said he's getting his Mercedes tuned up so he can pick me up."

"He drives a Mercedes," Hailey said, sounding impressed.

"Or says he does," Rob mumbled into his coffee. When Hailey moved her chair slightly, he caught her scent again, even over the coffee, or was he imagining that cool citrus underlaid with something hot and dangerous?

"I want to look my best, but I don't want to seem too eager." Julia turned to him. "What do you think? Jeans or dress?"

He wanted to bolt to the other side of the coffee shop and talk politics with the old guys. Instead he tried to recall to the last actual date he'd had. It would be dinner with Romona, after work but before bed. Romona looked hot in jeans, dresses, fancy gowns, and best in nothing at all.

Which didn't seem like information he wanted to share with two women he'd only just met.

"It depends where you're going for the date, I guess. But I like a nice dress on a woman."

Both women listened to him as though he might have the answer to life's greatest mysteries.

"It's more about chemistry than clothing. If you click, you click. It's a bizarre and unpredictable fact of life that sometimes you meet a woman and there's no spark, and sometimes, for no reason at all, there's this huge attraction between you."

Instinctively he glanced at Hailey. The inconvenient attraction was sizzling between them even now, in this crowded coffee shop with steamy windows from all the damp coats and sweaters drying off from the rain. Just the way her body curved into the chair turned him on. The way she held her coffee mug with two hands like a little kid. The way her head tilted when she listened. The sound of her laughter, the shape of her legs. "You have no control, even when it's the last person you want to be attracted to."

Their gazes locked and, as he felt the heat traveling back and forth between them, her lips parted, giving him a glimpse of white teeth and pink tongue.

She blinked and turned away, taking a quick drink from her china mug.

Julia gnawed some of her lipstick off. "I feel a huge

attraction to this guy and I haven't even met him. I can't imagine what will happen when we do meet."

"Neither can I," Rob mumbled.

Hailey reached over and touched her friend's hand while simultaneously kicking him under the table. Luckily his bad leg was on the side farthest from her. "I really hope this works out. He sounds perfect."

As opposed to this huge and inconvenient attraction he felt for Hailey that was far from perfect.

A smart man would keep his distance.

HAILEY RECEIVED A CALL the next morning from Diane, who said she had clients who might be interested in Bellamy House.

Hailey cleared it with Rob and showed up half an hour before Diane and her clients were due, to make sure he was as neat as he claimed he was.

After checking the downstairs rooms and sighing with relief that all she had to do was hide a coat and some boots in the closet and give the kitchen sink a quick polish, she hurried upstairs.

She walked into the master bedroom and discovered Rob had done away with the designer cushions Julia had placed on the bed. She unearthed them from where he'd stuffed them—under the bed.

As she was bending over, fluffing them as close to their original pristine state as she could get them, a voice said behind her, "Are you going to put mints on the pillows and turn down the bed?"

She turned abruptly. "Rob, what are you doing here?" And then her eyes widened. He'd emerged from the master bath in nothing but a towel loosely tied around his hips. His hair was wet, his chest hair clung in damp, dark curls to his skin and one water droplet slid down his shoulder in a way that fascinated her.

He smelled of soap and toothpaste but she could swear she got a whiff of hot, star-filled nights under a desert sky.

"You need to go. I've got a Realtor coming in twenty minutes."

"Her name Diane something?"

How could he know that? "Yes."

"She called here. Her clients couldn't make it today."

"She called here? She should have called me."

He shrugged. "She said she couldn't reach you. We had a good talk on the phone. She knows a lot about this neighborhood. She said she'd be interested in talking to me about the history of the house."

"Oh, did she."

"She also mentioned that you're pretty new in the business, and if I need any advice from a more experienced Realtor she'd be happy to oblige."

Hailey's blood began to boil, but she was determined to maintain her poise. "What did you tell her?" Please let him not have fallen for that phony snake's tactics.

"I told her she should be selling used cars down on Federal Way."

She was so surprised a snort of laughter erupted before she could stop it. "I wish I'd seen her face." She tried not to notice how gorgeous Rob was in nothing but a towel and a few lazy drops of water.

"I don't like those tactics."

"Good."

He took a step closer leaving a damp footprint on the rug. He had narrow feet with long toes. If she concentrated on those she wouldn't obsess about his near-nakedness and the big, tempting bed looming behind them.

"If I dump you for another Realtor it won't be to someone devious."

Her gaze connected with his, warm and intimate. "Are you going to dump me?" Her voice came out husky.

"I don't have you. Yet."

She flashed to an image of herself pushing him onto his back in that bed with one hand while the other rid him of his towel.

The thought was so compelling that she had to clench her fists.

They were inches away and she felt tingly all over. She tried to think of something completely unsexy to say.

"Why were you so negative to Julia about her date?" was the first thing she came up with.

"I wasn't negative," he said. "I told her to wear a dress, didn't I?"

"You sounded sarcastic."

"I have a hard time believing you can fall in love over the internet. The guy sounds like a dick."

"Why? Because he asks her what restaurants she likes? Doesn't drag her to his cave by her hair?"

He reached for his watch on the dresser and she wondered how hard she'd struggle if he tried to drag her to his cave. She suspected not very.

"No. Because he drops into the conversation that his Mercedes needs an oil change. Who does that?"

"He's trying to impress her."

"I think he sounds suspicious."

"You know you're not in a war zone now where every

other person could be a spy or the enemy. You're home. Maybe you should give your suspicion a rest."

He looked as though he wanted to say more. His eyes were a clear green in the morning light. His hair, now almost dry, was trying to curl. "Maybe."

"And maybe they are falling in love on the internet, like old-fashioned pen pals."

He turned to her, his expression intense. "You don't get attracted by words on a computer screen. Sexual attraction is raw and immediate. It's about a man and a woman seeing inside each other." His gaze grew more intense. "It's in the shape of her face, her expression in different lights, the way her hair falls." He reached forward and touched the ends of her hair with his fingertips. As he did so, he brushed her shoulder and she drew in a sudden jerky breath.

She tried to speak and couldn't. He was so close she saw the dark flecks in the depths of his eyes, the freckles on his shoulders.

"It's about the feel of her skin," he said, letting his fingers trace the line of her jaw. Rough fingers that hefted heavy cameras and schlepped equipment through gritty deserts. "The sound of her voice, the way she smells." His voice dropped to a near whisper, its tone deepening. "The way she tastes." And he closed the short distance between them and put his mouth on hers.

Even though she'd anticipated the feel of his kiss, nothing could have prepared her for the lust that punched through her system when their mouths connected. A light, teasing kiss turned hungry and hot in a nanosecond. His hand moved to the back of her head, fisting in her hair, tilting her head so he had better access. She made a little moaning sound in the back of her throat as she reached for him, wanting to feel the solid outline of his chest, to thrust her fingers into his damp hair. He tasted like the cool mint of toothpaste and the hot spice of lust, his tongue teasing and tormenting her, giving and taking in equal measure. She'd never been kissed like this. Never imagined anything close to this.

He kissed her, taking his time, not trying to rip off her clothes or talk her into his bed. He kept kissing her as though his whole existence depended on nothing but this moment.

Getting involved with Rob wasn't on her list or her agenda or anywhere in her short-term plans but she knew in that moment that her careful personal agenda had just been seriously screwed up.

When he drew slowly away from her, gentling his embrace, he grinned at her wryly. "You can't get that on the internet."

She'd have replied except that she was currently speechless.

When he turned to get dressed she scooted out of the room and said softly, "Or anywhere else."

6

JULIA'S HOME PHONE was ringing when she opened the door to her apartment. She'd left a bridal shower early to get home since Gregory generally phoned around this time. It seemed as though all her friends were either getting married or having babies and she wanted that, too. Excitement bubbled within her when her call display revealed an international number. "Hello?"

"Hi, sweetie."

"Hi yourself, Gregory. How was your meeting?"

"Long." The line crackled. "I miss you. I miss Seattle. Tell me what's going on?"

"It rained today. Nothing new there. Let's see. I destaged a house that sold, no doubt because of my excellent staging."

"Is the statue of Lenin still keeping watch over Fremont?"

She smiled into the phone. "Of course. Oh, and I was trying to decide what to wear for our date next week. I can't wait to meet you in person."

"I can't wait either, sweetie. I've never felt so close to a woman before."

"I know. I feel the same and it's so strange. We've

never even met." She moved a pot of rosemary on her windowsill, centering it. "I noticed you took your profile down."

"I'm not interested in anyone else."

She felt as though she'd endured years of feeling like second-best. Of giving out her number to men who never called her. Of seeing taller, thinner women walk off with guys she was interested in. So to have this man choose her, out of all the women on LoveMatch.com was incredible.

"I feel the same way," she admitted.

They never talked for long, but she always felt like the luckiest woman in the world when she hung up smiling.

She'd booked a hair appointment for Tuesday and then, thinking what the hell, added a mani, pedi and a facial into the mix.

When she imagined that beautiful, sexy man seeing her for the first time, it was easy to make sensible food choices. Dinner was a salad with oil and vinegar and a tasteless piece of broiled fish because she could still lose a pound or two by Tuesday if she remained disciplined.

She was contorted on her green yoga mat, trying to keep up with a Pilates DVD that would tighten her core, define her muscles and—something the cover copy had neglected to mention—make her sweat like a pig, when the ding on her computer signaled an incoming email.

Only too happy to give her core a rest, she leapt up to find, as she had hoped, that the email was from Gregory.

Hi sweetie,
I'm in a jam and I don't know who else to turn to. My ex-wife ran up all my credit cards so I had to cancel

them. My flight was canceled and I need to book a new one to get home in time for our date. I hate to ask, but could you wire me the money for the flight? It will be $1,200. I'll pay you back when I see you. Love, Gregory.

She read the email a second time, feeling worse by the second. *Don't jump to conclusions,* she scolded herself. He could be legitimate. Anyone could get stuck in a foreign country without a credit card. Although it was hard to imagine why his own company couldn't advance him the money for an airline ticket. In the background, the Pilates woman was encouraging everyone to "tighten those glutes as you lift your spine off the mat. And hold."

Julia sat down in front of the computer, nibbling her lower lip as she read the email yet again, then began typing.

Dear Gregory,
I have to admit your request has puzzled me. There are warnings all over the website about not sending money to strangers. Maybe if I'd actually met you, it would be different. How would I even send you the money?

Within a minute a response came.

Hi sweetie,
Please trust me. I want us to be together.

And then he'd included full instructions on how to wire money via Western Union.

And that's when she knew she'd been scammed.

"Do NOT SAY, 'I told you so,'" Hailey warned Rob. "Julia's very sensitive about what happened."

He held up his hands. "Hey, I was only trying to warn her. Not trying to score points. I didn't want the guy to turn out to be a scammer. She seems like a nice woman. I'm sorry it happened."

"Okay," she said more mildly.

His eyes crinkled at the edges as he faced her. "But to you, I can say it, right? 'I told you so.'"

"It was the lucky guess of a suspicious mind."

"Bull. It's an instinct honed by years of gathering and reporting news."

"We won't mention her getting scammed when she gets here. I don't want her to feel stupid. It could happen to anyone."

"Why is she coming, anyway?" And Hailey had a feeling there was an unspoken *and why are you here?* in his tone, as well.

Neither of them had mentioned that steamy kiss they'd shared in the bedroom yesterday. She was happy she'd had a dramatic story to impart the minute she got to Bellamy House so there were no awkward silences, no talking about something she preferred to ignore.

Even if Rob did look far too kissable in worn jeans, a much-washed and faded T-shirt advertising some band she'd never heard of and those bare feet that she found ridiculously sexy.

"I'm not happy about the way we've staged the small bedroom upstairs. It was fine to have it as a nursery when the MacDonalds were looking at it. However, most of the people who look won't have a baby so I'm thinking of turning it into an older child's bedroom with a single bed and a desk."

"Can't the people who look at houses figure out where their own stuff will fit?"

She thought about it. "Some can, I guess. Most only see what's in front of them. In this economy we want to do everything we can to make a home so inviting a buyer can't resist. Since this is a family neighborhood with schools nearby and that big park right across the street, it makes sense to stage it for a family."

"So you put a single bed and a desk in it. That's pretty much how it was when I grew up."

"I'm glad you approve of something we're doing. Which reminds me, you're going to have to make yourself scarce. Two sets of potential buyers are coming today between two and three o'clock."

He scowled. "We made a deal. You could keep the listing but I'd be living here."

"And I said I'd work around you. That means you leave fifteen minutes before the appointment time so I have a few minutes to clean up after you."

"Hey, I'm neat."

"I know you are. And what a relief that is, but I'll need to put your shoes away and hide your toothbrush. Stuff like that."

"You leave my toothbrush alone. A man's toothbrush is a personal thing. Handling it implies intimacy."

And just like that the intense lust she'd experienced during that kiss came roaring back. She was trying to forget it, and based on the way he was acting around her, so was he. Now he mentioned intimacy and she felt the warmth of his words touching her.

"Fine. Put away your own toothbrush."

"Okay," he said gruffly and she knew he'd been thinking about that steamy kiss, too.

They heard a knock and then the front door opening. "Hi," called Julia.

"Hi. We're in the kitchen." She put her finger over her lips as a reminder not to mention Julia's troubles.

Julia swept in with all the drama of an opera diva preparing for her final, tragic aria. "I feel so stupid!" she cried. "I am never, ever dating again."

Well, so much for worrying that Rob might bring up a difficult subject. She might have known Julia would be more than happy to share.

Even though her friend spoke in a tragi-comic tone, Hailey could see she'd been crying recently.

She wasn't going to sit by and let a good friend hurt. It was difficult for Hailey to make intimate friendships; she sometimes felt as though she'd never learned how. That's why her friendship with Julia was so important to her.

They'd met at a networking business event and they'd talked a little and laughed a little and exchanged business cards. She was startled when Julia had called her a couple of days later and suggested lunch, but she'd been pleased. They chatted about the industry, about their ambitions and then about men.

She liked Julia's frankness and honesty. Within a couple of weeks they were seeing each other regularly for a yoga class, a drink after work, shopping and brunch. Julia had a big, noisy family who'd lived at the same address for fifty years. She had friends she'd known since kindergarten. She had everything Hailey had never had and always craved.

She watched as Julia, her sisters, brothers and mother would argue, sometimes squabble like kids and then hug and joke minutes later. Julia took her in, made Hailey part of her life. Almost forced her to open up and share.

At some point she realized that Julia was her best friend. Probably the closest woman friend she'd ever had.

And if there was one thing she could do to thank Julia for teaching her what a friend was, it was to be one. So she said, "You are not giving up."

"I knew when I saw the photograph that he was too good-looking for me."

"That wouldn't be his real photo," Rob said. "You know that, right? He's probably a twenty-two-year-old Nigerian kid with a degree who speaks good English. They steal pictures of male models and hope nobody notices."

"I didn't," she moaned. "And I thought his accent was so cute. He said he'd been born in Manchester and moved around a lot. That's why his accent was different." She smacked her forehead with her palm. "And I believed him. I fell for the whole scam, hook, line and sinker."

"No. You didn't," Rob said. "You didn't send any money. So he didn't gain anything." Rob was a lot more direct than Hailey would have been but she could see that his blunt words had an effect. Julia looked slightly less beaten down. While she watched him talking to her friend she realized he was a truly nice guy, and watching his lips move reminded her that he was a great kisser.

And she hadn't been kissed in a long time.

He'd awakened her lusty, sexy side and she didn't think it was going back into hibernation anytime soon. What she was going to do about this, she had no idea.

She wasn't a casual woman and she didn't do casual sex. Still, an image of Rob and her in that big bed upstairs kept intruding. She pictured the two of them, limbs entwined, and a feeling of heat began to spread through her.

"Scammers only win when they get—"

He paused, turned to stare at Hailey, and she felt him sharing her fantasy as surely as if the two of them were naked and entwined at this very moment. The look he gave her was searing, intense. She touched her chest, her fingers resting on her collarbone, and his gaze followed as though he were the one touching her there.

Julia's expression was still bleak. "He gained my trust. I believed the guy. That's what hurts so much. I consider myself an intelligent woman. How could I be so stupid?" She shook her head and her red curls bounced. "Anyway, I'm done with LoveMatch.com."

Julia's pain broke the moment of intense lust and Hailey returned her attention to where it belonged.

"No," Hailey cried. "You can't give up so easily. Then the scam artists really do win. Come on. You're not going to let one bad apple wreck the whole orchard."

"I'm giving up on apples."

"Come on. Get your computer out. We're going to get you a date with a real guy who may not be the love of your life but who exists."

"Wow. How my standards are dropping. I used to think I couldn't date anyone who didn't appreciate Frank Gehry. Now all I ask is that he actually breathes."

Hailey laughed. "It will be fun. You'll feel a lot better once you put this behind you."

"I guess." Julia allowed herself to be persuaded to open her computer and log on to the site. Hailey leaned over her shoulder, watching every keystroke. "What about him?" she asked, pointing when Julia's possible matches appeared.

"I hate beards," she said, and deleted the guy's picture.

"What about him?"

Julia snorted. "The only good thing I can say about a guy that ugly is at least he's not a scammer who stole a male model's photo."

Hailey squinted to get a better look at the profile photo. "He's not that ugly."

Julie glanced up at her. "Would you go out with him?"

"Oh, look," she said, "Somebody's sent you a message. Two in fact. Click through."

Julia did. "*Bigbrownbear?* His handle is Bigbrownbear? I am so going into a nunnery." She clicked the message open anyway. It showed a man who could have been one of Santa's elves. His profile stated he was sixty, but he appeared a decade older. "Not big, not brown, not a bear. My luck continues," Julia said.

"He's a sculptor," Hailey read. "That's interesting. He says he'd like to meet for coffee."

"Maybe he wants to adopt me."

"Oh, look, another message just came through."

"From hotboy." She clicked the email icon and up came the message. She read aloud. "Lookin for a rockin' older gal. Do you go for younger guys?"

No one said a word when she clicked Delete.

"Okay, let's try John2012."

"What do you bet his name isn't even John?" Julia clicked on the message. A nice face looked out at them from the guy's profile photo. He'd sent a short message that said he'd be interested in getting to know her a little better.

Instead of deleting him, Julia clicked through to the man's online profile. He said he was recently divorced and worked in the computer industry. His hobbies in-

cluded sailing, ethnic restaurants and reading. Hailey
held her tongue and waited for Julia's verdict.

"He looks boring," she said. "And he has no style."

Hailey read over her friend's shoulder. "He sounds
nice. And you both like to eat out. You have that in common. What have you got to lose?"

"He probably thinks Frank Gehry is a football
player."

"Julia, at least meet the guy for coffee."

"Hmm. I don't know." All the same she pulled up
each of his three photos and studied them.

"Julia, go for coffee with this man. It's only coffee."

"What if we hate each other on sight?"

"Order an espresso so you can gulp it down if you
have to. You can always talk about books."

"I don't know." Julia made to close her laptop. Hailey prevented her. "Do it. Send him a message back.
Immediately."

"You are so bossy. If I have a terrible time I'm bill-
ing you at my hourly rate."

She squeezed her friend's shoulder. "There's someone wonderful out there for you. I know it."

Rob said, "Let me take a look."

Both women stared at him. "You're interested in Julia's matches? Maybe you and Bigbrownbear have a
future."

"Very funny. I want to look at Julia's profile."

"Why?"

"What is it with you two? I'm a guy. In the right age
range. I can tell you if your profile's any good."

"I don't want to appeal to you. No offense, but I
wouldn't date you."

"None taken. I wouldn't date you either." He held
out his hand. "Now give."

Hailey brought Julia's profile back up and handed over the tablet. He took his time, read everything she'd written and perused the three photos. Then he shook his head. "You come across as boring, too. This isn't you."

Julia tapped her fingernails on the tabletop. "Like I said, you're not my target market."

"What's bothering you about her profile?" Hailey asked. Maybe he and Julia wouldn't ever date each other but he was right. He was a man in the same age range. Also he was smart and well-traveled.

"The photograph is too businesslike. I bet it's the one you use on your staging website, isn't it?"

"Absolutely. I paid a lot of money for a professional portrait. Why not use it?"

"Because you're not selling your services as a stager, you're selling yourself as a sexual partner and possible marriage material. The business suit and heavy makeup aren't cutting it."

"But—"

"Wait right there." He got to his feet, grabbed his cane and limped over to his camera bag, taking out a smallish SLR camera and came back toward her.

"What are you doing?" Julia sounded alarmed and looked to Hailey for help.

"I'm taking your picture."

She flapped her hands. "I'm not dressed right. My makeup's terrible."

"You look great. You look like yourself."

Hailey nodded. "I agree. You dress with such great Bohemian style. You've got your favorite dangly earrings on, you're wearing a colorful sweater and you are having a good hair day. Swipe on some more lip gloss and you'll look fab."

After they'd both convinced Julia she didn't have

to post Rob's pictures if she didn't like them, they persuaded her to go into the living room and stand by the arrangement of flowers as colorful and vibrant as she was.

He got Hailey to move a lamp and then went to work snapping photos. He gave her quiet instructions about moving her chin down and what to do with her hands. He had her turn her body a little and Hailey watched her friend relax and get into the mood of the photo shoot. "Think about the greatest sex you've ever had," he said as he focused.

Julia's face softened and her smile grew intimate. *Wow,* Hailey thought, watching him bend and move, totally focused on his task. He might be injured, but everything apart from his leg was athletic, virile. She could imagine having the greatest sex ever with Rob. In fact it was all she could think about.

Damn. She had a problem.

He snapped a few more photos and then nodded.

"Okay. I'll email you the best of these and you can post a new profile picture. I guarantee it will help. Also, maybe make your written profile more—I don't know—personal. A guy's not too interested in where you went to school."

"What does he want to know?" Hailey asked.

"Will she be fun to be with? How much baggage is she dragging around? Does she play games? Is she looking for her kids' daddy? Is she sane? You know, stuff like that."

"Great," Julia said, pretending to type. "I'm fun to be with, the only games I play are Scrabble and Monopoly, I may want kids someday but there's no hurry, I'm a little bit crazy, but in a good way."

"Yep, that works. Only, substitute strip poker for Monopoly if you really want to pull."

She giggled. "Thanks. I'll get you one of my business cards so you can email me the photos."

He turned, still grinning, toward Hailey. "How about you? You want me to take some shots of you?"

"For what? A dating site?"

He shrugged, his eyes both teasing and challenging. "Sure, why not?"

She couldn't hold his gaze. Instead she began fussing with the flower arrangement. "I don't have time to date. I have a career to build."

She heard the snapping of the camera and glared at him. "What are you doing?"

"Candid photos. You might want something for your website. You look good with those flowers."

"Oh. Okay."

Julia returned, handed over one of her business cards and Rob slipped it into his wallet. "I guarantee plenty more Bigbrownbears will be beating down your door when you fix your profile."

"I can hardly wait."

Then she turned to Hailey. "Come on. We'd better get to work upstairs."

Hailey nodded. "And you, Rob, can make yourself scarce."

"Thrown out of my own home," he muttered, then looked at Hailey. "And I'm a cripple. What kind of woman throws a cripple out?"

"A woman who wants to sell this house."

He repacked his camera bag and then grabbed his cane. He'd been using the cane, she noted, on a regular basis and neither of them had mentioned it. She was glad he had it in him to be a little bit sensible.

They'd been working together only a few days but she'd started to look forward to coming here. She liked Bellamy House, liked its history, the neighborhood, its possibilities.

And, in spite of his annoying quirks, she liked the house's current owner.

When he looked at her with those white teeth set in his tanned face she thought maybe she liked the current owner a little too much.

"Have a nice afternoon," she called when he stomped out, making his limp as pronounced as possible.

"Don't sell my house to any losers."

7

JULIA'S HOPES WERE so low when she entered Beananza for her first actual date with a real man from LoveMatch.com that if they'd been any lower she'd still be in bed.

What was she even doing here? All right for Hailey to talk her into emailing the only man who seemed remotely in her dating range since she wasn't the one feeling like a complete fool.

The only thing that made a quick coffee with a complete stranger acceptable was that she could drink her favorite brew in her favorite location.

When the door banged behind her, she breathed in the coffee smell and glanced around.

She saw him right away, John2012. Sitting by himself at a table for two, a china mug in front of him. She glanced at the old-fashioned clock on the wall and realized she was ten minutes late. Oops.

She headed toward him and he stood up and held out his hand. "Hi. I'm John." Nice firm grip. At least she'd give him that.

"I'm Julia."

"I thought you'd stood me up," he said.

"No. Sorry, I guess I'm running a couple of minutes late." She glanced down at his half-finished coffee. "Were you early?"

"I like to be on time," he said.

"Oh." *This is going well.* She took a step toward the coffee bar, Hailey's suggestion of a quick espresso in her mind when he said, "What can I get you?"

"Oh, thanks. Tall, skinny latte."

"Coming right up."

He walked to the bar and she had a chance to study him. He was on the slim side but tall with muscular shoulders. There was something almost cowboy about him with his weathered skin, two deep lines running down lean cheeks, deep blue eyes and a prominent nose and chin. But who dressed him? That blue plaid shirt, faded from washing, was older than some of her friends. The jeans were the most unflattering she'd ever seen and had to be from a discount store, and when he'd stepped into a pair of truly ugly work shoe/boot things, he'd caught the back hems of the denim in them.

If he'd paid more than six dollars for that haircut he'd been ripped off since she suspected the barber learned his trade in an abattoir.

When John put in her drink order, Bruno glanced over and waved.

John sauntered back to her reminding her again oddly of a cowboy. All he needed was a Stetson and a way nicer pair of jeans. He set the mugs carefully on the table and she thanked him politely. Then almost choked.

Bruno's latte art topping her brew today was a question mark.

She gulped her coffee quickly, hoping John hadn't noticed. If she ever did this again she'd meet in an anon-

ymous coffee chain store. One that served to-go cups
in case she needed to make a quick exit.

They both sipped coffee and then he said, "This is a
nice place. I haven't been here before."

"I like it. The coffee's good."

Silence. Oh, man, this was tougher than she'd imagined. She loved new people. Always prided herself on
being able to talk to anyone, and here she was acting
like a self-conscious fool. She had to get a grip.

So many of her friends and family were getting married, having kids, moving on with their lives. Was she
becoming desperate? She hated the thought.

She tried to recall John's profile so she could at least
start some kind of conversation. "So, you like ethnic
restaurants?"

"I do," he nodded. "One thing we have in common."

"Do you have favorites?"

He shook his head, looking grim. "My ex only liked
fancy high-end places. I didn't get much chance to try
out smaller, ethnic places." Then he winced. "Sorry.
Great start to a first date. Talk about your angry, bitter divorce."

"Was it?"

"Angry and bitter?" he shrugged. "Is there another
kind?"

"I don't know. I've never been married."

They both took refuge in another sip of coffee.

"How 'bout you? I bet you eat out a lot?"

What? Was he suggesting she was so overweight
she must spend all her free time grazing at all-you-
can-eat buffets?

"No," she said. "Not really."

"Oh. You seem really cosmopolitan, as though you

know all the good places." He seemed a little disappointed to find out she wasn't that person.

But she *was* that person. She supposed she'd become so freaked out by the scammer that she wasn't giving a perfectly nice man a chance.

She glanced up and caught his gaze, realizing he was as uncomfortable as she. All of a sudden Bruno's caffeinated question mark, the pressure of too many friends' marriages and babies, the scammer, all of it seemed so ridiculous, she started to laugh. "I don't know about you but I'd really like to start over."

He nodded. "Can we consider that bitter-divorce comment deleted?"

"Done."

He let out a sigh of relief, and leaned back in his chair. And it was better. For no reason except that they'd been honest for a moment, it was better.

"Your profile said you work in computers?"

"That's right. I'm a programmer. My team works on software for the construction industry."

"Oh. I'm a home stager. That's sort of related to the construction industry."

"The way high fashion is connected to the silkworm."

"Okay. You made me smile. That's good."

So they talked about their respective businesses and she realized her coffee mug was empty and she hadn't had a terrible time.

"Well?" he asked, and she was reminded of Bruno's question mark.

"Well?" she asked back.

"You seem like a nice woman. I'd like to see you again if you're interested. Maybe we could try out one of those ethnic restaurants we both like."

Her silence dragged on a second too long while she processed the bad hair, bad clothes, and tried to imagine herself showing up to a decent restaurant with him at her side.

"I'm not sure we'd be a fit," she finally said, as honestly as she could without hurting his feelings, she hoped.

He didn't seem crushed. He merely nodded. "Tell you what, I'm not a big fan of emailing through a dating site. Here's my card with my personal email and my cell phone. If you ever want a friend to have dinner with or somebody to take in a movie or something, go ahead and call me."

She took the card and tucked it into her bag. "Thanks."

He rose and shook her hand again. "You heading out?" he motioned to the door.

She couldn't stand the idea of making small talk as they headed outside to their vehicles so she shook her head. "I'll have another coffee and check my email."

He nodded. "I enjoyed meeting you. Good luck." And was gone.

Since Bruno currently had nothing more pressing to do than fill the canisters with sugar, she walked up to him and said, "Well? What did you think?"

When Bruno turned to her he was wearing a T-shirt sporting a cup of coffee with these words printed on the surface: *Black as the devil, hot as hell, pure as an angel, sweet as love. Talleyrand.*

"Seemed like a nice guy. He a new squeeze?"

"No. I don't think so. We met online. This was the first time we'd seen each other in person."

"He's tall."

"Dresses badly."

"Mmm."

"He told me to call him if I want to go to dinner or a movie. I didn't feel much chemistry, but he seems like an okay guy. What do you think? Should I call him?"

Bruno neatened the packages on top of a silver canister. "Depends how desperate you get, I guess."

THE STATUE OF LENIN had been standing in the middle of Fremont for almost twenty years now, Rob supposed, as he wandered killing time, while strangers toured his grandmother's house.

He scowled at Lenin.

Lenin scowled back.

Rob still remembered the fuss when a local businessman bought the huge bronze statue and transported it to Seattle with the help of the original sculptor. Designed and installed in Czechoslovakia, the piece had fallen victim to the Velvet Revolution and would have been sold for scrap had not an English teacher from Washington agreed to buy it, perceiving it not as propaganda but as a work of art. He wondered how poor old Vladimir would feel if he could see the way Fremont treated his likeness.

He'd been decorated with Christmas lights, dressed up to resemble John Lennon and even dressed in drag for Gay Pride week. Today he was standing fairly peacefully, his revolutionary torch before him, Western capitalism surrounding him in the form of stores and restaurants, and trees blushing red as autumn deepened.

Rob had his camera bag slung over his shoulder, more out of habit than because he'd had any real intention of snapping photos. He'd learned long ago that a working photographer is always on. If a giant meteor fell out of the sky and crushed Lenin, he'd kill himself if he'd been right here, an eyewitness, and had missed documenting the event.

Not that any meteors seemed to be in sight. The sky was clear and sunny, unusual for fall in Seattle. The mild weather had brought people out to walk and chat and stroll.

Apart from tourists, nobody paid much attention to the formidable statue, all going about their business, living their lives. Once again he experienced that odd feeling of the similarity of most people's lives and concerns no matter where they live. Here came a mother chastising her son for something. The kid's expression was so bored as he slouched along at her side, Rob had his camera out before he realized his intention.

He forgot the pain in his leg, forgot his enforced exile from work, forgot the annoyance of two bossy women trying to sell his grandmother's house with the maximum disturbance to him, forgot even the inconvenience of his strong attraction to his uppity Realtor.

He snapped photos, tiny frozen moments in time, knowing the best ones would tell a story, evoke an emotion, bring strangers together in one fleeting moment of recognition. Maybe it was good for him to have this time. He discovered that without the heat of conflict, which was usually the environment in which he worked, he had more time to frame and set up shots, wait for the perfect moment.

The wobble of the chocolate gelato balanced precariously on a toddler's cone while mom and an older woman, maybe grandma, chatted together, the lick that sent the scoop tumbling, the splat, the wail of grief and despair.

The fussing women, the kid's tears.

He'd seen enough of kids' tears that he couldn't do

anything about but report whatever conflict the innocents had been caught in. This he could fix.

He quickly walked into the ice-cream store, paid for a replacement cone and made the teenage boy working behind the counter in a striped apron deliver it so there'd be no misunderstandings. No embarrassing gratitude.

He got his reward when the little kid stopped crying and took the brand-new cone with a hiccup and a lisped thanks, his heartbreak melting faster than the lump of ice cream on the pavement.

When Rob next checked the time, the sun was setting and he saw on his watch that two hours had passed with the speed of minutes. He packed up his bag, gripped his grandmother's cane and made his slow way to his grandmother's old Buick which he'd jump-started since the battery had gone dead.

He had no idea what he was going to do with the images he'd captured today, but he had the pleasant sensation of a good day's work.

He decided to reward himself with a good meal of the freshest Pacific Northwest ingredients. If he bought enough food for two, that was his business.

And since he was in town only for a short time, he carefully drove his grandmother's Buick to Pike Place Market. The place was bustling as usual and smelled of spices mixed with coffee mixed with the scents of artisanal cheeses and fresh flowers, all flowing around him and interweaving with memories of souks and farmer's markets all over the world.

His camera trigger finger began to itch until he gave in and once more pulled out his equipment. The personality of Pike's was as individual as the souks of Marrakech and yet...

He spent a happy thirty minutes or so loading up

on fresh ingredients for dinner. Because he was an optimist, he even bought wine. Which he would never drink alone.

WHEN HE ARRIVED HOME, Rob was pleased to see the lights were still on in the house. That meant Hailey was probably waiting for him.

Sure enough when he opened the front door and limped inside she came out of the kitchen with her suit jacket on and her bag in her hand.

"I was waiting for you," she said.

"So I see." He lifted the sack of groceries. "I'm cooking if you want to stay for dinner."

She fiddled with the button on her jacket. Glanced up at him, blushed and glanced back down. He was cold, tired and his leg throbbed but one glance from those blue-gray eyes and he was transported back to their steamy session in the bedroom.

"I—um— Maybe we should talk," she said.

"Uh-huh?" He put down his bags, slipped off his jacket and hung it on the old oak coat tree she'd stripped bare before the customers arrived, though if you asked him, a coat tree with no coats on it looked a damned sight stranger than one with a coat or two hanging from it.

"Dinner is, uh, unexpected."

"Not when it's dinnertime."

She gripped the handle of her briefcase. "What happened…" She stumbled to a halt and for some reason, he began to enjoy himself.

"You mean the kissing?"

He leaned against the wall, partly so he could take the weight off his injured leg and partly so he could watch her face.

"Yes. Yes. The kissing." She looked adorable, sexy, unsure, confused, a little irritated. "It was very unprofessional." She fiddled with that button some more. "It won't happen again."

Good. That was excellent news. Whatever crazy bug had bitten the pair of them, they'd both obviously come to their senses. Getting involved with a high-strung Realtor who was attempting to sell his house was a terrible idea. He'd had some bad ones, and this was up there with the worst.

So why did he have to be perverse? Why couldn't he simply agree it was a bad idea, shake her hand and promise to keep his distance if she kept hers?

Because he was a born fool, that's why. And kissing her again might be a bad idea, but not kissing her again seemed infinitely worse. "It won't happen again?"

She shook her head. "No."

"But what if I want it to happen again?"

Her lips quirked at that, and he could see her trying to reel in the smile. "I'm your Realtor. Our relationship has to be strictly professional."

"I see."

He regarded her for a moment, crossed his arms in front of his chest. "I suppose I could fire you."

8

"FIRE ME?" Hailey could not believe the words she'd just heard. It was the last thing she'd expected to come out of his mouth. In fact, she'd expected that he'd be as eager as she to put that unfortunate incident behind them.

At least she knew she would if she could only stop thinking about it.

It wasn't fair. She had plans. Two agendas keeping her life and her future on track. And nowhere, not in the electronic minder and not in the paper backup did she have time slotted in for a personal relationship.

Okay, she knew that these things happened in their own time. Of course she did. But her attraction to Rob wasn't only inconvenient in its timing, it was horrible on every level. Even if she could stand the idea of a relationship with a man when she really didn't have time for it, she would never choose a guy like Rob. Never. Not in a million years. He was everything she didn't want in a man. Restless. A wanderer. She'd had enough of wandering men.

With a father who'd moved his family twelve years out of thirteen she understood her need for stability. The very notion of being with a man who had those same itchy feet was inconceivable.

Her ideal man was a stay-put kind of guy—the kind whose idea of fun was puttering in the garden, working on home-building projects. A thrilling Saturday date would be wandering around a home-improvement store hand in hand, good-naturedly arguing about Brazilian cherrywood for the foyer as opposed to reclaiming the original oak. Naturally, they'd end up reclaiming the oak. She loved old houses that kept their original features. In her mind, Brazilian cherrywood should grace the homes of Brazilians.

Rob's idea of a Saturday afternoon was shooting footage of rebels in a country most people couldn't find on a map, never mind pronounce, and then getting shot himself.

So, in spite of the fact that one steamy kiss had disordered her plans, and intruded on her daydreams—and, okay, her night dreams, too, she had to be clear that it couldn't happen again. Once she'd told him that there'd be no future physical contact between the two of them, she was certain she'd stop thinking about it herself.

All he had to do was agree with her, maybe even apologize for getting carried away, though she knew perfectly well she'd been as crazed as he had. She blushed even to recall her own actions.

And did he make it easy for her?

Did he agree there'd be no future contact?

Did he apologize?

Hell no. He threatened to fire her. And with the most foolish, sexy grin on his face while he did it.

"You can't fire me."

"I believe I can."

"But—" Even though she knew he was toying with

her she still felt irritation pound through her veins. Why couldn't he make this easy for her? "But—" She shook her head. "You're not going to fire me."

He seemed to consider her words carefully. "No. But I probably want to kiss you again. Assuming you want to kiss me again, too, I don't think we should let a dumb thing like business get in the way."

"I don't want to kiss you again," she blurted, feeling more ridiculous by the second as this absurd conversation continued.

"Then we don't have a problem."

"Good. Okay."

He didn't argue, didn't fight for the opportunity to kiss her so senseless she could barely see straight. That was good. That was excellent.

"I still think you should have dinner with me."

She was so busy thinking of all the scorching kissing they weren't going to be doing that his request threw her. "What?"

He grinned at her. Leaning against the wall looking sexier than any man should.

"Have dinner with me."

"When?"

"Tonight."

"You're asking me for a date? Didn't you hear a single word I just said?"

"I'm not asking you for a date. I stopped at Pike Place Market and bought fresh sockeye, asparagus and potatoes. Seems like too nice a meal to eat alone."

She narrowed her eyes at him. "You don't know how to cook, do you? You want me to make you dinner."

"I happen to be an excellent cook."

"I'm not—"

"And you can tell me all about your showing today."

For some reason he was much cheerier than when he'd left hours earlier, and the feeling was oddly contagious.

"How come you came back in such a good mood? You were a complete grump when you left."

"When you kicked me out of my own home, you mean." He reached down and grabbed the white plastic grocery sack off the floor and started on his halting way to the kitchen. "I had an epiphany this afternoon."

"An epiphany? Don't tell me. You realized how lucky you are to have Seattle's finest Realtor at your beck and call?"

He turned to glance at her over his shoulder. "I thought becking and calling were out, as per our professional relationship."

She had to bite back an answering smile. He was just so easy to be with, so easy to flirt with, damn it. "So you *were* listening."

"Oh, I heard you all right. I just don't happen to agree with you. I think you can mix business and pleasure and make both more interesting. But that's me."

"Have you ever—" she began and then could have bitten her tongue. What was she thinking?

Having reached the kitchen he put down the sack and turned on the kitchen faucet to wash his hands. "Have I ever had a relationship with a work colleague? Sure. Haven't you?"

The stab of—what? Surely not jealousy—surprised her. It wasn't any of her business who he got involved with.

"No. Never."

He turned off the tap and dried his hands. Nice hands, she noted. Long-fingered and strong.

"How about a client? Have you ever been involved with a client?"

"Romantically?"

Even though his face was serious, his eyes laughed at her. "Yeah, romantically."

Apart from him? "No. I told you. I set rules for myself."

"Didn't you ever hear that nice old saying about rules being meant to be broken?"

"I bet you've broken a few rules in your time."

He chuckled. "One or two." He reached for the bottom of a set of three drawers and drew out an apron with the ease of somebody who's done it frequently. It was green cotton with sprigs of yellow flowers; obviously one of his grandmother's. When he popped the bib over his head and tied the string around his waist without any worry about whether he looked ridiculous or not, her heart melted a little.

He didn't look a bit ridiculous. He looked comfortable in his skin and his grandmother's apron which made her think he was also comfortable with his memories of her. Nice.

She removed her suit jacket, hung it over the back of one of the kitchen chairs, and then rolled up the sleeves of her silk blouse. "What can I do?"

He was taking items out of the bag. He placed a bottle of wine on the counter. "Can you open the wine?"

"Sure."

He'd bought wine. She wondered if this impromptu dinner date was actually planned. And whether she minded.

She opened the wine—a Washington pinot noir— and poured it into two glasses she found in the cupboard he gestured to.

"What else?"

"Want to sous-chef?"

"Why not?"

He reached for the drawer and took out a second apron. This one was cream sprigged with pink roses. He shook it out and then held the top strap for her, waiting until she stepped closer before looping it over her head. He turned her around, putting his hands on her hips in a gesture that was probably cheflike, but felt ridiculously intimate.

She was deeply aware of his hands moving behind her as he straightened the straps. "My grandmother was a little more stout than you," he said, and then brought his arms around her middle, doubling the straps around her waist. She felt him so close to her, felt his breath on her neck as he fastened the ties at her back. She wanted badly to lean against him, let the attraction she felt for him take them wherever it led.

"All done," he said, stepping away and breaking the spell.

"Thanks."

He passed her the asparagus and potatoes and, as she snapped the ends off the former and scrubbed the latter, he prepared a sauce for the salmon.

They worked companionably, side by side in the kitchen. "I bought a decent barbecue last time I was here. It's about the only modern thing in the place. I'll grill the salmon."

"Where did you learn to cook?" she asked.

"From my grandmother. Long before it became trendy she thought every man should be able to cook. The first time she saw Jamie Oliver on TV she said to me, 'There you are, Rob. I told you so. Men who cook make women swoon.'"

Hailey laughed. "Did she really say *swoon?*"

"Absolutely. I swear she actually did swoon when he started that program to get healthier lunches in schools. She was a former English teacher, you know."

"I didn't."

"You'd have liked her. I think she'd have liked you, too."

"I'm glad."

He reminded her a bit of one of those sexy celebrity chefs. Casual, assured, not bothering to measure things very precisely, but fully in control. She'd never seen a man in a flowered apron look so handsome.

"Do you cook much?" she asked.

"I don't cook when I'm away, and when I'm in New York I mostly eat out. With so many good restaurants, you could eat out every night and never get bored. I do most of my cooking here. In this kitchen."

He glanced around. "I'm glad you stayed. It's weird being here without her, you know?"

"I can imagine."

To lighten the atmosphere she said, "I'll set the table."

He looked at her as though she were crazy. "It's already set."

"The table's staged. You can't eat off this stuff or mess up the placemats and napkins. Julia would kill us both."

"My grandmother would not approve of staging," he said.

"If your grandmother was as smart as you make her out to be she'd love anything that got her more money for her house."

She knew she had him when he shook his head. "Damn, she really would have liked you."

"You miss her, don't you?" Stupid question, but sometimes she found the dumbest question was the right one.

His mouth twisted. "I keep thinking I'll hear her voice. She used to phone me sometimes but the biggest thrill was when she emailed me the first time." He chuckled at the memory. "She must have been eighty-two. She bought a computer and hired a kid to teach her how to use it. She wanted to surprise me. And hell, did she ever. I was checking my email in Istanbul and there's a message from her."

"Wow."

"I know. Funny thing is she always wrote emails as though they were formal letters. You know, 'Dearest Robert, I hope this finds you well.' That kind of thing. I got such a kick out of them." It would be a long time before he stopped expecting her to call him or, to his intense delight, email him. He caught himself before he went on. "Anyhow, she was a cool lady. And she had no time for men who were useless around the house. Therefore, I cook."

As she'd suspected, dinner was perfectly cooked. Simple and delicious.

The placemats were faded with age and the dishes clearly had been frequently used, in contrast to the designer linens and gleaming Denby china Julia had provided.

Once he'd lit a couple of candles, the atmosphere was cozy, romantic even, though she pushed the word out of her mind the second she thought it.

When she bit into the salmon she almost moaned with pleasure. "This is fantastic."

"So? Was my grandmother right? Am I the next Jamie Oliver?"

"Jamie Oliver doesn't wear flowered aprons."

He shrugged. "He has his style. I have mine."

Privately, she liked Rob's style. Which was a problem.

She did not want to have romantic feelings for Rob.

Which immediately reminded that she was not here for pleasure, in spite of the mouthwatering meal and good wine, but for business.

"I think the people who came today really liked the house."

He speared a potato. "Did they?"

"Yes. A nice family relocating from Connecticut."

"Hmm."

"You have a problem with Easterners?"

He chewed his potato. Swallowed. "No. Not at all."

"Good. The company transferring them is putting them up for three days in a hotel and in that time they hope to make a decision. They'd want a fairly quick closing date so they can move their family in and he can start his new job."

"How quick are we talking?"

"It's negotiable, of course, but I think a quick closing would be a big selling feature. They want their kids settled in before the school year is too advanced."

"Hmm. What happened to that other couple? The ones who interrupted my sleep?"

"The MacDonalds?"

"Yeah."

"They didn't like the angry presence in the house."

He laid down his knife and fork and drilled her with his gaze. "My grandmother would never haunt anyone. And she was never negative."

She sent him a thin smile. "They were talking about you."

"Weenies. The house wasn't right for them."

In fact she knew it was but what was the point of arguing? She hoped the Fergusons, Ted and Sue, and their three kids aged eight to thirteen might soon call Bellamy House home. Not only was she anxious to close a sale, but she was beginning to think that the less time she spent with Rob the better.

"I expect to hear from them tomorrow. They may want to view the property a second time. I hope you can accommodate them."

"Kicking me out again?"

"Believe me, as soon as the deal closes, you will be left in peace."

"Are you kidding me? I have to figure out what to do with all this stuff." He gestured vaguely around the kitchen, which she knew meant the things in drawers and cupboards that the stagers hadn't removed. Not to mention all the furniture and items currently in storage.

"You know, there are charities that could make good use of her things. And the valuable or sentimental pieces you could put into storage until you decide what you want to keep. I could put you in touch with the right people."

He nodded.

"Well," she said, "I hate to eat and run but I've got some paperwork I'd like to do tonight. I'll let you know when I hear back from the Fergusons' Realtor."

"You do that."

He got to his feet and, using the cane, followed her to the front door.

She turned to bid him goodbye and found him closer

than she'd have dreamed possible. He could really move with that cane.

"Thank you again—"

"About that kissing thing," he interrupted. Were they back to that again?

"What about the kissing thing?" she asked, half irritated, half intrigued.

"I want to give you some more information."

"More information? About kissing?"

"Not exactly. More about other things." He dropped his gaze to the cane. "I want you to know, in case you're wondering, that the bullet damaged some muscle and nicked a bone. Nothing that won't heal. Everything else is in perfect working order." He raised his gaze to hers. "In case you were wondering."

"I wasn't." Mostly because it had been perfectly obvious from their kissing that everything was working fine. As he must know.

"And about that kissing thing—"

"Oh, for heaven's sake. Would you forget about the kissing thing?"

She felt his nearness, his warmth, the stirrings of desire.

"No. Some things are unforgettable."

A tiny sound came out of her throat, unbidden, primal. Their gazes connected and it was like a match to dry tinder.

Her heart sped up, her skin began to tingle.

He moved closer; their mouths were in easy reach. With no order from any thinking part of her brain, her lips parted.

He moved closer. "I want to tell you that since you're

the one with the rules I'm going to leave the next move to you."

While she stood there astonished, he leaned past her to open the door. "Good night."

9

ROB WAS BEGINNING to find his forced sabbatical much more interesting than he'd ever anticipated, he thought, as he lugged his camera bag awkwardly down the old wooden steps to the unfinished basement. The smell of the lower floor was as familiar to him as a signature perfume on a woman. It smelled like dust and aging cement and years of layered memory. Down here he'd built his first model airplane with newspaper spread out to catch the glue drips though somehow they always ended up on him anyway. He supposed he'd had a man cave back before the term even existed. A boy cave in truth. A lumpy old couch still crouched in the corner. He'd hunched on it on rainy Saturday afternoons to read comic books. Later he'd snuck a girl or two down here for some heavy petting. And in between all of that his grandmother had allowed him to turn an old bathroom into a darkroom.

Now that his home had become a decorator's showplace everywhere but down here, he'd begun using the old oak desk in the corner. He fired up his computer and downloaded today's photos.

He began looking through his personal photo library,

hunting for the similarities he'd detected between these everyday scenes in the town he called home and the many scenes of daily life he'd witnessed in places far, far from home.

He'd read somewhere that the different racial characteristics had developed around ten thousand years ago. Before that man had been one small tribe in Africa. He'd begun to realize what human DNA demonstrated—we are more similar than we are different.

Over the next couple of weeks he worked on his idea. It gave shape to his days, a purpose to his idleness. He'd never in all his career had time like this to devote to a larger project. He'd become so accustomed to snatching a story in process, snapping photos that were more about capturing today's action than art. Now he had the time and leisure to do both. And to tell a story that wouldn't be old news in a few weeks but was timeless.

He'd caught up with a few of his old friends, and it was strange to see them settled, some with families.

"Still footloose and fancy-free, huh?" Mike Lazenby asked him as they hung out at Mike's place one Saturday afternoon while his wife shopped. The guy was pacing the living room, a squirming, fussy infant draped over his shoulder. A line of spit-up ran down his back like seagull poop. But there was no jealousy in his tone. While Mike had been a legendary womanizer and rabble-rouser back in the day, Rob sensed deep contentment in his old friend.

"Yep."

Wouldn't be his choice, but it was nice to see Mike happy.

He saw Hailey a few times whenever she dropped in to make sure the place was perfect before she booted him out for her showings. He took perverse pride in always being there, in making her boot him out. It was kind of a kick, as was the buzz of electricity between them every time they saw each other.

He was healing nicely. He was well rested, well fed and in far too frequent company with the sexiest Realtor he'd ever seen. He wondered when they were going to close the deal between each other.

From how she looked at him from time to time, he knew, whether she said so or not, that she was thinking the same thing.

She'd been pretty pissed with him when he'd told the Fergusons—truthfully—that raccoons nested in the trees in his yard. He used to have one that climbed right up to his window where he'd leave food out for it. Okay, maybe he'd overheard the little girl say she was scared of raccoons but he was certain that wasn't the only reason they'd chosen another home. He wasn't disappointed to lose out on a fast sale that would have left him homeless as well as jobless.

Since she'd found them another home and closed the deal, she'd gotten over that. Still, he had to be careful or firing her wouldn't be an issue. She'd quit.

It was a rainy Thursday and once again he was pushed out of his own home.

"Where are you going in this rain with a camera?" she asked him.

"I have a date with a troll," he told her.

She raised her brows but she had to know he meant Fremont's very own troll, the sculpture under the Aurora Bridge, which he was going to photograph. He had no idea what he was going to do, but was confident that creativity, luck and timing would be on his side.

Or else he'd go get a coffee at Beananza and read the paper.

"Have fun with your troll."

"I'd rather have fun with you. You thought anymore about that kissing thing?"

The door shut with a decided bang behind him. He chuckled. Trolls could turn up anywhere.

He got lucky. Some tourists had come to see the troll and after he took a few snaps of them with their camera, he asked if he could take a few with his. One day they might be published, he told them, though it would probably be on his website. If he ever got one started.

Then the Adopt-a-Troll group came by to clean up litter. He snapped a few more shots. And finally he photographed the gloomy guy all alone beneath the cavernous bridge.

He still had time to stop for a coffee before heading home.

HAILEY HADN'T BOTHERED to tell Rob that the family coming to view the place today were cousins of Julia's. It wasn't any of his business. Paige and Jay were expecting their first child. Likely the house was out of their price range but even if it was they might tell friends about the place. Hal Wilson at work was about to list a very nice town house that would suit Paige and Jay and a little one perfectly.

Naturally, when the doorbell rang there were more than two people standing there. Paige and Jay, Julia, Paige's sister Noreen and Julia's mother Gloria were already talking a mile a minute as she opened the door.

"Congratulations on the listing, honey," Gloria said, giving her a huge hug. Gloria was an older, heavier version of Julia. Dramatic, outspoken and deeply maternal.

"Thanks. Julia's staging really makes the house shine."

"I couldn't be more proud of you two." Hailey knew it was true and once more felt very fortunate to be considered part of this loving family.

"Come on in and see the house," she said.

The oohs and aahs were predictable. As was the moment when Paige said, "I feel overwhelmed. This place is too big."

Hailey nodded. "I think I have the ideal place for you. It's not even on the market yet. We can see it tomorrow."

She described the town house and immediately saw the couple exchange glances and nod. "Let's see it," Jay said. "I'd be a lot happier with a mortgage I could pay off in this lifetime."

"Since you're here, you've got to see upstairs. The master bedroom is my dream room."

While Julia showed Paige and Jay the rest of the upstairs, Gloria remained with Hailey in the big master bedroom, admiring the view of the backyard, the fireplace and the window seat. "What a beautiful room." She walked to the four-poster. "And the bed!"

"I know." Every time she was in this room Hailey experienced a sense of connection she couldn't understand. She'd simply come to accept it. She'd step into the room and immediately feel that it was somehow hers, her fantasies of her and Rob in that bed as vivid as though they were memories.

"Agnes Neeson was my English teacher in high school," Gloria remarked.

"Really? Was she a good teacher?"

"The best." She shook her head. "Her daughter was a real mess though. She dropped out of high school. Always in trouble. Sex, drugs and rock and roll. Poor Mrs. Neeson. It was really sad."

"That would be Rob's mother."

"The current owner?"

She nodded.

"How did he turn out?"

"He's… He's…" How to describe Rob? "He's a successful photojournalist. Works for *World Week*." Without thinking, she sat on the bed and Gloria joined her. "He's driven, ambitious, cares about people."

"Easy on the eyes."

"Oh, yeah."

"You two having sex yet?"

"Gloria!"

"What? You think I don't know you almost as well as my own kids? You're crazy about the man. I can hear it in your voice."

"I've thought about it." She blew out a breath. "I can barely think about anything else. But there'd be no future."

"I've never known a woman who spent so much time worrying about the future as you do. Maybe you should try living for now a little more." The older woman drilled her with a gaze that was like Julia's only with more life experience. "Have you had sex even once since your engagement broke up?"

She shook her head.

"Maybe it's time."

A shiver ran through her. Maybe it was.

"What if I fall in love with him and he breaks my heart?"

"You're doing it again. Forget the future and start living for today." She nudged Hailey with her elbow. "Or tonight."

Hailey knew herself too well to believe she could have an affair and not end up hurt. Maybe Gloria was right though. What if she indulged herself and Rob? Not for a long time, that could be dangerous.

But for a short time? Just to give in to the attraction that burned between them?

Could she play with fire and not get burned?

Maybe just one night.

THE LIGHTS WERE ON, as Rob had expected they'd be when he returned home from Beananza. Hailey always waited to tell him how her showing had gone. He liked to think she enjoyed their short visits as much as he did.

Remembering the door slam as he'd left, he called out, "Hi, honey. I'm home."

She came from the direction of the kitchen looking better than any Realtor should. He really wished she'd quit making them both wait for something she must know was inevitable.

Something seemed different about her. She glowed with suppressed excitement. With a sense of foreboding he prayed she wasn't going to present an offer on the house.

"How was the showing?"

"It wasn't right for them. Young couple with a child on the way. They need something smaller."

"Too bad," he said even as a feeling of relief slid through him.

If she hadn't sold his house, what was she looking so excited about?

"How's your leg?"

"Healing. Why?" He glanced at her with suspicion. "If you have some big-ass box that needs moving or furniture to unload I have to remind you I'm the walking wounded."

"What if I want sex?"

He was so dumbfounded he put all his weight on his bad leg and nearly went down. "What did you say?"

"It's a purely theoretical question. I was wondering whether you think your leg is strong enough for you to have sex?"

"Yes." The answer was definite.

"Theoretically yes?"

"Let's-go-upstairs-and-rip-our-clothes-off yes."

Hailey was enjoying herself. It wasn't a big surprise he'd so enthusiastically said yes. In fact, she'd have been stunned if he hadn't, given the level of sizzle between them recently. But to have amazed him like that, to have seen the look on his face go from suspicious to knocked out, gave her a huge charge.

Gloria was right. She'd been too cautious, too scared to get hurt. Too worried about a future that she couldn't predict.

Even as she watched, congratulating herself on shocking him so completely, the expression in his eyes changed. From stunned to…speculative. He took a halting step closer. He wasn't leaning so heavily on the cane anymore. In fact he didn't use it unless he was going out. "I've been wanting to get you upstairs in that big bed since the first moment I saw you," he told her, lifting a hand and playing with the ends of her hair.

She snorted. "When you first saw me you weren't too happy. You tried to kick me out of the house."

"That's true. Doesn't mean I didn't want you in my bed. A man can think two things at once, you know." He traced his index finger up the line of her hair, sending shivers up and down her body. "Especially if one of them is about sex."

He moved closer and she loved the feel of his

warmth, his personal space meshing with hers so you didn't know where one left off and the other began.

"Why the change of heart?" he wanted to know.

"The truth?"

"Of course."

If she was going to sleep with the man she ought to at least be able to tell him why, after informing him she wouldn't be kissing him anymore she was suddenly planning to become as intimate as two people can be. "I can't stop thinking about it," she said softly, shrugging. "It's getting in the way of my work. I'm usually not a daydreamer. I'm very efficient."

"I've noticed."

"I feel like if we just do it already I'll stop thinking about it."

"Such a romantic."

He'd think she was a complete die-hard romantic if he knew how much her fantasies revolved around that big four-poster. Ever since she'd first seen him stretched out all scruffy and gorgeous she'd associated him with the bed, and adding the two together equaled hot sex in her mind. Maybe she was being stupid, as she accused herself about six times a day, but the truth was she couldn't keep wasting time dreaming about having sex with the man. She'd be better to do it.

Why not? As Gloria had reminded her, she and Rob were both single, and she was young and healthy with a normal sex drive. Nobody was going to get hurt. Why shouldn't they indulge?

His mouth drew closer to hers and, as she lifted her face to his as though compelled, she retained enough sense to say, "I have some rules."

The forward motion stopped.

The sexual intensity in his glance dissipated replaced

by a glint of humor. "Of course you do," he said. "Do I need to go wash my hands first? Change the bedding? Brush my teeth?"

"No." She laughed. "Well, brushing your teeth is probably a good idea. I'll brush mine, too."

"You're a head case, you know that, right?"

"I wasn't going to say any of those things. I was thinking of setting some ground rules."

"Darling, the rules of sex are simple. Nobody gets hurt, and everybody has a good time." He stepped even closer. "And I will make damn sure you have a good time."

Warmth was stealing over her. He might be half joking, but the other half was dead serious. She had a strong feeling that this man would be generous in bed, making sure his partner had at least as much fun as he did.

"That's not— I mean, I'm sure you will but…" She shook her head. "Oh, this is ridiculous. The only rule I wanted to suggest is that we are very clear—this is one night only."

He seemed completely taken aback. "One night only?"

"Yes."

"But we'll barely get started."

"Well, I've thought about it, and that's all I want."

"I don't know." He scratched his cheek where stubble had formed. "I don't do my best work under pressure."

She glanced significantly at his injured leg. "Your profession is all about performing under pressure. I saw the pictures you took in Africa. During the gun battle when you got hurt. They're amazing."

"Thanks. But this is different"

What she didn't tell him was how she'd practically

trembled imagining him in that war zone in constant danger. She could never lose her heart to a man like that. She had to be so careful. Maybe she was stupid even to consider sleeping with him once, but she was suddenly tired of living so rigidly by her rules. Besides, her rules were designed for maximum efficiency of her time. If she was losing sleep having twitchy, hot fantasies about Rob, wouldn't it be easier just to sleep with the guy and be done with it? Then she could put her fantasies behind her.

He wasn't playing according to her program, however. He gazed at her as though she might be more than a little crazy. "I don't know. I've never been the type for one-night stands." He paused, "Well, not since college. I think I'd feel used."

She burst out laughing. "I'm not using you."

"A deal for one night of sex? Even if I want more? What would you call it?"

"I guess I thought we'd be giving each other pleasure for a night. Not that anyone was using anyone else."

"I don't see it that way." He took a step back. "This is probably a bad idea. I'm not at my best mentally or physically right now."

Her astonishment at being turned down by a man for uncomplicated, no-strings-attached sex evaporated when she searched his face and saw real hesitance there. He wasn't playing a game. And then suddenly his behavior made perfect sense.

All his bluster about feeling used, and his earlier comments about everything working properly came back to her.

He was worried about his performance. His leg was far from healed which meant they'd have to make some adjustments. Maybe he wasn't as certain everything was working as he'd told her he was.

He probably thought she was playing games when all she was trying to do was protect her heart. Maybe if she was contemplating being intimate with her body, she should at least let the man into some of what was going on in her head.

"Rob," she began, then didn't know where to go from there. "Rob. You are the sexiest, most interesting man I've met in a really long time."

He didn't appear to be over-the-moon flattered. He simply stood there and listened. She supposed it came from being a journalist. Listening was a skill and not jumping into speech kept the other person talking. As she knew well from her own profession. People often thought they wanted a certain kind of property but sometimes when she listened and encouraged them to talk a different vision would emerge. Not what they thought they wanted, but what would make them happy.

Now he was looking at her and she was going to tell him more than she'd intended. "The thing is I've got a busy career and I'm so focused. I don't want to be distracted by a relationship."

He shook his head. "Who said anything about a relationship? All I said was I'm not a big fan of one-night stands. I'm too old for that crap. I'd have thought you were, too."

"I am. I don't normally indulge like that either. But. Oh, this is so hard. I have this little problem where I… get involved with men I've been intimate with. I don't want to fall for you and then have you break my heart when you go back to war zones and put your life in danger again. So I need to balance the wanting to sleep with you against the fear of losing you. And the only way

I can reconcile the two things is to go into this with a very short-term goal."

"One night."

"Yes."

"That's the craziest damn thing I've ever heard."

She was more let down than she'd have believed possible. She'd really wanted to have one night with him, one night of memories she could enjoy without risking her foolish heart. "So you won't do it?"

He glared at her. "Of course I'll do it. I'm a man. I haven't had a woman in months. You're always underfoot smelling good and looking good. Yeah, I'll take the deal. But I don't like it."

She smiled at the grumpiness in his tone. And in relief. "I understand." She took a deep breath feeling a little shaky now they'd made the decision.

She pulled her electronic organizer out and clicked to her Week at a Glance. "Okay. When do you want to do this?"

A large and very masculine hand reached out and, before she guessed his intent, grabbed the organizer out of her grasp and set it ungently on the table. "How about now?"

"Now? But I was going to bring my nightdress and things over."

"You won't need a nightdress," he informed her stepping closer.

10

"I— OH," AND THAT WAS the last sound Hailey made for a long, long time, as his mouth closed over hers and he reminded her of all the reasons she'd been thinking lustful thoughts of him ever since they'd kissed in the bedroom.

It was different now. She had no frustrations about doing this. She'd made her deal, set boundaries she could live with.

Tonight he'd be her lover.

Tomorrow he'd be back to being her client.

It was fine. It was good. Oh, and the deeper he took the kiss, the more she knew how much she wanted him. She felt herself bending to him, melting against his body as he ran his hands up and down her back, stroking, enticing. His mouth toyed with her, seduced her.

He took her hand and led her up the stairs. He didn't take the cane but held the banister with one hand, and with the other, linked his fingers with hers. She felt the warmth traveling back and forth between their joined hands, felt her heart begin to hammer in anticipation.

She slowed her steps to keep pace with him even though she wanted to race up the stairs and dive into bed.

When they got to the top of the stairs and he tugged her toward the big bedroom she paused.

"What?" he demanded.

"I keep a toothbrush in the other bathroom," she admitted.

"Of course you do."

"Do you mind if I—"

"Five minutes. If you're not in my bed in five minutes the deal's off."

A little thrill went through her at his macho, caveman attitude.

"I'll be quick," she promised and scooted over to the other bathroom.

She brushed her teeth in record time, astonished, when she saw her face in the mirror, at how a little sexual buzz added color to her cheeks and a sparkle to her eyes. She managed to run a brush through her hair and grab a couple of the condoms she'd also stashed up here when she first started thinking thoughts that had nothing to do with buyers, sellers or amortization schedules.

She dashed down the hall and entered the master suite well within her allotted five minutes.

He came out of the master bathroom and stood in the middle of the room, watching her. The expression in his eyes brought a delicious heaviness to her limbs. With languorous steps, she walked to him, put her arms around his neck and kissed him.

She smiled against his lips, tasting fresh mint. "You brushed your teeth, too."

"Figured I'd get kicked out of bed if I didn't," he grumbled. Then took over the kiss, licking into her mouth, drawing her body against his so she could feel the full force of his passion.

Oh, my.

He raised his head. "Come on."

"Where are we going?" she asked when he took her hand and led her out of the master suite.

"My old room. I feel like I'd get in trouble if I had sex in my grandmother's bed."

"But your bed's a single."

"I know. I wouldn't feel comfortable is all."

"Okay." She tried to be understanding. Of course, grief did strange things to a person, and she respected his feelings, but she loved that four-poster. It was a bed for fantasies and she did not for one moment believe that Mrs. Neeson would begrudge her grandson pleasure. All the same he had to work through his loss in his own way so she went with him to his old bedroom, staged to sell but still containing only a single bed.

When they entered the room, she flipped on the bed-side lamp and turned back the coverlet on the ridiculously small bed. "Did you sneak girls up here when you were a teenager?" she asked.

"Truth is I snuck them downstairs to my man cave in the basement." He shot her a wicked look. "I still remember my moves down there if you want to give it a try."

"I am not going down two flights of stairs. And neither are you."

"Maybe later."

She raised her brows at him.

"We've got all night. Don't think you're going to sleep for one minute of it."

A tiny moan started in her throat and almost escaped. She bit it back in the nick of time. How did he do this to her? Driving her wild with no more than a promise of an action-filled night.

She was so hot she needed action now. When she

glanced up at him she got the strong impression he felt the same. He stepped closer and began kissing her again. He wasn't one for wandering all over the place, planting kisses on her cheeks and forehead and any old place his lips felt like landing. He seemed to be a man who liked deep, wet, hungry soul kisses. Which was fine with her. Their bodies strained together as the kiss grew more urgent.

She reached for the buttons of his shirt and began to undo them.

His skin was tanned, the hair on his chest wiry. His collarbones had to be kissed as they were prominent and demanded attention. Then the V where they met and dipped had to be kissed. His skin was warm and silky smooth for a guy who lived such a rugged life. The contrast of smooth skin covered with rough hair delighted her and she had to get the rest of his shirt off so she could play.

This was such a great idea. Play. Nothing serious. No future, just the fun of a sexy man to enjoy for a night before he wandered out of her life again and became no more than a fond memory. What could be better?

When she started tugging the shirt out of the waistband of his jeans, he took over, stripping it off quickly, balling it and chucking it into a corner. Next those big hands went to work on her shirt but he was so clumsy with the tiny buttons that she took over the job, taking her time, making a little striptease out of divesting herself of her top. No matter how passionate she felt she'd never toss her clothing on the floor so she took the extra few seconds to lay the garment neatly over the chair.

"That is a very sexy bra you're wearing," he said.

"Thank you." It was freshly purchased and she'd paid

an outrageous sum for a concoction of pale green silk, lace and underwire.

He lounged against the bed in jeans, bare feet, bare torso. Crossed his arms, showing off impressive biceps. "If I took it off I'd only throw it on the floor so you'd better do it."

The warmth and humor in his tone couldn't disguise the raw hunger beneath. The combination had her catching her breath. If she'd ever been this hungry for a man, she couldn't remember it. She licked her lips, glanced up at him from under her lashes and took her sweet time removing the bra. The way his gaze remained riveted, his breathing grew labored and his hands twitched, she saw she'd spent her money wisely.

When she slowly began to ease the bra down her breasts, feeling the slide of the fabric tease her nipples, he said, "I'm not sure I'm going to survive the night."

She grinned at him. "What a way to go."

She wasn't one to flaunt her body but he was so obviously enjoying her little show and his enjoyment only added to hers so she revealed her breasts slowly, taking his grunt as a sign of approval, then laid the bra over the back of the chair. With her back to him, she undid her skirt and wiggled the thing off her, giving him an enticing view of the matching thong panties, and the thigh-high stockings that weren't very comfortable but that made up in sexiness what they lacked in comfort.

"Who'd have thought," he said softly, "that under all that crisp business clothing, you were hiding that underwear. And that body."

Before she could turn around, his hands were on her waist and he was kissing the back of her neck, running his palms up her belly to cup her breasts. His palms were warm and a little rough, which felt delicious on her tender skin.

She felt the bulge of his arousal in his jeans as he bumped up against her and the feel of this denim-covered hot man rubbing against her near-nakedness had her turning to embrace him.

The jeans hung low on his hips, his long torso was tawny, sprinkled with sun freckles on his broad shoulders. He felt so solid that she leaned into him, rubbing herself against him shamelessly.

He stumbled.

Her big, strong, sexy guy stumbled and barely bit back a wince of pain.

Her hand flew to her mouth. "Oh, I'm so sorry. I forgot your leg. Did I hurt you?"

"No. Just got unbalanced," he replied gruffly.

She could have kicked herself for being so thoughtless. She knew better, though, than to make an issue of it. Instead she walked to the bed, knowing he'd follow her, and sat. When he came toward her, she leaned forward and kissed his belly where a line of hair arrowed into his waistband and then she tackled the fly.

She eased the zipper over the enticing bulge and began to ease the jeans down over his hips.

And soon realized he'd gone skimpier on the undies than she had.

He wasn't wearing any.

Staring back at her was the nicest cock she'd ever seen. Long and thick and standing proud. As she continued to stare, her hands halted as though frozen, she could have sworn it stood even straighter to attention, as though proud to have stunned her so thoroughly.

She couldn't stop herself; she had to touch it. Wrapping her hand around the hardness, she squeezed gently and heard him pull in his breath. "Remember, it's been a while for me. Don't want to embarrass myself," he said through gritted teeth.

"Right." She quickly let go and continued removing his pants. When she saw his thigh wound she had to bite back a gasp. She'd expected, if she'd thought about it at all, that the spot would be neatly bandaged. It wasn't.

The bullet had blasted a hole in the front of his thigh and another out the back. It was roughly stitched, but still red and raw-looking. "That looks so painful," she said, unable to help herself.

"I should have covered it up," he said. "Didn't know this was going to happen."

"No. It's okay. I'm only sorry this happened to you."

Now that she understood the mess his leg was in, she understood that she was going to have to be careful not to hurt him. Mostly in her experience, especially the first time, she'd let the man take the lead in the bedroom. Tonight she was going to have to take control, if only to stop him from hurting himself.

She kind of liked the idea of taking control, especially knowing it would make his night more pleasurable.

She eased herself off the bed, kneeling before him to continue pulling off his jeans. When he'd stepped out of them she pushed him gently back on the bed until he was half reclining looking up at her quizzically.

"What are you doing?" he asked, half belligerent, half husky.

She smiled at him, channeling every sexy siren who had ever gone before her. "Remember when you used to lie in your single bed in this very room and fantasize about a woman who would come to you and give you everything you desire?"

"Oh, yeah."

"I am your fantasy."

He reached out to cup the back of her head. His voice was husky when he said, "You have no idea."

In truth she wasn't the boldest woman in town but her desire not to hurt him was stronger than her fear of making a fool of herself.

Standing in full view of him she slowly slipped off her thong, enjoying the way his gaze stayed riveted on her every move. She tingled at the intensity of his gaze. And then, slowly, taking care not to bump his bad leg, she put one knee on the bed and straddled him.

"You're a take-charge kind of woman."

"Do you have a problem with that?"

He shook his head, "No."

"Good."

She smiled to herself thinking of all the fantasies she'd had of this moment. They'd taken place in the big bed in the master bedroom, or on the rug in front of the fireplace. And in every one of them, she'd been the one lying at ease while he pleasured her in ways that spoke to her deepest fantasies. Not one of which included her doing all the work.

And yet there was something enormously erotic taking charge. In knowing she had it in her power to give him pleasure. She felt free, powerful, sexy.

Tossing her hair over her shoulder, she leaned down to kiss him deeply, and, as she did, she took hold of his cock and began to rub it back and forth across her clit, bringing her to full enjoyment of the moment and torturing him a little along the way.

She'd never been much for living in the moment. A woman with two organizers tended to spend a lot of her energy on the future and usually Hailey was fine with that. But there were times, like now, when she couldn't do anything but live in the moment. If she looked at the future even as closely as tomorrow, this would all be over. This man lying beneath her, all warm and sexy and naked, wouldn't be her lover anymore. He'd revert to her client.

Clothed.

This feeling of joyful abandon would end. In truth she'd never been one for short-term relationships. They never seemed worth the effort, but to have an affair that was only going to last one night took all the anxiety away. There was no worry about tomorrow or his expectations or her expectations or whether he'd call and whether she wanted him to. There was no tomorrow, which meant there was only glorious perfect now. And as she slipped the condom onto him and sank, slowly, onto his jutting cock, she knew she'd never, ever had a more perfect now.

11

HE FILLED HER, made himself at home within her body, and then they began to move together. The connection between them when their gazes met was almost more intimate than their joined bodies. "This," she said, leaning close so she could brush the words against his lips like a kiss, "is a perfect moment."

"Oh, yeah, and it's about to get more perfect."

"Mmm." She'd have said he let her set her own pace except that it felt as though they were in perfect sync, rising and falling together as their bodies surged and ebbed.

His chest was rising and falling with the effort. She wanted to slow things down, to make this wonderful now last forever, but then he slipped a hand between them and began to touch her hot spot.

He'd barely touched her, brushing his fingertips across her clit, when she reared back, climaxing in a burst of heat that felt volcanic. She felt herself squeezing him, watched his blue eyes lose their focus, but still he kept touching her, easily, softly. She felt herself rising again and rode him hard. The bed protested. She didn't care if they broke the bed; she'd buy a new one.

He bucked beneath her, driving up and into her, hitting her G-spot and an entire alphabet of new erogenous zones she hadn't known she possessed.

He grabbed her hips when he came, arching up and taking her with him so her cries echoed his.

Fireworks exploded behind her eyes and for a moment she couldn't catch her breath.

The moment stretched to eternity and back again and then a glorious sense of peace filled her.

"Oh, my goodness," she said, slumping onto his sweat-damp chest, listening to the pounding of his heart. They remained connected intimately because she didn't want to let him go.

They didn't speak, both savoring the experience, enjoying the afterglow.

After a few minutes had passed, she kissed his neck, and wiggled her pelvis. To her surprise, a rock-hard penis still filled her. She lifted her head to look at him. "Didn't you come?"

He snorted. "Ah, yeah. In case you didn't notice, I did."

"But you're still hard." She heard her own puzzlement.

"It's kind of a thing I have," he said, looking vaguely embarrassed.

"What kind of a thing?"

"I can stay hard between sessions."

"You mean you can go again? Right away?"

"Yep."

She'd never heard of such a thing. "Are you, like, multi-orgasmic?"

"Are we going to analyze this or are we going to enjoy it?" he snapped.

She decided to let her actions speak for her and

reached down to cup his scrotum, stroking him. Then she began to play, exploring all the ways they could make love without putting strain on his wounded leg. With the first rush of need taken care of, they were free to take a leisurely pace and simply enjoy each other.

She'd never had so much fun in bed.

Ever.

He was earthy, giving, athletic and possessed stamina unlike anything she'd ever experienced before. She thought she'd be worn-out long before morning.

They dozed, then starving, raided the kitchen at three in the morning.

"What do you want to eat?" she asked, opening the refrigerator. His robe hung on her small frame, while he'd shoved only his jeans on so he was bare of chest and foot. Exactly how she liked him.

"Grilled cheese sandwiches."

"With pickles."

"I'll get the frying pan heating. You get the food."

They sat at the kitchen table munching sandwiches and pickles and drinking milk until they had enough energy to go back upstairs. They curled up together in that ridiculously small bed. As he played idly with her breasts, and she drew silly doodles with her fingers on his belly, they talked.

"How did you get into real estate?" he asked.

"When I was a kid we moved thirteen times in twelve years. My dad was in the army. He loved change and new places." She glanced at him. "Kind of like you."

"I guess."

"When you've never had something you can get pretty obsessed. I never felt like I had a real home." She loved the line of softer hair on his lower belly and she stroked it as she talked. "I mean, I always had a home, but eventually my poor mother just couldn't be bothered to unpack everything. What was the point? We'd only be moving again. We lived in military housing or rentals off base and never decorated or anything." She made a face. "When other kids were reading *Seventeen* magazine I read home-decorating magazines. And TV? I watched *The OC* for the houses, not the cute guys. I used to pretend that Martha Stewart was my mom and I lived in her house with her."

"Did your friends think you were nuts?"

"I didn't have any real friends. I've always envied those lifetime friendships women have. Oh, sure, I got over my shyness, learned to make casual friends and to protect my heart so it didn't break when I had to leave a place and start all over again in another."

He rolled over, cupped her face and kissed her softly. "That sounds so lonely."

"It was, but I also became pretty self-sufficient and independent. Good qualities in a Realtor."

"Where are your parents?" he asked.

"My dad passed away a couple of years ago just before he would have retired. My mom remarried and lives in California. She works in a furniture store and she never goes anywhere if she can help it."

"You feel that way?"

"No, I love to travel. But I want to know I've got a home to come back to. I suppose I have a little of both of my parents in me. I've been in the same rental for four years. I'm saving up to buy a place." She sighed. "I wish I could afford Bellamy House. This is my ideal. A home you could stay in for your whole life. Raise kids. Maybe get a dog. Get to know your neighbors."

"This is the place for that all right."

She was drowsy, so sated from sex that her body felt

limp and well-used. But she didn't want to waste any time sleeping.

It was nice, swapping secrets in the dark. "How about you? I saw a picture of your mother, but you never talk about your parents."

"Not much to tell," he said, staring up at the ceiling. "My parents got divorced when I was young. I never knew my dad. Mom was a hippie. A real free spirit. She had a lot of boyfriends. Usually the guys didn't want a little kid around."

A ball of anger began to form in her belly. Who would do that to a sweet little boy, the kind she was sure Rob would have been?

"She used to send me to my grandmother's for months at a stretch. That suited all of us. Then she'd end up single or miss me and haul me back."

In an odd way, she thought their backgrounds were more alike than she'd realized.

"Everything changed when I was fourteen." He turned, running his hand over her breasts, down her belly. "My mom had a new loser, a real piece of work. I wasn't a little kid anymore and I'd had enough. I hitch-hiked to the Canadian border. Had great plans about working up north on oil rigs. I'd heard you could make a pile of money. The border guards didn't think too much of my plans. I told them my mother was dead so they called my grandmother."

His hand slipped lower and she had to concentrate to hang on to the thread of the story. "She made a deal with me. If I finished school and lived with her she'd buy me a round-the-world ticket for graduation."

"What a smart woman."

"Oh, she was. She didn't yell at me or anything. She

got it. She also let me turn that bathroom downstairs into a darkroom and helped me buy my first camera."

"Wow."

"Could you spread your legs a little wider?"

She was happy to comply.

"After journalism school, when I was twenty-two, I took her up on that ticket. I was in the wrong place at the wrong time. Which for a budding photojournalist was exactly the right place at the right time. I was in Namibia. It was August 1999. The Caprivi Liberation Army claimed that the government was neglecting their region. Guerrillas attacked the Namibian military and police on August second. I'd only been in the region a couple of days. I was one of the first photographers on the scene and got some great footage."

"Wow. Some holiday." Then he moved his fingers and she sighed with pleasure.

"I sent my photos to Gary Wallenberg who was then bureau chief for Africa for *World Week.* Gary snapped them up. I started freelancing and then got hired on permanent staff. Like I said, right place, right time."

And the right talent, she thought.

"What happened to your mom?"

"She died. A few years ago. Cancer."

"I'm sorry."

"Yeah. Me, too. But the funny thing is, I miss my grandmother so much more. I guess in every way that counts, she was my real mother."

He kissed her, and the hand playing with her moved in earnest. Reaching over, she found him hard again. The guy was amazing.

It would soon be daylight, and she didn't plan to waste a minute of the night sleeping.

SHE DIDN'T THINK she'd been asleep but when her cell phone alarm chirped it jerked her awake. From the grittiness of her eyes and the almost light-headed feeling when she sat up, she suspected her night's sleep had been counted in minutes rather than hours.

Rob was instantly awake and sitting up, squinting at the window. Dawn had barely broken.

"What time is it?" he asked sleepily.

"Six-thirty."

"Do you have a meeting or something?"

"No. I need to get home and shower, that's all." In truth, she'd set her alarm deliberately early so she could avoid any morning awkwardness.

He wrapped his arms around her, drawing her back into the warmth of his embrace, his sleep-warmed skin cocooning her. "You could shower here," he said, kissing the back of her shoulders. "I'll wash your back for you."

She was tempted. Yet she knew she'd done the right thing in making such a big deal of only spending one night together. He was too sexy, too wonderful for her not to fall for him. And the last thing she wanted in her life was a wandering man.

She'd promised herself from the time she could understand why they moved all the time that she'd never get involved with a man who didn't stay in one place. By that very simple standard Rob was about the last man she should ever date.

So, reluctantly, she moved away, showed him a smiling face when she turned to him, kissed him once and then resolutely put her feet onto the floor. The hardwood was cold against her bare feet, and as she rose, she shivered. The sooner she got out of here the better.

"Will I see you later?" he asked sleepily.

"I'm not sure," she said in what she hoped was a businesslike tone. "I have a showing here tomorrow. I'll let you know for sure. As for today, unless somebody calls and wants a showing, I probably won't see you."

"You're really serious about this one-night thing, aren't you?" She heard disbelief in his voice. After the astonishing night they'd spent together she could understand how he thought she must be crazy. As she scrambled into her clothes she knew in her heart she'd be crazy to continue. Only pain would result if she ever let herself fall for a man like Rob.

"I have to, Rob. Don't you see? You're a rolling stone." He didn't argue with her, merely nodded slowly, a bleakness in his eyes she didn't want to see.

As she left the room, she said softly to herself, "And I'm moss."

12

ROB SCOWLED AT HIS COFFEE. It was his third cup of the day and it didn't seem to be doing the usual job of waking him up and energizing him.

After a night like last night he should be skipping and jumping like some guy in a Viagra commercial. Instead he felt the way he had done right after he found out his grandmother was dead. Bereft. As though something vital to his happiness had been ripped from him.

"Get a grip," he snarled to the French press, sitting on the counter with nothing but a sludge of pressed grounds in its glass bottom. That was kind of how he felt. As if someone, namely Hailey, had crushed every last drop of flavor and vitality out of him and left nothing but a squeezed-out lump of sludge behind.

He wasn't big on self-reflection, but for some reason she'd slipped under his skin and made him see himself in a light that wasn't entirely flattering.

Hailey had made it clear that she could never take a man like him seriously.

No. Not a man like him.

Him.

In her view, as a potential mate he didn't cut it. Not

that he wanted to cut it, but it was galling to know that she wouldn't sleep with him again because of that.

And she was right, damn it, he thought savagely as he tossed the dregs of his coffee down the sink. He wasn't mate material. Not for a woman like her, with plans for the future—and husband, kids and a family van written all over her. Probably he was irked simply because she'd decreed there'd be no more sex.

He thought of that sweet body convulsing around him, of the intensity of their night together, and he thought it was a crime, a class-B felony at least, to deny both of them pleasure like that simply because he wasn't a stay-at-home kind of guy.

Well, he wasn't a stay-at-home guy. The reason he was brooding, he suspected, was because he was bored and that made him twitchy. He needed to get back to work where he belonged and out of Fremont where he so clearly didn't.

He hobbled upstairs to his grandmother's bedroom and put on athletic shorts, sneakers and a workout shirt.

He'd been here for four weeks already. It was time he quit lounging and started working out. Once geared up, he headed out to the local running track. *A mile in six.* Trust Gary to punish him while he was on leave.

When he got to the track, there were only three other joggers. An overweight middle-aged woman shuffling along with earbuds hanging and two younger women who were chatting as they ran.

He started slowly, walking once around the track, trying to pretend there was no pain in his left thigh. Even though Hailey had—in her own sweet way—tried to keep from hurting him there was no way a man could have athletic sex and not use his thigh muscles. So he was sore.

Big deal. It had been so worth it.

He broke into a jog. Making almost a circuit of the track before sweat broke out on his brow and his leg felt as if shards of glass were being shoved into his thigh each time his foot hit the ground.

The obese woman passed him, huffing and wheezing, but outpacing him.

He made it another half a circuit by sheer grit before limping off the field cursing all the way home.

"WHAT THE HELL DID YOU DO?" Doc Greene demanded to know when he showed up for his appointment—an appointment it had almost killed him to make.

"I went jogging."

"Are you insane? It's been four weeks. I told you no running before six weeks."

"I'm a fast healer." He scowled. "Look, I lost the scrip for painkillers you gave me." He'd chucked it out but he didn't feel like sharing that information. "I need a new one, that's all."

Doc Greene glared at him from over his bifocals. "This injury involves an eight- to ten-week recovery. You are not in the condition to run."

Rob gritted his teeth. "I need to run a mile in six minutes before my boss will take me back."

"Pushing it too soon will only hold you back."

"There must be something I can do."

"What you want is physiotherapy."

It just got worse and worse. "Physiotherapy? I didn't put my back out. I got shot."

"I know. And your muscles need rebuilding. A good physio can get you back on the road sooner than you will by running yourself into the ground."

Rob couldn't describe the turmoil swirling around

his gut. He didn't mean to speak, yet he blurted, "I need to get out of this town."

"Why?" Doc gave him a penetrating look that made him feel as though he should be reclining on a couch reciting all the ills done to him in childhood.

He wasn't going to tell a septuagenarian doctor that a confusing mix of hot sex and no future with one stunning Realtor was driving him away so he said, "I don't belong here."

"Of course you do. You've lived most of your life here. People are proud of you. And you're the only living connection with your grandmother. She wanted you to stay. Why do you think she left you the house? It's not like you need the money with that fancy job of yours."

He'd never even thought about why Gran had left him Bellamy House. He'd assumed it was because he was her closest relative.

"What if I don't want to stay? What if I can't?"

"There are charities your grandmother supported who would love to get that house."

A light bulb went on inside his head. He wasn't rich, as Doc Greene seemed to be suggesting, but he did fine. Maybe that's what he'd do. Give the place to some deserving charity his grandmother had supported. That would take away this weird feeling he had that he had to choose the next owners, that the property should go to someone his grandmother would have approved of. If he gave the place away it would also sever his relationship with Hailey. He'd make sure she still got her commission for the sale. He owed her that. However, if he gifted the property to charity, he wouldn't be forced to see Hailey several times a week and relive their single night together like a particularly hot erotic movie that looped endlessly in his head.

Doc scribbled on a pad, ripped it off and handed him the page. "That's for the painkillers." Then he scribbled on another page. "And that's for a physio who is also a personal trainer. She'll get you doing your mile in six." He gave him a sharp look. "When your body is ready."

"Thanks, Doc."

He limped out. While he waited for his prescription to be filled downstairs in the pharmacy he noticed that the latest issue of *World Week* was on the stands.

He bought it along with the pills. Not wanting to go home, he headed to the friendly café down the road. Maybe a professional could brew him a coffee that would taste better than what he'd made himself this morning.

When he entered Beananza he had the place almost to himself. He'd missed the lunch rush and whatever rush was next hadn't started yet. He ordered an Americano.

"You're the guy who inherited Bellamy House," the barista said.

"That's right."

The guy wore a shirt that read Grounds for Divorce, and featured a cartoon of a woman in a business suit pouring coffee from a pot that was empty, while her suit-clad spouse sipped from a full mug.

"Why is it always the guys who are depicted as self-ish morons?" He wondered aloud, pointing at the shirt.

The barista looked down as though he didn't remember what shirt he'd put on that morning. "Maybe because they so often are."

He grunted. He'd like to get a shirt that said Men Should Stand Up for Each Other!

"Hailey and Julia are both friends of mine," the guy

in the offensive shirt added. "They sure have been thrilled about showcasing that house."

"They've done a great job," Rob said. Because they had. Hailey had also done a great job messing with his head and ruining his day. That, however, was nobody's business but his.

He took his coffee to a spot where he felt he'd be least likely to be disturbed. After popping a couple of the pain pills, he opened *World Week*.

Things were heating up in a Baltic state, one he'd been to before and knew well. The photographer Gary had sent had done an okay job, but he knew he could have done better.

The knowledge irked.

Famine in Africa. And the same obvious photos. The same tired stories. He was convinced he could have found something fresh in this latest heart-wrenching human tragedy.

Disasters were occurring all over the world and other people were reporting it, other cameras were capturing it. He felt like banging his mug down on the counter in frustration.

He flipped through the domestic news. Politics, more home foreclosures, the religious right—some days he wanted to crawl under the Aurora Bridge and live with the troll.

He left the magazine on the counter and went home. His cell phone rang. He saw it was Hailey and in his eagerness to answer he fumbled the phone. His bad mood and the pain in his leg vanished.

"Hi," he said. "And yes, I'm free tonight."

There was a tiny pause.

"Hello, Rob. I've got a new client who is very inter-

ested in Bellamy House. I'd like to bring him around
tomorrow around eleven."

Okay, she was putting on her professional act and
he got it. She'd done the same this morning though
she hadn't seemed quite so professional when she was
naked. Still, with every article of clothing she'd donned
he'd felt the warm, passionate lover easing away from
him and Hailey the Realtor taking her place.

Well? He'd taken the deal, hadn't he? Agreed to just
one night. How could he have imagined that one perfect
night could mess with him so badly? And now he had
to see her on a regular basis? Pretend they were only
business acquaintances?

He couldn't do it. He'd find a worthy charity to take
the house. And then he'd leave. So, he couldn't run a
mile in six. Or sixty the way he felt. But he could conva-
lesce in a hundred different places around the globe, not
one of which was full of memories. And where there'd
be no Hailey making him feel that he wasn't enough
of a man for her.

He made himself focus on the conversation.

"Him? A single guy? What does a single guy want
with Bellamy House?"

"Maybe he's planning to settle down and have a family," she said, all neutral, as though she weren't sticking a knife into him.

"Eleven is fine," he said. He didn't like the sound of
a single guy buying the property. He'd give Bellamy
House to a charity first. He wasn't about to share that
with Hailey just yet. He needed to do some research
first.

He also didn't like the tone she'd used with him.
Oh, it was professional and friendly enough. That was
exactly the problem. He didn't want professional and

friendly. He wanted sexy and intimate. She'd warned him up front how it would be; all the same it hurt to go from client to lover and back again within twelve hours. In fact it sucked.

He said goodbye, and, for the first time since they'd started working together, he determined to be far away from his own house for tomorrow's showing.

He'd thought his day couldn't get any worse, his mood any blacker when his cell phone rang again. He didn't recognize the local number.

"Robert Klassen?" a cool female voice inquired.

"Yes." Nobody called him Robert unless they were trying to sell him something and whatever it was, he wasn't buying.

"This is Keystone Funeral Home calling—"

"Thanks anyway but I don't plan to die for a while."

Weren't there enough deaths in the world? Did they have to troll for business among the young and healthy? He looked at his leg. Maybe this was targeted marketing after all.

"Mr. Klassen, I'm calling about Agnes Neeson. Your grandmother, I believe."

"Oh." Funeral home. Gran. He hated thinking of them together. He needed to end this call. "Didn't your bill get paid? Her lawyer took care of all the bills."

"Yes, payment was received. We've got her ashes. Mr. Klassen, you can come by anytime during office hours to pick them up."

"Her ashes? My grandmother's ashes?" He knew there'd been a celebration of her life shortly after she died. He'd never thought there were ashes somewhere waiting for a home. "What am I supposed to do with them?"

"Whatever you'd like, sir. We do have a memorial

field. Your grandmother's ashes would be buried under a tasteful plaque. We'd be happy to discuss placing your loved one in our memorial garden at your leisure."

A plaque in a field? He couldn't imagine anything worse. His grandmother wasn't going to end up in the middle of a lawn in a row of similar plaques, the last resting place of those with no imagination or a family who couldn't be bothered to scatter the ashes somewhere meaningful.

"Thanks. I'll pick them up."

His first instinct was to call Hailey and talk to her about the ashes. How had she done this to him? Turned him from an independent man who made his own decisions to someone who wanted to ask her where he should put his grandmother's remains? A woman she'd never even met?

The bizarre thing was that he was certain she'd have the right idea.

13

JULIA SPENT A MISERABLE evening deleting every single one of the emails from the guy she now referred to as her scammer.

Inevitably she couldn't simply delete the emails, not without reading each message over again. Nor could she put his photos in her computer's trash bin, not without gazing longingly at the man she'd believed was writing to her.

In the time since she'd discovered she'd been scammed she'd done research on the internet, something she should have done earlier, and learned there was an entire industry based on men creating fake personas to lure unwary women—such as herself—into sending them money.

The horror stories she'd read had practically made her hair stand up. Women had sold jewelry, antiques and family heirlooms to send more and more money to these men who professed love and made promises for the future if only they could send another thousand dollars for airfare or five thousand to pay for urgent medical attention—or some other bogus reason.

Once they'd taken the initial bait these women often

went into debt to keep their dream alive. It was ludicrous, these seemingly rational women sending their life savings off to men who didn't exist. How could they be so stupid? Now she knew.

Julia understood two things. One: there is no escaping the foolishness a woman will stoop to if she believes she's in love. And two: she, Julia, had to accept she wasn't as smart as she thought she was.

She knew in her deepest heart that there'd been a moment when she'd actually considered sending him the money, so deeply had she bought into the fantasy of him and of them together. That's probably what made her the maddest, knowing she'd been manipulated in the most humiliating manner and by someone who operated on the other side of the world and was virtually untouchable. All she could do was report her story to the internet dating site and admit to being one more fool for love.

Even as she accepted that she was a dupe, still she reread all the emails. Now that she knew the truth, she could see there was a certain generic tone to them. He'd been awfully quick to profess his affection for someone he'd never met.

And, gritting her teeth, she realized she'd been even quicker to accept his professions as genuine.

And those photos!

The guy whose pictures were so hot she worried he would be too good-looking for her, they were photos of a model, the likeness stolen and used to lure her.

She knew she should rip the Band-Aid off, chuck the emails and the photos and empty her computer's trash bin.

She knew that.

Still, she tortured herself going through it all again. It

was like looking at photos of a great vacation or studying pictures of someone you've loved who's died. That's
how she felt. She experienced the bittersweet sadness
of remembering past happiness. Because she had been
happy. She'd already written the story in her head. Their
first date, the first kiss.

How many idle moments had she spent wondering
when they'd first make love and where it would happen?
Fool!

After wallowing in her own misery for as long as
she could stand, she did what had to be done. Deleted
the emails and the photos into the trash. Purged the guy
from her life. Or the fantasy out of her life.

It was early evening, and she felt twitchy and out of
sorts. Maybe just to torture herself more, she logged
on to the dating site and checked to see if anyone had
tried to contact her. She had an email from a guy who
appeared to have spread his net pretty wide since his
home address was in Portland, Oregon, and she had
no interest in a long-distance relationship. She'd just
had one with a Nigerian and that hadn't gone so well.

She deleted Mr. Portland. And noticed the initial
message from John was still in her dating-site inbox.
She clicked on his profile, which was still active.

John wasn't romantic or exciting; she'd never worry
that he was too good-looking for her and he didn't make
her nervous with trying to make a good impression.
He was a nice man who was alone and she was a nice
woman who was alone. Maybe she should take him up
on his offer of dinner or a movie. Anything to get out
of her apartment and out of her own head.

Before she could talk herself out of what was probably a truly terrible idea, she'd dug out his card and
called him. He answered right away. After she identified

herself she didn't know what to say next. She fumbled around a bit and then said, "I'm having a lousy day. I was wondering if you'd like to go out and get some dinner with me? Or a drink or something."

There was a pause on his end and she closed her eyes, wishing she'd never dreamed up this stupid idea. What if he said no? Could she stand being rejected by somebody she wasn't even interested in?

Then he said, "I'm finishing something up. I could be free in an hour. Would that work for you?"

She was so relieved she said, "Oh, thank you."

He chuckled, but in an understanding way. "Day was that bad, huh? You like sushi?"

"Love it."

"You know Sushi Master?"

"I've never been there but I'll find it."

He gave her quick directions, then said, "Great. I'll meet you there at eight."

"Looking forward to it." When she hung up she found, to her surprise, that she was.

Since John was nice enough to accept a pity date with her she vowed not to be late. She was leaving her apartment only a few minutes after she'd planned to when she passed her computer. She took a step past it toward the door, then stopped.

"Do it!" she commanded herself out loud.

Without giving herself time for any foolish last thoughts, she emptied her trash and turned off her computer. A tiny pang of grief hit her when she knew the photos, emails and the dreams she'd spun around them, were gone forever.

AFTER SHE PARKED, she headed into the restaurant a respectable five minutes late. John was already sitting at a table, a beer in front of him. "You were early," she complained, when she settled herself across from him.

"No. You were late."

"Five minutes? That's on time in my books."

He shook his head. "How many planes have you missed?"

She made a big production of picking up the menu and opening it. A vast selection of rolls and sashimi and platters met her eyes. "What's good here?"

A waitress appeared. "Would you like something to drink?"

"Vodka tonic," she said, and then realized she didn't need to be on a diet anymore. She didn't plan to get naked with the cute blond guy since the closest she'd ever get to him would be seeing him on a billboard or a magazine ad somewhere. Thus, her caloric intake was her business. "No. Wait. I'll have a beer also." She gestured to his glass. "Whatever he's having."

"Sapporo?"

"Perfect."

Then she closed her menu. "Why don't we get a plate of assorted sushi and go wild."

"Sounds good to me."

She glanced around and found the decor to be pretty standard, but clean and full of clients, many of them Asian, on a Tuesday night, which suggested the food was particularly good.

John's hair hung over his forehead in a straight bang as though his mother had cut it using a bowl. His shirt was old, out of date and too short in the sleeves.

But he was here. And she was grateful.

"So, you had a lousy day."

"I did.'

There was a pause.

"Anything you want to talk about?"

"No."

"Okay."

There was another pause. She tried to think of something to talk about that was neutral and didn't involve the weather, which would be pathetic. She got the sense he was doing the same thing.

She let out a breath. "I did an unbelievably stupid thing, and I didn't want to be alone tonight to brood."

"Hey, don't beat yourself up. We all do stupid things."

"I never thought I'd be the kind of person to fall for... Oh, heck, I might as well just tell you." And so she did. The whole sad, sorry tale.

"I'm sorry," he said when she'd finished her story.

"That's all you have to say?"

"What do you want me to say?"

"I don't know. Make me feel better, I guess."

Their sushi platter arrived and he gestured to her to go first. She chose a California roll.

He went for the salmon, handling his chopsticks like a pro. He might dress like a goof but at least he could go out for sushi without making a fool of himself.

He certainly liked his wasabi, she noticed, as she watched him eat his roll. When he'd finished chewing and swallowed, he sat back and regarded her. "I think a lot of people go into online dating thinking they're going to meet the perfect partner. Maybe, though, there isn't a perfect partner. Maybe we need to be more open to trying new people, to thinking that it's okay to settle for someone you like who can fulfill a few of your needs without some romantic notion that there's a perfect match out there."

"You're saying that I bought into a fantasy."

"Absolutely. Romantic movies and Valentine's Day

cards, all kinds of fiction revolves around the idea that there's a missing half of us. That we'll find that other person and wow, fireworks! We'll be happy forever-more." He chose a dynamite roll. "It's so bogus."

"What if it isn't bogus? What if there is a perfect match?"

He stared at her, his food halfway to his mouth. "You can't still believe that?"

"I don't know," she said, kind of embarrassed. "I want to believe it. In spite of all that's happened. In spite of the fact that I'm...not as young as I used to be, I still believe there's a perfect someone out there for me. Don't you?"

"No, I don't. I think that all you can hope for is not to be lonely. At least some of the time."

"That's so depressing."

He shrugged. "I think of it as realistic."

"Let's get realistic. Tell me about your dating success. It's got to be so much easier being a man. There are so many more women in Seattle, you must have your pick of nice ones."

"Oh, you'd be surprised." He grabbed a piece of pick-led ginger deftly with chopsticks. Then glanced up at her. "Do you really want to hear this?"

"Yes. I do. I think we both know there wasn't any chemistry between us. I like the idea of having a male friend I can talk to about this stuff."

"It seems strange."

"After what I told you, nothing you could say would shock me. Really."

"Well, I wasn't scammed, at least not so far. So I suppose that's positive. Otherwise, online dating has been a pretty dismal experience."

She thought of the way she'd ditched him so quickly.

Realized that he was a really nice man. What he needed most was a makeover.

Or someone who could see past the bad hair, the worse clothes, the outdated glasses.

She really hoped there was a nice woman out there for John. He deserved her.

14

ONE NIGHT WASN'T SUPPOSED to change your life, Rob thought, annoyed. Or who you were.

It was ridiculous.

Sexual frustration, that's all he was feeling, and the weird notion that he'd been somehow rejected before he'd even got started.

If Hailey wanted to deprive them both of a satisfying few weeks of great sex while he was in town, that was her business.

One thing he knew was that he wasn't planning to be around when she had her showing today. Nope. He didn't want to experience the impact of those blue-gray eyes and remember how they'd softened to molten silver when she grew aroused or see her decked out in one of her fancy suits and know exactly what she looked like—felt like—without a stitch on.

He wasn't interested in torturing himself.

He was going to be long gone before the single dude showed up to look at his house. He didn't want to meet the guy and he didn't want to see Hailey. Not when she was treating him as though they'd never been any closer to each other than shaking hands.

He had enough problems, like a physiotherapist now added to the retinue of annoying women in his life, and then there was the box on top of his desk containing his grandmother's ashes. He had to figure out what to do with them. What she'd have wanted. Why could the woman not have left instruction in her will? Why leave it to him?

Women. He couldn't believe they could be almost as aggravating dead as were alive.

Still, it gave him an odd sense of peace to work on his project with that box in the corner. He hadn't gone so far as to talk to his dead gran though he'd stopped himself just in time not an hour ago. He needed to find her a better resting place.

The day was mild and the park across the street seemed like a great place to read the newspaper and have his camera handy for all the little dramas that might unfold. A little before eleven o'clock, Hailey drew up and got out of her car, one of the feature sheets she'd created for Bellamy House in her hand, along with the briefcase she carried around with her. Even from here he was struck by her beauty. A ray of sunlight caught her hair, lighting it gold. She was wearing a skirt and a suit jacket and heels that showed off the slim line of her legs.

He was overcome by the rushing sensation of recalling the feel of those legs gripping him as she rode him. He grew instantly hard at the memory and was thankful to have the *Seattle Times* as a shield. He vowed then and there that he and his hot Realtor were going to have a rematch. No way was that a one-night thing.

A second car drew up behind hers, a navy luxury sedan with rental plates. He watched a tall clean-cut guy wearing jeans and a sports jacket emerge from the vehicle. Hailey went toward him with her hand outstretched.

Watching him grasp Hailey's hand for way too long brought out a gut-deep urge in Rob to plow his fist into the guy's face.

Except he had no right. Scowling, he lifted the telephoto and focused in for a closer look.

Since the weather was nice, Hailey spent a few minutes pointing out the exterior features, no doubt giving a little of the house's history and describing the neighborhood.

The client nodded, asking a few questions.

Slick. That was the word that went through Rob's mind as he took him in. Salesman type. Clean-shaven, expensive haircut, slight tan in a face that had once probably been termed boyishly handsome. He looked to be maybe forty. Rob didn't wear expensive clothes, thought it was a pretentious waste of money, but he'd learned to assess a man's clothing. Where it was from, how much it had cost. It was part of his job.

He might not be able to name the designer, but he knew that jacket was made by one. British at a guess, worn over a black T-shirt. The loafers were Italian and so shiny you wondered if the guy walked anywhere. The jeans were from the good old U.S.A. The kind fools spent three hundred bucks for. The guy barely looked at the feature sheet in his manicured hand. All his attention was on Hailey. Rob didn't like it. Not one bit.

He'd seen enough. He started to pack up his camera, still keeping the couple across the street in view. A moving truck lumbered by, obscuring them momentarily from view. Traffic was light. A few cars drove by. A school bus, and no doubt Hailey took that opportunity to mention the excellent schools in the area. Even though the man didn't have kids.

A cop car came down the street. Mr. Slick turned quickly away so he had his back to the street when the cruiser drove by.

A million people would have seen that gesture and thought nothing of it. Those people hadn't been where Rob had been, hadn't seen the things he'd seen. As though covering his abrupt reaction to seeing a police car, Mr. Slick then pointed to the foundation of the house. Hailey walked closer to him and seemed to be answering questions. Rob swiftly raised the camera once more.

All he needed was... Yes, Mr. Slick turned to glance up the street and down again. Looking for more cop cars?

Luckily, the man didn't pay any attention to what was going on in the park. Rob shot off a few photos, with no clear idea why.

Then the Realtor and her client entered Bellamy House.

Now what?

Limp into the house and confront the guy? Threaten a complete stranger with his grandmother's cane?

Even though he felt an urge to do something stupid and dramatic, common sense told him that the man wasn't here to harm Hailey. For some reason he was interested in real estate in the area.

Still, Rob wasn't taking any chances. Whatever was up with her newest client, Hailey was not going to be alone with him any longer than Rob could help.

He packed his bag swiftly and crossed the street.

The same instinct that brought him here had him stashing his camera bag in the garage before entering

the house. He could hear voices upstairs and the idea of
that tanned weasel in a bedroom with Hailey had Rob's
hands tightening on the handle of the cane. He didn't
want it as a weapon, though he'd use the cane if he had
to, he wanted it more as a prop. A kind of disguise. By
leaning heavily on the thing and exaggerating his limp,
he would appear feeble and unthreatening.

He made his way to the bottom of the stairs. "Hi,
I'm back," he yelled.

The voices ceased. Then Hailey appeared at the top
of the stairs. "Rob. What are you doing home?" her
voice was friendly but he heard the steel beneath. She'd
told him to make himself scarce and he was anything
but.

"I have a physiotherapy appointment and my leg
hurts too much to drive. I was wondering if you'd drop
me off when you're finished here?"

"I—uh," she fumbled.

"If it's not out of your way?" Now he had a perfectly valid reason to stay in the house until Mr. Slick
was gone.

"Okay. Just make yourself scarce until we're done."

He wasn't at all surprised to find the prospective
buyer appear behind her. He'd want to check out another
male in the house, especially one who was friendly
enough with Hailey that she'd give him a ride.

"Hi," Rob called up the stairs, raising a friendly hand
while the other white-knuckled the cane. "I'm the owner
if you have any questions. Nobody knows the house
like I do."

"Thanks. It's a beautiful home." The accent was East
Coast. Upper-crust or faking it.

"Sure is. Too big for one person, which is why I'm
selling it."

"Yes. My sister is a single mother. She and her two kids live with me. Works out for now. Of course, when I get married and start a family," he said with a glance at Hailey, "there's plenty of room here to make a suite downstairs for my sister. So we'd both have our privacy." His attitude was friendly, but his eyes were cold and Rob had the impression he was being scrutinized thoroughly. He knew the feeling since he was doing some serious scrutinizing of his own.

HAILEY WAS FURIOUS and she let Rob know it as they drove the short distance to his physio appointment. "I am not a limousine service."

"You could have said no."

"And let my client think I was heartless? No, thank you."

"Sorry." But he didn't sound very sorry. "What's his story?"

She narrowed her eyes at him. "Why?"

Rob looked at her in a way that was a little too innocent. "I'm selling a house, he wants to buy one. I wonder if he's a serious candidate. That's all."

"He's some kind of consultant in the oil business. He's spent time in the Middle East, Mexico, Texas, Alberta, all over. He wants to settle in Fremont because his extended family lives in the area."

"He have a name?"

She hesitated, but she supposed it wasn't a national secret. And her client had appeared very seriously interested in the house. "Dennis Thurgood."

Rob tapped his knee for half a block. "He seemed more interested in you than in the house," he said at last. She didn't bother telling him that she'd been at the office when the new client came in. Next thing she knew she had a new client. The front-office receptionist had giggled when she'd told Hailey that the gentleman had first asked if Hailey were a Realtor, then asked for her name, then asked if he could be her client.

The path was a little unorthodox to be sure but he was a client who was only in town for a few days with the express purpose of buying a property. He had money, knew he wanted a large home in an established neighborhood and didn't drive her crazy with nit-picky criticism. She'd felt his interest in her as a woman and was flattered by it. But she was a businesswoman first, and he was an ideal client.

Unlike the one currently at her side.

She turned to glare at him. "I think he's a serious possibility." She raised her finger, schoolmarm fashion. "Do not sabotage this deal."

"I'm not going t—"

"You've scuttled every serious possibility."

"Have not."

"What about the MacDonalds?"

"What about them?" He looked sulky and wouldn't meet her gaze.

"You told them your grandmother died in the four-poster that's the centerpiece of the master bedroom."

"They weren't the right people for the home."

"And the Fergusons?"

"Whoever heard of a little kid being terrified of rac-coons?"

"And then as soon as you find that out you inform the kid that raccoons love to nest in the trees. And you had one that used to climb up to your bedroom window and you'd feed it."

"It was true."

"She made her mother take her back to the car and wouldn't come back into the house."

"I don't want anybody buying this house and not being happy here."

"It seems like everyone who's been interested hasn't been right for Bellamy House."

He scowled. "I want the right people, that's all."

She glanced over at him. He looked as though he weren't sleeping well. He barely glanced at her. She supposed it wasn't hard to figure out why.

They never should have slept together.

She'd never, ever fired a client, and with a listing as juicy as this one, she'd have a hard time doing it now, but the truth was, Rob was making her job difficult.

She sighed. "You know how you threatened to fire me?"

"I was never going to fire you." Their gazes connected and she felt a dangerous tenderness for him well up inside her.

"I think I might have to quit."

"Look," he said, "I'm having a bad day. Sorry. I shouldn't have asked you to drive me. I—I don't know how to do this. With you."

She sighed. "No. I'm sorry. Normally I'd offer to drive you to your physio. I really don't mind. It's just— I'm just—" She turned to him. Their gazes connected and everything she hadn't been able to say was right there. Between them.

She pulled up in front of the physiotherapy clinic. He didn't make a move to get out of the car.

She looked at him. He seemed to feel as lost as she did. It was all she could do not to reach over, cup his face in her hands and tell him she'd be here when he got out of his appointment. That she'd take him home to her apartment or take herself back to his place. Already her foolish heart was trying to attach to a man who didn't want commitment.

The silence stretched and then they both spoke at the same time.

"You know, I have this problem..." she began.

"I don't know what to do with my grandmother's ashes."

"I beg your pardon?" she asked.

"What?" he echoed.

It was so ridiculous she had to laugh. "You go first."

"I said, 'I don't know what to do with my grandmother's ashes.'"

She glanced at him. "Where are they now?"

"On my desk. In the house. I can't leave them there permanently obviously. I don't know where to put them."

She'd had the same problem when her father had died. Where did you put the ashes of a man who'd never belonged anywhere? In the end, she'd thrown them in the ocean at the junction of several currents in the Salish Sea. She thought that's what would have made him happiest, spreading himself all over the world.

Agnes Neeson, however, was a different person altogether.

"You know, I never knew your grandmother. Was there a place she really loved?"

He wrinkled his brow. "I can't think of any place special. That's the trouble. She was usually at the house or pottering in the backyard. That garden was a real showplace in its day.

"We used to go on holidays when I was a kid but that was for my benefit. She did most of her traveling vicariously through me."

"Rob, I think we both know where your grandmother would want her ashes to be buried. In the garden of Bellamy House."

He didn't argue. Hailey was right. It was so obvious. "She used to tell me how she and my grandfather had planned the garden, and she knew every tree. Every flower. They planted the mountain ash in the backyard because they wanted the berries to attract birds."

"Don't you think that's the perfect spot for her final resting place?"

"But people think the mountain ash is a garbage tree. They might chop it down. Pave over the whole backyard and churn my grandmother into tarmac. Then how would I feel? The new owners might pull down the old place and put up some big new McMansion."

"All you can do is your best, Rob."

"I guess. I'll think about it." He turned to her. "What were you going to say? Something about a problem?"

"I— Oh, I feel stupid now."

"More stupid than me asking what to do with a dead woman's ashes?"

"Right. Okay. Well, here's the thing. I have this problem. I think I've had it for a long time. Because we moved around so much, I became really good at fitting in." She fiddled with the key ring hanging from her ignition. It was a diamond slipper, given to her by Julia for her last birthday. "That's why I'm good at sales. I learned how to connect with strangers really fast. It's how I survived."

He nodded.

"The secret of being able to move when you've barely settled and start one more time in one more new school in one more new town is not to attach too securely." She glanced at him, "Does this make sense?"

He nodded.

"I made friends with so many girls along the way. Girls I didn't keep in contact with. Girls I probably wouldn't recognize if they walked past me on the street. I left one place and had to put all my energies in surviving in the next town. I couldn't waste energy on the past."

"Sure. Makes sense. You know, your voice, it goes higher when you talk about this stuff."

She touched her throat. Went "ahem" a couple of times to clear the constriction.

"It's hard for you to talk about. That's why your voice rises."

She nodded. Surprised he'd know something she'd needed a therapist to explain. As an interviewer he'd be acute to things like voice and tone. He could probably tell her that her shoulders were up a little higher than normal, too. She forced herself to relax.

"Why is that a problem? You seem fine now. You and Julia are obviously close."

She smiled. "Julia's the best friend I've ever had. Yet she had to work with me to get me there. She was the one who suggested counseling." Then she fell serious again. "That's not the problem. The issue I have is that somehow in my strange upbringing—or maybe I'm just hardwired this way—I can't do that with men."

He seemed confused. "What do you mean, exactly?"

"I attach. Weirdly and way too fast." She touched her chest. "I have to be so careful with my heart."

He felt a funny sensation in his own chest, a cross between a pain and an itch. He'd never had such a feeling in his life.

He also felt as though his collar was too tight. And

he wasn't wearing a collar. That feeling he'd had plenty. He edged closer to the door. "Are you saying…"

She shook her head, a wry smile on her face. "That I'm in love with you? No. What I'm saying is that I have to be very careful or I will be." She sighed. "And that can't end well for me."

He opened his mouth. Closed it again. Pondered. "Is that why you have that crazy-ass notion that you have to get your career going now and settle down later?"

"Mostly I just say that to protect myself. The truth is, if a local man was interested in me and he was a settling-down kind of guy, then I'd be interested."

"Like that guy looking at my house?"

She licked her lips. "Theoretically."

"He's asked you out, hasn't he?"

Damn, he was good. Those shrewd blue eyes didn't miss much. "Yep."

"Hunh. You're right. That is a problem."

15

ROB WENT THROUGH the photos he'd snapped of Dennis Thurgood, aka Mr. Slick, then uploaded several choice images to his computer.

The man had done nothing more sinister than act edgy around a cop car.

And ask Hailey out.

Maybe he'd have let it go except the man was coming back for another look at the house, which meant he'd be spending more time alone with Hailey. When she'd let slip that he wouldn't be needing a mortgage, Rob's suspicions had intensified.

Rob had no proof of anything. Yet…something about the guy was off.

Okay, he might be making a fool of himself. If his grandmother could speak to him from inside that box, he knew what she'd say. "Wouldn't be the first time."

He called his editor in New York.

It wasn't jealousy, he told himself, as he studied the images again. Listening to his gut instincts had saved lives, and not only his own.

Gary took the call right away. "Rob, good to hear from you. How's the leg?"

"Not bad. Healing."

"You running six-minute miles yet?"

"Funny. I'm in physiotherapy. She says she'll have me running in a week. Two tops."

"That's great. I could use you in the field."

"Yeah. I know. I follow the news."

Gary was one of the busiest people Rob knew so he didn't waste any more time in idle conversation. "Gary, I need a favor."

"What is it?" His tone sharpened. Rob could picture his boss pulling a notepad toward him, clicking open his ballpoint.

"I want you to run a check on someone."

"You're on sick leave. What the hell are you doing?" he said, sounding frustrated.

"I swear I didn't do anything. And I could be completely mistaken, but there's this guy who wants to buy my grandmother's house. I think something's shady about him."

He described the incident with the cop car.

Gary didn't sound impressed. "He could have unpaid parking tickets. Come on. You're not used to living in suburbia. You're bored. You're seeing things."

"I hope you're right. I really do. Could you do this for me? As a friend? For the guy who'd take a bullet to get you the hottest news."

"That is a low blow, even for you. What do you care who buys your house? So long as he's got the cash?"

There was a pause. Rob might bend the truth a little now and then, but he never lied to Gary. "There's a woman involved."

"Ah."

"I can't explain it. I think she could be in danger from this guy."

A long-suffering sigh traveled the miles between them. "What have you got?"

"Photos. And a name and occupation that may or may not be false."

"Send me what you've got. I'll see what I can do."

"Thanks."

"I'm making no promises. I'll see what I can do."

"Got it."

He emailed the photos and as much information about Mr. Slick as he'd been able to pry out of Hailey. It wasn't much but Gary had connections like nobody else. He never revealed how he got the information he did, and Rob never asked. All he could do was hope Gary would take him seriously.

And that—for once—his famous instincts were wrong.

He needed activity. He could go to the gym and do the workout his physiotherapist had created for him but he needed to be outdoors. The day was warm for September, short-sleeves-and-sunglasses nice.

He looked at his grandmother's remains and made a second call.

"Hi, Rob," Hailey said when she answered.

"Thanks for taking my call. I want to ask you something."

"What is it?"

"Would you come over and help me bury my grandmother? I feel like it should be special somehow. You're the only person I want to be there."

There was a silence and he felt all the things they couldn't say. How he wished he could be different for her. How she wished the same.

"Of course I'll come. I'm honored to be asked."

"Thank you."

She showed up an hour later with a bag from a local garden store. In it were spring bulbs and a small metal plaque with the gardener's prayer engraved on it.

He felt a rush of emotion fill him. "It's from a poem by Dorothy Gurney. My grandmother loved it." He felt such a connection between these two women. He'd made the right choice in asking Hailey to be part of this small ceremony to mark his grandmother's burial.

He dug the hole with a dirt-encrusted shovel he found in the shed. Neither of them said anything as he emptied the box of ashes into the hole. He wasn't a praying man but he felt an enormous sense of rightness in putting her ashes under the shade of the mountain ash.

Hailey helped him plant the tulip and daffodil bulbs. Then he covered over the hole and pushed the stake holding the plaque into the freshly dug earth.

He read aloud, hoping that somewhere his grandmother could hear him:

The kiss of the sun for pardon,
The song of the birds for mirth,
One is nearer God's heart in a garden
Than anywhere else on earth.

WHEN THE SIMPLE BURIAL was done, he turned to Hailey. She was wearing a flowered dress and he suspected she'd changed in order to wear the perfect outfit to say goodbye to a woman she'd never even met.

Rob had never felt more bereft.

"Don't go," he said.

She shook her head. Her eyes were luminous and he felt that she belonged here as surely as his grandmother did.

He walked to her, took her in his arms. She didn't resist.

Without a word, they walked into the house through the back door and, hand in hand, made their way upstairs.

This time he didn't hesitate. He took Hailey to the room he now thought of as his.

The big four-poster looked as solid as his grandparents' marriage had been. And Hailey's hand in his felt as solid, as true and lasting.

He wasn't sure he had it in him to give her what she wanted. What she deserved. Still he turned her to him, kissed her slowly and softly said, "I can't promise—"

He didn't finish. She laid a finger across his lips. "I know," she said. "It's okay."

He kissed that finger. Slid his own fingers along her palm and opened them so he could kiss her open palm, then her wrist where a pulse beat rapidly against his lips. The heat coming off her skin, the scent that was hers alone, intoxicated him.

As he undid the buttons at the front of her dress, he kissed the top of each breast following the lacy edge of her bra with his lips, making her sigh with quiet pleasure. When he had all the buttons undone, he eased the dress off her shoulders and it slid to the floor, resembling a pool of flowers.

Kneeling before her, he kissed down her belly, down to panties that were as lacy and erotic as that bra. When he slipped his thumbs into the sides and slid them down her legs she shivered. He could feel a trembling in her limbs, felt her arousal, mirroring his. He was so hard he felt he might explode. Knowing they'd end up making love on the floor if he continued doing what he wanted to, he rose, unhooked her bra, let himself enjoy the sight of her bare breasts, then pulled back the covers on the big bed and laid her down. It seemed to him as though the bed welcomed them with open arms.

"I want you naked," she informed him in a sultry tone.

She watched as he stripped for her, which he did in record time, and then he knelt between her legs and loved her with his mouth. Her hands tangled in his hair as he took her up, feeling her excitement build, tasting it on his tongue.

When she reached her first peak, she cried out, bucking against him, and then to his delight, she yanked on his hair. "I need you inside me," she moaned.

He managed to hold on to enough sanity to mumble, "Condom," and race to the bathroom. He brought out a handful and sheathed himself with fumbling hands. He'd never wanted anything as much as he wanted to be inside this woman.

He looked into her eyes, and, as his body entered hers, he let her see all the emotions he couldn't find another way to express.

As their passion built, she reached behind her, clasping one of the bedposts, as though it could keep her tethered to earth. He raised his hand, found hers and clasped it and the mahogany post as they rocketed to heaven together.

16

"I DON'T EVEN WANT to go home," John said. He and Julia were trying a new Thai place that had received good reviews. It was the second time this week they'd grabbed dinner. "My wife did all the decorating. I'm living in a box with beige walls and the furniture my ex didn't want."

"How bad is it?" Julia had to ask.

"Pretty bad."

He'd been good to her. So the online dating thing hadn't turned up much in the way of dates; she'd found a friend. And it was nice to have a man to go to a movie with and hang out with.

"I'd be happy to come over and give you some ideas."

"Really? Because I was totally hinting."

She chuckled. "I got that."

"Would tomorrow afternoon work? You could give me some ideas and then we could go for dinner somewhere."

"No hot dates?" she teased.

"Not hardly. You?"

"I'll be at your place at two o'clock."

"Great."

When she arrived at his house a little after two-thirty, she quickly realized he hadn't exaggerated. The place he'd bought was a standard bungalow with every interior wall painted the same shade of beige.

The place had definite possibilities though.

The rooms were a good size, the original oak floors had been refinished and large picture windows let in a ton of light.

The furniture, however, was pitiful. The kind of bad rec-room stuff you banish to the basement until you have the money to upgrade. Seemed like he and his wife had never got around to upgrading.

His bedroom furniture consisted of a queen-size mattress on the floor.

After ten minutes of walking through the house, she said, "I need a budget.'

"Already?"

"Yup. I need to know what you're prepared to spend." She took out her computer tablet. "There are emergency items, essentials and nice to have. We'll prioritize."

"Let me put it to you this way. If I let you do everything you want, how much would it cost?"

She smiled. "That's the sort of budget I like."

When he opened his mouth to protest—probably—she said, "Okay, okay. Here's where I want to start. First, the reason I was a teeny bit late is that I had some paint leftover from another job. And it's ideal for here. We'll do the main downstairs rooms in a color called linen. Don't worry, it's very neutral. Masculine in fact. You'll love it. I also snagged some mascarpone. That's for woodwork and trim. If you feel like a handyman project, you can do those horrible kitchen cupboards yourself. Otherwise, we send them out." She patted his shoulder. "So the paint's free."

"Why do I get the feeling that nothing else is?"

She tapped on the computer tablet in her hand. "I get a discount on furniture at several terrific places. Honestly, John, you need to get rid of this crap. Now."

He leaned against a beige wall and folded his arms. He had nice, muscular arms, she noticed. "That sounds like shopping. I hate shopping."

"You could give me your credit card and stay home."

"I can do shopping."

"Let's go then."

He looked alarmed. "What? Now?"

"There's no better time. And trust me. When you have a home that suits you and feels comfortable, you're going to enjoy being here."

"You're the professional. Let's go."

YOU LEARNED A LOT ABOUT a person when you attempted to remake their home as Julia knew from experience. In John's case he was easy to deal with, accepting all her suggestions and only quibbling when she tried to get him to move his big-screen TV out of the living room.

"Absolutely not," he said. "I watch games in here. I'm the one that does the living in the living room. What's the point of sticking me in a spare bedroom? The fireplace is out here. It's close to the kitchen. The big screen stays."

"Fine," she said. It was his house, after all, and his argument made sense. Once they'd chosen the furniture—well, she'd chosen, and he'd pulled out his credit card—they were ready for a break. As they headed for a local Mexican restaurant that she loved, they walked past a trendy menswear shop. She glanced in the window, then at her companion who wore his usual collection of unfortunate clothing choices.

Should she?

She glanced at him walking beside her. He had a great body, but he always camouflaged it in a series of clothing disasters. He'd been good about letting her redecorate his home. Maybe?

"John," she said, her tone tentative.

"I don't like that look in your eye. I'm not buying three identical white vases to place on the mantel."

"No. It's not about vases. Honestly. I was just wondering whether you'd like to check out this menswear shop."

He narrowed his eyes at her. "Why would I want to do that?"

She shrugged. "No reason. I think those jeans would look really good on you."

He wasn't fooled. "Are you trying to stage me, too?"

She nibbled her lower lip. Truth or not? She decided, since they were friends and not lovers, that she could afford honesty.

"I don't mean to be rude, but you could look so much better. You've got good bone structure, a nice body, but your clothes aren't doing you any favors."

"I like to be comfortable."

"And that was fine when you were married. Now that you're single, I think you should work on presenting your best package."

He snorted with laughter. Realizing what she'd said, she blushed. "I don't mean that package... Oh, you know."

He stared in the window. "If I put those jeans on, they'll definitely be all about my package. Those things are tight."

"At least try them on."

She coaxed him into the store and soon she had him

in a fitting room with a selection of jeans, sweaters
and shirts.

He emerged wearing jeans that actually fit. She
couldn't believe the difference. He had a seriously nice
body. And, she couldn't help but notice there did seem
to be a pretty nice package in there.

She pushed him in front of the full-length mirror.
"See how much better these look?"

"They'd better. They cost almost as much as that
sectional sofa you talked me into."

Still, he had a half smile on his face.

In half an hour she'd talked him into a pair of jeans,
black pants for going out, a casual shirt, a sweater and
leather shoes that could be casual or dressed up. As a
wardrobe went it was pretty basic. However, like her
decorating project, you started with the emergency list.
There were plenty more items she could add to bolster
his wardrobe. At least he had a start.

"And there's a really good stylist near my office
called Savoir Faire. Felix is the owner's name. He does
terrific men's cuts. I could—"

He held up a hand. "Enough. I can only take so much
improvement in one day."

"So HE HELD UP HIS HAND and said—" and here Julia
lowered her voice in a truly bad imitation of a man
"'—Enough. I can only take so much improvement in
one day.'"

Hailey laughed dutifully. Well, it was funny, but she
was having trouble concentrating. She really needed
to pull herself together. She and Julia were shopping.
Hailey for something to wear on her date with Dennis,
who'd checked out the hottest new eateries before inviting her. She liked that he'd taken the initiative, and

not used the fact that she was the local and he an out-of-towner as an excuse to make her choose the restaurant.

She'd heard nothing but rave reviews about Gastronome, raves on everything but the prices, which were steep.

Julia was shopping mostly because she loved shopping.

"John sounds like a nice guy," Hailey said to Julia, who was currently flipping through a rack of red and black tops as though she didn't already own enough black and red.

"Oh, he is." Julia glanced up. "And I think there's a surprisingly nice-looking man hiding under all that crap."

"Not for you?"

Her friend shrugged. "I'm regifting him to some deserving woman." Then she found a short black cocktail dress. "Ooh, I bet Dennis would love you in this."

Hailey would not feel guilty. She would not feel bad that she had accepted a date with her latest client. Why shouldn't she date?

It wasn't as if Rob had anything to offer her. Except the greatest sex of her life and an intimacy between them that was about so much more than sex.

If only he were a stay-at-home man.

Or she were a different kind of woman.

If there was one thing Rob had done for her, it was get her thinking about schedules and life plans and how perhaps hers was too rigid. It wasn't as though she could plan that in five years, when her business was more successful and she felt settled and ready, her ideal man would suddenly appear. Instead, she was beginning to realize that a little flexibility was a good thing, whether in life, in business or in love.

She was bending her own strict rules and dating a client. So what?

She found herself staring at a dress she didn't even like. "I don't know. I feel like I want to stay away from black."

"Right." Julia went to put it back on the rack, then said, "Maybe I'll try it on. I wonder if they have my size."

As Hailey flipped through dress after dress, she tried to imagine dating Dennis.

He was intelligent; he was charming; he loved Bellamy House almost as much as she did. What was it to Rob who bought the place? He clearly didn't want to keep his grandmother's house.

She tried not to contemplate what it would be like to date a guy who owned Bellamy House. One who wasn't Rob. She couldn't picture being with anyone else in that wonderful home. Somehow, in her mind, it would always be his.

Well, as Gloria had reminded her, she needed to stop wasting the present by worrying about the future. Everything would work out, she was certain of it.

Dennis had been suddenly called out of town for a few days but had made her promise she'd call him if any other serious buyers for Bellamy House appeared. She'd agreed. And had also agreed to postpone their date. Since she and Julia had already decided to go shopping, however, they'd kept that date.

She felt so torn. So messed up. And suddenly she realized that that was why women have each other. To talk to.

"Hey, how about we ditch the shopping and grab lunch early? I need to talk."

"Of course," her friend said, instantly putting the dress back.

Maybe a few days was exactly what she needed to get some perspective. Sleeping with Rob a second time had been the mistake she'd known it would be.

Well, she kind of thought her big mistake was sleeping with him in the first place. Her plan hadn't worked, not at all. Think about him less once she got him into bed?

She snorted at her own foolishness.

Over lunch at a little bistro around the corner she told Julia all of it.

Her friend opened her eyes wide. "You had sex on that single bed?"

"Yes."

"And that was the best sex of your life? On a single bed?"

She nodded.

"With a man with a bullet hole in his leg?"

"Uh-huh."

Julia stared at her as she sipped her tea. "Can you imagine what he'd be like in a real bed? With all his limbs working properly?"

They both sighed.

"Well, our second time was in the four-poster."

The teacup hit its saucer with a snap. "Second time? I thought you said—"

"I did. But we'd buried his grandmother's ashes, and he was so sad and so sweet, and he looked at me and I was lost."

"I know. Burying people always makes me hot."

She laughed. They both did. This was why it was so great to have a friend. For all her sarcasm Julia got it.

Their laughter died and she said, "In that big bed. I

can't explain it. The sex was so different. It was slower, the connection was so deep, it was like, like…"

"Like you were in love with him?"

Her friend's warm brown eyes were full of sympathy.

Hailey smacked her forehead into her palm. "I've gone and fallen in love with Rob. When I promised myself I wouldn't. It was only going to be one night. Just one night…"

"And now you're in love with him."

"Yeah."

"What about him? Is he in love with you?"

She thought about how he'd looked at her after they'd planted the tulips, how tenderly he'd made love to her. "Yes. I think he is. That doesn't change anything though. He's still the man with the camera on the other side of the world. And I'm still the girl who wants a stay-at-home guy."

"What are you going to do?"

As much as she didn't want to, Hailey knew she had to move on. "I'm going to date Dennis. And maybe a few other men I find interesting. And Rob will heal and he'll return to his globe-trotting existence. And I will try to forget him."

Her friend's response was succinct. "That plan sucks."

"Can you think of a better one?"

"Nope."

17

JULIA WAS IN A HURRY to see John's house completed, though not as much of a hurry as he was in, which made the project fun to work on.

She called in the painters she always used. They were fast and reliable, and more important, could come immediately. She'd chosen a chocolate color for his bedroom. During the week she'd spent extra time picking linens and a few accessories that she knew he wouldn't have been interested in.

The furniture was being delivered on Saturday and she was as excited as if it were her own home she was decorating.

When he called her Friday she assumed it was to let her know what time all the furniture was going to be delivered the next day.

It wasn't. "How do you feel about dinner?" he asked.

"Enthusiastic. I'm a big believer in three squares a day."

"Very funny. How do you feel about dinner tonight? With me?"

"Even more enthusiastic. I absolutely do not feel like cooking tonight."

"Seven?"

"Perfect."

"Pick you up?"

She hesitated. "Hmm. Tempting. I'm staging a place downtown. I don't think I'm going to have time to go home first. Why don't I meet you someplace?"

"Indian sound good to you?"

"Yes."

"You're a very easy woman to please."

She chuckled. "You're hitting all the right notes."

He named a place she'd heard of but never tried, and they agreed to meet at seven.

The staging job took longer than she'd anticipated. After she'd plumped the last cushion and fussed with the final flower arrangement she saw she was running a few minutes late. However, she absolutely could not be seen in public without retouching her makeup, which she did in the car once she'd parked near the restaurant.

When she walked in, she couldn't see John at first. There were two men sitting alone at tables, but a quick scan showed neither was him. Both were well-turned out, obviously waiting for their wives or dates. She glanced at her watch. Okay, she was a quarter of an hour late, but surely he wouldn't…

She started to nibble on her freshly lipsticked lip when one of the two men waved at her.

"John?" She couldn't have been more shocked. He stood and came toward her. "You look so different." She'd seen potential there, but even she hadn't seen how hot he could be. "What have you done?"

He was wearing the jeans she'd talked him into and the black sweater, which reminded her how good his body was.

But there was so much more he'd done to himself.

They returned to his table and he said, "I took your advice. I went to Savoir Faire and had my hair styled." He put air quotes around *styled* but he'd gone, hadn't he?

"I can't believe the difference a good cut makes."

"The guy who did the cutting is the one who recommended the eyeglass place."

"That's what else is different. Your glasses are from this millennium. They look good. You have beautiful eyes."

He seemed slightly embarrassed by her enthusiasm for his new look and quickly changed the subject.

"How did your staging go today?"

"Fine. The Realtor was really pleased. He's going to put photos on his website and mention First Impressions by name. It's always good to get a little free publicity."

While they talked, a woman walked by and Julia could see her checking John out. She wasn't used to seeing him ogled and she was surprised at how much she didn't like the experience.

"Have you had any dates since your makeover?" she asked him.

"A couple." Again that unusual stab of irritation. Why shouldn't he date?

"And?"

What was she doing, she wondered, offering her time and talents to turn John into a great-looking guy with a stylish home just so she could gift him to another woman?

He sat back, sipped the ginger drink they'd both ordered, and said, "The first one was nice enough. She was early for our date."

Julia thought of her own perpetual tardiness and hated this woman on principle. "She probably has no life," she commented.

"Could be. But then, if being early means you have no life, I guess I don't have one either."

"Oops."

"You know what's weird?"

"What?"

"I've got used to having that time to myself while I wait for you. I find it kind of relaxing. Have a drink, check email on my cell, settle in and study the menu. I didn't like this woman arriving at the same time as me. It threw me."

This was good. She was starting to feel better. "What about the other date?"

He shook his head. "I suggested coffee, but she wanted to go for a drink instead. Talked nonstop about herself while getting plastered. I put her in a cab two hours after we met. Longest two hours of my life."

"I'm only a social drinker," Julia said. Which was a stupid thing to say and completely irrelevant to the conversation. Especially as they'd already decided they were only going to be friends.

"I've noticed."

She looked up. Their gazes caught and held for a moment. She felt as though she were seeing him for the first time. He was already familiar to her, and yet, tonight he seemed different. Sexier. Surer of himself, maybe.

She glanced down again and the strange moment passed.

As dinner progressed the evening seemed more like a date. She found herself feeling flirty and felt a similar vibe coming from her companion.

A pleasant sense of uncertainty teased at her. They'd agreed they didn't have chemistry. Was it possible they'd been wrong?

Was it simply that they hadn't given each other a chance? She studied him across the table and saw not a fashion model nor a Greek god, but a real flesh-and-blood man. A heck of a lot better put together than the one she'd first met, but he wasn't a fantasy. She already knew that he was a stickler about time—though he seemed able to cope with her habit of being slightly late. She knew from his house that he was absurdly tidy—again, not something they had in common. She kept her place clean, but was always fighting clutter.

He enjoyed trying new restaurants. As did she. They could talk about anything and everything from places they'd traveled to bands they both liked or didn't to local politics.

He'd become a good friend. Could he be more?

Once outside the restaurant, they lingered a moment too long. She didn't want to leave him. He didn't seem in a hurry to leave her.

"It's a funny thing about dating sites," he said. "You end up judging people so fast. It's like you have these ideas about what you want and like and if the other person doesn't hit a bunch of the things in the first few minutes of meeting, you move on."

"Sometimes too fast, maybe."

"Yes. Exactly." He stepped closer to her. "I have to make a confession."

Her pulse sped up. "What is it?" She hoped it wasn't something bad. She *really* hoped it wasn't something bad.

He said, "I was attracted to you the first time we met."

"You were?"

"Yep. You obviously weren't into me so I figured friends was still good."

"I was caught up in my ridiculous fantasy." She closed her eyes. "I was so naive."

"Do you still just want to be friends? Or are you open to something more?"

In response, she stepped even closer to him until she could see the black flecks in his blue eyes that were staring into hers with an intensity that she felt throughout her being. She raised herself on tiptoe. She'd intended to kiss him. Somewhere along the line, though, he took over, drawing her in tight and kissing her long and hard. It was a kiss that could make a woman forget to breathe.

When he pulled away, she touched his face. "Oh, I am definitely willing to consider more."

"Good."

She fiddled with her car keys. "I've got some linens I picked up for you in the car."

"The bedroom furniture arrived today. Do you want to come and see it?"

His gaze was tender, and she didn't feel like speaking, maybe wasn't able to. She just nodded.

He nodded back. Sometimes you didn't need words.

She climbed into her car and followed him back to his place. She felt jumpy and strange, but also keenly excited. She was pretty sure they were going to do more with that bed than put linens on it. Luckily, her gym bag was in the car so she had toiletries, a few cosmetics, a toothbrush and a change of underwear—an unexpected benefit of belonging to the gym.

When she walked into his house she cried out in delight. Against the freshly painted walls rested the new furniture. Clearly the bedroom suite wasn't the only furniture that had been delivered a day early.

"The sectional is great there. And wasn't I right about

the paint color and those black-and-white photographs? Masculine but stylish. Even the TV fits in now."

Even though this was her business there was huge pride when her design worked out. As this one had.

"What do you think?" she asked him.

"Beautiful," he said, not looking at the freshly painted walls or the brand-new furniture. He was looking at her.

She held the bag of linens in one hand, her gym bag and purse over the other shoulder. He walked over, took the bag from her hands. "Would you like to see the bedroom?"

"Very much."

When they entered his bedroom, she barely noticed the decor. All she saw was that splendid Mission-style bed. Already made.

"It looks fantastic," she said.

"I haven't slept in it yet."

To be the first in his bed was a wonderful thing, she decided. "New beginnings are good."

He took her into his arms, kissed her slowly, and then he knelt and scooped her up.

"What are you doing? I weigh a ton."

"No, you don't." And he laid her down on his bed.

He left the bedside lamps on, and for once, she didn't insist on darkness. If he was brave enough to lift her, she figured he knew she had a pound or ten she'd love to get rid of. He hadn't groaned or toppled under her weight. He didn't even seem to be breathing hard. She supposed he could handle her.

He took his time undressing her. When her full breasts spilled out as he took off her bra, he made a sound of pleasure and reached down to pop a plump nipple in his mouth. She felt lazy, content to be toyed with, as he learned her body, explored her hills and valleys, coaxing her slowly until she didn't feel lazy anymore. He slipped a hand between her thighs, drove her up higher until she crested the first peak crying out against his mouth.

"You're dressed," she said, when she could focus once more.

"Not for long."

She watched him, taking as much pleasure in eyeing his body as he had in revealing hers.

"You don't care at all that I have a few extra pounds on me, do you?"

"I like you exactly the way you are."

She sighed with deep contentment. Then she reached for him. "Let me show you what a woman with a few extra pounds can do with them."

18

Rob decided to be cool. So Hailey had a date with a smarmy twit who didn't like cops? It wasn't like she would go back to his hotel room or something on the first date.

He upped the weight on the leg press and powered through a few more reps. He didn't even think about the pain, only about getting strong again. Getting his mobility back.

Rob needed his quad muscles to be completely functional. Not only did he need to run a mile in six, he needed to be strong enough to run away from Fremont, from his memories, from Bellamy House, and most of all, from Hailey.

It bothered him even to admit how that woman had burrowed under his skin. No, when he thought about it, she hadn't burrowed at all. She'd blasted into his system with the same impact as that bullet. And there were moments when he thought the damage she'd done wouldn't heal as fast. Or be as relatively painless.

"You using that bench?" a gym-jock grunted at him, indicating the bench where he'd rested his towel.

He shook his head. Kept pushing. Five more reps.

He'd do five more reps then he'd take a break. As beads of sweat slid down his temple, he hunched a shoulder and wiped it onto his T-shirt. Three more. He could do it. He'd push through the pain.

The sooner he was out of here the better. He'd head back for New York. Pick up the pieces of his normal nomadic life. He tried to picture a reunion with Romona, but the fantasy wouldn't come. He could only think about Hailey. How he'd started out enjoying the challenge, the teasing to get the woman into his bed and the utter mind-blowing passion they'd experienced together once he had.

She'd warned him that she was afraid to fall in love and he'd tried to respect that, backing off out of courtesy to her.

Okay, they'd fallen into bed one more time but neither had planned that. He couldn't stop thinking about those hours in that four-poster and how everything had felt so utterly right. A final puzzle piece had fitted into place. Click.

One more rep. Every muscle in his body was bunched as he pushed up against the weight. It felt as if he were lifting a million pounds with his ankle while someone was stabbing this thigh with a hot poker.

The irony was they'd both worried about her heart. Who'd given a rat's ass about his?

Nobody, that's who. And now look at him. Trying to build up enough strength to run.

Because the truth was it wasn't Hailey who was in trouble here. It was him.

Mr. Lighthearted, the traveling guy who never stayed in one place long enough to get caught. And here he was, as caught as any man could be.

He was so in love with that woman he ached with it. But that didn't change who he was.

He hobbled off the machine, grabbed his towel and dried his wet face.

And that didn't change who she was.

Nobody knew better than he did that love wasn't enough.

He showered and returned home, driving Gran's Buick down streets as familiar as his own memories. He was pulling into the drive when his cell phone shrilled.

"I ran a mile in eight minutes yesterday," he said.

"Hello to you, too."

"Merv?" He checked his cell again. "What's my agent doing calling from my editor's office?"

"We were talking about you."

"I know he wants me back. I'm ready. Really."

"Rob, I'm not the HR department. Gary and I were talking about your photojournal."

"Photojournal?"

"That's what we're calling it. *My Neighborhood.* A photojournal. We're both excited about the possibilities. You've captured how people have parallel interests and concern wherever they live, whatever their relative wealth or political situation. It works because you always come back to your own hometown. Fremont becomes the central character in the book. And the photos are some of your best work."

"Oh, right. The book idea." He'd almost forgotten he'd sent Merv the photos and idea.

"More than a book idea. Gary and I talked about doing something interesting. *World Week's* parent company, Anvil Media, also has a book publishing arm, as you know."

"Sure."

"Gary and I are discussing a book that also has a magazine and website component."

He shut the engine off. Got out. Wandered toward the mountain ash tree. "Not sure I follow."

He wanted his grandmother to hear this. He settled himself on the cool ground, his back leaning against the tree trunk, his throbbing leg stretched out before him.

"It's simple. Anvil publishes the coffee-table book, you agree to do a number of features for the magazine based on the same idea. Cross publicity for the book and the magazine. Maybe a few extra pieces exclusive to the web."

"I don't do features. I cover hard news."

"Until a few weeks ago, you didn't write coffee-table books either."

"What kind of money are we talking?"

Merv told him. His eyebrows rose. He repeated the sum for his grandmother's benefit. "That's a nice chunk of change."

"You bet. Think about it. Gary says you'll still be a hard-news guy but this gives you a little more breathing room. Might stop you from burning out."

Or getting bored. He nearly jumped out of his skin. He could have sworn his grandmother's voice had uttered those words.

And, as so often, he thought she might be right.

He wondered how much of his travel bug had been simple boredom? The truth was, since he'd been home this time he hadn't felt bored once. With Hailey trying to sell the house to hordes of the wrong types and *My Neighborhood* to keep him busy and wanting to get Hailey into bed, enjoying the greatest sex of his life when he did, then wishing he could get her back into his bed, he hadn't had much time to be idle.

He patted the ground where tulips would bloom come spring and he wouldn't be here to see them.

Unless.

He realized he needed to tell Hailey his good news.

He called her.

"Hi, Rob."

"Hi. I want to talk to you about something." He didn't want to tell her his news over the phone. He wanted to watch her face, to share his excitement. "How would it be if I take you for dinner?"

"When?"

"Tonight."

There was a tiny pause. "I can't tonight. I already have a date."

His good mood dimmed as though a light had been switched off. "A date."

"Yes."

"Would this date be with Dennis Thurgood?"

"Yes."

"I don't think you should go. I don't trust that guy."

"You met him for five minutes. You don't know a thing about him."

"I saw him. When you were showing him the house. He turned his head when a cop car went by."

This time the pause was longer. "Were you spying on us?"

"No. Not exactly. I happened to be across the street at the park."

"With a telescope?"

"A telephoto lens. It was purely coincidence."

"And through studying a man through a camera lens for a couple of minutes you've decided...what exactly?"

"I don't know," he admitted. "How he turned his

head as the cruiser went by looked suspicious. An innocent man doesn't care if a cop gets a good look at him."

"That's it? That's your entire reason for telling me
not to go out with a man? There might be a million reasons why he turned his head. Maybe he thought he was
going to sneeze. Or he was checking out the state of the
siding. He is interested in buying the house, you know."

"I have a bad feeling."

"You're paranoid."

He traced the words of that poem on the plaque she'd
bought. "I was right about your friend and the Nigerian
scammer."

"Even she figured that one out."

"Don't go."

"Give me a better reason why I shouldn't go."

"I want to talk to you. I—I…" What was the use?

She sighed. "I need to get going. I'll talk to you tomorrow."

"Where's he taking you? On this date?"

"So you can turn up with your telephoto lens? I don't
think so," she said, ending the call.

ROB SHOWERED, CHANGED INTO a clean pair of jeans and a
gray sweater and decided that if it was date night here in
Seattle he didn't feel like spending it sitting around in
the house feeling sorry for himself with nothing better
to do than imagine Hailey out with Mr. Slick.

He didn't feel like hooking up with one of his old
friends.

There was a neighborhood watering hole not far from
here where he could sit at the bar, enjoy a beer, get
something to eat and watch the Mariners.

He looked at the keys to the Buick and decided that

one beer might too easily stretch into three. He'd leave the car and grab a cab.

Rain was falling when he stepped out. Ridiculous city. Always dripping. Who'd want to live in a rainforest? Not him.

He gave directions and the driver said, "Going to the bar to watch the game, huh?"

"Absolutely."

And he was treated to the cabbie's views on the Mariners. He experienced a strange sense of disconnection. He could so easily be one of those guys who followed teams and put money on fantasy leagues and whatever men who lived in one place for extended periods of time did.

He'd never missed that sort of life because he'd never envisioned it. Still, as the cab splashed its way through the wet streets, he began to warm up to the idea.

Hell, it was a cold, wet night and the idea of some male bonding over a game sounded good.

He paid the driver and entered the noisy place. There was one seat left at the bar. Empty because it was closest to the big screen and he'd have to crane his neck to see. Since his other choice was standing and his leg hurt like a son of a bitch, he took the barstool.

After ordering a beer, he started to watch the game. Groans, shouts of encouragement, cheers punctuated the play. They were the people of his neighborhood, he supposed, if he'd ever really had a neighborhood. They were professionals with ties bunched in their pockets, stopping to watch some baseball on their way home from work. They were soccer moms and dads. The plumbers and electricians he'd call if something needed fixing. They were groups of guys who liked to hang out together and a few singles like him who didn't want to sit home alone.

Especially not when the woman he'd fallen in love with was out on the town with another guy.

He took a pull of his beer, cold and smooth going down his throat. He rubbed the back of his neck, wishing the prickling sensation would go away. Hailey was fine. Maybe she had terrible taste in dates but she wasn't in a jungle surrounded by rebel forces wanting to harm her. She was an intelligent woman in a big city.

She'd be fine.

He tried to concentrate on the game but he couldn't stop thinking about her. About everything she was communicating to him by dating another man.

And what had he communicated to her? By stepping out of the way and letting her go?

Maybe that's what his irritation was about. It wasn't her in danger, it was him. In danger of losing the most amazing woman he'd ever met.

"What a fool!" he suddenly blurted aloud.

"I know, man," the chunky guy beside him said. "He totally shoulda seen that comin."

They both had their eyes on the screen. "Yeah," Rob agreed. "He should have seen it coming."

Tomorrow, he'd call her.

And what?

Was he really thinking about changing his life dramatically? For a woman?

His pocket buzzed and he realized it was his cell, which he'd put on vibrate. He glanced at the call display. "Gary? Why you calling so late?" He calculated it must be after eleven in New York.

"Where are you?"

"What? Oh, in a bar."

"Go somewhere quiet. Now."

19

GARY WASN'T A MAN to give orders without serious reason. Every nerve in Rob's body went into heightened alert. He rose from the bar, tossed money on the counter and walked out to the relative quiet of the street.

"I'm outside. What is it?"

"Those pics you sent me? Of the guy you wanted checked out?"

His fight-or-flight response was on full alert. Only there was no flight. It was all fight. "What about him?"

"Is he still in Seattle?"

"He left for a while but he's back. Why?"

"Your instincts are the best I've ever seen. Dennis Thurgood is a person of extreme interest to Interpol, the CIA and the DEA."

"Holy shit. What'd he do?"

"He's a real bad dude. Drugs and arms mostly. He almost got caught in a big bust in Paris a few months ago. Nobody knew he'd snuck into the States. The best guess is he's trying to hide out."

Rob thought of the fact the man had said he wouldn't need a mortgage. "You can add money-laundering to the list."

"Any idea where Thurgood is now?"

He wanted to punch something. "Out with my girl."

"Where?"

"I don't know." Fear, anxiety, anger churned in his gut and he had to tamp them down or he was no good to anybody. He forced himself to calm down. Think.

"They were going for dinner. I'll find out where."

"You call me when you find out where they are and I'll relay the information to the right people."

"Yeah."

"Do *not* be the hero. Let the pros handle it."

He didn't waste time arguing. There was no time. He ended the call.

Hit the button that would connect him with Hailey. "Come on," he urged. "Pick up."

She didn't pick up. Instead, he got her chirpy message telling him that she would love to talk to him but unfortunately couldn't take his call right now, blah, blah, blah. He stood there, watching as raindrops hit puddles and when the tone sounded for him to leave a message, he said: "Hailey. I need to talk to you. It's urgent."

Much as he was tempted to tell her to get away from Mr. Slick, and fast, he couldn't take the chance that he might somehow intercept the message.

He cursed.

If only she'd told him where she was going.

Fortunately her best friend Julia's business card was still in his wallet from when she'd first met him.

To his relief she answered right away. "First Impressions, Julia sp—"

"Julia, it's Rob. Hailey's in trouble."

"What?"

"I need to know where she is."

There was a pause and he got the feeling Hailey was one of those women who tell their BFF everything. Which was confirmed when Julia said carefully, "I'm sure if Hailey wanted you to know where she is she'd have told you."

Once more he had to tamp down the surge of emotions that threatened to choke him and make him do something stupid like scream at Julia.

"Listen. The guy she's with? I got a bad feeling about him. I snapped a few photos and sent them to a friend of mine who has connections. Turns out he's a real bad dude. We're talking international criminal here."

"Rob? Have you been drinking?"

"No. I'm serious. Please. Your friend is in real danger."

"I don't know."

"I'm a hard-news reporter. I have instincts honed by years of reporting on guys like him. And I have connections."

"Maybe I could just call her."

"I tried that. Her phone's off."

He heard her curse, knew she was worried about Hailey, but not sure whether it was her date or Rob who was the real problem.

How could Rob help her? Every second that ticked by was another second Hailey was at the scumbag's mercy. He said, "I'm going to give you the number of my editor at *World Week*. He'll confirm what I'm saying."

"How will I know it's really him?"

"You can look him up on Google!" Frustration careened through him. "Here's the number."

"Okay. I'm sorry to be difficult, but I have to look out for my friend."

"Then make sure you do. She's in real danger."

"WHAT'S UP?" John rolled over, lazily stroked Julia's back.

She snuggled up against him, glad to have his comfort and warmth. "That was the weirdest phone call." She relayed what Rob had said to her.

"You don't believe him?" he asked, frowning.

"I don't know. I don't want to cause Hailey any embarrassment."

She called her friend's cell. As Rob had told her, it was off. She left a message. "Hailey. It's Julia. Hope your date's going well. Call me the second you get this. Love you."

Then she rapidly texted a similar message.

"I didn't tell Rob where she is in case he's a crazy-ass stalker."

"What if he's telling the truth?"

She nibbled her lower lip. "He gave me his editor's phone number in New York. How do I even know it's his editor?"

"Seems like a pretty elaborate plan to get to a woman he sees almost every day anyway."

"I know. I just…" She turned to him, her new lover, and found there was something so reassuring and solid about him. It was wonderful to have a man she could trust. "The story seems so far-fetched. How many times does a girl end up on a date with a—a—terrorist?"

He drew her in close and kissed her cheek. "It seems to me that if there's even the smallest chance of it being true you need to warn her."

Julia jumped out of bed, grabbed her panties and stepped into them. "You're right. Come on, get dressed."

"I had plans for round two."

She dimpled at him. "Later. Right now you are taking me out to dinner at a very expensive new restaurant."

"Might this be the expensive new restaurant where your friend is on her date?"

"Yes."

He reached for his shirt. "So, we tell her she might want to ditch the date."

"You got it."

"And then round two?"

"And then round two."

"Are you going to tell Rob?"

"I don't think so. His instincts tell him this guy's bad news. Fair enough. But I have instincts, too, and they tell me that Rob crashing Hailey's date is a terrible idea."

HAILEY BELIEVED IN the power of positive thinking. And that meant that if she was determined to have a good time, she ought to have a good time.

The hollow feeling in her stomach must simply be hunger.

She pinned the bright smile back on her face as she listened to her date grill the wine waiter—no, sommelier, as he'd made a point to call him—about a certain vintage.

She suspected he was trying to impress her. She knew she should be flattered, but actually she was bored.

She didn't care about the microclimate where the grapes grew or the weather that summer or the phases of the moon when the fruit was harvested.

She liked to go to a restaurant, pick something that sounded good to eat, maybe have some wine and get on with it. She'd never been out with someone who took the menu apart and put it back together again and then approached the wine list—in this case an entire book—

like a battle of wits between him and the poor guy who simply wanted to take their wine order and move on.

This whole thing had been a bad idea. There was a reason, she reminded herself, why she never got involved with clients.

Gastronome, the trendy new eatery, was busy, but not crowded. The decor was sleek and modern. Her date had insisted on a table in a shadowed corner. "More private," he told her, touching her wrist. She'd smiled politely but didn't want to be private with him. She didn't even know him.

Once they were seated, he'd scanned the restaurant and she could have cursed Rob for putting stupid suspicions in her head. So what if Dennis preferred a dark corner, sat with his back to the wall and checked out the place with the vigilance of a spy who might need to make a quick getaway?

He was probably merely admiring the decor.

"Tell me why you chose Seattle?" she asked him once he'd finally approved the wine and she'd agreed with him that it was a very good vintage. As if she knew. Or cared.

"I'm ready to settle down," he said, relaxing back into his chair, sipping his wine. "This seems like a great city. It's cosmopolitan, but close to the outdoors. I like all the recreational opportunities. The climate's good. Mild."

She pointed to the picture window behind them where raindrops chased each other. "Except for all the rain."

"Yeah. First thing I'm going to do when I buy Bellamy House is hire an architect. I want a garage large enough for three cars."

"You're planning to tear the house down?"

"The value's in the land. And most of it is wasted on gardens and those trees. I'm going to build a place that has all the bells and whistles. Heated floors in all the bathrooms. Entire place wired for top-of-the-line electronics, home theater room, a gym." He sipped his wine thoughtfully, spinning the stem of the glass so the liquid swirled. "Temperature-controlled wine cellar, too."

"Wow. You have big plans."

"I've worked hard in my life. It's time to enjoy the rewards." He leaned closer to her. "And I'm definitely interested in finding someone to share my life with."

The gesture should have been sexy, but there was something calculated about it. He was good-looking, obviously rich, and someone who seemed to want what she wanted. A stable home life. Permanence.

She knew already there wouldn't be a second date.

And she strongly suspected there wouldn't be a home sale either. Once she told Rob about his plans to knock down Bellamy House she knew he'd never sell to this man.

In truth she didn't want Bellamy House to be redeveloped either. She loved the place. She'd grown to appreciate its quirky charm. And what of the garden where Agnes Neeson's ashes rested? Was Rob's grandmother going to end up underneath a home theater? The very notion was an outrage.

She glanced surreptitiously at her watch, wondering how soon she could eat her dinner and get out of here.

"You look so beautiful tonight," Dennis crooned. "That blue dress really brings out your eyes."

"Thank you." After the shopping trip with Julia had ended up in a long lunch and girl talk, she'd decided to forego a new outfit and wear one of her favorites. The blue silk was elegant without being overtly sexy. Dennis was a client, after all.

"And you're tall. I like a tall woman. I'm tall so we look good together."

Had he actually said that? And did she want a laundry list of obvious compliments?

She recalled the way Rob looked at her. He didn't gush about her eyes but his expression as he gazed at her made her feel beautiful.

Dennis Thurgood, by contrast, covered her in compliments the way a baker might cover a cake in sticky-sweet frosting. However, his eyes didn't warm when they looked at her. If anything he seemed to be calculating. How many years until her skin wrinkled? How well would she keep her slim figure after childbirth? She couldn't shake the notion that she was being studied and evaluated like the wine he'd chosen. Or the house he was planning to buy to raze and rebuild.

No, she thought, she really didn't want to be one of his possessions, like the original art he'd boasted of, the cars he'd described that would fill his garage and the rest of his carefully chosen possessions.

She wondered how she'd ever found him interesting.

And how soon she could make her escape.

20

ROB STOOD IN THE RAIN. Behind him the door of the bar opened periodically letting somebody in or out, along with a burst of bar noise. Once he heard a cheer.

He willed his cell to ring.

It remained stubbornly silent.

Julia should have figured out by now that he was telling the truth. Why hadn't she called him to tell him where Hailey was?

A cab pulled up and a young couple in jeans and raincoats made a run for the entrance. Before the cab drove away, Rob hailed it. Ran to the door and opened it. "You know the city well?"

The driver was between fifty and sixty with stubbled cheeks, a ball cap pulled low and eyes that had seen it all. "Yeah."

"What's the hot new restaurant in town?"

The guy shrugged. "Depends what you're looking for."

Rob climbed into the back of the cab. At least while he waited for his phone to ring, he could be doing something. "I'm meeting a woman at a restaurant and I can't remember the name of it." He held up his hands as if he were a typical, clueless dude.

"That sucks. She's waiting for you?"

"I think so."

The cabbie pulled out into traffic. "Why don't you call her?"

"I tried. Her phone's turned off. She's going to be pissed if I don't get there soon."

"Do you know anything about this place?"

He tried to think like a hardened criminal trying to pass as a normal guy. More than that, a catch. Rob recalled the expensive car the guy had rented, the designer duds, the Italian loafers. "Best restaurant in town that's also fairly new."

The driver reeled off a few names. Since he'd never heard the name of the restaurant they were of no use to Rob. "Of those, which one's the most expensive?"

"Oh," the driver said, catching his eye in the rearview mirror. "She's one of those women."

He shook his head. "You know, she's really not."

"Well, I'd say it's down to two. Gastronome or Luminous. Both are high-end. The first one I've heard has better food. Luminous is showier."

"Luminous. Let's try that one."

"You got it."

They headed downtown and hit traffic. Rob cursed every vehicle, every gnarl of construction, every fool who should be home and not out clogging the streets. Sweat crawled down his back as he imagined all the things a thug like Dennis Thurgood was capable of.

When they didn't move through an intersection in the space of two traffic lights, he banged his fist into his palm. "Come on!"

"This girl's really got to you."

"Yeah."

"You planning to propose tonight or something?"

As he sat there, pulled to knots by anxiety over this woman, Rob waited for the horror of the notion of marriage to sink in. It didn't. Instead he was struck by the rightness of the idea.

She belonged to him. He knew his famous instincts had been right about her date tonight, but what his famous instincts had forgotten to reveal was that he was miserable with jealousy, and that he and he alone, should be wining and dining Hailey. Wooing her—and there's a term his grandmother would have liked. Marrying her.

Now, all he had to do was find her, get her out of the clutches of a dangerous man and prove to her that he was the right man.

And he was determined to do that, if it took the rest of his life.

"I'm planning to marry her. If she'll have me." And the idea didn't stick in his throat. He had a book deal now. He could afford to spend more time at home.

After about ten million years of crawling through traffic, they finally arrived outside Luminous. "Hang here for just a sec," he snapped as he bolted from the cab.

He yanked open a heavy glass door, dashed inside, and knew almost instantly that he'd guessed wrong. The place was too brightly lit, and if a man had to make a quick exit, it was going to be difficult with all the columns and gold mirrors and what not.

"Just looking for a friend," he said as he jogged past the maître d' and in less than two minutes he was jogging back out. Back into the cab. "Nope. Let's try the other place."

They crawled back into heavy traffic. He groaned.

"How far is the other place?" he asked after five more minutes had moved at glacial speed and the cab had traveled ten feet.

"Three blocks that way." The driver pointed to his left.

"Okay. I'll walk it."

"Likely be faster."

He paid the guy and hopped out, heading in the direction indicated. Run a mile in six? The way his adrenaline was pumping he'd do it in four. He didn't care that his leg was sore. Didn't care rain was stinging his eyes and blurring his vision, didn't care that passersby glanced at him as though he was deranged.

He ran.

His leg burned, his lungs burned, every cell in his body pushed him forward. He had to get to her. Had to.

Common sense told him she couldn't be in any real danger, but common sense had no control over his gut instinct to get to her fast.

He jogged around a couple holding hands under matching umbrellas, dashed across a street against the light and got a screeching horn as a dark car seemed to come out of nowhere and slam on its brakes.

The driver rolled down the window and cursed fluently. He waved—in a kind of acknowledgment, apology, and *I don't have time to stop, this is an emergency* way—and kept running.

HAILEY WONDERED IF she'd ever been on a less successful date. Neither the exquisite food, nor the fancy wine, nor the discreet decor and exceptional service could change the fact that she didn't like her dining companion. He was boastful, rude to those he considered inferior, like the waiter, who looked as though he'd like to carve out her date's liver with a butter knife, and so full of sugary compliments to her that her teeth were starting to ache.

When they'd first arrived and been shown to their seats she'd surreptitiously scanned the place to see if there was anyone she recognized or anyone famous. But there was no one. So she was beyond surprised when an extremely familiar voice said, "Oh, my gosh, what a surprise!"

She glanced up.

"Julia!" If anyone was surprised, it was she. She'd told Julia not three hours ago when they'd had a wardrobe consultation, where she was going. Julia had declared her envy but made no mention of eating at the same restaurant tonight.

She wasn't even dressed for it. Julia, who always gowned herself in dramatic fashion, was wearing the same skirt and top she'd worn to work. Her lipstick was worn off and she had a bad case of bedhead. Her companion wasn't much better. He'd thrown a blazer over a denim shirt that was buttoned wrong, and he sported one blue sock and one brown.

Both of them had strange expressions on their faces. "Is something wrong?" she asked.

"No, of course not," Julia said, fake-casual. "I just—"

"Are these people your friends?" her date demanded.

"Yes. This is Julia Atkinson. The woman who staged Bellamy House. And her friend." She held out her hand. "I'm sorry, I've never met you. I'm Hailey."

"John. Pleasure." When she shook his hand, he squeezed. The guy either had some kind of neurological problem or he was trying to warn her about something. Based on the bizarre way these two were dressed and acting, she went with the latter.

When they were both introduced to her date, he sent them his bland smile and said, "Please. Join us."

"This is a table for two," she said, but he actually snapped his fingers at their waiter. "Two more chairs. Our friends will be joining us."

"Oh, no. Really…" Julia began.

"They probably want to be alone," she suggested.

"Nonsense. I insist. Dinner is my treat." As though money was everything. Or nothing.

They hovered, and then Julia said, "Could I talk to you for a minute in the bathroom?"

"Of cou—"

"Oh, I don't think that's a good idea at all," her date said. Still smiling, but with his teeth locked together. He put a hand on her arm to stop her from moving.

Hailey had had enough. Enough of being polite to this turkey, of spending time with a man she wasn't interested in, of men in general. She glared at her date. "Please take your hand off my arm."

His hand tightened. "You're causing a scene. Sit down. All of you."

There was something in his tone that made them all comply. She couldn't have described it without using hyperbole. *Deadly intent* was the closest she came. Which would be ridiculous if you hadn't noticed the utterly cold expression in his eyes.

"You two were obviously roused out of bed to come here," he said in that same cold tone.

"That's not—"

"Your clothes are a mess, your makeup is smudged and you have a hickey on your neck."

"I had a busy day, I—"

His voice sliced through Julia's words. "Cut the crap. Why are you here?"

Hailey glanced up and saw a sight that made her heart leap. Heading toward them was Rob. He was soaked to the skin, his leg a little stiff so she knew it was paining him. From the way he was panting he'd been running.

She had never been so happy to see anyone. In that moment their gazes connected and she saw such fierce, passionate love in the depths of his eyes she wondered how she had ever doubted his feelings.

As he closed in on their table, he said, "Why don't you cut the crap?" to her dinner date.

"What the hell's going on here?" Dennis asked. His expression was hard suddenly, his eyes scanning the area behind Rob. It was as though a mask had fallen off. The smug, look-how-rich-and-successful-I-am, I-want-to-settle-down-and-I-might-choose-you act was gone. As she stared at the cold, hard man, she wondered how she'd ever thought him charming. Or good-looking. What she saw in his face made her skin prickle.

Rob looked tougher than she'd ever seen him. "Let's just say your date is over. Come on, Hailey." He held out his hand to her. There were so many messages he was trying to send her, but she only received one. Loud and clear. *Come now, I'll explain later.*

Oh, and I love you.

Julia and John were already rising, Hailey started to stand, held out her hand to Rob. Soon she'd be out of here.

In that brief second before they could reach each other, another hand clamped on her arm.

Again.

She did not like being manhandled, she did not like having spent an awful evening with a crummy date and she most of all did not like the knowledge that something bad was happening and she had no idea what.

She bared her teeth and swung around to Dennis. "Let go of me."

To her fury, he didn't let go. He tightened his grip and yanked her hard so she lost her balance in the damn high heels she'd worn, hit her hip on the table and fell into his lap, knocking most of his glass of wine on top of both of them.

She tried to scramble up, saw Rob coming for her, and then out of the corner of her eye saw the flash of black metal.

A gun.

21

"OH, SHIT," ROB SAID when he saw the gun and stopped in his tracks, his hands clenching at his sides, even as she felt the hard metal press into her side.

"Sit. Down," Dennis said to Julia and John.

Julia looked as though she were going to cry. She sat. John sat.

Dennis Thurgood motioned Rob to Hailey's now-vacant chair.

Rob hesitated, and then sat.

She could feel the tension in Dennis in the rigidity of his muscles. Otherwise he seemed cool and unruffled, as though he took his dates hostage by gunpoint all the time.

His calmness was almost as frightening as the gun.

The wine seeping through her skirt made her skin sticky.

"What we're going to do is leave this restaurant together. You—" he nodded to Rob "—go first. Open the door for all of us. You two go next. Hailey and I will exit last. I'm sure I don't need to tell you to act normal. I wouldn't want anybody to get hurt."

"Then what?" Rob demanded. "After we're outside, then what?"

"I will take my date home like a gentleman. And you three have a nice night."

"I don't—"

She gasped as the man with the gun jabbed it into her ribs.

"This is not negotiable."

"Okay," Rob said. "Okay."

Rob got up slowly. Began to walk to the door.

"Now you two," Dennis said.

Julia and John rose and followed Rob. John reached for Julia's hand and clasped it.

"Now get up slowly and don't do anything stupid. I am in no mood to dispose of a body tonight. Understand?"

She nodded. It was awkward getting out from behind the table with the gun and the man both pressing against her. She felt angry and helpless. She couldn't imagine a worse combination.

Her eyes searched desperately for their waiter. If there was one person who'd love to cause this guy trouble, it had to be him. He was nowhere to be seen.

She felt sweat prickle at her hairline, tried to make eye contact with other diners, staff, anyone. However, it was one of those discreet places where every diner had the illusion of privacy and the staff did their best to be invisible.

Great. Just great.

Rob was ahead of them, taking his sweet time getting to the door. John and Julia were following his pace. Her heart was beating uncomfortably fast and she felt as though she couldn't breathe.

The hand holding the gun was rock-steady. The notion that he'd killed before crossed her mind, only to be banished. She'd end up a blithering basket case if she let herself think like that. She had to keep her wits about her. She wasn't alone.

She wasn't alone.

Even if this turned out to be the last evening of her life she had the blinding realization that she wasn't a rootless army brat anymore. She had Julia, a friend so firm that she'd risk her life for her friend.

And she had Rob. For as long or as short as their future might be, she knew that he loved her and that he'd do anything to keep her safe.

Her eyes threatened to mist as she discovered she already had what she'd been looking for. A home. People she could count on.

Roots.

And no creepy, self-centered, gun-toting thug was going to take that away from her.

There was a way. There had to be. Somebody would see them, he'd lose his focus for a moment. That's all it would take.

Even as she had the thought, one of the waitstaff stopped playing by the invisible rule. And, thank God, it was their waiter.

"Excuse me, sir. I think you forgot to pay your bill," he said in a loud voice.

Yes!

She felt her companion go absolutely rigid. As she'd guessed he'd completely forgotten they hadn't paid yet.

Then he turned them both. She could feel him put on his fake smarm act. "My girlfriend's not feeling well. Let me get her outside for some air. I'll be right back."

The waiter glanced at her and she widened her eyes trying to yell "Help!" without saying a word.

He looked more skeptical than heroic. As if they were dine-and-dash artists who pulled stunts like this all the time. Her evening went down another notch, if it was possible.

"Her friends could take her outside while you take care of the bill," the waiter said. As she'd hoped the commotion had caused a few of the diners to start paying attention. If anything at least now people had a reason to remember them.

Rob had stopped inside the door, Julia and John standing with him.

Two older women had finished paying and were rising from their table, handbags in hand.

Rob said something to Julia and John and began to push open the door.

A chorus of sirens penetrated the quiet restaurant as the door opened.

She felt the change in her captor. His heart began to bang and his breath came in harsh pulls. "Shut that door and get back inside," he snarled.

John shut the door and maneuvered himself so he was standing in front of Julia.

The older women headed for the front desk, their coat-check slips in their hands.

"Sit back down," Dennis ordered them.

One turned, a silver-haired elegant woman wearing a black suit and pearls the size of gumballs. "I beg your pardon?"

"I said sit down." And he pulled out the gun for all to see.

The woman looked at him for a steady second, then

said in a firm tone pitched loud enough that Hailey suspected her friend was hard of hearing, "Come on, Mavis. I think we'd better sit down."

The other woman had her back to them. "But we've got ballet tickets, and I am *not* missing the opening." And she continued on her way.

For a second, the awful pressure of the gun pressing into her was relieved. She barely had time to shut her eyes and scrunch her shoulders when the gun blasted.

A big chunk of plaster rained down from the ceiling.

The woman referred to as Mavis shrieked and turned.

"You're not going anywhere. This restaurant is in lockdown." Then Dennis began hauling Hailey backward, away from the front door and Rob, back to the kitchen.

"Those of you pulling out your cell phones, don't forget to tell the cops I have a hostage."

He dragged her back, even as the older woman with the pearls said, "You'll never get away with this."

Hailey searched for Rob, wanting the reassurance of seeing his face, but to her dismay, he was ducking out of the front door.

No, she silently cried. *Don't do it, Rob. Don't be a hero.*

She knew in that moment that he was going to try and run around the building and cut them off. However, he was an unarmed man with an injured leg. Her captor was a hardened criminal with his own gym and the definite advantage of a handgun.

He was so familiar with his way to the back entrance to the restaurant that she had to assume he'd checked out the layout before he ever made a reservation here. She wondered what it would be like to live like that, always ready to run. Ready to kill. Never entering a front door until you knew how to get out the back.

The hallway bypassed the kitchen, where, from the bustle and sounds of pots banging and food sizzling, she had to assume the drama playing out in the front hadn't penetrated. He dragged her down the hall, past the bathrooms and a storage closet to a fire door.

"Open the door," he snapped.

No one had followed them though she had to believe police and help were on their way. For now it was only the two of them here. She had no options.

She pushed the metal bar of the fire door and eased it open.

He held her and peeked around her shoulder, shielding himself with her body in the reverse fashion to John and Julia.

No flashing police cars greeted them. The lot was quiet. His car was exactly where he'd left it.

"Head for the car." He hit the button on the keypad that unlocked his fancy rental. "You'll be driving."

As she began to move to the car she heard the scuffling of shoes and Rob came running around the corner toward them.

"What the—"

"Dennis!" Rob yelled. "Leave her behind. Take me instead."

"Why would I do that?"

"Because I'm a high-profile guy. My company would do a lot to make sure I was safe. I'm a media personality. You can use that as leverage to get away."

"Why don't I take you both?"

"It's not practical," Rob was panting from the effort of getting here so fast.

"You don't have time to secure one of us and two hostages put you in more danger. You know that."

"Come closer, let me see you."

"No, Rob. Don't," she cried, feeling her captor's hatred for the man she loved.

Rob was walking forward, hands held up and high as though he were surrendering.

"That guy really pisses me off," Dennis Thurgood said and fired.

"No," she screamed, even as the bullet hit Rob in the chest, knocking him down and backward.

As the man she loved hit the dirt, something snapped inside her. A terrible scream was ripped from her throat and anger so red and hot rushed through her that she had no conscious thought—only action. She grabbed his gun hand before Dennis could fire again, squeezing it with both hands, driving her knee up into his groin with every bit of adrenaline-fired strength in her body. She caught him off guard and he grunted and swayed but didn't let go of the gun.

They wrestled for it, and she knew her superstrength couldn't last for long and he'd only be incapacitated for a few seconds. She had to get that gun. She bared her teeth and fastened them onto his wrist like a frenzied pit bull.

She had no thought of her own safety, was only determined that he wouldn't get a chance to hurt Rob anymore.

Rob wasn't dead. He wouldn't be dead. He couldn't be. Life without Rob was not an option. And she was going to put everything she had on the line, including her life, to make sure that Dennis didn't have a chance to finish him.

He kicked her but she didn't let go. She tasted blood and bit down harder. If she could just get the gun out of his hand....

Suddenly she wasn't alone anymore.

A shadow appeared in her peripheral vision. There was movement. Impact.

Dennis gave a grunt and the gun dropped.

"You can let go of his arm now," Rob said gently.

She did. Realized Rob was standing with the gun trained on Dennis who was sagging against the nearest car.

She took a few steps away from him, tried to figure out how Rob could be standing, decided that believing in miracles was a healthy option and bent over to draw in some deep breaths.

Rob pulled out his cell phone. She heard him say, "The fugitive has been subdued, the hostage is safe. The man holding the gun is friendly. Understood?"

And within minutes, all the sirens and flashing lights she could have wished for converged.

Rob was quickly relieved of the gun, her client/date/ kidnapper was led away in handcuffs. While a number of people in various uniforms were suddenly swarming, giving orders, asking questions, Rob put up a hand. Turned to her.

He took a step forward. She took one and suddenly they were in each other's arms. As she grabbed him tightly into a hug he winced.

"Oh, I forgot. He shot you. How did you…"

He lifted his shirt and she saw the dark vest. "Kevlar," he said. "I wear it in the field. Decided to throw it on tonight. Most of the time you don't need them, but once in a while—"

"They can save your life."

She touched the spot where the bullet had hit. "You'd have been killed."

"Probably."

Her eyes filled. The stress and pent-up anger and fear of the evening roared up. "What would I ever do without you?"

"Hailey, God willing, you are never going to have to find out."

As she looked up, she found him smiling down at her and then they were kissing, hungrily.

Yes, everything inside her shouted. This was so right. Yes.

"WE'LL WORK IT OUT," he said, holding her so tight she could feel that he was trembling, too. "I got a book deal. I can stay home more."

"I love you enough to let you go."

"And about Bellamy House…"

"I don't think Dennis Thurgood is going to buy it," she said, with a faint laugh that would go hysterical if she wasn't very careful.

"Nobody's going to buy it," he informed her.

Hope filled all the places where fear had lived a few seconds ago. "No?"

"I'm taking it off the market. I'm keeping it."

"Oh, Rob."

"I don't know exactly how all this is going to work. But I'm not losing you. I can't lose you."

"But your job…"

"It's only a job. The thing is, I thought I was like my mother. I thought I couldn't settle down. But I'm not. I was running away. I've been running away since

I was fourteen years old." He touched her face where a raindrop skidded down her cheek. "I don't need to run anymore."

"Mr. Klassen?" a uniformed cop asked, coming close.

"Yes."

"We're going to need to talk to you both down at the station. Get your statements."

"Tonight?" Rob turned, looking tired and frustrated. "Can't it wait until the morning?"

"I'm sorry sir, but—"

"Of course it can wait until the morning," a firm and somewhat familiar voice said.

Hailey stared to see the elegant woman with the pearls step carefully over the puddles to reach them.

"I'm Judge Eleanor Hanover," she said. She handed them each a business card. "We've got plenty of reasons to hold that man in custody. Let these two get some well-earned rest."

"Of course, Your Honor."

"Thank you," Hailey said.

She smiled at them. "That was quite an eventful evening. If you could come by the precinct at nine o'clock?"

They both nodded. She couldn't imagine arguing with this woman.

Julia and John arrived next.

Julia grabbed her friend in a hug so tight Hailey's ribs threatened to crack. "Oh, honey. I am so glad you're okay."

"Me, too."

"And Rob. I'm sorry I didn't believe you. Exactly."

A wry grin twisted his mouth. "You were looking after your friend. I get that."

"No hard feelings?"

He shook his head. Julia put out her arms to hug him.

"Not too hard," Hailey warned. "He got shot."

"Again?"

"It's kind of a bad habit," Hailey said, on another hysterical giggle.

"One that's going to stop," Rob promised.

"We haven't met. I'm John."

The men shook hands.

And then they stood there. The sirens were muted. Most of the cop cars had left. Dennis Thurgood had been taken away.

"Do you need a ride home?" John asked.

"Yeah. Actually, we do," Rob said.

On the way home Hailey demanded to be told the whole story. Between getting three different versions of the tale, she finally pieced together that Rob's instincts had been right all along; that Julia was the best friend she'd ever had and that John was Julia's perfect match.

It felt like the middle of the night when they reached Bellamy House, but when she checked her watch it was only a little after eleven. The stress had exhausted her.

She and Rob pretty much helped each other up the stairs into the master bedroom.

When Rob undressed, she cried out when she saw the bruise already spreading where the bullet had hit the vest. One more wound for a man who couldn't help being a hero.

She kissed the spot.

And he kissed her wrist where Thurgood had left bruises.

They lay together, simply holding each other. Hearing him breathe was such a gift, knowing he was warm and alive and hers, at least for now.

"Rob," she said after a while.

"Mmm?"

"I love you."

"I know."

Her eyes prickled. "I love you enough to let you go."

He turned to her and she saw again the depths of his feelings for her. "And I love you enough to stay."

"But—"

"I didn't have time to tell you about it, but I've been working on this idea. How all over the world, people have the same problems. They may be different colors and live in mud huts or McMansions but deep down we live similar lives. Where to live? How to earn a living? Courting, raising kids. It's mostly told through pictures. My agent said Fremont comes across like one of the characters. And I realized that I do have a home. I've always had a home. I just never had a strong enough reason to stay." He touched her face. "Until now."

"But your work—"

"Well, first I'll be writing about a certain arms dealer. A *World Week* exclusive." He chuckled. "Gary will love it. That's my editor. And they want me to write some features around the book. I've got a big enough advance that I can afford to take some more time here."

He touched her breast and she sighed. "You're firing me again, aren't you?"

He chuckled. "Yeah. I guess I am. I'll make up your commission somehow."

She let her own hands wander. Felt his arousal. "How?"

"I could give you half of Bellamy House." Her hand clutched so suddenly he winced. "Are you saying…"

"That I want to marry you? Yes."

"Oh, Rob." They kissed for a long time, and then she said, "I am such a good Realtor. I always end up with the right people for a house."

"I don't have all the answers yet, but we'll work it out. If we love each other, we'll work it out."

"Do we?" she smiled at him tenderly. "Love each other enough?"

He traced her lips with his fingertip. "Oh, yeah," he said, and then he pulled her against him.

* * * * *

Dear Reader,

Have you ever wanted desperately to connect with some-one, yet not known for certain whether they'd accept you? That's the uncomfortable position in which Wyatt Locke finds himself as he drives toward the Last Chance Ranch in the first SONS OF CHANCE book. Yes, folks, Wyatt's story kicks off another three-book parade of gorgeous cowboys!

Although Wyatt longs to be friends with his half-brother Jack Chance, he's so afraid of rejection that he doesn't notify Jack that he's coming. That plan doesn't work out as he expects, but in Wyatt's shoes, I would do the same.

In writing about Wyatt, I longed to protect him from get-ting hurt, so I gave him Olivia Sedgewick, someone who sympathizes with his desire to connect with family. But even Olivia can't stand between Wyatt and disappoint-ment. As it turns out, getting hurt and learning from the experience is how people grow.

And just so you know, Wyatt doesn't start out the story as a cowboy, but before long, he's wearing the jeans, the boots and the hat. They're borrowed, but they do the trick. Taking yummy-looking guys and turning them into yummy-looking cowboys is what I do.

Welcome back to the Last Chance Ranch, and thank you for joining me there once again! It's going to be a great winter because my cowboys are saddled up and ready to ride straight into your heart!

Warmly,

Vicki Lewis Thompson

LONG ROAD HOME

BY
VICKI LEWIS THOMPSON

First published in Great Britain 2012
by Mills & Boon, an imprint of Harlequin (UK) Limited,
Eton House, 18-24 Paradise Road, Richmond, Surrey TW9 1SR

© Vicki Lewis Thompson 2012

ISBN: 978 0 263 89391 5
ebook ISBN: 978 1 408 96943 4

14-1112

Harlequin (UK) policy is to use papers that are natural, renewable and
recyclable products and made from wood grown in sustainable forests. The
logging and manufacturing processes conform to the legal environmental
regulations of the country of origin.

Printed and bound in Spain
by Blackprint CPI, Barcelona

New York Times bestselling author **Vicki Lewis Thompson**'s love affair with cowboys started with the Lone Ranger, continued through Maverick and took a turn south of the border with Zorro. She views cowboys as the Western version of knights in shining armor—rugged men who value honor, honesty and hard work. Fortunately for her, she lives in the Arizona desert, where broad-shouldered, lean-hipped cowboys abound. Blessed with such an abundance of inspiration, she only hopes that she can do them justice. Visit her website at www.vickilewisthompson.com.

To my wonderful readers, especially those of
you who've been with me from the early days.
Your e-mails and letters mean the world to me!

Prologue

August 22, 1978
From the diary of Eleanor Chance

JONATHAN IS MARRIED, and my heart is heavy. We had a small ceremony this afternoon at the Last Chance because that's all he and Diana wanted. There's no pretty way to say this—a baby is on the way, and after several months of debate, Jonathan and Diana decided to get married. If you're in love, you don't debate such things, so I've concluded they're not in love and I hate that for both of them.

Oh, they say they love each other, but I think that's so Archie and I won't be upset about this marriage. Jonathan is our only child, and of course we wanted him to end up with a woman he adores, who also adores him. We hoped she'd share his devotion to the ranch and look forward to raising children here. Our grandchildren.

Instead he has Diana. She looks like an Indian princess, which makes sense because her mother was Shoshone. Other than that, she hasn't volunteered much about her parents except to say they're both gone.

I have to wonder what her upbringing was like, because she's the least nurturing person I've ever come across. She pretends to be happy about the baby, but I can tell she's not.

She confessed to me that before she found out about her pregnancy, she'd been saving her tips from waitressing to finance a move from the Jackson Hole area to San Francisco. She'd dreamed of getting out of Shoshone, which she calls a one-horse town, and living a more sophisticated life.

Instead she's stuck here, and I can tell that's exactly how she feels, too. I seriously doubt she looks forward to living on the ranch for all her born days, and if she stays with Jonathan, that's what she'll have to do.

I'm torn because I don't think the marriage is a good idea, but she's carrying my grandchild. For that reason, I want her to stay right here and learn to love being a mother to my grandbaby and a wife to my son. I plan to do everything in my power to help that cause.

1

IF WYATT LOCKE BELIEVED in omens, his return visit to the Last Chance Ranch had disaster written all over it. Rain drummed on the roof of his truck and sluiced over the windshield faster than the wipers could sweep it away. Every so often lightning would strike close enough to deafen him while providing a camera-flash view of the muddy road and the soggy Wyoming countryside.

The storm had come on quickly, ambushing him after he'd already committed to the rutted dirt road leading to the ranch. The weight of his camper shell and the gear in the back helped keep him on the road, but trying to turn around now would almost guarantee he'd end up axle-deep in mud. Going forward was his only option.

He slowed the truck to a crawl and kept his headlights on, although they didn't accomplish much. Still, he'd hate to run into something. A pair of taillights winked in the distance to let him know he wasn't the only fool out here. But then the rain got serious again and reduced visibility to about fifteen feet in front of him.

If his twin brother, Rafe, could see him struggling through this deluge, he'd laugh himself silly. Rafe had tried his best to talk Wyatt out of this harebrained scheme, but once Wyatt latched on to an idea, he couldn't let it go. Jack Chance was his half brother, damn it, and they should get to know each other. Jack was Rafe's half brother, too, but Rafe wasn't interested in cementing any family ties.

The rain let up for a second and there were the taillights again, several yards in front of him. Probably one of the ranch hands coming back from town. Could even be Jack.

Wyatt's gut tightened as he thought about his half brother. He probably should have alerted Jack that he was coming, but he knew exactly why he hadn't. He'd been afraid Jack would tell him to stay away.

Wyatt had shocked the hell out of him the previous summer by dropping by the ranch to introduce himself. He'd shown up without warning that time, too, not sure until he'd knocked on the ranch house door that he'd go through with it. Realistically, he should have expected Jack's chilly response.

No doubt Jack hadn't believed him at first. He would have believed Rafe right away because the two men looked so much alike, both having inherited their mother's dark hair and eyes. But Wyatt and Rafe were fraternal as opposed to identical twins, and Wyatt had ended up with his dad's sandy hair and gray eyes.

Eventually Jack had seemed to accept that Wyatt was his half brother, but he'd remained suspicious, as

if Wyatt might want to cash in on the financial success of the Paint horse breeding operation at the Last
Chance. No, and hell no. Wyatt had a profitable wilderness trekking company based in San Francisco and
wasn't the least bit interested in Chance money, but Jack
couldn't know that.

The money issue wasn't the biggest reason for Jack
to be prickly, though. Finding out that the mother who'd
abandoned him had subsequently married a successful
businessman and raised two more kids couldn't be an
easy pill to swallow. Worse yet, she'd kept Jack's existence a secret from her second family until last year
when the divorce from Wyatt and Rafe's father had apparently loosened her tongue.

Hiding the fact she'd had a kid thirty-odd years ago
was pretty radical, even for his mother. But it wasn't
totally out of character. Diana had always been evasive
about her past, as if she was ashamed of it. She claimed
that she'd been through hard times and nothing more
needed to be said. Yeah, well, she'd put Wyatt and Rafe
through some hard times as they tried to deal with a
completely self-absorbed mother.

The taillights disappeared again as the rain redou-
bled its effort to drown this part of the country. Wyatt
had years of experience handling every kind of weather,
and he'd be damned if he'd end up in a ditch this afternoon and have to call the ranch for help. That wouldn't
improve his rep any.

And he wanted his rep to be solid, wanted Jack and
everyone else on the ranch to think of him as a competent outdoorsman, even if he wasn't a cowboy. Maybe he
and Jack would have things in common other than the

obvious connection of having the same mother. Wyatt liked the idea of being related to a rancher.

He'd always felt out of place in the circles his parents preferred. Rafe, with his business degree and his talent for investing, fit right in. Not Wyatt. He'd taken up hiking and camping as a teenager to escape charity balls and gallery openings.

Jackson Hole had some of that high society element going on, especially within the Jackson city limits. But the little town of Shoshone about ten miles from the ranch was definitely more Wyatt's style. A collection of small businesses and a single traffic light at the only major intersection—that was urban enough for Wyatt.

If he chose to, he could relocate his company here. Adventure Trekking could operate as well—or maybe even better—from the Jackson Hole area as it did out of San Francisco. If he lived here, he could spend time at the ranch and get to know the Chance family. He had a feeling he'd fit in with them better than he ever had with his own family.

But before he made any drastic changes, he needed to find out if Jack had mellowed toward the idea of Wyatt's and Rafe's existence. Jack's resentment could be a major obstacle to Wyatt's plan. The guy had obviously been hurt when Diana had left him, but in Wyatt's opinion, Jack might have been better off without her in his life. Wyatt had asked around town, and the guy seemed to be doing just fine.

Sure, his father had died a while back, but he still had his stepmother, Sarah, and two half brothers, Nick and Gabe. They all owned a part of the ranch and, according to what Wyatt had heard, everyone got along great. Jack was happily married now and had a kid of his own.

Wyatt planned to keep that last bit of info to himself. He wasn't sure how Diana would react to finding out she was a grandmother, and Jack didn't need to have her suddenly appear and claim her grandmotherly rights. She might not care a whole lot about the baby, but she loved being the center of a drama.

If Jack had a baby, that made Wyatt an uncle. He smiled at the idea. It was kind of cool to think about. Maybe he should have brought something for the baby, especially because he was once again arriving unannounced. But he hadn't....

Lightning flashed, nearly blinding him with its intensity. For a split second the road was lit up like a movie set. A crack of thunder followed, loud enough to make his ears ring. But in that brief moment of full light, he'd seen a Jeep Cherokee off on the side of the road up ahead, its right wheels buried in mud, the taillights still on.

He hadn't been able to tell if the vehicle was occupied, but he guessed it was if the lights were on. Once he was alongside it, he stopped and lowered his passenger side window to get a better look.

The driver's window on the Jeep slid down, too, which gave him his answer even before he saw the pretty woman with the hopeful expression gazing over at him. Her shoulder-length hair was streaked with red and blond, obviously a salon job and not her natural color, but it looked good on her. The Cherokee's taillights must have been the ones he'd followed down the road.

"Seems like you're stuck!" he called out over the sound of the rain.

"Yep! I was about to phone the ranch. Maybe somebody can come get me."

"I'm headed that way, if you want a ride." He knew what he was suggesting wasn't a perfect solution. That salon hairdo would be dripping with water by the time she made it into his truck, and her shoes would be covered with mud. But she'd be in the same fix if someone drove out here to get her. Trying to hitch a tow chain to her Jeep in this downpour with lightning flashing all around wasn't reasonable.

A couple of seconds went by with rain coming in his open window and hers, too, probably. He had a chance to study her a little, which added to his initial impression that she was pretty—high cheekbones, rounded chin, full lips and very blue eyes. He wondered if she was worried about accepting a ride from a stranger. "My name's Wyatt Locke," he said. "I'm Jack Chance's half brother visiting from San Francisco."

"Sarah didn't mention anyone coming to visit today."

Wyatt wondered if Jack's stepmother would be annoyed because he was dropping in. "It's a surprise. But if you want to call the ranch and double-check that I'm legit, go ahead. The surprise isn't that important." And they couldn't tell him to leave with this gully-washer in progress, even if they wanted to.

She smiled, revealing even white teeth with a tiny space in the middle. "I'm sure you're perfectly safe, Wyatt Locke. Serial killers don't usually come out in weather like this." She glanced at the seat next to her before turning back to him. "But I have a couple of bags of stuff I need to take up to the ranch house."

"Will it get ruined if it gets a little wet?"

"Not really, but—"

"You can't carry it all in one trip," he said, making a guess.

"Right."

"Hang on. I'll help." Leaving the motor running, he opened his door and stepped out. He was drenched immediately. Cold water soaked his Adventure Trekking T-shirt and hiking shorts, and burrowed into his hiking boots.

"Wait!" she called out. "You don't have to—"

"Yeah, I do. Can't leave a damsel in distress." He slogged around the front of the truck, his boots making a sucking sound with every step. First he opened his passenger door and then turned toward her Jeep. "Let's get your bags in there first. Do you have an umbrella?"

"No such luck." She opened her door and passed him two large zippered totes.

"Got 'em." Water ran in rivulets down his face, but now that her door was open he could see the rest of her if he blinked the rain away. She had a great figure, nicely showcased by jeans and a black scoop-necked top. Then he noticed her feet. Dear God, was she wearing high heels? Not good. "Stay put. I'll come back for you."

"No need. I'll take off my shoes and roll up my pant legs for the trip over."

"It'll be better if I carry you," he called over his shoulder as he navigated the short but muddy stretch between her Jeep and his truck. He put the totes on the floor of the cab and turned back to her.

She had one bare foot propped on the edge of the seat as she rolled her pant leg up and her toes had some sort of glittery stuff on them. Her left arm and leg were already wet from the rain coming in the open door.

"You really don't want to step out here. It's nasty."

"It's only mud." She glanced up at him, her blue gaze resolute. "You can go back to your truck. I'll be right there."

"But I'm already a mess. If I carry you over, you won't have to be."

She looked him up and down. "Yes, but the footing is terrible. You could easily slip, and then where would we be?"

He swiped the rain away from his eyes. "I won't slip." By now his boots were so full of water they'd keep him well stabilized.

"I'm sure you wouldn't *mean* to slip, but how often do you carry a person who weighs a hundred and… twenty through the mud?"

He couldn't help grinning. Women and their weight issues. "More often than you'd suppose. I'm a wilderness guide, and I'm certified for search and rescue. In other words, I'm a professional."

"Oh. That explains the Adventure Trekking logo on your truck and your shirt."

"Exactly. I could carry you even if you weighed one-thirty." He was guessing at how much she'd subtracted from her actual weight.

Her cheeks turned pink and her chin lifted. "One-twenty-six."

She wore it well, too. "Come on. Just let me do my thing. It would be a shame to get those sparkly toes all covered with muck."

"They'd wash off, but…all right, Wyatt Locke of Adventure Trekking. You're getting soaked, and you've convinced me I'm just being stubborn."

"I wasn't going to say that."

"I believe you, and that kind of restraint is impressive." She smiled at him. "Let me put my shoes in my purse before you hoist me out of here."

He waited as the rain plastered his clothes to his body. He hadn't been this wet fully clothed since the time he'd fallen in the Snake River on a canoe trip two years ago.

"Ready." She hung her purse strap around her neck and scooted out from behind the wheel. "Can you get the door once I'm out?"

"Uh-huh." Moving into a half crouch, he slid one arm under her knees and the other behind her shoulder blades. She felt warm, soft and infinitely huggable. If it were up to him, she wouldn't lose an ounce of that one-twenty-six. "Put your arms around my neck."

She did, bringing with her a tantalizing scent of jasmine.

He was starting to enjoy himself. "On the count of three. One, two, *three*." He lifted her, taking care not to bang her head on the door frame, and stood slowly as she nestled against him. "Okay?"

"Yes."

He was more than okay. Coming to the aid of a beautiful woman—he'd upgraded her from pretty to beautiful—was a rewarding experience. Besides getting points for gallantry, he was required to cuddle with said woman for a brief time, all in the name of a heroic rescue. He turned toward his truck.

"Don't forget the door."

"Right." Which he had. The sensual pleasure of holding her had short-circuited his brain.

Rotating in place, he nudged the door with his left knee. The sideways tilt of the Jeep meant gravity was in his favor, and the door swung closed with a solid clunk. But using his knee to close the door threw him slightly off balance.

She let out a little cry of alarm and tightened her hold on his neck. "Don't you dare drop me!"

"Easy does it. We're fine." He regained his balance and adjusted his hold. God, she felt good in his arms. Part of that was her welcome warmth against his chilled body, but he could get that from a hot water bottle. She was a lot more satisfying to hold, and he was reminded that he'd been so busy working in the past year or so that he'd abandoned his social life.

The trip to his truck took maybe five seconds, and he cherished every one. Too soon he had to lean down and slide her onto the fabric seat, which was also wet after having the door open so long. "There you go."

"Thank you." She scrambled onto the seat and unhooked her purse from around her neck. He thought she'd go for her shoes, but instead she put the purse on the floor with the bags and started running her fingers up through her wet hair as if trying to save the look she'd started out with.

Shrugging, he closed the door and sloshed around to the driver's side. A woman's concern with her appearance was usually a warning signal for him after all the years he'd spent watching his mother obsess about her hair, makeup and clothes. But he didn't know this particular woman well enough to make snap judgments.

Hell, he didn't even know her name. Climbing into the truck, he closed the door and fastened his seat belt. She was still futzing with her hair. "It looks fine," he said.

She laughed and finger-combed it back from her face. "I'm sure it doesn't, but thanks for saying that. I'm Olivia, by the way. Olivia Sedgewick. And I appreciate you rescuing me and keeping my feet clean."

"You're welcome, Olivia. Nice to meet you." And he meant it sincerely. He flashed her a smile for added emphasis.

"The thing is, I'm a beautician, so I like to arrive at an appointment somewhat pulled together."

"You have an appointment at the ranch?" He put the truck in gear, and after a moment's hesitation while the tires worked out of the mud, it moved forward.

"Uh-huh." She took her trendy heels out of her purse and slipped them on her feet. "Sarah hired me to come out and give everyone manicures."

"Everyone?" Wyatt had only spent about ten minutes with Jack, but he couldn't picture the guy getting his nails done.

"All the women, I mean. Most of the guys are out of town this weekend at a horse show and sale, so Sarah decided to schedule a night of beauty for herself and her daughters-in-law, plus a few other women connected to the ranch in one way or another. I'm going to try and get a few pedicures in there, too."

"Oh." Wyatt wished to hell he'd pushed past his fear of rejection and called ahead. "I assume that means Jack's gone, too."

"I'm afraid so." She glanced at him. "Sorry. Kind of messes up your surprise, doesn't it?"

"It kind of does." He stared out the windshield. Maybe the storm had been an omen after all. Not only had he missed Jack, he'd landed in the middle of a girls-only beauty shindig. He had bad timing all the way around.

2

OLIVIA FELT SORRY FOR her hero. Wyatt Locke seemed like a really nice guy, besides being serious eye candy. His wet T-shirt clung to muscled pecs and washboard abs that made her little heart go pitty-pat.

The trip from her Jeep to his truck had been a true delight. She couldn't remember the last time she'd been carried, let alone by a guy with such a hard body. On top of that, he had nice eyes, a great smile and he hadn't dropped her in the mud.

But now, after his outstanding rescue, he wouldn't get to spring his surprise on his half brother, at least not immediately. She tried to come up with a consoling statement. "Jack can still be surprised when he comes home tomorrow night."

"I guess. But once the weather clears up, I'll head back to the Bunk and Grub for tonight."

Although the Bunk and Grub B and B wasn't far away, she was still surprised he had a reservation there. "You weren't planning to stay at the ranch?"

"Uh, no."

"But I thought you said you were Jack's half brother."

"Yeah, well." He sighed. "It's complicated."

Olivia was beginning to understand the Chance family was full of complications. Although she'd only arrived in Shoshone from Pittsburgh last fall, her job in the local salon, To Dye For, guaranteed that she heard all the gossip.

Within a couple of months she'd found out that each of the Chance men had a different mother. Jack's mom had left when he was two, Nick had been the result of a brief affair and Gabe was the only biological son of Sarah, Jonathan Chance's second wife and now his widow. But according to everyone in town, Sarah treated all three as her own.

Now here came another half brother, but he'd only made reference to Jack. "This is really none of my business," she said, "so you don't have to answer, but I'm curious as to how you and Jack are related."

"We have the same mother."

"Ah." So that was the much-maligned Diana who'd taken off all those years ago. Any time her name was mentioned, people made a face. "And is she…"

"Alive and well in San Francisco."

"Hmm. I take it she and Jack aren't close?"

"They've had no contact since she left the ranch."

Olivia considered that for a moment, trying to imagine such a thing. Nope, couldn't do it. "But you're here now."

Wyatt heaved another sigh and stretched his arms against the steering wheel. "I didn't find out Jack existed until last summer, and I…I'd like to get to know the guy."

"She kept Jack a secret?"

"Yep."

Olivia didn't say what she thought about that because Diana was his mother, after all, but apparently the people who made a face at the mention of her name had good reason. "Does Jack know you exist?"

"Yeah, because I paid him a short visit last August. We left the situation sort of open-ended. I decided to come back and see…"

The longing in his voice made her heart ache. "Are you an only child?"

"No. I have a twin brother named Rafe." He paused. "He thinks coming here is a dumb idea. And maybe it is."

"No, it's not a dumb idea," she said softly. "I don't have any brothers or sisters, but if I suddenly found out I had one tucked away somewhere, I'd be making tracks for wherever that person lived. I mean, they're your blood. That has to count for something."

He sent her a look of gratitude. "I think so."

Rain continued to pound the roof of the cab and splash against the windows, cocooning them from the rest of the world. A sense of intimacy enhanced by his impressive rescue almost made her comfortable enough to touch his arm in a gesture of understanding. Almost.

"You said you don't have brothers or sisters, so you must be an only child," Wyatt said after a moment of cozy silence.

"I am. My mom died soon after I was born, and my dad never remarried."

"Were you lonely?"

Yes, achingly lonely. But she gave him the answer

she always gave. "Not really. My dad's an inventor so he worked at home. He kept me company."

"An *inventor*." Wyatt sounded impressed. "You don't hear that every day. Has he invented anything I'd know about?"

"Actually he came up with a razor blade that never wears out."

Wyatt gave a low whistle of surprise. "Is it available? Because I would buy that in a second. I have to shave twice a day."

That comment directed her attention to his strong jaw. He must have shaved recently because no stubble showed, and now that he'd mentioned shaving, she remembered that she'd noticed a mint scent when he'd carried her to his truck. "Sorry, but the blade's not available."

"When's it coming out?"

"It's not. One of the big companies, and I'm not allowed to say which one, bought the patent because they didn't want that product on the market. They said it would wreck their profit margin."

"Damn. Can I just buy one from your dad?"

"'Fraid not. He had to destroy everything, including his research notes, in order to get the payoff. But it was a lot of money. That's why we're here, actually. He always wanted to live in Jackson Hole, so once he had the means, we pulled up stakes and left Pittsburgh."

"You live with him?"

Olivia shook her head. "God, no. I had to deal with his cluttered lifestyle when I was a kid, but I don't have to now. I live nearby so I can keep an eye on him and make sure that he eats, but I have my own place."

"He sounds like an interesting guy."

"Interesting, maddening, funny. He looks like that picture you've probably seen of Albert Einstein, white hair sticking out everywhere."

"Really?" He glanced at her. "But Einstein was old in that picture. You can't be much over twenty-five."

"I'm twenty-eight, and Dad was fifty when I was born. His hair was already turning white then, and now it's a hot mess. Besides being a nail tech I also do hair, but he won't let me give him a decent haircut. He'd rather cut it himself with my mother's old sewing scissors."

"At least he's not vain."

That made her laugh. "No, he certainly isn't. I've tried telling him how handsome he'd look if I trimmed his hair, and he just shrugs and says he doesn't care about that."

"Speaking of your work, I really don't see myself hanging around during a night of beauty."

"Maybe not, but I don't think Sarah's going to stand for you staying at the Bunk and Grub, either. It's a very nice B and B and it's almost like being with family because of Pam's connection, but still, Sarah's going to want you here, I'll bet." From what Olivia knew of the woman, she was virtually sure of it. A long-lost half brother wanting to connect with kin would touch Sarah's heartstrings.

"Pam Mulholland is part of the Chance family?"

"You didn't know that?"

Wyatt shook his head. "There's probably a lot I don't know. And I want to."

"She's Nick Chance's aunt, his late mother's older

sister. In fact, Pam will be at this thing tonight, assuming she made it over before the storm hit."

"She probably did. Somebody else checked me in this afternoon and said Pam would be gone overnight."

"Pam didn't recognize your name when you made a reservation?"

"She didn't act like she did. Jack and Sarah are the only people I met when I came here last August. Maybe they decided to keep my visit quiet."

"Maybe." Although intimate details of people's lives were freely bandied about in Shoshone, Olivia figured the town had its share of secrets, too. Wyatt might be one of them. "I'm guessing you didn't leave a phone number or an address with Jack."

"No. To be honest, he was so abrupt that I wasn't sure I'd come back. I understand why he might not welcome me with open arms, but like you said, we're blood. I'd hate to miss out on...well, friendship, at the very least, and a deeper connection if such a thing is possible. Rafe doesn't hold out much hope and doesn't seem to care whether Jack accepts us or not. But I...I do."

Olivia turned to him. "I like your courage and persistence, Wyatt Locke. I'm glad you decided to come back and give the brother deal another try, because it means we got to meet."

He grinned at her. "Same here, Olivia. But no matter how much I like you, and I do, I'm still not up for a night of beauty with the girls."

DESPITE THE DIFFICULTY he'd had driving through the storm, Wyatt was sorry when they reached the circular drive in front of the two-story log ranch house. He felt that he and Olivia had made a connection during that drive, and now that it was over, he wasn't sure how to keep it.

He really did plan to head back to the Bunk and Grub the minute the storm passed. There would be no advantage in hanging around. Olivia would be busy doing her job and he just didn't fit in with an evening of foot massages and nail polish. Maybe he'd drive into town and get a beer and a burger at the Spirits and Spurs, Shoshone's local bar.

Several trucks and a couple of SUVs were parked to the left of the ranch house. "A lot of people are here," he said. "Who did you say was coming?"

"Well, there's Pam, as I mentioned, and Mary Lou, the ranch cook, and Sarah's three daughters-in-law—Dominique, Morgan and Josie. They each have homes on the ranch, but it's not really walking distance so I'm sure they drove in. Then Morgan's sister Tyler will be there—she's married to Josie's brother Alex."

"Everybody's sort of connected, aren't they?" It sounded nice to Wyatt. Really nice.

"It's a close-knit group. Oh, and I'm pretty sure Emily will be there. She's the daughter of the ranch's foreman, Emmett Sterling, and she married Clay Whittaker this past spring. He runs the stud program at the ranch. I did everybody's nails for that wedding. Great party."

As Wyatt had suspected, this was exactly the kind of family he'd always longed for and never had—informal and good-hearted. But they might not let him in. He quickly shoved away that thought, which was way too depressing to contemplate.

The house itself looked as massive as he remembered. The barn, corrals and other outbuildings were located down the hill to the right, and were nearly obscured this afternoon by a heavy curtain of rain.

Over the winter months, Wyatt had pried some information out of his mother about the place. When she'd moved in as a bride, the house had a two-story center section plus a wing on the right, a wide front porch running the length of the house and a circular driveway. The two medium-sized spruce trees she'd mentioned being located in the middle of the circle now stood at least thirty feet tall.

After Jack was born the family had added the wing on the left and extended the porch. On each side porch a row of rockers, shiny with rain, moved gently in the wind. Rain had flattened the plants in the flower beds on either side of the wide front steps, and water gushed from downspouts to puddle in the gravel driveway.

Both wings were set at an angle like arms flung open in welcome, and lights glowed from the windows on this stormy afternoon, inviting travelers inside. Wyatt figured some travelers were more welcome than others. And his category was still in question.

Olivia looked over at him. "I don't think it's going to let up. We'll have to make a run for it."

"You're right." Wyatt wondered if he could get away with dropping her off and heading back down the road. Not likely. That would force her into breaking the news that he was here and he'd look like a damned coward for leaving. "Let me pull up closer to the steps. Then you can unload without having to walk on that sloppy gravel in your nice shoes, and I'll move the truck once you have everything out."

"Believe me, I'm regretting the shoe decision, but at the time I was going for stylish."

"They are that." He put the truck in Reverse, backed up a ways and cut the wheel. Then he pulled forward and edged right up next to the steps.

"But if I'd worn sensible boots, you wouldn't have had to haul me over to your truck." She picked up her purse and one of the two bags.

"I enjoyed it."

She gave him a quick smile. "Me, too."

That comment made him bolder. "Listen, I'm not sure how this visit will turn out for me, but can I give you a call before I leave town?"

"Sure." She zipped open her purse, rummaged around in it and came up with a business card. "My cell's on there."

"Thanks." He took the pink card, which advertised the beauty salon, To Dye For, but also gave Olivia's name and number. "I've toyed with the idea of relocating here."

"Really?" Her gaze met his. "That would be nice."

"Meeting you gives me some extra incentive."

Her blue eyes warmed. "Good."

He had the craziest urge to kiss her, but it was too soon, and he didn't want to ruin everything by overstepping.

Then, to his amazement, she leaned toward him and quickly brushed her lips against his. "Thanks for rescuing me today." She pulled right back, as if to signal it was a one-time shot.

The kiss came and went so fast he didn't have time to close his eyes, much less reach for her. "You're welcome." His voice sounded a little rusty, which wasn't surprising since he was busy processing the soft feel of her mouth.

"I'll come back for the second bag in a sec." She opened the door and let in a gust of wind and rain. "Man, it's some storm!"

"Yep." Wyatt watched as she navigated the rain-soaked steps to deposit her purse and the first bag beside the door. As far as he was concerned, it was a wonderful storm. Without it, he would have arrived at the ranch, discovered Jack wasn't there, and driven back to either the Bunk and Grub or the bar. He might have met Olivia in passing but they wouldn't have talked, not when she was there to create nail magic.

Instead they were well on their way to becoming friends. Wyatt was really starting to like it here. The country was beautiful, even in the rain, and the local residents, including a certain blue-eyed beautician, interested him a great deal.

Leaning back in, she grabbed the second bag. "Okay, that does it. I'll meet you inside."

"Right."

She paused, and her eyes narrowed. "You *are* coming inside, aren't you?"

"Yes, I am, but I'll leave my muddy boots on the porch. I actually considered asking you to make my excuses, but I didn't think you'd appreciate that."

"Good guess. And besides, you don't want to miss the food."

Wyatt imagined finger sandwiches and tea cakes

washed down with wine coolers. "That's okay. Once the storm lets up, I'll go into town and—"

"No, really. You don't want to miss the food. See you inside." She started to close the door but opened it again. "Can I say that you're here? Or do you want to make a grand entrance?"

He chuckled. "Do I strike you as a grand entrance kind of guy?"

"No, but you did mention this was supposed to be a surprise."

"That was a smoke screen. I was just too chickenshit to give Jack advance warning in case he told me not to bother. So, yeah, go ahead and announce that I'll be in after I park the truck, but please tell Sarah I'm not planning to stay and interfere with this night of beauty she's set up."

Olivia looked amused. "I'll tell her. But don't blame me if she vetoes your decision." Then she shut the door, ending any further debate on the matter.

Pulling carefully away from the front of the house so he didn't accidentally take out a chunk of the wooden steps, he drove over to the area where everyone else had parked and turned off the engine. So he was here. Considering he'd met Olivia, he was glad he'd come.

But no matter what, he wouldn't stay at the ranch tonight. He'd made it out here, and he could make it back to the paved road, too. When Jack came home from the horse show tomorrow, Wyatt would drive over and try this routine again.

A flash of lightning followed by a crack of thunder that sounded like a mountain being split in two made him jump. The house went dark. Well, damn. What kind of guy marched into a house that had just lost power and announced he was taking off?

He needed to go in and find out what he could do to help before he left. Climbing out of the truck, he ignored the rain pelting him as he walked around to the rear and opened the back window of his camper shell. Fortunately his battery-operated lantern was within easy reach of the tailgate.

Lantern in hand, he sloshed through water and gravel and climbed the front steps. The cool, rain-scented air smelled of wood smoke, so a fire must be blazing inside. He unlaced his boots, toed them off and peeled away his wool socks, which were soaked.

When he came out—*if* he came out—he'd just wear the boots out to the truck and carry the socks. Taking a deep breath, he knocked on the door.

It opened soon afterward. "There you are!" Olivia stood holding a brass candlestick with a lit candle. She looked like an angel. "Come in. I told everyone who rescued me and they're all dying to meet you. Well, I guess Sarah has already met you."

"Briefly." He remembered a stately silver-haired woman in her sixties who had a warm smile and kind eyes. Stepping into the entryway, he closed the door behind him. "I'm dripping. I should stand out here on the mat for a minute so I don't mess up the hardwood floors." The musical hum of female voices and laughter filtered in from the living room, along with the clink of glasses and the snap and crackle of a fire.

"Maybe I should get you a towel."

"That's not necessary. I really can't stay." He threw the comment out there, although his escape hatch was closing fast. "But I brought a lantern in case the power's out for a while." He held it up.

"If the lightning hit a transformer, and Sarah thinks it might have, then the power will be out for the rest of the night."

"Doesn't the ranch have a backup generator for emergencies?"

"Yes, but it's not working right now. The men were planning to buy the part in Casper and repair it after they came back. I guess this storm was a surprise to everyone."

"Oh." Although intellectually Wyatt knew that the women on this ranch were unlikely to be helpless females who couldn't look after themselves during a power outage, he still couldn't picture himself driving away, knowing he'd left them in the middle of a blackout that might last until morning.

"Sarah wants you to stay, and I think you should. Pam's fine with it, and she won't charge you for a night at the Bunk and Grub, either."

The escape hatch closed with a bang. "I'm happy to pay her anyway, but yeah, I'll stay. Although I don't have anything with me like clothes and stuff. I left it all at the B and B."

"I'm sure that can be worked out. A place with this many men on-site must have some old clothes somewhere."

"I suppose." Wyatt felt something warm and wet on his bare feet. Glancing down, he discovered a low-slung, brown-and-white spotted dog with floppy ears licking his toes. "Who's this?"

"Rodney, Sarah's recently adopted dog. She got

him from a shelter in Colorado, and he's a mix but he's mostly basset hound."

"Not the kind of dog I'd expect on a ranch, but why not?" Wyatt crouched down and scratched behind the dog's oversized ears. "How's it going, Rodney?"

"His full name is Rodney Dangerfield."

Wyatt lifted the dog's muzzle and looked into his sad eyes. "Appropriate. Can't get no respect, can you, Rodney?"

The dog whined and wagged his white-tipped tail.

"You and me, we'll hang out tonight, buddy. We'll find us a baseball game on TV—"

"No power," Olivia said.

"Oh, right. No worries, Rod. With that face, I'll bet you're great at poker. We'll play cards by candlelight."

The dog whined again.

Olivia glanced up at him with a smile. "That's enough of the stall tactics. You've stopped dripping, so it's time to come inside and meet everyone. I told them how you rushed to my rescue, so I suspect you're going to be the man of the hour."

Wyatt groaned inwardly. Just what he didn't want. He followed Olivia into the living room with Rodney trotting at his heels. Wyatt wasn't sure of his welcome with Jack, but at least he'd scored with the dog.

3

OLIVIA GUESSED THAT WYATT had agreed to stay because he was unwilling to leave a group of ladies caught in a power outage. If chivalry kept him here, that was fine with her. She wouldn't mention that these were resourceful ranch women who didn't need a man to babysit them in an emergency.

But judging from what the women had said after she'd arrived, nobody should be out driving tonight, not even a can-do wilderness guide. Sarah's battery-operated weather radio had predicted high winds and hail would follow on the heels of the heavy rain. She and Wyatt walked into the living room, where a fire burned in the large rock fireplace and candles positioned around the room illuminated a comfortable collection of brown leather furniture and sturdy wooden side tables.

Conversation stopped among the eight women gathered there. Eleven-month-old Sarah Bianca, Morgan Chance's little girl who was known as "SB," continued to babble to her stuffed dinosaur, and four-month-old

Archie, Josie Chance's son, slept peacefully in his carrier. All other eyes turned toward Wyatt.

Olivia understood why. Firelight and candlelight bronzed his wet T-shirt look with an erotic glow that was truly mesmerizing. The women had good reason to stare, especially after hearing Olivia's tale of being carried through the rain by this fine specimen of manhood.

Sarah was the first to break the charged silence. "Good to see you again, Wyatt, but my goodness, you're soaked!" She set down her wineglass and walked toward him, all smiles. "We need to do something about that before you settle in."

Olivia swallowed a bubble of laughter. What Sarah really meant was that if she didn't reduce the sexual wattage of that impressive physique by giving him something dry to wear, the women would be distracted the entire evening by the resident beefcake.

"I have some of my sons' old clothes I was going to take to a rummage sale in town," Sarah said. "Come on back to the laundry room with me. Something should fit you."

"Thanks. I appreciate it." Wyatt set his lantern on a side table and followed her down the hallway to the left with Rodney close behind, his short legs moving rapidly to keep up.

"Whew." Josie Chance, Jack's wife, flipped her long, blond braid over her shoulder. "Don't anybody tell Jack I said so, but that guy's hot. I had no idea. Jack just said he was a typical hiker type with sandy-colored hair."

Morgan Chance, Josie's redheaded sister-in-law, laughed as she took the dinosaur her daughter handed her. "Of course he said that. You think he's going to describe his half brother, or any guy, for that matter, as good-looking?"

"I wish I could have snapped off a couple of shots before Sarah dragged him away." Nick Chance's wife, Dominique, a tall brunette with short hair, was a professional photographer who always had her camera handy. "But that would have spooked him, I'll bet."

"Oh, you think?" Mary Lou, who'd been a cook at the ranch for years, shook her head and grinned. "You ladies better take it down a notch or he's liable to spend the evening in a back room playing with the dog."

"That would be a shame." Olivia had returned to setting up her mani-pedi station in a corner, but she glanced over at Dominique. "Still, I would have loved a picture of him in that wet T-shirt. I can see it framed and hanging in your gallery. You'd sell a few prints of those, girlfriend."

"But you and Dominique would be the only ones who could get away with having that picture," said Tyler, Morgan's dark-haired sister. "I don't think Alex would take kindly to me pasting it up on the inside of my closet door. Those days are over for this married lady."

Emily, a petite blonde, lifted her chin. "I don't need a picture like that. I have Clay."

"Spoken like a woman who's only been a bride for two months." Morgan winked at her. "Just because we ogle once in a while doesn't mean we don't adore our guys. There's no harm in a little recreational voyeurism. Right, ladies?"

"Right!" everyone chorused, except for Emily.

"I can't believe I didn't recognize his name when he made his reservation at the Bunk and Grub." Pam Mulholland, a curvy woman who counted on Olivia to keep her gray hair looking blond, sipped her wine. "Sarah told me about his visit last summer, and you'd think I'd have made the connection."

"It's probably just as well you didn't." Josie walked over to peek at a still-sleeping Archie before retrieving her glass of mineral water. "If Jack had known he was coming, that might have changed his plans for the Casper horse show."

"True," Morgan said. "And I think it's great that they all went and took so many Last Chance horses. Gabe was looking forward to putting on a cutting horse demonstration."

"And Jack didn't have time to get all discombobulated at the idea of Wyatt returning," Josie added. "So I'm glad it didn't occur to you, Pam."

"I'm certainly not complaining, either." Olivia pulled her stainless-steel footbath out of one of her zippered totes. She'd organized the area with a comfy chair and a small desk for manicures and a second cozy chair for pedicures. She'd roll back and forth on the office chair Sarah had brought out.

"I'll bet you're not complaining," Morgan said.

"He seems really nice." As Olivia took inventory of the stack of towels Sarah had provided, she almost mentioned that Wyatt might move his business here, but she thought better of it. He wanted to relocate, but he might not appreciate having her give out that information prematurely.

"Yes, he does seem nice," Josie said. "I hope that everything—well, never mind. I hear them coming back down the hall."

"So!" Sarah clapped her hands together as she walked into the living room with Wyatt and the ever-present Rodney Dangerfield. "Let's get this party started!"

Olivia straightened and turned toward Sarah and Wyatt. Whoa. She was more than ready to party, all right, but she wished it could be a private one featuring her and the hunk of burning love who'd just walked in. The wet T-shirt had showcased Wyatt's glorious muscles beautifully, and she hadn't thought Sarah could improve on that.

Oh, but she had. The yoked gray Western shirt was a smidgen too tight and tucked into worn jeans that fit like a second skin...ooo, baby. Olivia licked her suddenly dry lips.

A scuffed but serviceable tooled leather belt with a plain silver buckle brought her attention to the fly of his jeans, and she looked away quickly before she could be caught staring. A pair of Western boots that showed some wear completed the outfit. He'd left the room a wilderness guide. He'd returned a cowboy.

SARAH INTRODUCED WYATT to everyone and he did his level best to keep them all straight. Josie, Jack's wife, would be important to remember. She was the one with the long blond braid. Their baby, Wyatt's new nephew, was named Archie, after Jack's grandfather. Archie was asleep in his carrier, so despite Wyatt's curiosity, he kept his distance, not wanting to wake him.

Morgan, a busty redhead, was obviously the mother of a little redheaded tot named Sarah Bianca, SB for short. Morgan's dark-haired sister, Tyler, had married

Alex Keller, Josie's brother. Wyatt decided when he had access to paper and pencil he'd write some of this down.

Then he met Dominique, a tall brunette who was the third daughter-in-law, and Emily, a petite blonde who had just married the guy who ran the stud program. That took care of the women in his generation.

He recognized Pam, a blonde in her fifties, from hearing her voice on the phone when he'd registered at the Bunk and Grub. By process of elimination he knew that the gray-haired woman with the jolly smile had to be Mary Lou, the cook. Yes, he would definitely write all this down before he went to sleep tonight.

But he should be okay for the evening while the introductions were fresh in his mind. Maybe this wouldn't be so awkward after all. He'd thought he'd be uncomfortable wearing somebody else's clothes but he'd been wrong. These cowboy duds felt great.

Sarah had offered him several shirts and pairs of jeans along with clean underwear. Neither of them had talked about the need for underwear, but he was soaked through.

Once Sarah had handed over the clothes, she'd waited outside the laundry room while he tried them on. He'd chosen the first things he'd put on for expediency's sake. But the longer he wore them, the more right they seemed.

When he'd asked her who the clothes had belonged to, she'd confided that they'd all been Jack's. Now that Jack was relaxed, happy and enjoying married life, he'd put on a little weight and couldn't wear them anymore without straining the seams. She'd made Wyatt promise not to mention the weight gain to Jack, because he swore the clothes had shrunk in the wash.

Apparently Wyatt was about the size that Jack had been a year ago, before he'd married Josie. Knowing they were so alike in build, if not in coloring, had pleased Wyatt. But meeting Jack while wearing his old clothes might be weird. Wyatt planned to drive back to the Bunk and Grub and change into his own stuff before Jack came home.

In the meantime, he liked the way Olivia had looked at him when he'd first come into the room. He hadn't thought about whether she had a soft spot in her heart for cowboys, and if so, he might decide to brush up on his riding skills and pick up some Western wear of his own. Re-creating that sparkle in her blue eyes would be worth the effort.

Sarah finished the introductions and turned to Olivia. "So who would you like to do first?"

In what looked like a purely unconscious move, Olivia glanced at Wyatt, and he swore he could read her X-rated response. Heat rocketed through him. Wow. He was definitely buying Western clothes before he left town.

She turned bright red before she looked away. "Why don't I start on Josie's nails while little Archie is asleep?"

"That's fine with me, but he sleeps through anything," Josie said. "But I guess if you do my nails first, they'll be dry in case he does wake up."

"I just thought of something." Sarah looked worried as she glanced at Olivia. "You'll want warm water for your finger bowl and the foot bath. The hot water heater's electric, so we have hot water now, but we won't for the rest of the evening."

"We can hang a kettle over the fire like people did in the old days," Mary Lou said.

Sarah brightened. "Sure we can. Problem solved. Let's get that kettle going now so it'll be ready when the water from the heater turns cool."

Talk of manicures and footbaths galvanized Wyatt into action. "I think it's about time for me to take Rodney and vamoose."

"Oh, no, you don't." Mary Lou smiled at him. "Now that we're in full swing, I could use some help getting the food laid out."

"We can help, Mary Lou," Dominique said. "Morgan has her hands full with SB, but the rest of us can schlep things from the kitchen."

"Hey, I'm glad to do it," Wyatt said. "I'm the party crasher around here, so it would make me feel better if I can be useful."

Dominique put down her wineglass. "Okay, but we can still help."

"Absolutely," Tyler said. "I'm actually good at this kind of thing."

"Ladies, ladies." Mary Lou held up both hands. "Your offer is much appreciated, but I think you should let this nice young man do the honors. I've had my eye on him since he walked in. I said to myself, *Oh, good. There's our muscle.*"

Wyatt pretended not to hear the muffled laughter that followed that remark. "Then it's settled. Everybody relax and I'll handle it." Considering how hungry he was and how many delicious smells had invaded the laundry room while he was changing clothes, he was more than willing to facilitate the food situation. He could always disappear after the meal part.

"Great," Mary Lou said. "Come on back and I'll show you where the large folding tables are stored. We need a couple set up in the living room so we can create a buffet. That way everyone can munch whenever they feel like it. Since the stove's electric, I need to move the hot food into chafing dishes and bring them out here."

"Sounds like a plan." Wyatt was aware of everyone eyeing him with amusement.

"Oh, and I'd appreciate it if you'd bring that light of yours into the kitchen, too."

"Sure thing." Wyatt grabbed the lantern from where he'd left it and followed Mary Lou down the same hall he'd recently traveled with Sarah. The left wall was a bank of windows, which now looked out on rain and streaks of lightning. But each time the lightning flashed, it lit up the other wall, which was covered with framed photos.

"What are all those pictures?" Wyatt asked.

"Family." Mary Lou kept walking. "No sense in trying to show you now, though. We'd have to use your lantern and we should probably conserve the batteries. But the entire history of the Chance family is there in those pictures."

"I'd like to study that." His mother would never allow a wall of pictures to spoil her ultrachic decor.

"I'm sure you would. Come down in the morning and I'll give you a guided tour." Mary Lou kept walking, but she glanced over at him. "I wish you well, Wyatt Locke. Your mother caused a lot of pain in this family but that's not your fault. It took guts for you to come back here, and that tells me you'd fit in a lot better than Diana ever did." She caught her breath. "Oh, I shouldn't have said that. It wasn't respectful. I'm sorry."

"Don't be sorry. I know my mother's not a popular person around the ranch." He hesitated, torn between truth and disloyalty. "She's a complicated woman. Being her son hasn't always been easy."

"Well said." Mary Lou reached over and patted his arm. "I personally think you'll be good for Jack. I only hope he'll be good for you, too."

"We'll see, Mary Lou. We'll see."

After that they didn't have time for philosophical discussions. Wyatt carried the folding banquet tables back down the hall and set them up while Mary Lou used his battery-operated lantern to light her work space in the kitchen. Because the ranch was used to serving hot food outdoors for barbecues, Mary Lou had an assortment of warming pans heated by gel packs instead of electricity.

As Wyatt helped her bring in the food, he laughed at his assumption that it would be finger sandwiches and tea cakes. This was hearty ranch fare—baked beans, ears of corn, coleslaw, fried chicken, mashed potatoes and a giant platter of chocolate frosted brownies for dessert. The only nod to what Wyatt considered girly food was a big bowl of salad and a relish tray of carrot sticks, celery, radishes, pickles and green onions.

Sarah told Wyatt where to find a high chair for little SB, and he brought that in along with an oil cloth he spread under it to catch food fallout. Then he helped Morgan settle the little redheaded girl into her seat, along with her stuffed dinosaur and a bowlful of dry Cheerios. He'd never spent much time around little kids and he was surprised that he instinctively took to it.

Mary Lou announced the food was ready and the women didn't hold back. Laughing and talking, they loaded their plates and refilled their wineglasses. Wyatt, being gentlemanly and an uninvited guest, waited until they'd all gone through the line. That included Olivia, who'd finished Josie's manicure.

"I'll fix your plate for you," Olivia said to Josie. "You need to be careful of your fingernails."

"I can do it for Josie," Wyatt said. "You go ahead and eat, Olivia."

"Why, thank you." She gave him such a dazzling smile that he temporarily forgot what he'd volunteered for. He was fascinated by that tiny space between her front teeth. Adorable.

"You're making points fast," Josie said to him. "Gallantry counts around here. Are you sure you're not a cowboy?"

When she spoke, he refocused on his task and picked up a plate. "My brother and I used to pretend to be cowboys when we were kids." He grabbed a napkin and utensils, too. "Does that count?"

"Absolutely." She pointed to the steaming baked beans. "Lots of those, please. Light on the potatoes and heavy on the coleslaw."

Wyatt loaded Josie's plate as instructed and carried it over to an empty chair next to the baby carrier sitting on the floor. Archie slept on, despite the racket.

After making sure Josie was all set and hadn't ruined

her manicure, Wyatt crouched down next to the baby carrier. "Looks like he took after you more than Jack."

"I think so." Josie gazed with fondness at her son. "He has Jack's nose, though, and of course he's only four months. His blond hair could get darker, but he definitely didn't inherit Jack's coloring."

Wyatt studied the tiny face, so sweet and soft. Something about the nose reminded him of Rafe's baby pictures. "He looks...familiar."

"He should. You're related to him." Josie laid down her fork and looked at Wyatt. "I hope you'll be patient with my husband. He puts his shields up when it comes to you, even though it's not your fault that your mother...well..."

"Abandoned him." Wyatt met her gaze. "It's okay. You can say it. There's no good excuse for what she did and I promise I won't try to make any."

"I'm sure that will help. At one time I thought Jack had accepted his past, but meeting you has stirred it up again. Unfortunately I think he resents the fact that she started another family while continuing to pretend he didn't exist."

Guilt pricked him. "I don't want to create problems."

"You're not the one who created the problem. Diana did. Jack knows about you and your brother now, so you can't put the toothpaste in the tube again. Coming back was the right move, in my opinion."

"Thanks, Josie. Jack's a lucky guy to have you."

"We're lucky to have each other," she said softly. Then her glance shifted as she looked over his shoulder. "Too bad you can't see the expression on Olivia's face right now. Women get all mushy when they see a guy crouched down next to a baby."

Warmth crept up the back of his neck and he resisted the urge to turn around. "But I wasn't doing it for—"

"I know. I can see that you're the real deal, Wyatt. Olivia can, too. We all can. Even Rodney."

Upon hearing his name, the dog padded over and pushed his nose against Wyatt's leg. Wyatt ran a hand over the dog's silky head. "Yeah, I know, Rod. I promised you we'd hang out and here I am ignoring you."

Josie chuckled. "Now Olivia's *really* got a sappy look on her face. Kids and dogs. I'm telling you, Wyatt, you have a gift. Not that it's any of my business, but is there a girl back home?"

"No, actually, there's not. I've been pretty busy getting my business up and running."

"In that case, I suggest you grab a plate of food and go sit by Olivia while she has a moment to herself."

Wyatt smiled. "Believe I will. Come on, Rod. Apparently you're an asset to the cause."

As Wyatt headed to the buffet table, Mary Lou handed him a cold bottle of beer. "Most times the guys prefer this to wine," she said.

"Thanks, Mary Lou."

"There's more where that came from. I brought in a small cooler and put it under the table. Consider it your reward for all your fine work."

"You're a gem." He tucked the beer in the crook of his arm, filled a plate with food, and walked over to where Olivia sat on a leather-covered ottoman.

She glanced up, welcome in her blue eyes. "Hi, there. I'd offer you a seat, but there isn't one."

"No worries." Setting his plate on a nearby end table, he crouched down next to her. Rodney took a spot right by his feet. "I'm used to making do." He unscrewed the cap on his beer and took a swallow. "That's quite a spread Mary Lou put on."

"See, I told you to stay for the food."

He didn't say what he was thinking, that he'd eat twigs and leaves if he could be near her while doing it. "You were right." He noticed that Rodney was staring up at him as if he hadn't had a decent meal in a week. "The dog thinks so, too."

"Don't feed him anything. Sarah has him on a special diet. He's overweight."

"How can you tell with a basset hound? They're all sort of roly-poly."

"Beats me, but she wants him to be able to fit into his life vest and it's still a little tight."

Wyatt blinked. "His *what?*"

"One reason she wanted to adopt him, besides the fact he's adorable, was his tracking ability. Sarah's always wanted a tracking dog on the ranch. Butch and Sundance, the two mixed breeds living down in the barn, aren't particularly good trackers."

"So what's that got to do with a life vest?"

"There are streams and ponds all over the property, and basset hounds can't swim. Their bones are too dense."

"They are?" Wyatt looked down at Rodney. "I didn't know that."

"Me either, but Sarah researched it. If she wants to turn him loose to do his tracking, he has to wear a life vest so he won't accidentally fall in the water and drown."

Wyatt took another swig of his beer and glanced down at Rodney. "I'm getting quite a visual here, Rod. I'm thinking YouTube video star, aren't you?"

Olivia laughed. "I think you're on to something. Definitely bring a camcorder next time you come to the ranch." She picked up her empty plate and stood. "Well, time for me to get back to work. You can have the ottoman."

Wyatt rose, too. "Actually, I think I'll take my plate, my beer and the dog into the kitchen. I'll just be in the way out here."

"I heard that." Morgan, little SB on her hip, walked toward him. "Don't think you can sneak out of here that easy. I'm sure I speak for everyone when I say we'd love for you to hang around."

"Yes, we definitely would," said Dominique from her spot on one of the couches.

Wyatt wasn't sure where this was headed. He glanced over at Olivia, but she was already settled into her chair and preparing for her next customer. "Hey, I'll just cramp your style," he said to the room in general. "Rodney and I will be fine in the kitchen, right, Rod?"

The dog gave him a doleful look.

"Our style isn't that easily cramped," Morgan said. "And we need somebody to tend the fire and add wood. We'll all have fresh manicures and can't do that." She looked up at him. "Unless you're planning to get a manicure, too, in which case we—"

"I'm not getting a manicure."

"See? So you'd be perfect, then. Instead of a designated driver we need a designated fire tender."

Wyatt had to hand it to these Chance women. They were very good at maneuvering a guy into doing what they wanted. "Then I'd be honored to watch the fire for you."

"Excellent." Morgan beamed at him. "Besides, it's not every day we get the opportunity to talk to a single guy without our husbands around to kibitz."

He gave her a wary look. "Talk about what?"

"What else?" Morgan's green eyes twinkled. "Men!"

4

OLIVIA ALMOST FELT SORRY for Wyatt, who looked somewhat like a cornered animal. But he was a big boy, and besides, she was curious to see how this would turn out.

"I'm not sure what you mean," he said.

"Let me explain." Morgan shifted SB to her other hip. "Most of us in this room are married, and the ones who aren't are getting closer by the day."

"Not true," Mary Lou said. "I'm never marrying that old fool Watkins, and you can quote me on that."

"Emmett still has a burr under his saddle about the size of my bank account," Pam said. "So I don't see us tying the knot anytime soon, either."

All attention focused on Sarah, the remaining single lady other than Olivia. Sarah was blushing.

Morgan paused expectantly. "Well? Do you have news at long last?"

She cleared her throat. "I guess it's okay to say something."

Dominique laughed. "At this point, I think it's required to say something, Sarah. We're all dying of curiosity. Have been for months."

"Well, Pete and I have talked about it, but we haven't set an actual—"

Squeals of joy erupted as everyone ran over to hug Sarah. Olivia, who didn't feel she knew Sarah quite well enough to be part of the hug fest, motioned Wyatt over to the manicure table so she could fill him in on the meaning of the uproar.

He walked over, carrying his beer. "Who's Pete?"

"Peter Beckett. He's a local philanthropist. He and Sarah put together a youth program that begins here in two weeks. They'll be boarding several problem teens and giving them a chance to work at the ranch for the summer."

Wyatt's eyes widened. "Hey, that's cool."

"It is. Really cool. And everyone's suspected a romance between the two of them, but Sarah always denied it before."

"She looks happy. Is this Peter guy good enough for her?"

"Her sons all like him, so I'd say he has the Chance stamp of approval."

Emotion flickered in Wyatt's soft gray eyes. "I have a feeling that's not so easy to get."

"Don't worry. It'll work out between you and Jack." She gazed up at him. "You already have a lot of support right in this room."

"I hope so. I'd enjoy being part of life around here."

"Even when you're about to be put on the hot seat?"

"Yeah." He massaged the back of his neck. "I'm not sure what that's all about."

"After all my years as a beautician listening to women talk, I can make an educated guess. Husbands are more prone to say what they think their wives want to hear. These gals are hoping you might actually tell them the truth about what guys are thinking."

"But it's only one point of view."

"Yes, but you've established yourself as one of the good guys and that makes your point of view worth exploring." She pushed back her chair. "I'll get you another beer. That should help."

Before he could protest, she'd hurried over to the buffet table and snagged another bottle out of the ice-filled cooler Mary Lou had brought in.

"Here." She handed it to him and then stepped closer. "Listen, before I make a complete fool of myself, I need to ask you something."

"What's that?"

"Are you involved with anyone?"

He looked into her eyes and his gaze was straightforward. "Nope, I'm not. Not at all. Are you?"

"Not yet." Rising up on tiptoe, she gave him another one of her drive-by kisses. She was fast becoming obsessed with his mouth, but she didn't dare linger. "I have to refresh my soaking solution." She picked up the crystal bowl she used for that purpose and headed toward a bathroom located just down the hall on the right.

If she'd ever met a more adorable guy than Wyatt, she couldn't recall who it might have been. If he truly wanted to relocate to Shoshone, Wyoming, she'd do whatever she could to help him make that happen.

ONCE AGAIN, OLIVIA HAD GOTTEN the drop on him. Wyatt vowed that the next time he'd be ready for her when she did that and he'd get in some lip pressure of his own.

In the meantime, he stood there holding one full bottle of beer and one nearly empty one while he gazed after her like some love-struck adolescent. He finished off the almost-empty beer and looked for a place to put the bottle.

"I'll take that." Morgan appeared at his elbow with her red-haired mini-me propped on her hip. "You need to finish your meal because we really do have some burning questions."

If Wyatt had hoped Morgan had forgotten her original plan in the flurry of excitement over Sarah's admission, that hope was now officially dashed. "I'm really not very knowledgeable about—"

"Now don't be modest, Wyatt. You're eligible and you're gorgeous, which puts you in the perfect position to give us some insight into how guys think these days." She gestured to an empty chair. "That seat's available. I'll be right back."

Wyatt glanced over at Olivia, who'd just started working on Pam Mulholland's nails. Olivia looked up with an encouraging smile. She'd told him he had support in this room, so maybe he should stick around. Retrieving his plate, he sat in the chair Morgan had indicated and began to eat. He probably needed to keep up his strength.

With a little doggy sigh, Rodney plopped down on the floor beside him.

Kids and dogs. Wyatt realized he hadn't had much to do with either because his mother hadn't wanted any messes in her perfectly decorated house. All his playing as a kid had been at the school yard or somebody else's place.

Pets hadn't been an option either. Once Wyatt became a wilderness guide, he'd given up any thoughts of getting a dog even though he no longer lived with his mother. He traveled too much. But if he was based in Shoshone and was welcome at the ranch, he could interact with the dogs and horses here.

As he was polishing off the last of his dinner, Morgan sat in the chair next to his and settled her daughter, who was drifting off to sleep against her shoulder. "Okay. I get the first question. Inquiring minds want to know…what's the most important thing a man looks for in a woman?"

"For what?" He figured hedging was a good tactic.

"For anything. Conversation, working together, bedroom games, whatever."

"I can only speak for myself."

Tyler, Morgan's dark-haired sister, dropped onto a sofa nearby. "Tonight, my friend, you're speaking for every man."

Wyatt took a fortifying sip of his beer, which bought him a little more time to think. Finally he settled on his answer. "Enthusiasm."

"Can you be more specific?" Tyler combed her dark hair back from her face. "Enthusiasm for what, exactly?"

"I think he's talking about sex," Morgan said. "You are, aren't you, Wyatt?"

"Not just sex." He slugged back some more beer. "It's fun to be with someone who goes all in with whatever she's doing. And sure, that goes for sex, too, but—"

"I think he means sex," Pam called over from the manicure station.

"Not *only* sex." Wyatt sat forward in his chair and gestured with his beer bottle. "I'm talking about enthusiasm for her work, and if she plays any sports then I hope she plays them with all she's got. If she has hobbies then I hope she loves doing them. I want her to be passionate about whatever she's doing."

"I'm here to tell you I'm not enthusiastic about housework," Dominique said.

"That's something I think men should be enthusiastic about." Josie held her hands out in front of her and gazed admiringly at her pink fingernails. "Then maybe this manicure would last awhile."

"Wyatt." Morgan gazed at him. "Do you clean your own place?"

"Uh, yeah." He felt a trap was about to be sprung.

"Enthusiastically?" Tyler asked.

"Not exactly, but—"

"Aha!" Dominique pointed a finger at him.

Wyatt glanced over at the fire. "Gee, will you look at that? I need to tend the fire. If you'll all excuse me." Setting his empty beer bottle down, he stood and walked over to the fireplace.

"Be sure and tend it enthusiastically!" Morgan called after him, which made everyone laugh.

"Oh, you know it, ladies." As he moved the screen aside, he started whistling some snappy tune he'd heard recently on the radio. He often whistled on long drives to amuse himself, so he was pretty good at it by now. Then he added a few dance steps when he picked up a log from the rack beside the fireplace. The women began clapping rhythmically.

At that point he felt he had no choice. Instead of

backing off, which any sane or less inebriated man would have done, he turned the fire building into a hip-swinging, foot-stomping routine worthy of Chippendales. He'd never actually seen a Chippendales routine but this was how he thought it might go, minus the logs and the fireplace tools.

Where he got the inspiration was a mystery, although it might have been the beer he'd had. It also might have something to do with Olivia being in the room. He wanted her to know he was up to the challenge thrown down by these women.

He finished with a flourish that won him loud applause. Amazingly, both babies slept through the whole thing. He met Olivia's gaze for one quick moment and had to look away. She'd obviously liked the performance, and that sizzle passing between them was liable to attract unwanted attention.

Returning to his chair, he sank into it gratefully.

"Well done," Morgan said.

"Relax and have another beer." Dominique brought it to him this time. "Girls, let's stop picking on the poor guy for a while. He's acquitted himself admirably, and besides, we have brownies to eat."

"And beauty to accomplish." Josie smiled at Wyatt. "You should at least have Olivia give you a pedicure."

"I don't think so." When Olivia finally touched him, he didn't want her to start with his feet.

"Maybe he'd agree to just a foot massage," Olivia called over from the manicure table. "I give great foot massages."

He'd just bet she did. The thought spiked his blood pressure because anyone who gave good foot massages was into sensuous contact of all kinds. He shifted his weight in the chair and told himself not to think about it.

"Pam's done," Olivia said. "Who wants to be next?"

Mary Lou waved her hand in the air. "I'd love a pedicure."

"Then come on down, Mary Lou." Olivia stood and squirted some liquid soap into the stainless-steel bowl in front of the second chair. "I'll go fill the footbath."

"No, *I'll* fill the footbath." Wyatt left his seat and walked over to take the bowl from her. He hadn't given enough thought to how much work this night would be for Olivia. He couldn't paint nails, but he could fetch water.

"Thanks." The look in her eyes told him he'd done a good thing.

"Any instructions?"

"Test the temperature on your wrist. It should feel warm but not scalding. I think the water coming from the faucet in the tub should still be warm enough, but if it's not, leave room so I can add some from the fireplace kettle."

"Got it." Following her directions, he soon returned with a sudsy pan of water, which he placed carefully in front of the chair where Mary Lou already sat barefoot with an eager expression on her lined face. She immersed both feet with a sigh of pleasure. "Thank you, Wyatt."

"I'll be in charge of the footbath from now on, Olivia."

From the group of women gathered in the seating area came a long, drawn-out "Awww."

"I swear to God, Wyatt," Tyler said. "You are redefining the word *hero*."

"I have to admit he's setting the bar pretty high," Josie said. "I—" She paused as the theme song from *Pirates of the Caribbean* started playing. "That would be Jack on my cell."

Wyatt tensed as Josie located her purse, pulled the phone out and answered it. Holding the phone to her ear, she talked quietly as she stood and walked down the hall he'd just come from. In an instant he went from feeling welcome and appreciated to thinking of himself as an intruder.

Conversation flowed again after the interruption, and Wyatt joined in as if that phone call didn't occupy ninety-nine percent of his thoughts. Josie would mention his arrival. It was the right thing to do in an open and forthright relationship, and Wyatt believed Josie and Jack had that.

Fortunately for Wyatt's sanity the call was short. Josie walked back into the room looking calm. That was promising, he told himself.

"Is everything going well in Casper?" Morgan asked.

"Very well. They've sold several horses and Clay's written up quite a few orders for semen delivery."

Emily's face seemed lit from within. "That's so great. He had high hopes for this trip and I'm so happy for him. Well, and for the Last Chance, of course."

"That is good news," Sarah said. "How's the weather down there?"

"Not bad at all, and that's why Jack called. He heard about the storm hitting Jackson Hole and wanted to know how we were doing. I told him the power was out but we were coping fine." She looked at Wyatt. "And of course I told him you were here."

Wyatt's gut tensed. "What did he say to that?"

"Not much." Her voice gentled. "But that's Jack. He's not chatty on the phone. He said he'd be home late tomorrow afternoon."

Wyatt nodded. "It'll be good to see him." At least Jack hadn't said that Wyatt had better be gone by then.

5

By the time Olivia had finished six manicures and
three pedicures she should have been exhausted, but
having Wyatt around kept her energy level high. For one
thing, he insisted on emptying and refilling the footbath
and the soak bowl, which saved her some time and effort. But just looking across the room and exchanging
a glance with him was enough to recharge her batteries whenever she started to drag.

Besides helping her, he carried the chafing dishes
back to the kitchen once everyone had finished eating,
took down the folding tables and worked with Mary Lou
on cleanup duty. After Archie woke up and was fed and
changed, Wyatt took a turn at holding the little guy.

Although holding a baby seemed to make him nervous to begin with, soon he relaxed and began making
faces at Archie. That activity entertained both the baby
and the women gathered around sipping the last of their
wine and exclaiming over the beauty of their nails.

Olivia finished her last manicure, a pale peach shade
for Emily, and began packing up her supplies. Rain still
pounded on the roof and slashed at the windows. Sarah

had called down to the bunkhouse and the few hands who were there reported that the horses were fine and the barn didn't seem to be leaking, so they were all going to bed.

Olivia had brought pajamas and a change of clothes, but she didn't know where Sarah planned for her to sleep. One of the recently constructed bunks upstairs would be fine. Growing up in the chaotic household of an eccentric father had made her flexible when it came to sleeping accommodations.

As if reading Olivia's mind, Sarah set down her empty wineglass and stood. "I see some droopy eyelids, and I'm about ready to turn in myself."

Josie yawned. "Yep. It's been great, but I'm ready for some shut-eye."

"Go on up whenever you want." Sarah waved a hand at the upper floor. "The only ones who don't know where they're bunking down are Wyatt and Olivia, so now would be an excellent time for me to show them." She picked up a candle sheltered inside a small glass chimney. "Come on upstairs, you two."

Olivia knew Sarah hadn't meant to link them together as if they'd be sleeping in the same room, but the image stuck in her mind anyway. She didn't know Wyatt well enough to sleep with him…yet. But she intended to further the acquaintance. All the signs pointed to the possibility that something wonderful could develop between them.

Leaving her tidying, she stood and followed Sarah toward the wide, winding staircase. Archie Chance, little Archie's great-grandfather, had been a master carpenter who'd constructed the graceful wooden stairway leading to the second floor. Olivia had wanted to climb that staircase from the first time she'd seen it, which had been at Emily and Clay's wedding.

That day she'd had no reason to go upstairs. But now she had a chance to sleep in one of the rooms and she was thrilled about it, even if she wouldn't be sharing with Wyatt. The Last Chance Ranch house seemed like the height of casual elegance to her.

Wyatt was right behind her on the stairs, and she was superaware of that fact. The attraction between them seemed to be growing rapidly, at least from her perspective, and sleeping under the same roof tonight would be tantalizing. She wouldn't allow anything to happen and she doubted he would either, but the forced proximity heated her blood.

Sarah reached the landing and waited for them both to join her. "As Olivia knows, we've converted some of these rooms to dormitory-style spaces to accommodate the teenagers who are coming—God help us all—in two weeks."

"Olivia told me about that." Wyatt stood close, but not so close as to imply they were a couple. "I love that idea."

Olivia imagined she could feel his body heat, but that was probably her hyperawareness kicking in. "I'd be perfectly happy in a bunk," she said. "Put me wherever."

"Actually, the others are in the dorm spaces. They all know each other so well, so I assigned Morgan and Josie to one room, along with a couple of portable cribs for SB and Archie. Dominique, Tyler and Emily are in another dorm room. Pam's downstairs with me and Mary Lou has her own apartment off the kitchen."

Olivia would have been happy to squeeze in with the other women, but this was Sarah's call, so she kept quiet.

"So I'm putting you in Roni's old room, Olivia. That's one we decided not to convert, so you have your own bath attached."

"Roni's the mechanic for a NASCAR team, right?" Olivia was grateful for all the gossip in the salon, which had filled her in on the players at the Last Chance.

"That's her, the runaway teen we took in years ago. Come to think of it, she kind of foreshadowed this program Pete and I have created." Surrounded by the glow of her candle, Sarah started down the hall to her right. "Occasionally Roni comes home for a visit and brings her husband, Judd, with her, so we like to keep her room available. But it's yours for the night." She reached a doorway on the right side of the hall, stepped inside and lifted the candle up. "I think it'll work for you."

Olivia glanced into the room and could make out a race car motif on the bedspread covering the double bed and repeated in the curtains and the pictures hanging on the walls. It wasn't her style but she didn't care. Any room at the Last Chance was special.

"It's perfect," she said. "Thank you for putting me up."

Sarah stepped back into the hall and wrapped an arm around her shoulders. "Thank you for agreeing to participate in our little party. Everyone had fun, and our nails look fabulous."

"I was happy to do it, Sarah." But now Olivia couldn't help but wonder where Wyatt would be sleeping. Considering that she'd be in this wing with the other women, she had a suspicion…

"I'm putting you in the other wing, Wyatt," Sarah said.

Bingo. That would have been Olivia's guess. Underneath it all, Sarah had a touch of old-fashioned propriety, and Olivia respected that. She wasn't about to violate the unspoken rules.

"Anywhere is fine," Wyatt said.

"You're going to be in Jack's old room." Sarah walked to the other side of the house, with Olivia and Wyatt trailing behind. "Eventually we may turn this side of the house into dorm rooms, too, but for now they're just guest rooms. Jack's enormous bed is gone but I bought something to replace it." She held the candle aloft once again.

Olivia released a little sigh of pleasure. In the pool of candlelight she could see that the room was furnished in soft greens and browns—a man's room, and yet the kind of room a woman would love to slip into and be seduced by that man. Olivia repressed a tug of longing and promised herself that she would not, would *not,* lie in bed tonight and picture Wyatt stretched out under that fluffy hunter-green quilt wearing…probably nothing. He had no clothes of his own here, and anyway, he didn't seem like the pajama type.

"It's a very nice room," Wyatt said. "I'll only be here one night, of course, but thanks for letting me—"

"Don't be silly." Sarah turned to him. "You're family, and I won't have you paying for a room somewhere else, even if it's in Pam's B and B. I've already discussed it with her and she's fine with having you move over here."

"But I just appeared, without notice," Wyatt protested. "You shouldn't feel the least bit obligated to put me up under the circumstances."

"It's not a matter of obligation," Sarah said gently. "It's a matter of welcoming those who are related to us." She paused. "And much as I hesitate to say this, that would go for your mother if she were inclined to visit."

Olivia's breath caught. Really? Sarah would house Diana under her roof?

"I would never expect that of you," Wyatt said. "That you would even say such a thing speaks to your generosity of spirit, but my mother has forfeited any right to stay in this house."

"You're wrong." Sarah's voice was low but firm and her gaze steady. "No matter what she's done, she's still Jack's mother and little Archie's grandmother. If it would help Jack heal the wounds that I'm afraid still fester in him, I would welcome the devil herself into my home."

Wyatt stared at her in silence for several seconds. "That might be an accurate description of Diana."

"Careful. She's your mother."

"I know. Believe me, I know."

The silence stretched between them.

"And Archie's grandmother." Sarah took a deep breath and shook her head. "I don't know what to do about that. After all, little Archie is her grandchild, more hers than mine if we're talking about a biological link."

"Blood isn't everything."

"No, but it counts."

"In this case I don't think it counts for much," Wyatt said. "I'd recommend keeping the baby info quiet for now. It's probably enough that Jack has to deal with me."

Sarah gave him a knowing smile. "Wise words." She glanced over at Olivia. "Bet you didn't expect to get mixed up in a family drama, did you?"

Olivia spoke from her heart. "I feel privileged that you've included me in the discussions, and I promise you I won't gossip about anything I've heard here."

"I know you won't. I trust you. But I'd hate to think we've made you the least bit uncomfortable by airing our dirty laundry."

"Not at all. Ever since I moved here, I've wanted to learn more about the Chance family. You're legendary in Shoshone."

Sarah's cheeks turned pink. "Well, I don't know about that."

"It's true, Sarah. Being asked to come out for Emily and Clay's wedding preparations was an honor considering I'd only been here for six months. When you suggested tonight's manicure party, I was thrilled. I can't imagine ever regretting the opportunity to be part of whatever's going on here."

Sarah's eyes had regained their old sparkle. "That's quite a compliment."

"I know what she means," Wyatt said. "I felt something special the minute I stepped inside the ranch house last summer. You've built something here that you should be proud of. Archie and SB represent the fourth generation of Chances on this land, right?"

"Yes, they do." Sarah couldn't hold back a smile of

satisfaction. "And I am proud of that. Archie and Nelsie would have loved knowing that we're still here." Her expression softened. "So would Jonathan. He'd be so proud of what his boys have accomplished since he's been gone."

"I wish I could have met him," Wyatt said.

"I wish you could have, too." Sarah appeared to consider that possibility for a moment, and then she shook her head and laughed. "No telling how he would have reacted to meeting you, though, so maybe we shouldn't think about that too wistfully. Anyway, we've delved into this mess enough for one night. Let's go back. I just wanted each of you to know where you were laying your weary heads tonight."

On the way downstairs they met Josie and Morgan coming up, each carrying her child. Morgan had located a flashlight and was using it to light their way. Wyatt stepped aside to give them more room to pass while Sarah and Olivia continued on down.

"We're packing it in," Morgan said. "The others are cleaning up the last few things before they come up. Pam's already gone off to her room, and I think Mary Lou's in bed by now. We tried to get Rodney to go out to pee, but he won't. We weren't sure if you were ready to bank the fire, either, so we left it."

"I can take care of the fire," Wyatt said. "I'll make sure it's okay before I go to bed. And I can take the dog out, too. Maybe it'll let up a little and he'll be more willing."

Sarah reached the bottom of the stairs and turned back to smile up at him. "That would be wonderful, on both counts. Thanks for all your help."

"Seems like the least I can do."

"You're a pleasure to have around, Wyatt." Sarah laid a hand on his arm once he joined her. "In fact, if your brother Rafe is anything like you, then—"

"He's not. He's a lot harder and tougher than I am, at least on the outside. When we were kids he was always telling me not to care so much."

Sarah nodded. "Sounds like Jack."

"If you put the two of them in a room together, you'd know they were brothers immediately. It's not only that they look so much alike, but they seem to have the same attitude."

"Which explains why you came to the ranch and he refused." Sarah gave his arm a pat. "I'm so glad you did."

"Me too."

"And now I'm off to bed. Sleep well, both of you." With a little wave, she headed down the hallway toward her room.

Dominique walked toward the stairs, trailed by a sleepy-looking Tyler and Emily holding candles. "We're going up, too," Dominique said. "Thanks for a fabulous job, Olivia."

"Yeah, thanks!" Tyler said. "Loved it."

"You're welcome, all of you."

"And thanks for the floor show, Wyatt," Emily added with a laugh.

"Anytime."

"The dog has to pee," Tyler said over her shoulder as she trudged upstairs. "We couldn't make him go out."

"We'll handle it," Olivia said.

"There's rain boots, slickers and a flashlight by the

front door!" Tyler called out before disappearing down the hall.

After the women were out of sight, Olivia took a deep breath before looking up at Wyatt. "I don't know about you, but I wouldn't mind relaxing by the fire a little longer."

"Listen, don't worry about me. I really can take care of the dog."

That wasn't quite the response she'd hoped for. Maybe he wasn't in the mood for company. "Or, maybe you'd prefer to sit by the fire alone."

"I didn't say that."

"Well, except for Rodney. Maybe you'd like to do the man and his dog companionship thing."

Alert to the sound of his name, the dog padded over and stood looking up at them.

"Olivia, I—"

"Or, maybe you'd like to toddle off to bed and let me take care of the fire and the dog. I used to have a dog, so I can handle Rodney. And my father's a scientist. I understand the principle of banking a fire."

That produced a smile. "Let's not bank the fire yet. Let's put on another log."

"Okay." Now, that was more like it.

"You haven't had a chance to put your feet up all night. I think I should give *you* a foot massage."

Her first thought was that would be heaven. Her second was that she was the foot care professional and Emily had suggested it would make a good payback for having him rescue her. "No, really, I should give you one in exchange for pulling me out of the ditch."

He rolled his eyes. "Tell you what. I'll massage your feet first, and then you can massage mine. How's that?"

"I like it."

"Good." He took her by the hand and led her to the couch with Rodney following behind. "Take off your shoes and get comfortable while I build up the fire."

"Gladly." She sank down to the soft leather cushions as he walked over to the hearth and moved the screen aside. "I enjoyed your floor show, too, by the way." She eased her shoes off.

"If that's a hint, I'm not putting on another one." He grabbed a log and laid it in the middle of the bed of embers. "Basically I'm too shy to do that, but I'd had a fair amount of beer on an empty stomach."

Damn, but he was cute. She had a serious crush going on, made more intense by that wounded part of him he tried so hard to hide. "I wasn't asking for a song and dance routine," she said. "I'd just like to talk and get to know you better."

He replaced the screen, dusted off his hands and turned back to her. "I'm all yours."

She knew he wasn't, not really. But he'd just stated her ultimate goal. She'd been too passive in her dating life and had allowed men to choose her. Then she'd gone along with their decision to become a couple. But for the first time in her life, she was making the choice, and she wanted Wyatt Locke.

6

WYATT COULDN'T IMAGINE a more beautiful sight than Olivia relaxing on the cushy leather couch, firelight dancing over her skin and gilding her curves as she waited for him to join her. He wished he'd met her under different circumstances, when he wasn't dealing with the emotional issue of his half brother, Jack. But if not for that issue, he might never have met Olivia at all.

He sat at the opposite end of the couch and turned to lean back against the rolled arm. Drawing his leg up onto the cushion, he reached for her left foot and brought it into his lap. Her sparkly toes rested inches from his crotch, but he vowed not to think about that.

"You'll have to give me some pointers." He took hold of her foot with both hands and ran his thumbs up the curve of her arch. "You're the professional."

"That feels nice. It's nearly impossible to do it wrong unless you're tentative. Firmness is everything."

He grinned. "Sort of like sex." Whoops. He hadn't really meant to introduce that topic. The words had slipped out, probably because he was thinking so hard about how they would not get sexual tonight. "Sorry. Shouldn't have brought that up."

"Why not?"

"Inappropriate." Cupping her heel in one hand, he began working on each individual toe. Touching her feet was great, but he couldn't help thinking how nice it would be to touch the rest of her.

"I wouldn't say that. Neither one of us is committed to anyone, and speaking for myself, I'm very attracted to you."

"I'm very attracted to you, too." He used a more gentle pressure as he rubbed the top of her foot. "But under the circumstances, we can't do anything about that. Not tonight, anyway."

Her expression grew serious. "No, we can't. I think Sarah made that clear when she put me on the girls' side of the house and you on the boys' side."

"Yeah, I got that message." He worked his fingers into the crevice at the base of her toes.

She moaned softly. "That feels terrific."

He chuckled. "Anybody listening might misinterpret that moan and comment, you know."

"Do you think anyone is?"

"Don't know. They all looked pretty tired to me."

She gave him a secret smile. "I think everyone's fast asleep, but just in case, I'll keep my moans discreet. You are doing a fabulous job, by the way. I suspect you've massaged a woman's feet before."

"A time or two." He concentrated on a spot next to the ball of her foot. When he'd first pushed against it, she'd looked almost orgasmic. And he didn't need to think about *that* subject, either.

He searched for a more general topic. "So, how many broken hearts did you leave back in Pittsburgh?"

"Three."

"Oh?" He hadn't expected such an instant and precise answer.

"At least I assume their hearts were broken—temporarily—and I'm truly sorry for that. My heart was broken, too, because I'm the perennial relationship optimist, so I convinced myself we were meant for each other. But just so you know, I always gave back the ring."

"The *ring*?" He was so startled he stopped rubbing her foot. "Are you saying you were engaged to all three of these guys?"

"I was. And each time I thought it was for keeps, but then…I realized it wasn't going to work, and I'd have to break off the engagement. Which was all terrible and sad for both of us."

"I'm sure it was." Knowing she'd accepted a marriage proposal three different times was sobering. Then she'd rejected each of those guys and returned the ring. He hoped never to have to go through something that painful.

She glanced down at her foot. "Ready to switch?"

Her revelation had made him completely forget about massaging her feet. "Um, yeah. I'll work on the other one now."

"I really appreciate this. I can't remember the last time a guy offered." She pulled her left foot back and gave him her right.

"I'm happy to do it." He wondered if any of her three ex-fiancés could have saved the day with a decent foot rub. He reapplied himself to the task at hand, but in the back of his mind he was still assimilating the fact that Olivia could commit and uncommit far more easily than he could. That was important to know.

"I think I figured out the problem, though, and I don't expect to go through that again."

"And what's the problem?" He pushed with both thumbs as he worked his way up her arch.

"Oh, that's *heaven*." She closed her eyes. "Please do that again, Wyatt."

He did, but he was in serious trouble. She was turning him on with her breathless comments. He could see why her exes had become involved with her. He knew exactly why they'd shown up with a ring in their pocket and no doubt a *firmness,* as she'd put it, in their Jockeys.

She was beautiful and sensuous, which was attractive to most any man. Besides that, she had the quality he'd mentioned earlier while being grilled by the women. She was enthusiastic. And yes, he was thinking about sexual enthusiasm, damn it.

So what had she been talking about before she closed her eyes and moaned like a woman in the midst of sexual ecstasy? He searched his lust-soaked brain. Oh, yes.

And he really wanted to know the answer to the question, too. "So how are you going to avoid broken engagements in the future?"

"Simple." She opened those gorgeous blue eyes and gazed at him. "I'm going to pick the man instead of waiting for the man to pick me. I'm going to take my time about it and make sure it's what *I* want and I'm not just going along with his idea."

"I see."

"I've had a reasonable amount of interest from men."

"I'm sure you have." He massaged her toes, working from the base to the tip, and watched a dreamy expression steal over her face. He should get a medal for not seducing her right now. She was becoming more relaxed by the second, and a relaxed woman was usually a willing woman.

"And that's the problem. I've allowed them to pursue me and catch me. I was never the pursuer, only the pursued. They wanted me, so I convinced myself that I wanted them, too, because I was flattered and it made life easy."

So the poor saps were screwed from the get-go. "Just so you know, I don't want you at all."

Her smile was damn near irresistible. "Yes, you do."

He wanted to kiss her so much his throat ached. "No, I don't. What you see going on is a case of indigestion. Lust and indigestion look remarkably alike, especially in the human male."

"You don't have to pretend indifference, because the thing is, I decided hours ago that I wanted you."

After what she'd just said about choosing her potential husband, he needed some clarification. "How do you mean that, exactly?"

"It's okay for you to want me. It's a mutual attraction. I'm not just going along with what you have in mind. I want what you want."

"We're just talking about sex, right? Not rings and weddings and stuff like that?"

She laughed. "Absolutely! No way am I ready to choose a husband, but I have to start being more proactive with men in general. So to be perfectly clear, we're just talking about sex."

"Which we can't have tonight." Still rubbing her foot with one hand, he slid the other inside her pant leg and caressed her smooth calf.

Her lips parted slightly and her eyes grew unfocused. "True."

He brushed her soft skin with his fingertips. "So I won't be peeling off your jeans and exploring what's under those silk panties."

She swallowed. "How do you know they're silk?"

"Sparkly toes, stylish shoes, designer jeans. They're silk." His cock grew hard.

"Good guess."

"And they're pink." Why he was torturing himself, he wasn't sure.

"Lavender."

"I was close. Trimmed with lace."

Nodding, she met his gaze. "And wet."

He groaned and squeezed his eyes shut. "That was a low blow."

"Yeah." Her voice was husky. "Sorry."

He opened his eyes and looked at her. "I doubt it."

"Okay, I'm not sorry."

"Olivia, we're not going to make out on this couch. I'm not about to have Sarah come to investigate strange noises and discover us writhing around naked on her furniture."

"I'm not, either."

"She's my hostess."

"She's my client."

"Which settles that issue." He withdrew his hand from her pant leg. "Shall we go to bed?"

"We're not doing anything upstairs, either."

"I'm aware of that. But I think we'd be wise to separate before we start something we feel compelled to finish."

"Right."

He gently—and reluctantly—placed her foot back on the leather cushion and stood. "Going upstairs to our separate rooms and closing our respective doors seems like the only solution."

"But first we have to bank the fire and take Rodney out to pee."

He shook his head. "No, *I* have to do those things. I'm the one who said I would. You can go on up."

"I'm not letting you struggle with the dog by yourself. It's still raining."

"Yeah, well, it won't be the first time I've been wet today."

She winked at him. "Me, either."

"Stop it, Olivia."

"Oh, come on, Wyatt. Isn't this kind of exciting? When was the last time you were under the same roof with a woman you wanted and you were forced to restrain yourself?"

He had to think about that. "I try not to get into those kinds of situations," he said at last. "I have to go back to my teenage years for a memory like that."

"Look at it this way. We'll get together eventually, so it'll be that much more fun when we finally accomplish it."

He sighed and levered himself off the couch. "I'm

not sure I agree with that reasoning, but if you're determined to help me deal with Rodney, then I accept
the offer. I know a lot more about banking fires than
taking dogs out to do their business."

"Like I said, we had dogs while I was growing up. I
think my father hoped a dog would keep me from missing a mother quite so much."

"Did it?"

"Probably. But nothing takes the place of having a
mother."

"Unless she's my mother."

"Even then. At least she was there."

"Physically, maybe, but—" Wyatt caught himself.
He didn't want to talk about his mother any more tonight. "I'll get the fire bedded down for the night. Do
you know if Rodney has a leash?"

"I'm sure he does. I'll go see if it's hanging by the
front door." She grabbed her shoes and got up. "I'll get
him over there while you handle the fire. We can do
this." She patted her thigh. "Come, Rodney! That's a
good boy."

Wyatt wasn't nearly as confident as Olivia. He'd
never dealt with a rain-averse dog and a bedtime potty
issue. But if Olivia had grown up in Pittsburgh with
dogs, then she had to know about getting them outside
in rain, sleet and snow.

After he was satisfied with the condition of the fire
he set the screen in front of it. Once he did, the room
was considerably darker, so he moved a votive candle
to the stone hearth to give them a little light when they
came back in. Then he walked over to the entryway
where Olivia stood with Rodney on a leash.

Wyatt reached for a yellow slicker hanging on a peg. "Ready to suit up for the rain?"

"I have an idea. How about taking the flashlight and going back to the kitchen to find him a treat?"

"Like what?" He took the flashlight she handed him.

"Something bite-sized that we can give him as a reward. Maybe get a piece of chicken and tear some meat off it. But don't bring a whole chicken piece. They can't handle the bones."

"I know that much. All right. I'll see what I can find." Hanging the slicker back on its hook, he switched on the light and headed toward the dark hallway. At the end of it he passed through a large dining room that Mary Lou had explained was where the hands ate their midday meal.

In the kitchen his lantern was still sitting on a counter, so he turned off the flashlight and switched on his own light. He had the refrigerator door open and the lantern held high when someone tapped him on the shoulder. He jumped and yelled as if he'd been hit with a cattle prod.

When he spun around, he found Mary Lou standing there in a red silk nightgown that he never would have imagined her wearing. He lowered the lantern, although she hadn't looked particularly embarrassed to be caught in a negligee.

"What the hell are you doing, boy? If you're after a midnight snack, then forget about it. We're not supposed to open that refrigerator any more than we have to with the power out."

He felt like a kid caught raiding the cookie jar. Then again, it was kind of a good feeling. As a kid, he'd raided the cookie jar, which had only held bakery cookies, hundreds of times. Nobody had noticed. People around this ranch paid attention. They cared about what went on, and he liked that.

"We have to coax Rodney out to do his business," he said. "Olivia thought we should bring a treat, like a hunk of chicken or something."

"Well, that's easy. Close that refrigerator door and shine the light over on the cupboards to the right of the stove."

Wyatt did as he was told, like any twenty-something guy would do when confronted by a grandma-type giving orders.

"There's a jar of dog treats on the second shelf. Just take a couple of those and you'll be good to go."

"Thanks, Mary Lou." Wyatt found the jar with no trouble, unscrewed the top and took out a couple of bone-shaped biscuits. "Sorry if I woke you."

"You didn't. That damn-fool man Watkins decided to leave his warm bunkhouse and knock on my door. But when I heard someone banging around in my kitchen, I had to investigate. See you in the morning."

"Okay. Thanks again." Wyatt decided not to think about whatever was going on between Mary Lou and Watkins in her apartment. The image might stay burned in his brain forever.

"Oh, and you and Olivia make a cute couple. You should pursue that."

"I...um...she doesn't want to be pursued."

"Hogwash. Any woman likes to be chased after."

"Not this one. She says that was the problem with

her other guys. Now she wants to be the one doing the pursuing."

"Then I guess you'll have to figure out how to get her to chase you until you catch her."

"There's the trick, all right."

"And don't dither around about it. Women like her don't grow on trees, you know."

"I do know." Sticking the dog biscuits in the pocket of his jeans, he turned off the lantern, picked up the flashlight, and made his way back through the dining room and the hallway lined with pictures. He'd known Olivia was special from the moment she'd lowered the window on her Jeep Cherokee. He might not be able to explain exactly why he knew, but he did.

He couldn't say that to her, though. She'd think he was coming on too strong. How ironic that he'd stumbled across a woman he thought might be right for him, and he couldn't go after her or he'd risk ending up like the other three schmucks she'd dumped.

Logically, all three men who had proposed to Olivia might have been ninety-nine percent sure she was the one. But they'd seriously miscalculated. Wyatt cringed at the idea of offering a ring to a woman who later returned it. When he presented a ring to someone, he expected it to stay on her finger for the rest of her life.

He knew from his parents' lives that his preferred scenario wasn't necessarily the norm, but that didn't stop him from being determined that it would be the norm for him. He'd seen marriages that worked for the long-term. He suspected there were some in the Chance family, his mother and Jonathan notwithstanding.

He found Olivia crouched down next to Rodney. She

had rain boots on her feet and a slicker over one arm as she talked earnestly to the dog.

"You need to empty your bladder, Rodney," she said. "It's not good to hold it too long. I've made that mistake a few times when I was working and couldn't take a break. It's not good for you."

Wyatt couldn't help smiling. Olivia might have dumped three guys, but she wasn't without compassion. She would probably argue that leaving them had been an act of kindness because they would have been unhappy in the marriage.

She glanced up. "Did you find some treats?"

"Thanks to Mary Lou, I have a couple of dog biscuits in my pocket."

"She wasn't asleep?"

"No, and please don't ask why. I'd rather forget what I know. In fact, if the Men in Black could come through and zap my memory, I'd be a happy camper."

Olivia giggled. "But you're already a happy camper. Adventure trekking. That's what you do."

"True enough. Ever been camping?" Bracing a hand against the wall, he pulled off one of his boots.

"Nope."

"So you weren't a Girl Scout?" He took off the other boot.

"For a little while, but money was tight and I dropped out."

"I didn't think it was that expensive." Money was one thing Wyatt hadn't worried about when he was growing up.

"It isn't really, but I saw my dad's face when I told him I needed a uniform, and it wasn't worth having him angst over it. Consequently, the only tent I've been in was a blanket draped over a clothesline in the backyard."

"Ever wanted to try camping?" He took the rain boots she handed him and shoved his feet inside.

"Is that an invitation, Mr. Wilderness Guide?"

Play it cool, dude. Let her chase you. "I guess it could be, if you're interested." He stomped his feet to adjust the fit of the rubber boots.

"I'm definitely interested if I can do it with a pro."

He was glad the darkness hid his smile of triumph. "Then we should go camping sometime. Not right away, because I'm hoping Jack will agree to go out with me for a night or two this week, but I'd be happy to take you when we're both free."

"Alone in a tent." She stood. "That could be fun."

He pictured Olivia naked on a down sleeping bag. With great effort, he kept his tone nonchalant. "It definitely has promise."

7

IMAGES OF SEX IN A TENT with Wyatt got Olivia so hot she was eager to go outside and cool off. Without further comment, she put on the yellow slicker and flipped up the hood. "I'm taking the umbrella." She grabbed a collapsible black umbrella leaning in the corner by the door. "If I keep the rain off him, he might be more cooperative."

Wyatt fastened the snaps on his slicker and picked up the flashlight. "I'll bet most dogs go out in the rain no problem."

"Not necessarily. Some dogs love it and some dogs hate it. Just like people." She tucked the umbrella under her arm. "I'll go out first. Give me one of the dog biscuits and I'll coax him down the porch steps."

Pulling up his slicker, Wyatt dug in his pocket and handed her a biscuit. Rodney brightened and wagged his tail.

"See? He wants that treat. If I can tempt him down the steps with the first one, we'll give him the second one as a reward." She opened the door and rain-freshened air cooled her face.

Stepping out on the porch, she crouched down and held out the dog biscuit. "Come on, Rodney. Out the door, big boy."

Nose twitching, Rodney ventured out onto the porch as Olivia backed away toward the steps.

"Smells good out here," Wyatt said as he came out and closed the door behind him. He flicked on the flashlight. "Rain, wet pine needles and smoke."

She paused at the edge of the steps and put up the umbrella. "Rain smells better here than it did in Pittsburgh. Okay, if you could hold this over him as we walk, I'll handle the leash and the treat."

"Sure thing." He took the umbrella, positioned it over the dog and swept the area with the beam of light. "No tree branches in your way."

"Thanks. I'll bet sometimes you camp in the rain."

"Sometimes. It's tricky working with a fire when it's raining, but it can be done."

Watching him in his element would be a turn-on, she thought. Of course, as ramped up as she was right now, just watching him breathe was a turn-on.

But she was here to help the dog, not fantasize about sex with Wyatt. Holding the treat in one hand and the leash in the other, she tugged gently as she edged backward down the first step and into the rain. "That's it, Rodney. Down the steps." The rain fell steadily, but not quite as hard as earlier in the evening. "Wyatt will cover you with the umbrella so you don't get quite so wet."

With painstaking slowness the two of them maneuvered the dog down the steps and onto the gravel.

"My plan is to lead him over to one of those spruce trees," she said.

"All that way?"

"He's a boy. He needs something to lift his leg on."

Wyatt chuckled. "I can see you're determined to do this right."

"It's that or risk an accident in that beautiful house. I'll keep a tight hold on the leash, but if he shows signs of backing up, block him from behind."

"Okay. If I have to, I'll break out some of my old football moves."

"You played?"

"Nearly every sport I could squeeze into my schedule. It got me out of the house. And it was a legitimate way to get sweaty and dirty."

"I was the opposite, an indoor, playing-with-dolls kind of kid. I set up a beauty shop and spent hours on their hair." She waggled the biscuit as she backed across the gravel drive and used the flashlight beam to watch for big puddles. Rodney followed. Although he whined a couple of times in protest, the umbrella seemed to give him a feeling of protection. "I played beauty parlor with the dogs, too."

Wyatt's boots crunched on the gravel as he followed close behind Rodney and sheltered him with the umbrella. "So that's why you became a beautician? Playing beauty salon with your dolls and your dogs?"

"No." She waggled the biscuit again. "I got into it because I practically lived at a salon called A Cut Above. My dad had no idea what to do about my hair and the salon was only a couple of blocks away, so he took me there when I was two. After that I went once a week, sometimes twice, until I graduated from high school. Those women were my substitute moms."

"Now *that* must have been expensive."

"I'm sure they felt sorry for him and gave him a smokin' deal. Plus I started helping out when I was old enough to fold towels and sweep the floor. Then of course I went to work there after I graduated from beauty school."

Talking about A Cut Above always swamped her with nostalgia. For a while the only sounds were the patter of the rain and the soft crunch of their boots on the gravel.

"I'll bet it was hard to leave that place," Wyatt said at last.

"Yes, it was." It was the hardest thing she'd ever done. She'd known some of those women for twenty-five years. But her father's heart had been set on moving to Jackson Hole, and he'd convinced her that they were in a rut living in Pittsburgh. "I still call back there once a week." Glancing behind her, she saw that they'd reached the edge of the gravel. "This part might be harder because of the mud. He won't want to walk through it."

Wyatt gave a resigned sigh. "I already figured that out. If you can hold the umbrella and take over with the flashlight, I'll carry him to the tree."

"All right." She had to hold the umbrella and the biscuit in one hand and the flashlight in the other, but she managed the trade-off.

Leaning down, Wyatt scooped Rodney into his arms. "Oof. You are heavy, dog. I can see why Sarah put you on a diet."

"It's just that his bones are dense, remember?" Olivia

held the umbrella over man and dog as they squished through grass and mud to the nearest spruce.

"It's just because he's porky, is what I'm saying."

"He'll be lighter on the way back."

"He damned well better be." Wyatt lowered him to the ground under the tree. "I don't think you need the umbrella right here. The branches are shielding him."

"You're right." Setting the umbrella on its side on the ground, she offered Rodney the dog biscuit. "Here you go. That's a good boy. Now do your thing."

Rodney chomped happily on the biscuit, swallowed it, and stood looking up at them and wagging his tail.

"Go ahead, Rodney." Olivia made shooing motions with the flashlight beam. "Do your business."

"I swear to God this is turning into a three-act play." Wyatt tossed back his hood and crouched down next to the dog. "Want me to show you how it's done, Rod?"

The dog whined again and licked Wyatt's hand.

Olivia burst out laughing.

"Well, I'm not gonna demonstrate, because there will be no unzipping of flies out here. It could lead to something else."

Olivia nearly choked on her laughter, but a hot river of lust sluiced through her at the thought of Wyatt's potentially unzipped fly. "Honestly."

"Well, it could."

"Not likely, considering the rain and the mud factor."

He rose to his feet and turned to her, his face in shadow. "Then I guess you've never done it up against a tree."

"Uh, no." Her pulse raced. "Can't say that I have."

His voice was low and filled with repressed desire.

"We might have to remedy that if we go camping to-gether."

She wanted him so much she could barely breathe. "Promises, promises."

"Those are the kind I like to make." Dropping the leash to the ground, he anchored it with his boot as he took the flashlight from her and shut it off.

She trembled in anticipation of his next move. "It's dark out here without a flashlight."

"Are you afraid of the dark?" A rustling sound indicated he'd shoved the flashlight in the back pocket of his jeans.

"Not when I'm with a professional wilderness guide." Her heart beat so fast she felt dizzy.

"There you go." He brushed back the hood of her slicker and cradled her head in one large hand.

"Are you going to kiss me?"

"Thinking about it." His tone was lazy, almost casual. "How would you feel about that?"

"I kind of like the idea."

"I sort of do, too." Cupping her damp cheek in his other hand, he settled his mouth firmly over hers.

The fuse had been burning within her for hours. With his deliberate kiss the flame reached the keg of gunpowder, blowing away all thought and leaving only heat and fire. She moaned and wrapped her slicker-clad arms around his neck as her mouth opened in surrender.

He took what she offered, thrusting his tongue inside, mimicking the connection they both wanted, yet were denying themselves. With several loud pops he unfastened the snaps down her front and cupped her breasts in both hands. She pressed against his palms, desperate for his touch.

He lifted his mouth a fraction from hers as he massaged her breasts through her shirt. "The whole time I was rubbing your feet, I really wanted this."

"I wanted this, too. Oh, Wyatt, kiss me. I want your mouth on me."

He kissed her eyes, her cheeks, the tip of her nose. "Where do you want my mouth, Olivia?"

She groaned. "Everywhere. All over. Wyatt…" His name turned into a wail of frustration. "You're torturing me."

His breathing was heavy. "No more than I'm torturing myself. Right now we have to settle for this." He deepened the kiss, ravishing her in a way that left no doubt what he would like to do once they were free to explore each other.

The wind picked up and blew a shower of water down from the pine needles, drenching them. Wyatt just kept kissing her, his mouth supple, wet and intoxicating. She squirmed closer, wanting more, wanting everything.

A series of sharp barks jolted them out of their frenzied kiss. Wyatt let her go. She put her hand to her chest and struggled to remember their original purpose in coming out here. Oh, yes, Rodney.

Leaning down, Wyatt scooped up the end of the leash. Then they both looked at the dog. Rodney had been hit by the same splash of water as they had, but he didn't seem nearly as pleased with the erotic feel of it.

Slowly he lifted his muzzle and began to bay in true hound-dog style.

"No, Rodney!" Olivia dropped to her knees and held his mouth closed. "Don't do that! You'll wake up the whole house!"

"I think he mostly wanted to get our attention."

Olivia glanced up at Wyatt. "Guess that wasn't so easy to do."

"Nope." His grin flashed in the dim light. "You are one great kisser, Sedgewick."

"Speak for yourself, Locke. I'm surprised you didn't create a layer of fog around this spruce tree from all that steam."

His grin softened. "I loved kissing you, Olivia. I could do it all night. And it's going to be hell trying to sleep when that luscious body of yours is right down the hall. But we need to get back to the house and do our damnedest to be respectful houseguests."

"But what about Rodney? We stopped watching him. Now we don't know if he did anything or not."

"You're right, so I'll take him up to my room, which will serve a couple of purposes. If he didn't go just now and ends up peeing on the floor, I'll be the one to clean it up. Also, I won't be tempted to creep down to your room when I know this dog would probably start howling if I did."

"Rodney's a canine chastity belt."

"Something like that." Wyatt lifted up his slicker and fished out the second treat from his pocket. "Here you go, Rod. Sorry about the unexpected shower."

"I'll bet he went, after all. I'd hate to think we did all of this for nothing."

Wyatt's eyebrows lifted. "Nothing?"

"I didn't mean it like that. I just—"

"I'm perfectly willing to let the dog wait in the rain a little longer. I'd hate for you to leave here feeling all let down and disappointed."

She held her breath, wondering if he'd pull her into his arms again. "I don't feel let down and disappointed. I feel keyed up and horny, and if you kiss me again it'll only get worse." And wouldn't that be fun?

But instead he backed off. "Wouldn't want that."

"Right." Oh, yes, she would.

LATER THAT NIGHT, AS WYATT tossed and turned on a mattress built for two, he wondered if he could maintain the facade of coolness with Olivia. Their kisses had raged through him like a brush fire, and every time he thought of the way she'd responded, his cock turned to granite. Instead of sleeping, which was the smart thing to do, the thing Rodney was doing on the braided rug beside Wyatt's bed, he imagined making love to Olivia.

He wondered if she had plans tomorrow. He didn't know a lot about beauticians and salons, but he was reasonably sure that they wouldn't be open on Sunday, especially in a small town like Shoshone. Olivia could have things to do on her day off, though.

Still, she might be willing to spend time with him, and Jack wouldn't be home until late afternoon. As he thought about what they might do together, he admitted to himself that mostly he wanted to get her alone somewhere. Would that be too obvious?

And if he succeeded in working out a way they could be alone, then he needed his stuff from the Bunk and Grub. Specifically, he needed one certain item, something he carried with him, although only God knew why he did. He hadn't had a girlfriend in over a year.

Actually, he did know why he kept condoms on hand and had done it for years. Funny he hadn't figured that out before. His mother hadn't bothered to have any heart-to-heart talks with him except once, and the subject had been birth control.

She'd handed him a box of Trojan condoms, which had embarrassed the hell out of him, but she'd insisted that he listen to what she had to say. A lecture about unplanned pregnancies had followed. She'd emphasized how such a disaster could change someone's life forever.

Now he knew where that lecture had come from. She'd married Jonathan Chance because she'd been pregnant with his child. These days people didn't always believe that a marriage had to follow a pregnancy, but his mother had believed it back then.

Even after only a few hours at the ranch, Wyatt could understand why she'd thought marrying Jonathan was her only option. She'd conceived the heir to the Chance legacy. And when she'd finally made up her mind to leave, she couldn't take that heir with her. Jack belonged here.

She should never have had more children, but he couldn't very well wish she hadn't or he wouldn't exist. But she had not been a good mother, certainly not to Jack, and not to her other boys, either. One lecture about birth control didn't balance out years of indifference. But it had prevented him from making the same mistake she had.

As he lay staring into the darkness, Rodney whined. At Olivia's insistence when they'd started upstairs,

Wyatt had taken the flashlight while she took the votive candle. She'd argued that he had the dog and might
need it.

Apparently he did. When he turned it on, Rodney
looked for all the world like he had to go outside. Well,
crap. Climbing out of bed, he walked to the window.
Rain no longer ran in rivulets down the pane, so maybe
it had stopped. Maybe Rodney knew that.

"All right, Rod." Wyatt put on his briefs and the jeans
and shirt he'd borrowed. No sense in bothering to put
on Jack's boots when he was planning to wear the rubber rain boots outside. He left his shirt unsnapped, too.
This would be a quick trip.

"At least it better be quick," he told the dog as they
left the bedroom, lighting the way with the flashlight.
He let Rodney walk to the top of the stairs, but he carried him down because a long flight of steep steps
wasn't really Rodney's thing. Once on the ground floor,
he put the dog down, and Rodney padded right over to
the front door.

"I'll be damned. Okay, let me get some boots on."
He abandoned the slicker option, snapped on Rodney's
leash and opened the door. Cool air greeted him, soothing his heated skin. Maybe this wasn't such a bad idea
after all.

Without coaxing, the basset hound trotted across the
porch and made his way down the steps while Wyatt
gave him a lit path with the flashlight. Crossing the
gravel drive took no time at all. But at the muddy area
on the far side of the driveway, Rodney paused.

"I'm not sure how you're going to be a tracking dog if
you can't stand mud, my friend." But Wyatt picked him

up and transported him over to the tree, where Rodney hiked his leg and did what everybody had been trying for hours to get him to do.

"Feel better, now?"

Rodney yipped his answer.

Wyatt stood under the tree for a moment reliving his encounter with Olivia. His groin stirred. Either they'd find some time alone tomorrow, or he was going to be one frustrated guy. But suggesting a picnic seemed lame, especially when the ground would be wet and muddy after all this rain.

At some point he'd help her get her Jeep out of the ditch, but he couldn't imagine parlaying that into anything cozy. Then inspiration struck. The night breeze must have blown the cobwebs from his brain because he had the perfect solution.

In describing the ranch, his mother had mentioned a sacred Shoshone site a short drive from the house. The marker was a large, flat rock about the size and length of a pickup truck and it was laced with white quartz, a stone that was thought to conduct special energy and sparkled in the sun.

He'd been a little surprised that she'd talk about the site because usually she downplayed the fact that she was half-Shoshone. That made him a quarter Shoshone, though he didn't look the least bit Native American. And he wanted to see this site.

Apparently the tribe didn't visit the spot anymore, even though the Chance family had given them permission to do so whenever they wanted. Times had changed. But many years ago, the rock had been the location for tribal ceremonies. Inviting Olivia to drive out there with him was the perfect excuse to get her alone, and—if he was a very lucky guy—naked.

8

8

OLIVIA HAD HEARD WYATT go outside with Rodney because, big surprise, she'd been unable to sleep. Most of the clouds had drifted away, leaving the moon and stars to play hide-and-seek behind the ones that were left. Kneeling by her bedroom window and resting her arms on the sill, she watched him move across the gravel. The flashlight bobbed rhythmically as he walked in that loose-hipped way that told her a man knew how to use those hips in bed.

His shirt billowed out, which meant he hadn't bothered to fasten the snaps. She intended to stay here until he walked back. An opportunity to catch a glimpse of his bare chest was worth the wait.

She liked that he hadn't left his shirt open for a calculated macho display of muscles. He thought he was alone with the dog and had no idea she was at the window, her attention glued to his every move.

At the far edge of the drive, he switched off the flashlight, leaned down and scooped Rodney into his arms just as the moon came out from behind a cloud. She had a great view of his buns in the borrowed jeans that were delightfully snug. Ordinarily she'd feel shallow for obsessing about a guy's body like this, except that she also admired the person inside, so ogling didn't seem quite so awful. She admired his cheerful attitude and his courage in coming here and trying to become friends with Jack.

He was risking rejection and she hoped to hell that wasn't going to happen. She didn't know Jack very well. Everybody knew his wife, Josie, because she owned the Spirits and Spurs and still worked there regularly. But Jack spent his time on the ranch, so Olivia had limited knowledge, mostly gained during Emily and Clay's wedding two months ago.

Jack had cut loose a little at the wedding, and people had told her that he'd been quite the party animal in his younger days. But after his dad died he'd retreated into a workaholic shell. Josie and little Archie had brought him out of that shell, apparently, but the whole issue with his mother still affected him. His initial response to Wyatt proved that.

But Wyatt had come back, wearing his heart on his sleeve. She wished she could protect that vulnerable heart somehow, because she wasn't convinced that Jack would be any more cordial than he had been before. Maybe she'd find a reason to hang around tomorrow, if nobody objected, so that she could be there when Jack arrived.

After spending quality time with Rodney in the shadow of the spruce tree, Wyatt emerged carrying the dog again. Damn. That dog was obscuring her view of Wyatt's most excellent pecs and abs. But then he reached the gravel, set Rodney on all fours and straightened.

The moon and clouds were still involved in a dance, but they separated long enough to illuminate Wyatt— divine intervention as far as Olivia was concerned. Her breath caught at the beauty of him. Men weren't supposed to be beautiful, but Wyatt was.

Moonlight painted him in shades of gray, as if he were the subject of an artistic black-and-white photo. Dominique would be able to capture this on film, but Olivia would have to rely on her memory. No problem. She wouldn't soon forget how the light sculpted his contours and added soft smudges of chest hair that formed a blurry line that disappeared beneath the waistband of his jeans.

Her fingers itched to touch him, but he was out of reach tonight. He would soon be back in his room and right down the hall, but he might as well be on another continent as far as Olivia was concerned. The thought of causing Sarah any embarrassment gave her heartburn. No matter how much she wanted Wyatt, and that was a whole lot, she wouldn't breach the invisible barrier Sarah had erected between the two wings of the upper story.

As Wyatt crossed the gravel drive he glanced up toward her window. She doubted he could see her there, but she liked knowing he'd thought of her during his late-night ramble. But she was dead serious about how she'd handle their relationship beyond the initial sexual involvement. If she and Wyatt turned out to be more than friends with benefits, she wanted to make damned sure that it was her idea and not his to take it to the next level.

Wyatt and Rodney reached the porch and disappeared under the roof. The front door creaked open, and the sharp sound of the dog's toenails on the hardwood floor and the softer thud of Wyatt shucking his boots told her they'd soon be trudging up the stairs. She had to talk long and hard to herself to keep from walking out and meeting them at the top of those stairs.

That would accomplish nothing except to frustrate both her and Wyatt even more. Climbing back into bed, she listened for Wyatt's footsteps and knew from his heavy tread that he was carrying the basset hound. It made an endearing mental picture.

Then they reached the second floor, and the dog's nails clicked along the hardwood while Wyatt's progress was virtually silent in his bare feet. How she yearned for him. But she would have to wait. Morning seemed an eternity away.

RODNEY TURNED OUT TO BE a damned fine alarm clock. Before the sun was up, he'd begun pacing the floor and whining as if he had to go out again. Mumbling in protest, Wyatt left his warm bed and started pulling on his borrowed clothes. He hadn't expected to sleep at all, but eventually he'd drifted off.

His dreams had been excellent, filled with a very naked and willing Olivia, and pulling the jeans over his morning wood was not a fun exercise. "You're worse than a new baby, Rod, old chum. I've never had a new baby, but I understand they interrupt your sleep a lot."

Rodney came over and started licking his bare toes.

"And you can knock that off, too, Rod. The only person I want licking my toes is sleeping down the hall. At least I hope she is. I hope everyone on this frickin' ranch is asleep because it's barely light out. This is beyond early, and I know early."

Opening his bedroom door, he staggered out into the hall. Josie appeared coming from the other direction, Archie clutched in her arms. "Gotta deal with the baby," she said in a sleep-roughened voice.

"Gotta deal with the dog." Wyatt let her go down the stairs ahead of him.

"You'll make a good dad, Wyatt," she said over her shoulder.

"I already feel like one, except this guy needs to lose some of this baby fat." With a sigh, he picked up Rodney and carried him down the winding staircase. Then he clipped the leash to his collar and opened the front door.

Although he wasn't overjoyed to be roused out of bed this early after so little sleep, the minute he stepped out on the porch, his weariness vanished. The front of the house faced a spectacular view of the Grand Tetons, still snow-covered as spring moved into summer.

The view had been obscured by rain yesterday, but this morning the pale pink of an impending sunrise bathed the jagged peaks and took Wyatt's breath away. Knowing his mother had walked away from such beauty underscored how different they were.

San Francisco had spectacular views as well, but his mother had never mentioned that as her reason for living there. She'd wanted an urban life and a rich husband. Not that anyone would have called Jonathan Chance a pauper. Any fool could see that the Last Chance was worth a lot of money, but the family would have to sell in order to tap those millions. His mother obviously preferred ready cash.

Accompanying Rodney across the gravel drive to the dog's chosen spruce tree, Wyatt shivered in the morning chill and wished for a jacket. But other than the temperature, it was glorious out here. He savored the scents of pine and wet earth and glanced up as a hawk wheeled overhead.

Just as Rodney finished anointing the tree trunk, Wyatt heard activity down at the barn and several paint horses appeared in the pasture, manes and tails flying as they celebrated their freedom. The barn dogs Olivia had mentioned bounded out and ran up to greet Rodney.

Thanks to leather collars hand-tooled with their names, Wyatt was able to identify them. Butch was a medium-sized dog, a mixed breed with short hair that was mostly tan except for a patch of white on his snub nose. Sundance was slightly smaller with a curly black coat and floppy ears.

All three dogs participated in a round-robin of nose-to-tail greetings, but Butch and Sundance also trotted over to Wyatt seeking attention. Crouching down, he ruffled their coats and scratched behind their ears. "Guess Rod must have vouched for me, huh?"

Panting, the dogs both grinned at him. A whistle from the barn sent them racing back down, probably for their breakfast. Wyatt realized he was smiling. He could easily lose his heart to this ranch and the surrounding countryside. And that wasn't even taking into account the woman he'd kissed last night under this very tree.

Rodney started back toward the house, obviously

interested in his next meal, too. Wyatt was attached to Rodney by the nylon leash but the dog was far more eager to go in than Wyatt was. The rockers lining the porch were still wet, but he could imagine coming out here with a cup of coffee and just...appreciating. No doubt that's why the chairs were there.

The minute he walked through the front door he caught the scent of coffee and wondered how someone was accomplishing that if the power was still off. But if there was coffee in the making, he'd sure like to find a towel and wipe off one of those rockers.

He wasn't sure where his boundaries lay, though. Sarah had insisted that he stay here, but that didn't mean he could act as if he owned the place. He had to be very careful about that, in fact.

Rodney, on the other hand, had no such hang-ups. Once Wyatt unhooked the leash from his collar he trotted down the hall toward the kitchen as if the Last Chance had been built expressly for his comfort. Wyatt followed him, figuring the dog gave him an excuse to investigate what was happening in the kitchen.

In the early morning light he could see the pictures on the wall, but he wouldn't know most of the people. He needed that guided tour Mary Lou had promised him. He also needed coffee.

He found more people in the kitchen than he would have imagined this early. Josie had Archie in his carrier on the table and was rocking him gently while she sipped from a steaming mug. Mary Lou, wearing a fluffy white bathrobe, also sat at the table cradling a mug, and the third person was a fully dressed middle-aged cowboy with a handlebar mustache. He had coffee, too.

"Hi, there, Wyatt!" Mary Lou smiled at him. "Want coffee?"

"Yes, but what kind of magic did you use to make it?"

"Cowboy magic." She glanced at the man sitting next to her at the table. "Watkins, I'd like you to meet Wyatt Locke, Jack's half brother."

Watkins shoved back his chair, stood and extended his hand across the table. "Pleased to meet you, Wyatt."

"Same here, Mr. Watkins." Wyatt shook the cowboy's hand and kept his expression carefully neutral. So this was the "old fool" Mary Lou had no intention of marrying, the same guy who'd knocked on her door in the rain and caught her wearing, probably not by accident, a red negligee.

"Just Watkins, son. That's all I go by. Coffee's in that big thermos over there. Take as much as you want. I'm about to head down to the bunkhouse and reload it."

"Thanks." Wyatt walked over to the counter where a large carafe stood.

"Mugs are in the cupboard above," Mary Lou said. "Need cream? I hope not, because we're limiting how often we open the refrigerator."

"I don't use cream, thanks." Wyatt took down a plain white mug, stuck it under the spigot and pushed on the top of the carafe. A stream of dark, fragrant coffee poured out. Heaven.

When he was finished, Watkins came over and lifted the carafe. "Yep, nearly empty. I'll be back."

"Thanks, Watkins," Josie said. "You're a lifesaver."

"It's the hands who get the credit. They weren't about to go without their coffee this morning."

"So what did they do?" Wyatt asked.

"Hauled out the old campfire coffeepot and turned on the propane barbecue grill," Watkins said. "They'll be cooking bacon and eggs soon. I'll bring some of those up when they're ready."

Wyatt grinned. "Exactly what I would have done. In fact, I didn't even think about the little camp stove I have in the back of my truck. Should I get that out?"

Watkins smoothed his mustache. "Thanks, but I think we've got it covered. They're having fun, as a matter of fact. It'll be their pleasure to feed the ladies. Well, and you, of course. Be right back." Carrying the carafe, he left the kitchen by the back door.

"Look at that Rodney," Mary Lou said. "Waiting so patiently for his breakfast. At least we don't have to cook that." She stood and walked back to the laundry room. "Come on, boy."

Rodney covered the same distance faster than Wyatt would have thought possible on such short legs. "That was a popular suggestion, Mary Lou."

"He loves his food, which is why he's got love handles."

Josie glanced up at Wyatt. "Have a seat, cowboy."

"Oh, I'm not a cowboy." But he pulled out a chair and sat at the oak kitchen table anyway.

"Hey, you wear the clothes, you soon get the attitude. We've seen that happen before, right, Mary Lou?"

Mary Lou chuckled as she returned to her seat at the table. "We certainly have. Your brother Alex, for example. Oh, and Logan Carswell."

Wyatt recognized the name. "Logan Carswell? You don't mean the former catcher for the Cubs."

"One and the same." Mary Lou sounded proud of the fact. "He and Alex were best friends growing up in Chicago, so he came out for Alex and Tyler's wedding last summer, fresh from forced retirement. He turned into a darned good cowboy, don't you think, Josie?"

Josie laughed. "He's so hooked on the cowboy life-style that he had to go to Casper with the rest of the guys even though he doesn't own any horses and doesn't ride competitively, either. But he couldn't stand to be left out. His wife, Caro, would be here tonight but she needed to spend time with her grandmother in Jackson this weekend."

"Huh. Logan Carswell." Wyatt sipped his coffee. The ranch was full of surprises.

Josie eyed him across the table. "You and Olivia seemed to hit it off."

Startled, he met her gaze. Welcome to the other side of this cozy family situation. People felt free to give advice and commentary.

Josie looked amused. "If you'd rather not talk about it, that's okay. Around here we have a bad habit of poking our noses where they don't belong."

"I told him last night that he should stake his claim," Mary Lou said.

Wyatt decided to use the system to his advantage and find out more about Olivia. "Does she date much?"

"No." Josie reached over and started rocking Archie again when he began to fuss. "I think after breaking off three engagements she's turned over a new leaf and is getting choosier."

"She told me about the three engagements," Wyatt said. "And about being more in charge of her love life from now on."

Josie continued to rock Archie's carrier. "Did she tell you why she broke those engagements?"

"Just that it didn't work out."

"Each of those bozos managed, eventually, to make a disparaging remark about her father."

"Oh." That put a new light on the situation. No wonder Olivia wanted to make the choice next time. "He sounds like he's...different."

"He is, and she'll be the first to say it, but woe unto anyone else who pokes fun at him. I find that kind of loyalty admirable."

Wyatt nodded. "So do I. Thanks for telling me."

"Consequently, I don't think she's planning to rush into another engagement any time soon."

"Rushing into an engagement is a bad idea, anyway," Wyatt said. "I want to be pretty damned sure when I ask somebody to marry me."

Mary Lou gazed at him over the rim of her mug. "Sounds like you've never taken that plunge."

"Nope. Like I said, I want to be really, really sure before I drop to one knee in front of a woman." When neither of them responded, he raised his eyebrows. "You don't agree with that?"

"I don't know if you can ever be that sure," Josie said. "You can be crazy about somebody, but there's still a big risk involved. Sometimes you have to be willing to leap and hope the net will appear."

"Or you can be like me." Mary Lou set down her empty mug. "I had your attitude about marriage. Still do, actually. Can't see any reason for it, so here I am, still single at fifty-two."

Josie gave her a nudge. "Watkins would take care of that issue for you in a heartbeat."

"Watkins." Mary Lou blew out a breath.

"Did you call my name, Lulu?" Watkins came through the back door without knocking, a testament to the freedom Mary Lou allowed him in her domain.

She sniffed. "I told you not to call me that."

"Then I'll call you sweetie pie." He held the coffee carafe in one hand and a metal container covered in foil in the other. "Time to break out the chafing dishes. I'm bringing home the bacon."

"I smell coffee and I smell food!" Olivia's cheery voice preceded her as she walked into the kitchen. "Good morning, everyone!"

Wyatt stood up so fast he had to steady his chair to keep it from falling over. Wow, did she look great. She'd tied her hair up in some kind of sassy ponytail that made her look about sixteen, and the impression was enhanced by her bare feet, jeans rolled at the cuffs, and a light green T-shirt with the words Nail Techs Do It with Polish on the front.

As far as he was concerned, she could do it any way she cared to, if she promised to do it with him.

9

THE AROMA OF COFFEE HAD finally drifted up to the second floor, which had roused Olivia out of a very erotic dream involving a certain Wyatt Locke. Knowing a sexy guy like Wyatt was around certainly could cause a girl to rush through her morning ablutions. Cold water could do that, too, and she'd danced her way through a freezing shower.

At least her skin would look pink and healthy after that onslaught. But the hair dryer she'd brought wouldn't work, which had meant towel-drying her hair, which wasn't the optimal method for fluff. She'd wanted to look cute for him, so she'd taken a little extra time to create a bouncy ponytail. A light application of makeup and she'd been good to go.

Her outfit couldn't be changed. She'd brought something fun to wear, thinking she'd just be hanging out with the girls until she went home this morning. She had, however, forgotten to bring another pair of shoes, and the heels just didn't go with her casual clothes. She'd opted for no shoes at all, figuring she could borrow the same rain boots she'd worn before if she needed to go outside.

She'd heard Wyatt's voice as she'd walked down the hallway that led through the dining room and into the kitchen, and that soft baritone had jump-started her pulse rate. By the time she'd arrived she'd been slightly out of breath, strictly from nerves. The size of her crush on him was growing by leaps and bounds.

His smile when he saw her was encouraging, and the light in his gray eyes was even more encouraging. He hadn't shaved yet and she enjoyed the fact that he had a beard going on. There was an intimacy involved in knowing this was the Wyatt she'd see in the morning if they spent the night together in a tent.

She shouldn't be entertaining such thoughts while they were in a crowd of people, though, a crowd that grew larger by the moment as Morgan showed up with SB, followed by Tyler, Emily and Dominique.

Then Sarah and Pam walked in and Sarah immediately took charge of the situation. "Time to move into the family dining room for breakfast."

Olivia had never seen the room Sarah referred to. The main dining room with its four round tables that could each accommodate eight people didn't seem like the right venue for a family meal. Instead Sarah led everyone through double doors that Olivia hadn't noticed before. Then she hit the light switch and muttered a soft curse.

"That's okay," Mary Lou said. "I can fix this." Shortly she returned with a candelabra, each taper lit. "Voilà."

"Breakfast by candlelight," Emily said. "I love it. I'll have to try that with Clay after he gets home."

Olivia was entranced. The flickering candles revealed a table perfectly sized for the number of guests eating breakfast. In no time Sarah, Pam and Mary Lou had everyone set with dishes, utensils and cloth napkins, all matching.

The food arrived in shifts, and Olivia soon realized that the hands down at the bunkhouse were cooking on the barbecue grill. She recognized Watkins, Mary Lou's sweetheart, as the delivery man. The meal was chaotic, fun, and somehow she ended up sitting next to Wyatt.

His knee touched hers under the table, and when he didn't move it, she decided he'd meant to do that. The point of contact felt warm and sent squiggles of awareness through the rest of her.

Wyatt unfolded his napkin and laid it in his lap before glancing over at her. "How did you sleep?"

It could have been an innocent question, a simple conversation-starter, but she knew it wasn't. "Fine."

"Really?" He sounded disappointed.

"You didn't want me to sleep well?" She couldn't keep the teasing note out of her voice.

"Well, yeah, of course I wanted you to sleep well. I'm glad you did. That's great." He passed her a platter of scrambled eggs. "Want some eggs?"

"Thanks." She started to take it from him.

"Go ahead and dish yourself. I'll hold it for you."

"Okay." She took a couple of spoonfuls. Apparently lust made her hungry, because she could hardly wait to tuck into the food.

The bacon came around next, followed by hash

browns and then toast. Each time Wyatt repeated his gallant gesture of holding the platter while she loaded her plate. He was so cute. She had the strongest urge to lean over and kiss him on his bristly cheek, but that wasn't appropriate in front of all these people, even in the subdued light of candles.

Conversation flowed around the table. Most of it had to do with family matters that didn't concern them, so after the food was all served Olivia and Wyatt were free to continue where they'd left off.

"I trust you slept well, too," she said.

He chewed and swallowed a bite of toast. "Like a baby. Didn't move all night long."

She lowered her voice. "I know that's not true. You took Rodney outside again."

"And how would you happen to know that?"

"I watched you walk him over to the spruce tree."

"Hmm." He didn't look at her, but his cheek creased in a smile. "That was a couple of hours after you went to bed, Olivia."

"So, maybe I didn't sleep quite *that* soundly."

He continued to eat without looking at her. "I guess not. I was pretty quiet going downstairs."

"The stairs creak."

"Not much." He concentrated on his meal for a few moments. "So you heard me go downstairs and went over to the window? Is that what you're saying?"

"I was just curious."

"And awake."

"Maybe."

"Too bad you didn't slip on a bathrobe and come out

there with me. It was nice. A half moon, some stars, a few stray clouds, the sound of a dog tinkling…"

Fortunately she didn't have a mouthful of food when he said that or things would have turned ugly. As it was she got the giggles and had to use her napkin to wipe her eyes.

"What's so funny over there?" Dominique asked.

"Rodney," Olivia said between fits of laughter.

"Rodney's in the dining room?" Sarah glanced around. "We need to move him out of here, then. We're trying to break him of begging, but it's slow going."

"Rodney's not in here," Mary Lou said. "I made sure he was in his bed asleep in the kitchen before we all came in. I think he had a hard night."

"Yeah, how did that go?" Tyler asked. "We could *not* get that dog to go outside in the rain. He was like this immovable object."

"They used dog treats," Mary Lou said. "Right, Wyatt?"

Tyler smacked her forehead. "Brilliant. So he went, then?"

"Uh, no," Wyatt said. "We got him out there, but he didn't go. At least I don't think he did."

Olivia did her best to look nonchalant during Wyatt's explanation and hoped to hell nobody could tell from her expression that some hanky-panky took place under that spruce tree.

"I took him up to my room so I could keep an eye on him," Wyatt continued. "A couple of hours later, he started pacing, so I took him out again. This time the rain had stopped, so we had liftoff. Or 'lift-up,' I guess you'd say."

"I can see why Olivia was so entertained." Dominique grinned at him. "You're a funny guy, Wyatt. I'm glad you decided to pay us a visit."

"Me too," he said. "And I apologize for the scruff at the breakfast table. I took Rod out first thing and then was lured into the kitchen by the smell of coffee so a razor blade never made it into the mix."

"Hey," Tyler said. "Without hot water, this girl is not getting in the shower, so you can be as scruffy as you want to be, dude. I won't complain."

Sarah beamed at him. "Besides, anyone who's been that dedicated to my dog's bathroom needs is not going to get a lecture from me about appearing with whiskers at the breakfast table. Thank you, Wyatt."

"Anytime." He drank the last of his coffee. "But I'm starting to feel like the hobo who appears at the back door for a handout, so if you'll all excuse me..."

"The water will be cold," Tyler said. "I know you're a wilderness guide and all that, but if you want my advice, you'll wait for the power to come back on."

"I don't mind cold showers." He pushed back his chair. "Oh, wait. My shaving kit's over at the Bunk and Grub."

Sarah waved a hand dismissively. "No problem. I'm sure there's a pack of disposables and a can of shaving cream in the bathroom next to your bedroom. Just use what you need. But I agree with Tyler. Wait until the power's back on."

"But there's no predicting when that will be, right?"

"No," Sarah admitted.

"Then I'll take my chances with the cold water."

"If you must, you must, then. I can't remember what

else is up there, but I've tried to keep travel-sized toiletries in that bathroom for whoever's staying in that wing. Help yourself."

"I appreciate it." He paused. "I, um, heard there's a sacred Shoshone site on the ranch. I'd like to go see it this morning, if that's okay."

"Of course it's okay," Sarah said immediately. "That's part of your heritage, after all. It's easy to find, but if you'd like somebody to go with you…"

"I'm sure I can find it." Then he turned to Olivia. "Have you been there?"

She wasn't prepared for a direct question and stumbled over her answer. "No, but I thought…I mean, that's really only for…I've never been invited to go, so I—"

"For heaven's sake, go, both of you," Sarah said. "It's a lovely spot, and you should see it, Olivia. We haven't opened it up to tourists and never will, but friends of the family are definitely free to go out there. I think that's a great idea."

"Good." Wyatt pushed back his chair and stood. "I can use my truck to pull Olivia's Jeep out of the ditch after we get back. That'll give the sun a chance to dry up some of the mud."

"No rush." Coffee mug in hand, Sarah relaxed against her chair. "Unless you have plans, Olivia, you're welcome to stay as long as you want."

"What a lovely offer." Sarah's warm welcome felt good, very good. "All I have is chores at home. Well, and checking on my dad. But I'm off tomorrow, too, so I have leeway."

"Speaking of chores," Wyatt said. "I'll help with the

dishes before I get cleaned up. With the power out, there's no dishwasher."

As if in direct response to his comment, the hammered metal chandelier lit up. Everyone cheered and clapped for the return of life as they knew it.

Olivia was happy that no one else would have to take cold showers like the one she'd endured, and that the dishwasher could take care of the breakfast dishes. Electricity was a good thing. But she'd enjoyed doing without it since yesterday.

With candles and a fire the evening had been more romantic. And she agreed with Emily that breakfast by candlelight was an awesome idea. Wyatt seemed like the perfect guy to share those things with, too.

ONCE WYATT KNEW THAT supplies had been left in the upstairs bathroom in what was essentially the guys' wing, he decided to do a thorough search. Maybe he wouldn't find what he was looking for, but then again, someone might have left a box behind.

In the cupboard under the sink he hit pay dirt, a box with six foil packages inside. They were even the brand he normally bought. If he took two, he'd replace them later.

Maybe this was a forgotten box that would never be used. But if some guy had left them here thinking he'd have a stash for a future event, Wyatt didn't want to leave him in the lurch. These had been available when Wyatt desperately needed them and he'd pay it forward.

He wasted no time showering and shaving, although from now on every time he used a razor he'd mourn for that perpetually sharp blade Olivia's dad had invented.

Some might say her father shouldn't have sold out, that if he'd persisted in bringing his blade to market, he would have contributed to the advance of civilization.

Wyatt couldn't fault the guy for the way he'd handled things. Economics was Rafe's department, not Wyatt's. For all he knew, a perpetually sharp razor blade might cause companies to fold and stocks to plummet.

Then there was the selfish part of the equation. The money from the sale of that invention had financed Olivia and her father's move to Shoshone. That action had put her, literally, in Wyatt's path. He wasn't about to criticize her father for selling out.

He wasn't about to criticize her father for anything now that he knew how sensitive she was about her eccentric dad. Wyatt wondered if it bothered her that he was far less loyal to his parents, especially his mother. Surely the commitment level of the parent factored into a child's loyalty.

From what he'd gathered, Olivia's father had been completely committed to Olivia, which was why he'd hustled her off to a beauty salon when he'd recognized his shortcomings in the matter of hairstyling. That whole story touched Wyatt's heart, from the initial tragedy of losing Olivia's mother to the warmhearted beauticians who had welcomed a motherless little girl into their midst.

Olivia's story was nothing like his, and although she'd lost her mother, she'd had buckets full of love to compensate for that loss. He'd had…not much. His father had worked long hours in an attempt to keep up with his wife's spending. Any free time had been split between his sons and the endless demands of a narcissistic wife. Rafe and Wyatt had come out on the short end of the stick.

Harlan Locke had done the best he could but Rafe and Wyatt had basically been on their own. That's what he wanted Jack to understand, once he could talk to him in a neutral setting, maybe around a campfire. Wyatt had great hopes for a camping trip with his half brother.

But Jack wouldn't be home until the end of the day, and Wyatt had plans for the hours between now and then. Putting on another pair of Jack's jeans and a black Western shirt, he thought again about how right the clothes felt. Even the boots fit, which was an unusual coincidence.

But after he and Olivia visited the sacred site he'd make a quick trip over to the Bunk and Grub for his clothes. Whistling, he descended the stairs and found Olivia sitting in the living room waiting for him. No one else seemed to be around.

She stood and walked toward him, her ponytail swaying and rain boots on her feet. She held out a gray felt cowboy hat. "Sarah wanted you to borrow this. She tried to get me to take one, but a hat won't work with the way I did my hair."

"I have a baseball cap in my truck. You could pull your ponytail through the hole in the back."

She made a face. "Then I'll end up with hat hair. I'm not really a hat sort of person."

"Suit yourself." He smiled at her as he took the hat. "It's your nose, so it's up to you if it gets sunburned."

"Won't happen. My makeup is SPF 45."

Personally he thought the baseball cap was a more reliable option, but he knew all about choosing appearance over practicality. His mother did it constantly. Fortunately he recognized that sharing a single trait didn't make Olivia like his mother. Olivia's every action proved that she was not a self-centered egotist.

"Sarah drew me a map." Olivia patted her jeans pocket. "She said the road will be muddy, but your truck should make it fine." She gazed up at him with those incredible blue eyes. "I'm honored that you're taking me out there, Wyatt."

He thought of the foil packages he'd brought along and felt guilty. If she was thinking of this as a spiritual experience and he was focused totally on sex, that would be bad. "Um, I need to confess something." He cleared his throat. "I do want to see the site, but the main reason I suggested the trip is so that we—"

"I know that."

"You do?" He wasn't sounding particularly intelligent.

"Of course. Last night we were ready to rip each other's clothes off. Unless you've had a change of heart, we're both still in that mode."

He sighed in relief. "I haven't had a change of heart. And there was a box of condoms in the upstairs bathroom."

"Oh!" Her eyes widened.

"Did I shock you?"

"No." She moistened her lips. "But you sure as hell ramped up the excitement level for this trip."

He settled the hat on his head. "Then let's take off, little lady."

She laughed. "You really do look like a cowboy, Wyatt."

"I'll take that as a compliment."

"It was meant that way. My dad romanticized the West so much that I've always had a thing for cowboys."

He'd gathered as much the night before, and now she'd admitted it. "You realize once I get my stuff from the Bunk and Grub I'll be wearing boring old hiking clothes again. I could lose all my appeal."

"Unless you take another approach."

"I'd rather not spend the rest of the day shopping for cowboy duds, if that's what you have in mind."

"Nope, that's not what I meant." Her eyes held a mischievous gleam.

"What, then?"

"I'm thinking you might want to just forget about the clothes entirely. Go with the natural look."

"Oh." White-hot lust shot through him. He grabbed her by the hand. "Come on. Let's get the hell out of here." With every moment he spent with Olivia, she became more perfect for him. He just couldn't let her know that.

10

As Olivia rode shotgun in Wyatt's truck for the second time in two days, she thought about how everything had changed since the first time they'd shared the cab of a truck. She couldn't remember ever getting sexual with a guy so soon after meeting him, but getting sexual didn't mean they were headed for the altar. She'd made that clear, at least.

No question that Wyatt had to be the yummiest guy she'd ever run across, though. He was clean-shaven again and had that mint scent going on. When he'd put on the cowboy hat she'd nearly swooned with lust.

"Want the windows down or up?" Wyatt asked.

"Down is fine."

"Good." He lowered both windows with the buttons on the driver's side. "Didn't want to cause a hair issue with the wind."

"I'm not *that* focused on my hair. I just don't like hats."

"Or hat hair," he said with a grin.

"I'm a beautician. I practically grew up in a salon. I think about these things."

"I know. I'm just teasing you. You agreed to go camping with me sometime, so I know you can't be totally a girly-girl."

"I'm pretty much a girly-girl, but I realize I'm not in Pittsburgh anymore."

"So what was so important about moving out here for your dad, anyway? It sounds like Pittsburgh was home."

"It was, but my dad loves old Western movies, has a whole library of them. From the time I was a little kid, he always said if he ever came into money he'd move out to Jackson Hole, Wyoming. So the money arrived and here we are."

"And is he happy with the move?"

"Delirious." Olivia smiled fondly as she thought about how happy her father was these days. "When he's not working in his lab, he sits out on his front porch swing and stares at the mountains."

"What about the cowboy thing? Did he take up riding or get all duded up?"

"No. Says he's too old to start learning to ride and he really doesn't care about clothes. Trust me on that one. Just being here seems to be enough." She glanced over at him. "Why?"

"I'm sort of fascinated by his story, I guess. And if this is what he wanted, I'm glad his razor blade invention gave it to him. I'm also glad he talked you into coming along."

"Once I knew he was completely serious, I couldn't imagine sending him out here by himself. Besides, as I said, he'd watched cowboy movies for all those years, so for me, cowboys were heroes."

"So you came out to find yourself a cowboy?"

"Not exactly. Maybe more to window-shop."

"How's that working out for you?"

She reached over and ran a hand over his denim-covered thigh, causing the muscles to contract under her palm.

He sucked in a breath.

"So far, so good." Wow, he was pure dynamite. Touching him sent flames licking through her.

"Better cut that out if you want to actually make it to the sacred site." His voice roughened. "I've already got sex on the brain."

"I have sex on the brain, too." She gave his thigh a squeeze and moved her hand. "But I want to see the sacred site. It was mentioned when I was here for Emily and Clay's wedding, and I've been curious ever since."

"Then we'll definitely see that site before we get naked, but I'm warning you, I do intend for us to get naked. I have a bed in the back of this truck and I know how to use it."

Olivia's laugh was a little breathless. "I hadn't really thought about where we'd do the deed."

"Believe me, I have."

"Do you even care about the sacred site?" She was fast losing interest, herself.

"Sure I do, but given a choice between admiring the sacred site and admiring your naked body, I'd ditch the site in a second."

"Fortunately we don't have to choose. We're not on a timetable so I think we have a couple of hours to mess around out here, which can include viewing the site and...other things."

"Which is very lucky, because if for some reason

we're thwarted and *don't* have sex, I'm going to have to find another outlet for my frustration. Maybe I can chop a few cords of wood for Sarah."

"A cord is a lot of wood. I've learned that since living here."

"I know how much it is. I'm not exaggerating. If I can't get you naked soon, I'm liable to turn into freaking Paul Bunyan, only instead of having a blue ox, I'll have blue—"

"I get the picture." Dominique was right. Wyatt was extremely entertaining, besides being sexy as hell. "Maybe we have to just do it so you won't turn into a wood-chopping maniac. It might be my civic duty to make sure you're sexually satisfied before we drive back to the ranch."

"That's what I'm saying. I barely slept last night, and here's the kicker—I wasn't slightly interested in relieving the pressure on my own. Usually that's a reasonable option when I'm hot and bothered, but I didn't just want a climax. I wanted you."

"Same here," she said softly.

"Yeah?"

"Yeah, and I don't know what that's all about. We've only known each other since yesterday. That's crazy."

"Probably just hormones."

She nodded. "Or the phase of the moon."

"Or my cowboy outfit."

"Well, there's that. Maybe you should leave the hat on while we do it."

Wyatt smiled. "Whatever it takes, Olivia. Whatever it takes."

She didn't think it would take much, and the hat really wasn't necessary. Wyatt was hot no matter what he wore, or didn't wear.

WYATT WAS RELIEVED THAT his questions about Olivia's father hadn't aroused her suspicion. Now that he knew what had tanked her other relationships, he wondered how weird her dad actually was. But any man who had tried so valiantly to be a good father had earned Wyatt's respect before they even came face-to-face—if they ever did. Given the stakes, Wyatt felt somewhat nervous about that prospect.

But he wouldn't worry about that now because he'd been telling the truth about his lust level. Her hand on his thigh had topped it off nicely, and now he was at full capacity, the needle veering steadily toward the red zone.

He checked the truck's odometer. "We should be getting close according to the mileage on that map Sarah drew for you."

"It's off to the right, she said, and doesn't stick up very far. We're looking for a gray, flat rock." Olivia gazed out through the windshield. "I think that could be it, up ahead." Leaning forward, she put both hands on the dash. "Yep, I think so. Pull over."

He didn't need to be told twice. There was a spot on the side of the road that had been cleared of vegetation. Ruts made by previous vehicles still held some water, so he eased the truck over carefully, loathe to get stuck out here after claiming he could make it out and back on his own.

Once he was off the road he killed the engine. Ahead lay an impressive slab of granite that stuck out of the ground a foot or more. There were no markers, but he hadn't expected any. The Chance family and the Shoshones before them had wanted to keep this area on the down low.

"Let's get out." Olivia unsnapped her seat belt. "From what I heard during the wedding, you're supposed to stand on it to get the full effect."

"I tried to get my mother to tell me what this rock was all about, but she said it was stupid superstition. She's not particularly in touch with her Native American side."

"It has to do with the veins of white quartz running through the granite." Olivia opened her door. "They're supposed to give you mental clarity."

"Hang on. It's muddy out there. Let me come around and help you out."

"I'll be careful." She started down.

So much for gallantry. But at least she had on the rubber rain boots this time. He, on the other hand, was wearing Jack's old boots, and he didn't want to ruin them. Unfastening his seat belt, he opened his door and stepped down, looking for whatever footing he could find where he wouldn't sink ankle-deep.

"Wyatt, you have to come and see this!"

He glanced over and discovered she'd already made it to the rock. Sitting on the edge of it, she pulled off her boots and left them sitting in the mud as she swung herself up on the granite slab and walked barefoot to its center. "I love it," she said. "This is a special place. I can feel it."

He wasn't sure if he loved the site or not, but he loved watching her standing there, feet spread, toes flexing against the smooth stone. She might have spent most of her life in beauty salons, but she would adapt to the outdoors. He sensed an adventurer's spirit in her.

But he'd be wise not to comment on that, either, in case she'd think he was trying to mold her into his perfect companion. Funny, but he'd always imagined he'd end up with a fellow hiker, someone who already owned boots with a serious tread and a GPS. Instead he was weaving fantasies about a beautician who'd never been camping in her life.

He chose a route over to the rock that would minimize the amount of mud he'd get on the boots. In retrospect, he should have worn the pair of rain boots he'd used last night. But they didn't look as cool as Jack's cowboy boots, and now that he knew Olivia's weakness for cowboys, he couldn't help wanting to fit the image.

"Just a suggestion," she said as he approached, "but I would sit on the edge and take off my boots, if I were you. And your socks, too. I think the way to experience this rock is barefoot."

"You're experiencing something?" He agreed there was no point in tracking mud on the weather-polished surface of the rock, which had recently been washed clean by rain, so he sat on the edge and took his boots and socks off, as she'd suggested.

"Yeah," she said softly. "I am. I feel...lighter."

Swinging around to face her, Wyatt got to his feet. He'd heard the theory that certain rocks transmitted energy, and he couldn't deny that in the iron-rich red rocks of Utah and Arizona he'd felt something vibrant in the air. Some of his clients wouldn't hike in those areas. They said the red rock agitated them too much.

This was different, though. The rock felt cool and soothing under his feet as he walked toward her. A gentle sense of peace flowed through him and he let out his breath in an easy sigh.

"Look at how it sparkles in the sun." Olivia pointed to the veins of white quartz running like zebra stripes through the granite.

As Wyatt's glance roamed the surface of the rock, the quartz glittered beneath his feet. "That's kind of pretty."

She held out her hand. "Come closer."

When he touched her warm skin, something flowed between them, a light current that pulsed through his system, making him aware of his surroundings as if he'd never quite seen them before. The green of the trees seemed richer and the blue of the sky grew more intense.

He picked up the scent of wildflowers just beginning to bloom and the quiet drone of bees. He was hyper-aware of Olivia watching him, her pink lips parted, her blue eyes filled with wonder. He heard her soft breathing and found himself matching that rhythm.

He didn't realize that he'd gradually closed the distance between them until she lifted her face to his and all he had to do was lean down for his lips to touch hers in a slow, easy kiss. Nothing in his life had ever been this innocent, this sweet. His breath caught.

Pictures flitted through his mind—Olivia walking down an aisle strewn with flowers, Olivia laughing on a beach somewhere, Olivia cradling a newborn baby. Lifting his head, he looked into her eyes and saw his future. He opened his mouth to tell her.

But then, even though the gauzy pictures lingered

in his mind, he remembered. If that future was to become reality, he couldn't go after it. He couldn't pursue the dreams that tempted him so. He had to let them
come to him.

"Come back to the truck with me." His voice was
rusty with emotion. "I need you."

"I need you, too."

That was all he had to hear. Swinging her up in his
arms, he carried her back across the smooth rock. He
stepped into the mud, not caring, and took her to the
back of the camper.

He was forced to set her on her feet in the mud while
he opened the back window and let down the tailgate.
Then she climbed in and he climbed after her, muddy
feet and all. Nothing mattered but the fever in his veins
and the hope that if he made this ultimate connection
with her, the wispy images that had taunted him as they
stood on the rock would gain form and substance, would
have a chance to become reality.

She started taking off her clothes. Thank God she
was as eager for this as he was, because undressing her
in the cramped quarters would have been a challenge.
Although he'd insinuated that he knew how to use his
camper as a seduction site, he never had. He'd only
slept solo back here.

Tents were infinitely better for making love, but desperate times called for desperate measures, and she
seemed to understand that. Sitting on the quilt covering his double mattress in the back of his truck, she
pulled off her T-shirt and unhooked her bra.

He yanked open his shirt and wrenched it off before sitting on the tailgate to get out of his jeans and his

briefs. He stuffed his clothes in a corner after extracting the all-important condom from his pocket. Then he set his borrowed hat on top of the balled-up jeans.

"You're not going to wear it?"

He gazed into the dim light of the camper's interior. She was stretched out on the quilt, propped up on one elbow, every scrap of clothing gone. His heart thudded wildly in his chest. She was...incredible.

He had to clear the emotion from his throat before he could speak. "The condom, yes. The hat, no. If I have to wear a Stetson to make an impression on you, then I obviously need some lessons in how to please a woman."

"You're right. It would only get in the way."

"Exactly." Tearing open the condom package, he took care of that chore so he could concentrate all his attention on her. He happened to be down by her feet, so he decided to start there. "You got a little muddy."

"I don't care."

"I can fix that." Using a corner of the quilt, he wiped the mud from her feet. Then he kissed each sparkly toe before moving to her ankles. Such sexy ankles. Lifting each one, he paid homage to it with his mouth and his tongue.

She moaned and arched against the quilt. "How long...before you get...to the good stuff?"

"It's all good stuff." He traced the curve of each calf with his tongue and angled her leg to reach the backs of her knees.

"But I want—" She gasped as he kissed the inside of her thighs, drawing ever nearer to his ultimate destination.

"I know." He blew softly on her moist curls. Light

brown. Now he knew what color her hair *really* was. "But didn't you say anticipation made it better?"

"No fair using that against me."

Sliding up the smooth length of her body, he looked into her eyes. "I promise never to use anything against you. That's not what friends do."

"Wyatt." She cupped his face in both hands. "When we were standing on the rock, did you…was there a feeling of…?" Her uncertain gaze searched his.

"Don't analyze it, Olivia." He didn't want to scare her away. "Just let me love you." He kissed her then, thoroughly, with lots of tongue, while he stroked her full, glorious breasts. Instinctively he'd known she'd feel like this, her skin pulsing and warm beneath his fingers as she arched into his caress.

Her response threatened to end his control and turn him into a rutting beast concerned only with his own satisfaction. He reined in the impulse to abandon the seduction and take her in one satisfying thrust. Lifting his mouth from hers, he began moving down, taking each nipple in his mouth, coaxing her to reward him with soft cries of delight.

She was a banquet, and he was the honored guest. His heart rate jumped as he kissed his way down the valley between her ribs, paid homage to her navel and settled at last between her thighs. Her intoxicating scent rose to meet him as her breath grew ragged.

"Wyatt…"

"I'm here." He lowered his head. "Right…here." He touched down, and she cried out in complete abandon. And that was what he was after, total surrender. He used his tongue to pleasure her and wrenched another cry from her lips. And another, and another, until she filled the morning air with her cries and came in a rush of sweet moisture, her body taut and quivering beneath him.

He'd achieved his initial goal of giving her a climax, but those dreamlike pictures in his mind wouldn't materialize unless they achieved a more basic connection, soul to soul. Rising above her, he sought her pulsing center and drove home.

11

TREMBLING FROM HER ORGASM, Olivia had no breath to ask for what she wanted. She'd come in a shower of pleasure, but an ache remained, one that could only be filled if he would just…yes. He was there. One swift movement of his hips and he was buried deep, joined with her in the way she'd longed for. She hugged him close and wrapped her legs around his, drawing him in tight.

"Easy." His breath was warm against her ear. "Don't hold me too tight or I can't move."

She gulped for air. "I don't want you to move. I want you right there."

He rocked forward. "There?"

"Yes." She lifted her hips, pressing her sensitive trigger spot against his body, pressing, squirming, until… the explosion came again, making her buck in his arms and gasp out his name.

"Ah, Olivia." His soft chuckle tickled the inside of her ear. "My amazing Olivia. Loosen your hold and we can do that again."

Lost in the wonder of her shuddering response, she heard him as if from a distance, but she relaxed her grip, allowing him to move. And move he did, easing away and sliding home in slow, steady strokes.

She moved with him, surrendering to his rhythm, loving the sweet feel of his cock caressing her so intimately. Lovely. Not mind-bending like before, but if this was good for him, then she'd— *Oh*...he shifted, came in from a slightly different angle.

She moaned as he made contact with a spot deeper, more elusive. He sought out that spot again, and yet again. A coil of tension wound within her.

"Tell me." His voice was a low growl. "Is that good?"

She began to pant. "Yes."

"How good?" He moved faster.

"Very...very...oh...Wyatt..."

"This time will be for both of us." His breathing roughened. "Come for me, Olivia. I can't hold off much longer."

She rose to meet him, glorying in the power of each stroke. "Don't wait," she murmured. "Take what you need. Take it!"

With a bellow of satisfaction he pushed deep, and that was all she needed to be hurled over the edge with him. Her spasms blended with his as they clung to each other in the whirlwind they'd created...together.

Gradually his tense muscles relaxed as he settled against her. She welcomed the feel of his warm chest covering her, although he kept the pressure light, not giving her his full weight. She wasn't surprised that he'd be considerate when he was in bed with a woman. He was that kind of guy.

Stroking his back, she listened to his breathing as it evened out and her thoughts returned to her experience on the rock. Standing there with him had felt so…so *right*. If the rock was supposed to give a person mental clarity, then the message she received had been crystal clear. Wyatt was good for her.

She wasn't about to base her whole future on a feeling she'd experienced standing on a piece of quartz and granite, but for that one moment, she'd been convinced Wyatt was the one. Probably just a hormonal reaction.

But something she did know for sure—he was incredible in the sack. She hoped they'd find time for more of this particular activity. Once Jack and the rest of the guys came home, though, that might be tricky.

Outside the truck a bird gave a little concert, trilling and warbling like crazy. "I feel like that bird," she murmured.

"No, you don't." He caressed her bare shoulder. "A bird has feathers."

"I meant I feel like that *inside*."

"That's not true, either. I've been inside, and you're smooth, and warm and very wet, but no feathers."

"You're ridiculous." She pinched his butt.

"Ow."

"I'm trying to tell you I feel happy."

"Good." He nuzzled the side of her neck. "Me too."

"But we probably should head back. I don't want anyone to get worried and come looking for us."

"Good point." Wyatt propped himself up on one elbow and gazed down at her.

She smiled. "But I wouldn't mind doing this again sometime."

"Excellent." He dropped a quick kiss on her mouth. "I'll get dressed outside and leave the camper to you."

His gray eyes glowed with warmth. "See you in a few minutes." Easing away from her, he left the truck.

She took a deep breath. Wow. What a great guy. She sure hoped things worked out with Jack, because she wouldn't mind having Wyatt make that move to Jackson Hole.

On the way back to the ranch Olivia got a little more background on Wyatt's life when he was a kid growing up in San Francisco. He spent way more time describing his friends from high school and college than he did talking about his family. She could understand. Between having a mother like Diana and dealing with her recent divorce from his father, Wyatt would probably like to avoid discussing his family.

When they walked back into the ranch house they met Sarah coming from the wing where her bedroom was located.

"You're just in time for lunch!" She beamed at them as if they were cherished guests. "That hat looks terrific on you, Wyatt."

"I appreciate the loan, but I should give it back to you—"

"Not yet. Keep it until you get one of your own. Anyway, to catch you up on the doings, Pam's gone back to the B and B, but the girls all decided to stick around here for the rest of the day because we don't see as much of each other as we used to now that everyone has her own place. Come on back and have some lunch."

Olivia felt a pang of uneasiness. "You're sweet to invite us, Sarah, but it seems like this is family time."

"Don't be silly. You're like family. Come on down to the dining room with me."

"Olivia's right," Wyatt said. "You deserve some privacy with your daughters-in-law and your grandkids. Besides, we both have things to do and we might as well get them accomplished. I need to go back over to the Bunk and Grub to pick up my stuff, and on the way I can pull Olivia's Jeep out of the ditch."

"Good plan." Olivia appreciated him coming up with a reason to leave.

"Well, I suppose you will have to do those things eventually, so you might as well get them out of the way now, before the men come back."

"Exactly," Wyatt said.

"But I'm inviting you for dinner tonight, Olivia. We'll have a big celebration for the guys coming home from their successful trip. You can either drive yourself or have Wyatt bring you, whatever makes sense. But I've so enjoyed having you here. You fit right in, like you're one of my girls."

For one embarrassing moment Olivia thought she might burst into tears. She'd missed the mothering she'd received from the women at A Cut Above more than she'd realized. She cleared the unexpected emotion from her throat. "Thank you," she said. "I'd like that."

"Good. It's settled, then. What did you think of the sacred site, by the way?"

Olivia's cheeks grew warm. "Fascinating," she said. "Absolutely fascinating."

Sarah gazed at them with a knowing smile. "I thought you'd like it out there."

"It was great." Wyatt's tone was nonchalant, as if all they'd done was take a drive to see the sights. "Thanks for giving us directions."

"You're welcome. Well, I'm sure Mary Lou wonders where I am, so I'd better get back to the kitchen. See you both later. Make sure you get here before dark. That road desperately needs grading after the rain, but you'll find it easier if you can see the ruts."

"Will do," Wyatt said.

Once Sarah was gone, Olivia turned to him. "Nicely handled."

He grinned at her. "You, on the other hand, turned the color of a stop sign."

She groaned. "I know. I'm sorry."

"Don't worry about it. I think Sarah knows something is going on between us. After all, she's raised three boys, so it's not like she doesn't understand. If she disapproved, we'd know it right away."

"I guess so." She glanced at him. "That hat really does look good on you."

"Maybe so, but I doubt I'll be wearing it again. A Stetson doesn't go with hiking shorts and a T-shirt, which is what I'll have on once I've picked up my clothes from the Bunk and Grub."

"I'm guessing you don't want Jack to come home and find you wearing his old clothes."

"Good guess. Or his hat."

"Then let's get on with that program. I'll run upstairs and grab my totes." As she hurried up the stairs, she couldn't help feeling a little sad that she wouldn't be sleeping here tonight. But she had a perfectly fine house that she liked, even if it didn't have the ambiance of the ranch house.

She hadn't realized until staying overnight that part of that ambiance was the scent of varnished logs permeated with wood smoke, overlaid with the aroma of leather and lemon oil furniture polish. The house not only looked like it belonged on a ranch, it smelled as if it did.

She quickly gathered her bags and made sure she hadn't left anything in the bathroom. Maybe Sarah would decide to have another night of beauty at the end of the summer, after the teenagers had left. Olivia hoped so. She'd like to be invited back.

But as she reached the top of the stairs and gazed down at the man waiting for her, she realized that he'd been a big part of the reason she'd loved staying here. She couldn't imagine this place without Wyatt, and yet his continued presence on the ranch wasn't assured. She hoped he wouldn't turn into a bone of contention between Sarah, who wanted him here, and Jack, who hadn't acted as if he did.

Wyatt was right to insist on changing into his own clothes before Jack came home. Sarah might not think anything of it, but if Jack already considered Wyatt an interloper, seeing him in his clothes would make everything worse. Wyatt did look great in them, though. Just looking at him made her hot.

He watched her come down the stairs, a gleam in his eyes that suggested he was having similar thoughts. "Ready?"

She laughed softly. "For what?"

"You're a bad girl, Olivia."

"Don't pretend you're not thinking the same thing, because I can see it in your face."

"Who, me? All I'm thinking about is getting your Jeep out of a ditch."

"Then the prospect of doing that must really turn you on, cowboy."

"I'm not a—"

"Can you ride a horse?"

"Yes."

"Do you respect women?"

His gray eyes twinkled. "Yes."

"Are you kind to old people, kids and animals?"

"Yes." He began to laugh.

"I've watched hundreds of cowboy movies with my dad, and you just passed the test. Plus you look great in those clothes, so I now pronounce you a cowboy."

"If you say so. Now let's go see about your Jeep."

"Oh, that's the other thing. You rescue damsels in distress. Can't forget that."

"Nope." He held the door for her. "I'm not likely to forget it, either. That was the first time I got my hands on you. Here. Let me carry those for you." He took her totes just as music started coming from one of them.

"Let me keep that one. My dad's calling."

"I should have known when I heard the theme from *The Good, the Bad and the Ugly.*"

"Oh, yeah. He loves those old Clint Eastwood spaghetti Westerns. Excuse me a minute." Pausing in the gravel driveway, she answered her phone.

"Hey, Livy. Thought you might be home by now."

"Not quite, Dad." She usually spent a couple of hours with him on Sunday playing chess, but she'd warned him she wasn't sure how this Sunday would turn out. Boy, had that been on the money. "Do you need anything?"

"Just wondered if we'd get in that chess game."

"Um, let me give you a call when I get home. I've been invited to come back here for dinner, so I'm not sure how much extra time I'll have."

"Oh, that's okay, Livy. We can skip it."

"Maybe we can schedule it for tomorrow instead."

"If you have time, but don't worry if it doesn't work out." He sounded cheerful, as he always did. She'd never seen her father in a bad mood.

"I'll call you when I get home, Dad. Bye for now. Love you."

"Love you, too, sweetheart."

She disconnected the phone and glanced up to discover Wyatt watching her, and the gleam of desire in his eyes had been replaced by something more poignant. He seemed almost...wistful. "My dad and I usually play chess on Sundays for a few hours," she said. "He just wondered if the game was on or off."

Wyatt perked up. "So you play chess?"

"I do. You?"

"I've been known to. Maybe we should play sometime."

She smiled, recognizing immediately that he was into it. "I warn you, I've been taught to play by a guy who tests out at the genius level on a standard IQ test. But if you're ready to be beat, I'll happily take you on."

"Okay. And just so you know, I can lose to a woman without whimpering."

"Good to hear, because I hate that. Whimpering puts a real damper on my sex drive. Maybe we could take a chess set when we go on that camping trip."

"I'll plan on it."

"Great." But her mind was no longer on chess. From

the moment her dad had called she'd been mulling over a somewhat radical idea. She liked Wyatt. Really liked him. What if he turned out to be like the others she'd thought were nice until they made fun of her dad?

The closer she and Wyatt became, the more she'd worry about that. But not if she took action now. True, she'd risk ending something that had been great so far, but if she didn't take this step she'd risk future disillusionment and heartache. It was a no-brainer.

But she'd have to sound übercasual about it. "After we get my Jeep out, how would you like to follow me home and see my house?"

"Great."

"I probably should stop by my dad's, too, and see if he's low on groceries. I usually check that out when I'm there on Sundays. You can come along, if you want."

"Uh, okay."

She noted he sounded less enthusiastic about that part. "No big deal." She laughed. "It's not like I'm officially taking you to meet him or anything. It's just that I'd like to spend time with you this afternoon, but I should probably at least poke my head in and check out his food situation. You could always wait for me at my house, I guess."

"No, no, I'll go with you." He was making a valiant attempt to cover his reluctance.

She gave him points for that. Her suggestion obviously had taken him by surprise, but he was rolling with it. The more she thought about this plan, the better she liked it.

Her dad was...different, and people couldn't seem to resist commenting on his eccentricities. She could tolerate it when the comments came from casual acquaintances, but not from a guy she had feelings for. Much as she was resistant to admit it, she was beginning to have feelings for Wyatt.

She thought about warning him that most likely the house would be a mess and her dad would be roaming around in his "lab coat," which was really a ratty white bathrobe he loved to wear. If they were lucky he wouldn't offer them something to eat. His food inventions usually combined ingredients never meant to coexist.

But she decided against issuing any warnings or making any defensive statements. The less she said about her father at this point, the more she'd discover what kind of guy Wyatt really was.

12

WYATT CARRIED A TOW CHAIN in his truck and the road had dried enough that hauling Olivia's Jeep out of the ditch didn't take long at all. She seemed impressed with his efficiency and he didn't mind winning more points, but it wasn't a particularly heroic feat.

Meeting her dad would be a much bigger test of his worthiness. Yeah, he was a little apprehensive about that. If it had been up to him he would have put the moment off a while longer. Then again, maybe it was a good thing to get out of the way.

Deciding to pick up his clothes from the Bunk and Grub on the way back to the ranch, he followed Olivia to her house, a neat little two-story Victorian on a side street a block away from Shoshone's central business district. On a Sunday afternoon the streets were deserted.

He parked behind her in the driveway next to the house. The place was old enough to have a detached garage, but someone had kept the property in tip-top shape. The house was painted a sunny yellow with white trim. Two hanging baskets of petunias brightened the front porch along with a couple of white wicker rockers.

Wyatt liked the whole rocker-on-the-porch concept, although he still hadn't taken advantage of the ones at the ranch. He couldn't complain, though. He'd much rather have spent the morning having hot sex with Olivia than lounging on the porch at the Last Chance.

She climbed down from her Jeep and then pulled her totes out. "We can walk to my dad's from here," she said. "I called him from the road and I'm afraid he insisted on making us lunch. I tried to talk him out of it, but in the end it was easier just to agree."

"That's fine." He had a hunch that an eccentric genius might come up with some oddball combinations, but at least the guy sounded hospitable. Good thing Wyatt had a cast-iron stomach.

"I appreciate you being flexible. I just need to put my bags inside. Come on in and see the place."

"Thanks." He followed her over to the small porch, curious to see what her house would look like.

"I'm still getting settled." She opened the screen door and shoved the key in the lock. "I didn't bring much with me from Pittsburgh. What I had wasn't really worth moving, the kind of secondhand stuff you buy when you're starting out."

"Right." He'd have to take her word for it. When he'd moved into his first apartment, his mother had insisted he take all the rec room furniture, which she pronounced "ruined" after the one and only party he'd had for friends after graduating from college. One coffee table had a slight scratch. Technically it was secondhand, but not the way Olivia meant it.

He followed her through the front door with its leaded-glass insert and found himself in a room full of rainbows. Sunlight streamed through the living room windows and the faceted crystals she had hanging in them.

"Beautiful," he murmured.

"Cheap decorating. It kind of makes up for the lack of furniture."

"Yeah, but what you have is great." An overstuffed sofa covered in denim with a couple of colorful throw pillows was the only piece in the room other than a cabinet holding a small flat-screen TV. It was what Wyatt thought of as a make-out couch—long, wide and cushy.

Too bad he and Olivia had other things to do. He had no trouble imagining how he could draw her down on those plump cushions and coax her out of her clothes. He still had a condom burning a hole in his pocket.

"We should go," she said gently. "I told my dad we were on our way."

He snapped out of his erotic daze.

Olivia had put down her bags and was gazing at him with amusement.

"Sorry. But it's a great sofa."

"I thought so when I bought it."

He decided there was no point in being subtle. "I was thinking about how much fun we could have on it."

"I could tell."

He noticed that her eyes were about the same color as the sofa. She'd look awesome lying naked on it. "I want to kiss you so much right now, but if I do it would lead to the sofa. So let's head outside before my self-control disintegrates and I grab you."

She smiled. "Okay."

He felt very noble as he followed her out the door. "Going to lock it?"

"Nope. That's another thing I love about this place. I can run down to my dad's for a while and not worry about locking up. When I'm going to be gone longer than that, I usually do, just so the wind won't blow the door open and let in the birds and the squirrels. But I don't worry about thieves."

Wyatt took her hand as they started down the tree-shaded sidewalk. "I'd like living like that. It's not an option in my apartment building in San Francisco."

"I can't picture you in the city."

"I'm not there much. I always figured it was as good a home base as any for Adventure Trekking, since most of my clients come through my website. I've never thought it mattered where I lived, but then again, I never look forward to going home either."

"It's good to have a place that welcomes you when you walk through the door."

"You've certainly accomplished that."

She laughed. "I didn't realize how seductive that sofa was until you stepped inside my living room. Suddenly all I could think about was rolling around on it with you."

"I'm glad I wasn't the only one with a one-track mind." He squeezed her hand. "But if I'm about to meet your father, I need to get that image out of my head. In my experience, dads have a sixth sense for identifying guys with designs on their daughters."

"Not mine. He assumes that if I allowed you into my life, then you're A-okay."

"So he trusts you." Wyatt now understood why a disparaging remark about her father would cause Olivia to cut that person off at the knees. Given the unwavering confidence her dad had placed in her, she wasn't about to let him be hurt by an unkind comment.

"He does trust me," she said. "And I don't take that lightly."

"I'm sure." He loved how the sunlight brought out little flecks of gold in her blue eyes. "I'm having another one of those I-want-to-kiss-you moments."

She reached up and pressed her finger gently against his mouth. "Later," she murmured as she came to a halt on the sidewalk. "We're here."

The brick bungalow wasn't as cheerful-looking as Olivia's house, but the front yard was neat and the porch had a swing. The front door was painted dark purple.

"Interesting door," Wyatt said cautiously as they approached the house.

"Dad's choice. He thinks it's a good color for wizardry."

"Ah." Wyatt hoped to hell he was up for this. "So do you knock on the door, or say magic words, or what?"

"Nothing. He knows we're here and he'll open the door."

"He was watching at the window?"

"Nope. We just tripped a laser beam about six inches above the top porch step. It sounds a chime inside the house."

The purple door opened and Wyatt decided that Olivia's father was indeed a wizard, or at least a good impersonation of one. Tall and thin, he wore a long white robe and black sandals. His white hair puffed out from his head like dandelion seeds about to take flight. Wire-rimmed glasses perched on his long nose, which brought Wyatt's attention to piercing blue eyes. All the man needed was a staff topped with a dragon's head and he could audition for a *Lord of the Rings* production.

"Hi, Dad." Olivia stepped forward and kissed his cheek. "This is Wyatt Locke, the guy who pulled me out of a ditch this morning. Wyatt, I'd like you to meet my father, Grover Sedgewick."

Wyatt stuck out his hand. "It's a pleasure, Mr. Sedgewick. Or is it Professor Sedgewick?"

"Nope, nope." His grip was firm. "Dropped out of college. Never could get the hang of academia. And call me Grover, son. It sounds friendlier. Come on in. Lunch is ready."

Wyatt followed Olivia into a house that smelled sharp and tangy, as if it had been soaked in vinegar. The living room was chaotic, with papers and books scattered on the floor and covering the furniture. Stirring classical music played in the background, the kind with lots of drums and French horns.

Among the books and papers Wyatt caught glimpses of gadgets—creations involving wires and batteries and strangely shaped pieces of metal. The only orderly surface he could find was the wall opposite the front door.

There, marching in neat rows in an area at least four by eight feet, were framed pictures of Olivia from babyhood to womanhood. A few looked quite recent. Then the display moved on to certificates from elementary school through high school for things like spelling bees, making the honor roll and good citizenship. Wyatt had never seen more touching evidence of parental pride than this.

"That's my girl." Grover swept a hand toward the wall, just in case Wyatt might have missed it. "She's a corker."

"Yes, sir, she is." Wyatt couldn't help smiling. *Corker* was an old-fashioned word, but it fit Olivia.

Instead of being embarrassed because her father insisted on splashing her early history all over his living room wall, she simply put her arm around him and gave him a hug. "Thanks, Dad." She gazed at him with fondness. "You're a corker, too."

As she stood serenely in this disaster of a house with a father who greeted a guest in his bathrobe, Wyatt looked at her with new respect and admiration. He'd always known this was a woman he could like, and certainly a woman he could lust after. At that moment, he realized she was also a woman he could love.

THEY ATE IN THE DINING ROOM, where Olivia's father had cleared off enough of the papers to make room for three plates. Olivia watched Wyatt swallow a hot dog and peanut butter concoction without a grimace or complaint. He didn't flinch when her father brought out his "bug juice" as a complement to the meal, even though it was a ghastly shade of blue.

Lunch was a slightly larger test than she'd planned on, but she was impressed with the way Wyatt soldiered cheerfully through the meal. After having suffered through her dad's cooking all her life, she knew the food could have been worse. She was relieved that today's lunch was at least recognizable.

Conversation revolved around Wyatt's job and his reason for coming to the area. Grover seemed pleased that Wyatt was Jack Chance's half brother and might end up moving to Shoshone. Because her dad wasn't privy to community gossip, he didn't know that Wyatt and Jack's mother was persona non grata in town. Wyatt didn't bring that up, which kept the tone positive, the way her father preferred it.

As the meal wound to a close, her dad glanced over at Wyatt. "You strike me as a chess-playing man."

Wyatt sent Olivia a questioning look.

She held up both hands. "I didn't mention it. If my dad likes somebody, he usually asks if they play chess."

Wyatt seemed pleased with that. "As a matter of fact, Grover, I play a little."

"Care for a game?"

Olivia crossed her fingers. If her father suggested a chess game, that meant he wanted to get to know Wyatt better. Grover believed in learning about people by observing them during a chess match.

Once again Wyatt glanced at Olivia. "Okay with you?"

She shrugged, as if it didn't matter one way or the other. "Sure."

"All right, then, Grover. Let's set up the board."

Olivia relaxed. She hadn't realized until that moment how tense she'd felt as she'd watched the two men interact. But it would be okay. Anyone who could eat Grover's cooking with as much grace as Wyatt had could also handle being annihilated in a chess game.

To her surprise and delight, Wyatt played a decent first game. Her father still beat him handily, but then her father beat everyone handily. A couple of times in the twenty years she'd been playing him, she'd come really close to winning a game. Anyone who could give her father even a slight challenge was aces in his book.

In the second game Wyatt actually managed to make her father pause and stroke his chin, a sign that he didn't immediately know his next move. Olivia gazed at Wyatt with new respect. Not many accomplished that.

"Did I stump you, Grover?" Wyatt took another sip of his blue drink.

"Momentarily." Her dad studied the board. "Aha." Then he proceeded to take command of the game once again.

As Wyatt went down in flames for the second time, taking his defeat without excuses and complimenting her dad on his playing, Olivia longed to wrap her arms around this amazing guy and hold on tight. She thought of the way he'd looked at her sofa, and glanced at the time on her phone. The afternoon was getting away from them.

"I hate to break this up." She thought the lie was forgivable under the circumstances. "But Wyatt and I need to get moving if we're going to finish our other little chores before we head back to the ranch for dinner."

Wyatt pushed back his chair. "Guess so." He held out his hand to Grover. "You're a tough competitor and I'm looking forward to a rematch."

"Any time." Grover stood. "Any friend of Olivia's is a friend of mine."

"She mentioned that, and I feel lucky that she considers me a friend."

Grover nodded, his white hair bobbing. "You are

lucky. I need to warn you that she's picky, though. She's given three men the boot already, back when we lived in Pittsburgh."

"Because they were jerks," Olivia said. She hadn't told her father the exact reason she'd broken up with all three of those guys, and she didn't intend to.

"I think there was a little more to it than that," her father said with a smile. "But I guess it helps if you don't act like a jerk."

"I'll do my best not to, sir."

"I hope so. I'd like to keep you on as a chess partner. Now run along, both of you. I know you have things to do. Thanks for spending some time with an old man."

"You're not old, Dad." Olivia gave him a hug and a kiss on the cheek. "You're timeless. I'll call you tomorrow."

"I'd like that."

Once they were out the door, Olivia laced her fingers through Wyatt's. "Thank you. You were terrific."

Terrific didn't even cover it. He'd passed this test with flying colors, but she had to be careful not to overdo her compliments or he might suspect he'd been set up.

"You say that like I was making some sort of sacrifice. I had a blast."

"Well, I could see you were engaged in the chess game, and he is an outstanding player, but I can't believe you were okay with the food."

Wyatt laughed. "It was like being back at Scout camp when we used to dream up every gross combination we could think of. I'm pretty sure we had hot dogs and peanut butter once. It tasted very familiar."

"You really didn't mind it?"

"Hell, no! Even the bug juice made me nostalgic for those days at camp. Considering my home life, I *loved* camp. One of the counselors taught us how to play chess. I was in my element just now."

She hadn't expected that kind of response in a million years. "Then maybe I shouldn't have dragged you away."

"Oh, yeah, you should."

"But if you were having so much fun, you probably wanted to stay and wallow in nostalgia some more."

"I might have, if I hadn't known there was a certain cushy sofa waiting for us over at your house."

Now she felt better. "You think that's why I suggested we had to leave? So we could roll around naked on that sofa?"

"I hope so, because if that's not what you have in mind, then I'm going back for another game of chess with your dad."

She tightened her grip on his fingers. "My dad's had his time with you. Now it's my turn."

13

OLIVIA'S HEART RATE HAD skyrocketed by the time she and Wyatt reached her front door. "We'll have to lower the blinds," she said.

"I'll leave that to you." His voice was low and urgent. "I'm feeling so desperate I might pull the damned blind right out of the window casing, and then what would we do?"

"Go back to my bedroom." Nothing was going to stop her from having her way with him.

"Maybe we should do that in the first place. Just because I have an image of you naked on that sofa, doesn't mean—"

"Yes, it does. Anybody can do it on a bed." She drew him through the door. "Let's make some memories on the sofa."

"Yeah, let's." Shoving the door closed with his booted foot, he pulled her into his arms and kissed her feverishly as he began divesting her of her clothes. He behaved as if he couldn't get enough of her.

"The blinds…" she gasped between kisses. "We have to…"

"I know. In a minute. I just need to—" Pulling her T-shirt over her head, he unhooked her bra.

"You're crazy," she murmured, but she was just as busy unsnapping his shirt and running both hands up his lightly furred chest. "I love how you feel."

"I love how you feel, more." Cupping her breasts, he leaned down and sucked an aching nipple into his mouth.

She forgot all about the blinds. Nothing mattered but his hands, his mouth, his tongue. They wriggled out of their clothes, laughing as her zipper stuck and his boots refused to come off his feet. Her zipper finally gave way but his boots weren't so cooperative.

"I can do this with my boots on, damn it. And my jeans." He stripped hers away. "At least one of us is naked." His voice was thick with need. "The most critical one."

"I don't know about that." She was panting by the time she flopped back on the sofa. "I think you should be—"

"—kissing you all over." Kneeling beside the sofa, his shirt and his jeans unbuttoned and unzipped but still on, he proceeded to do exactly that. "You've covered with rainbows."

"That's because the blinds...are still up."

"I can't bring myself to care." He circled her nipple with his tongue.

Neither could she. She abandoned herself to the sensuous pleasure of lying naked on her sofa while Wyatt hovered over her, bestowing erotic kisses.

"There's a rainbow here." He licked the underside of

her breast. "And another one here." He touched down just beneath her navel. "Oh, and one more here."

She didn't know whether a rainbow rested at the sensitive spot where he put his mouth last, but she wasn't going to question his word. She'd experienced his expertise at this endeavor before, and she was willing to believe a rainbow had guided him there.

She was willing to believe anything he told her when he was doing…oh, yes…*that*.

"I love how you taste," he murmured, his breath hot against her moist skin. He slid both hands under her. "And how you make that little noise in the back of your throat when I do this." He settled in and began to get serious.

She had no idea what little noise he meant, because her brain had turned to mush. She probably made that noise, along with several others, as he nibbled and licked and generally drove her insane. She vaguely remembered begging him to make her come, and he did… gloriously.

As she vibrated from the intensity of it, she heard boots hit the floor and the clank of a belt buckle followed. A foil package was ripped open and then he was there, managing the gymnastics necessary to make love to her on a sofa that was almost, but not quite, long enough.

Or wide enough. She put one foot on the floor and so did he. They maneuvered and shifted, their laughter breathless, their excitement building along with their frustration.

"I know what," he said at last. "Let me sit on the sofa and you—"

"Brilliant." Which was how she ended up straddling him in the center of the middle cushion, her hands braced on his shoulders as she rode him to glory, both his and hers.

Gasping for breath, they touched foreheads.

"I love this sofa," he said. "Don't ever get rid of it."

"I won't." She gulped for air. "It's a part of history now."

"Yeah." He slid his hands from her hips to her waist. "Our first ride together."

She probably should be worried that they were talking about furniture as a history of their relationship, as if it was destined to last a very long time. But he'd been so great with her dad, and in her warm, postorgasmic glow, she couldn't be bothered to worry about anything.

True, she hadn't known him very long, and she'd promised herself that she'd take time about singling out another guy. But Wyatt had shown himself to be a hero in so many ways already. What could possibly go wrong?

ALTHOUGH WYATT WASN'T crazy about the idea of driving back to the ranch separately, he couldn't argue with the logic of it. Olivia wanted time to shower and change clothes, and he needed to go back to the Bunk and Grub and get his things. He'd called the ranch and the travelers weren't expected for at least another hour, so he had time to shower and change, too.

After dinner Olivia would go home. Not knowing how tonight would turn out, Wyatt thought it was probably best if they each had their own transportation. He expected to spend the night at the ranch, but if things went south with Jack, Wyatt could always ask if Olivia would take him in temporarily.

With a mental promise to return at some point in time, he left the yellow house with the white trim, the rainbows, and the most excellent blue denim sofa, not to mention the amazing woman he'd made love to there. He was comfortable with the term *made love* when it came to Olivia. Their connection deepened with every moment they spent together.

He would not, however, pursue her. He would love her with everything he had to offer and hope that she would pursue him. It wasn't the way he normally handled events in his life, but he was willing to adapt to the situation.

When he arrived at the Bunk and Grub, he sought out Pam in the little office she'd created right next to the living room.

She turned in her wooden swivel chair with a smile of greeting. Her blond bob shone in the afternoon light coming through a window. "I knew you'd show up sometime, but I wasn't sure when. I have your duffel bag over in the corner, ready to go. How has your day been?"

"Incredible." As he said it, he realized he'd put a hell of a lot of emotion into that one word. Probably too much if he wanted to keep things under wraps.

"It's Olivia." Pam wasn't asking. It probably only took one look at his smiling face to know, especially after seeing them gravitating toward each other last night.

"Yeah." He sighed. "It's Olivia."

"She's great. I hope you two continue to get along. Listen, do you have a minute to sit and talk?"

"Sure." He levered himself into a wingback chair in the corner of Pam's tiny office. "But first off, I want to pay you for the nights I booked here. It's not right to reserve a room and then cancel at the last minute."

Pam gazed at him. "I don't know how much you know about me."

"A little. You own this place, and you're Nick's aunt, and from what you said last night, there's some connection to Emmett Sterling, the ranch foreman."

Pam chuckled. "Oh, there is. I've had a serious crush on that guy for years, which isn't surprising. He looks like Tom Selleck and is a real sweetheart and a good dad to Emily. But he's not what you'd call wealthy, and I…am."

Wyatt nodded. "My dad's around that age, and I don't know if he could accept being with a woman who was richer than he is."

"I intend to keep working on Emmett, but the real point I wanted to make is that I don't need the money from that reservation. But if you're determined to pay it, I'll accept on one condition."

"What's that?"

"As you can imagine, Sarah and I had a couple of conversations about you."

Warmth crept up the back of Wyatt's neck. "I'm sure she's worried about whether my presence will cause trouble. That's one reason I wanted to stay with you, but Sarah wouldn't hear of it."

"Of course she wouldn't. Jack may be part owner of the ranch but Sarah still wields most of the power over there. You came with good intentions, and she wants you to feel welcome. She doesn't think anyone should tiptoe around Jack on this issue."

Wyatt nodded. "Okay. I respect that."

"But she realizes that having Jack come home to find you in his old clothes might start things off on the wrong foot."

"Exactly. That's one of the main reasons I'm picking up my things, so I can go back to the ranch and change into my own stuff."

"Shorts and T-shirts, right?"

"That's what I live in."

"It's anyone's guess what the best strategy is when it comes to Jack, but Sarah and I think it might be better if you looked less like a California dude and more like a cowboy. Besides, you can't ride a horse in shorts, and if you want to bond with Jack you'll do it best on horseback. That's where he feels most at home."

"Guess I'll go shopping first thing in the morning, then. I'd thought about doing that, anyway." Not so much for Jack, but for Olivia, who seemed to like his cowboy look.

"Or..." Pam left her desk and opened a small coat closet. "You can accept these things I picked up today in Jackson." She took a shopping bag out and brought it over to where Wyatt sat, openmouthed. "Once Sarah knew you fit into Jack's old clothes, she was able to give me the size. I've taken all the tags off because I want you to consider them a gift. I wasn't lucky enough to have kids of my own, so I spoil those Chance boys rotten and I'd be tickled to do the same with you."

Wyatt looked from the bag to Pam. She'd driven

to Jackson and spent her valuable time and money on him, someone she barely knew. He was overwhelmed by her thoughtfulness and generosity. "I don't know what to say."

"Say, 'thank you, Pam,' and then hop in your truck and head out to the ranch so you can change clothes before Jack and the other guys get home."

"Thank you, Pam." He stood and gave her a hug. In the past twenty-four hours Sarah and Pam had acted more like mothers to him than his own ever had.

"If you don't like anything I can take it back, even without the tags. They know me there."

He grinned. "I'm sure they do, but I'm not giving anything back. I'll proudly wear every stitch until it falls off me."

"One other thing. I didn't buy boots, but I don't think wearing Jack's will be a big issue. And I didn't get you a hat, either. That's something you should probably pick out for yourself. A cowboy's hat is kind of like his signature."

"Got it. Thanks, Pam. You're the best." With a heart full of gratitude he picked up the bag, grabbed his duffel from the corner, and left the Bunk and Grub.

Olivia had told him he had support in his quest to make friends with his half brother and his extended family. Apparently that was true. Now all he needed was for Jack to arrive home feeling mellow from the success of his trip and in the mood to give friendship one last chance. If Jack would just meet him halfway, Wyatt was willing to do the rest.

LESS THAN AN HOUR LATER, Wyatt finally had his first opportunity to sit on the ranch's front porch in one of the wooden rockers. After taking a quick shower and putting on one of his new pairs of jeans and a pale green yoked shirt, he'd come downstairs and discovered everyone had gathered on the porch with wine, beer and snacks to await the arrival of what Sarah had dubbed "our returning heroes."

Apparently the final tally of horses sold and stud fees collected was very good financial news for the Last Chance. Wyatt got the impression that the family sometimes struggled with being land-rich and cash-poor, but that wouldn't be the case this summer. He was happy for them.

Peter Beckett, a tall, distinguished guy in his mid-sixties, had come for the welcoming party. Sarah introduced Peter, and Wyatt liked his easy smile and firm handshake. Wyatt wasn't sure if he was supposed to congratulate them on their engagement or not.

"Sarah tells me the cat's out of the bag," Peter said, ending Wyatt's uncertainty. "Looks like I'll be joining the family soon."

"I heard that," Wyatt said. "I haven't been here long, but I can already say that anyone who's allowed to hook up with the Chance family is one lucky SOB."

"I totally agree."

"Thanks, Wyatt." Sarah leaned over and gave him a kiss on the cheek. "You look great."

"Pam's a persuasive woman." He smiled at her. "Like I said, hooking up with the Chance family comes with all sorts of benefits."

She beamed with happiness and linked her arm through Peter's. "I'm glad you think so. Now, go get yourself a cold beer and snag yourself a seat. They should be here soon."

"You bet." Feeling as if this might go well after all, he pulled a beer from a much larger cooler stocked with far more bottles than Mary Lou had provided the night before. This was shaping up to be quite a party.

Josie called him over to an empty rocker next to her. He couldn't help thinking that the chair had been saved for him because Josie wanted Jack to see immediately that she'd accepted Wyatt. Rodney padded over and plopped down at his feet. Wyatt grinned and leaned down to scratch behind the dog's floppy ears.

Josie glanced over at Wyatt as she bounced little Archie gently on her knee. "Nice duds, cowboy. Glad to see you accepted Pam's generosity."

"You knew about that?"

She chuckled. "Oh, yeah. Sarah told us what she and Pam had cooked up and we all speculated as to your reaction. You made the right choice. Pam would have been crushed if you'd refused."

"I was touched that she'd do such a thing when she barely knows me."

"You made friends here last night, Wyatt. We all want this to work out for you. Even the dog."

"Thanks, but don't feel you have to step into the breach if it starts going downhill with Jack. As I said before, I don't want to cause a problem, either between you and Jack, or Sarah and Jack."

"Then Jack will just have to behave himself, won't he?"

Wyatt smiled at her. "Guess so." He uncapped his beer and glanced toward the road. From the moment

he'd come down he'd been watching for Olivia's Cherokee and hoping she'd show up before the men did. But
the road was still empty.

He turned back to Josie. "Did you have a good day?"

"We did. Between working at the Spirits and Spurs
and taking care of Archie, I don't get much chance to
hang out with Sarah and my sisters-in-law." She smiled
at him. "But you could have stayed for lunch, you know.
Sarah said you were afraid you'd be intruding."

"Yeah, I did feel that way. And then it turned out I
got to meet Olivia's dad."

"Really." Josie stopped bouncing Archie. "She's very
careful who she takes over there, for obvious reasons.
Does she know that you know why she broke up with
her fiancés?"

"Nope." He gazed down the road.

"Well, I won't say anything. What did you think of
him?"

Wyatt took a sip of his beer. "He's a genius, is what
he is. You don't meet many of those."

"True." Archie began to fuss so Josie went back to
jiggling him on her knee. "You like her a lot, don't you?"

"Yeah, I do."

"I have a good feeling about you two. It's early yet,
but if you didn't run for the hills after meeting Grover,
that's a good sign." She picked up Archie and scooted
out of the rocker. "Time to walk around with my little
guy. He's getting restless."

Wyatt set his beer down next to his rocker and stood.
"Why don't you let me do that? My nephew and I need
to get better acquainted."

"That would be lovely." She handed him over. "But if he gets too fussy bring him back."

"He won't be fussy, will you, Arch?" He adjusted the baby in his arms and Archie looked at him with wide blue eyes. Wyatt felt a tug of recognition. Archie really did look like Rafe's baby pictures. "Come on, kid. Time to see the sights with Uncle Wyatt."

Carrying the little boy, he walked carefully down the steps, mindful of not stumbling with his precious cargo. Archie seemed to enjoy the movement and change of scenery, so Wyatt walked away from the house and down toward a corral next to the barn where a couple of paint horses milled around. Archie might like watching them.

As he drew closer to the corral, the little kid started crowing and bouncing in his arms, obviously excited about the animals. Wyatt was congratulating himself on being a really cool uncle when he heard the rumble of a truck's engine.

He turned to see a cherry-red semi tractor rig pull in, hauling a large horse trailer. Wyatt watched with a feeling of inevitability as air brakes hissed and the semi came to a halt. Jack Chance climbed down from the driver's side.

14

JACK STARED AT WYATT in obvious disbelief. "You've got my kid!"

A couple of other smaller trucks pulled in behind the horse trailer and Josie hurried down the hill, followed by the rest of the family. Even from this distance Wyatt could see the panic in her expression.

"Hello, Jack," Wyatt said. "Nice to see you again, too."

"What are you doing with my kid?"

"Giving Josie a break. Archie was starting to fuss, so I offered to—"

"You come to my house unannounced when I'm not even here. Don't you own a cell phone?"

"I should have called in advance." Guilt stabbed him.

"Damn straight you should have. This is the second time you've shown up without warning, and I don't like being caught off guard. Not only that, but I arrive home to find you toting my son around like you and he are the best of buds. I don't know much of anything about you, Wyatt Locke, except that you're Diana's son, and that's not much of a recommendation."

Josie reached him, puffing slightly from her short jog. "Jack, I told Wyatt he could carry Archie around."

"Well, if it's all the same to you, I'd rather he didn't do that." Jack closed the distance in two strides and pulled Archie out of Wyatt's arms.

"Wyatt is Archie's uncle, Jack."

Jack glanced at her. "Yeah, and that makes Diana Archie's biological grandmother, which is a sickening thought." His gaze swung to Wyatt. "Did you tell her about Archie?"

"No."

"That's a damn good thing because she has no right to this kid. He's a Chance."

"Jack..." Josie put a hand on his arm.

Jack ignored her and continued to glare at Wyatt. "You, on the other hand, are not. So keep your hands off my kid."

"You arrogant SOB." Anger curdled in Wyatt's gut.

"Jack, stop this!" Josie grabbed hold of his arm.

"Stay out of it, Josie."

"Then give me Archie." Her voice was laced with fury.

"Yeah, take him." Keeping his attention on Wyatt, Jack handed her the baby. "Get him out of here."

Wyatt clenched his fists. He wasn't going to throw the first punch, but he was sorely tempted now that Jack wasn't holding Archie. "How dare you taunt me with not being a Chance, like I had a choice in the matter? Like you did? It's all an accident of birth, Jack."

"This is *my* property, and I dare whatever I damn well please."

"Oh, yeah, the mighty Jack Chance. Judging from your arrogant attitude, I'm glad I'm *not* a Chance!"

"If that's the way you feel, why the hell did you come back?"

"God knows. But I'll tell you this. You should get down on your knees every day and thank God that my mother left you here."

"Oh, but she didn't leave *you*, now, did she?" Jack's expression was thunderous. "You didn't have to wake up one morning and find out that your mother was gone and she wasn't coming back! You didn't have to—"

"You didn't have to grow up with a mother who didn't give a damn about you! And a father who was so busy trying to please her that he barely noticed you either!" Wyatt's blood ran hot in his veins. "No, you were surrounded by people who loved you—your dad, your grandparents and later on Sarah, and this…this whole fricking *ranch!* Yeah, let's compare notes and see who had the worst of it, shall we?"

Archie started to wail at the top of his lungs.

"Get off my land." Jack's face was like granite.

"Don't worry. I've lost any desire to be here." Adrenaline pumping through his system, he stormed past Jack and the rest of the family. Sarah called out to him, and he gave her a wave that he hoped would let her know he heard her, but he couldn't respond. Not now.

When he reached the drive, Olivia had just pulled in. She hopped down, took one look at his face and came running over. "Wyatt?"

"I'm leaving, Olivia." He started up the steps. He felt as if someone had his chest in a vice and was jabbing his head with an ice pick. "You should stay, though. It's going to be a good party, and I know how much you like these folks."

"So do you!" She went up the steps with him. "Are you going to let Jack run you off?"

"I don't stay where I'm not wanted, Olivia." He drew a breath that made his lungs burn. Then he opened the front door and held it for her because she seemed determined to follow him. "Jack was here first, and all I'll do is cause tension if I stay." He didn't break stride as he headed upstairs. "I still love the area, so…we'll see."

Olivia kept pace with him. "So you're not going camping with Jack, I take it?"

His bark of laughter sounded loud in the quiet house. "Hardly."

"Will you take me, then?"

"What?" He reached the second floor and walked quickly down to the room he'd been assigned.

"Camping. Let's go."

"That's crazy." He hadn't taken time to unpack, so all he had to do was throw a few things in his duffel and zip it. He took the bag of clothes Pam had given him as well. He wasn't sure what to do about those, but he could decide that later. "We can't just go off camping."

"Why not?"

"Because…" He actually didn't have a good reason. He had some dehydrated food in the truck, plus water he always carried. He glanced at Olivia's outfit, noticing for the first time that she'd worn sneakers with her jeans and shirt, and she was carrying a zip-up sweatshirt.

"I'm not going to stay for the party if you're leaving," she said. "I came to be with you."

"I don't think I'm going to be very good company."

But the idea of heading off into the woods appealed to him. He'd cancelled his reservation at the Bunk and Grub, and he wouldn't want to stay there anyway.

"Let's do it, Wyatt. I don't have to work tomorrow. Let's spend the night together in a tent. You can teach me how to camp."

"You've been the best part of this whole experience, Olivia."

She smiled at him. "Thanks."

"All righty, then. Let's go camping. You can follow me out, and once we're off the ranch we'll figure out our next move."

"Works for me."

But when they descended the steps, they found Sarah waiting for them. Wyatt looked around for the others but Sarah appeared to be alone in the house, at least for now. She looked extremely determined.

Wyatt's gut tightened again as he walked down the stairs toward her. "Sarah, I'm really sorry. I hate that I spoiled your great homecoming celebration."

"You didn't," she said. "My son did, and I'm sure eventually he'll apologize to you for that."

Wyatt stared at her. "You're kidding, right?"

"No. One of the things I've instilled in all my boys is good manners. Jack forgot his just now, but I have every confidence he'll remember them soon."

There was a hint of steel in her words, but she kept her voice so even that it took Wyatt a moment to realize that she was furious. She did not, however, apologize for Jack. The glint in her eyes made it clear he would be expected to do that for himself.

Wyatt had no stomach for watching a battle of wills

between mother and son, not when he was the bone of contention. "It's okay, Sarah," he said gently. "You've been great to me and I appreciate that."

"I'd rather you didn't leave."

"We're going camping," Olivia said. "So I won't be here for dinner, after all. Thank you for asking me, though."

Sarah frowned. "Camping? Just like that? What about food?"

"I always carry emergency rations in my truck. We'll be fine for one night."

"That's ridiculous. Come back to the kitchen with me."

"No, really." Wyatt didn't want to linger. "We should just go. It's better if we—"

"No one's coming up to the house until I give the okay, so don't get nervous. I instructed them all to stay down by the barn until I'd had an opportunity to talk with you. Pete's in charge of making sure that's the way it goes."

"Wow," Olivia said. "You really are in charge around here."

"You bet your sweet bippy. Now come along. I'll give you some real food so you don't have to eat that reconstituted junk." Sarah marched down the hall toward the dining room and kitchen area.

Wyatt glanced over at Olivia and shrugged. Crossing Sarah right now didn't seem like a wise idea. He set down his duffel and bag of clothes, took Olivia's hand and followed Sarah to the kitchen.

Moments later they came back down the hall. Wyatt carried a soft-sided ice chest filled with frozen gel packs and stuffed with homemade spaghetti sauce, eggs, bacon and cheese. Olivia had a bag that contained a box of pasta, a loaf of homemade bread, a box of crackers and a box of red wine.

Wyatt mentally calculated whether he could get everything in his pack. He might need Olivia to carry some of the food in his spare backpack, but he'd make sure her load was light. He wanted to hike in a ways before they made camp. Getting away from civilization had never seemed more necessary than now.

"Thank you, Sarah." Wyatt glanced at Olivia. "Would you be okay with returning the ice chest and anything we don't use?"

"I expect you to return it, Wyatt," Sarah said. "I can understand that you want to go off and lick your wounds, but you need to come back."

Wyatt faced her. "I'm not sure I even want to—"

"Now you listen to me, Wyatt Locke. You started this thing, and I intend to see that you and Jack are on civil terms before you leave the ranch."

"But—"

"Just leave Olivia's Jeep here, take your truck and drive on up the road past the sacred site. The terrain rises some, and I'm sure you'll find good camping up there."

"I don't want to stay on ranch land."

"Oh, for pity's sake. Of course you do. It's getting late, and you need to make camp before it gets dark. You really don't have time to mess around looking for some other spot, Wyatt. Besides, this way you can come back tomorrow and sort this thing out with Jack."

"I don't think Jack wants to sort it out."

Sarah met his gaze and her jaw firmed. "He will."

Wyatt had never met a woman like Sarah Chance. She was one of the most loving people he'd ever known, yet also one of the toughest. He now understood why she hadn't crumbled when her husband died unexpectedly.

He still didn't believe that he and Jack would mend any fences but he wasn't going to convince Sarah of that, at least not now. Might as well go along with her plan for the time being, especially when he couldn't refute her logic. He might have trouble finding a good camping spot before dark if he insisted on leaving Chance land to do it.

"All right," he said. "I'll take your suggestion. Thank you for everything, Sarah."

"You're welcome. See you tomorrow." She stood in the doorway as they walked down the porch steps and over to Wyatt's truck.

He was aware of her watching as they loaded everything and got into the cab. Once he put the truck in gear and started toward the road leading to the sacred site, she came out on the porch and waved to the group of people waiting down by the barn.

In his rearview mirror, Wyatt saw them trooping back up to the house except for one lone figure. Wyatt was pretty sure he recognized Jack standing there, staring after the truck. His gut twisted again. He'd wanted Jack's goodwill more than he'd realized. But despite Sarah's determination, he doubted he'd ever get it.

OLIVIA WASN'T SURE WHETHER to talk to Wyatt or leave him in peace to mull over his situation. They rode with the windows down, which at least kept the drive from being silent. Small birds twittered in the meadows they passed and a hawk circled overhead and added its piercing cry to the lilting music below.

"The hawk is probably planning to eat one of those songbirds," Wyatt said.

"Now there's a cheerful thought."

"I warned you that I might not be very good company."

Olivia sighed. "Then I say let's talk about what happened instead of sitting here in silence."

"Not much to tell."

"How did everything get nasty so fast? It looked to me as if they'd just come home."

"Bad timing, maybe even poor judgment on my part. We were all sitting on the porch and little Archie started to fuss, so I told Josie I'd walk with him a little, give him a change of scenery."

She could imagine what came next. Poor Wyatt. "Let me guess. Jack came home when you were strolling around with Archie."

"I don't know why I didn't think that might happen. I was just enjoying taking the little guy down to see the horses, and somehow it didn't occur to me that Jack might not react well to me doing that. The minute I heard that heavy-duty engine, I knew I was screwed."

She reached over and rubbed his thigh. "I'm sorry." Then she paused. "Are these new? They don't feel like jeans that have been worn a lot."

Wyatt smiled for the first time since she'd met him coming up from the barn. "I think you should feel that material again to make real sure it's different from the jeans Sarah loaned me."

She was encouraged by that remark. Leaning over, she stroked his thigh again. "These are not the jeans you borrowed from Sarah."

"So do you like this feel better than the ones I had on before? Go right ahead and fondle them again if you're not sure. I don't mind."

She walked her fingers up and down his thigh. "I'm trying to solve the mystery as to how you have a pair of new jeans when you were with me practically all day and the stores in Shoshone aren't open on Sunday."

"Two words. Pam Mulholland."

"She bought these?"

"Plus two other pairs, and two more shirts. She gave them to me when I went to pick up my clothes. Too bad it was a wasted effort. She and Sarah thought it would be better if I had riding clothes so I could go out on horseback with Jack."

"Don't give up on that, Wyatt. Sarah is a powerful woman."

"I don't think even Sarah can bring Jack and me together. The gap is huge."

"How huge? You didn't tell me what was said."

"It wasn't pretty." The truck hit a rut and Wyatt wrestled with the wheel until the vehicle settled down again. "First he accused me of walking around like I owned the place."

"Ouch. That's harsh."

"Then he made it clear I wasn't a Chance and I'd better keep my mitts off his kid."

"I'm sorry, Wyatt. Didn't anyone come to your defense?"

"Josie tried but Jack was on his high horse, staking his claim to this land and letting me know I didn't belong here. So I told him to thank his lucky stars that my mother had left him here."

"Oh?"

"Yeah, I let him know that living with her had been its own kind of hell. I offered to compare situations any day of the week. Not long after that Jack ordered me off *his* land."

Olivia winced. She could see why the confrontation hadn't gone well, but she didn't think Wyatt would like what she had to say about it. He was convinced that dealing with his mother had been as bad or probably worse than being left at a tender age as Jack had been.

She was on Wyatt's side in this because he'd made the gesture toward friendship with his half brother. But that gesture would be worthless if he insisted that his life had been more miserable than Jack's. It wasn't a contest to prove who had suffered more.

But she chose not to say all that right now. They were heading up into the forest, Wyatt's favorite environment. Maybe when he was surrounded by nature he'd be able to open his mind to a new way of looking at his situation with Jack. If he stubbornly held to his current thinking, his cherished wish to unite with his half brother was doomed.

She hated that prospect for many reasons. It would mean Jack and Wyatt would miss out, but so would Sarah and the rest of the family. Wyatt was a warm and caring man, and he could enrich the family dynamics in so many ways.

But someone else would miss out, and that was her. Much as she wanted to believe Wyatt would consider settling in Shoshone whether his half brother approved or not, Olivia knew the reality. Jack's animosity, if it continued, would eventually kill Wyatt's urge to move his business here.

As for her, she was in Shoshone for the duration. It was her father's dream, and she wasn't planning to leave Grover Sedgewick to his own devices. Ever.

15

WYATT DROVE UNTIL HE spotted a trail going off to the left and up a hillside. He and Olivia didn't have much daylight left, so they needed to set up camp soon. Much as he hated to admit how right Sarah had been, leaving the ranch boundaries to find a camping spot wouldn't have worked. They'd started too late to be particular.

Fortunately he had plenty of experience in getting an expedition moving down the trail. After taking the time to switch out his borrowed cowboy boots for hiking boots, he quickly loaded most of the gear on his aluminum rack. Then he parceled out the rest for Olivia to carry in a small backpack. Locking the truck, he pocketed the keys and led the way up the trail.

Jeans weren't as comfortable for hiking as shorts, especially new jeans, but he relished the feel of the trail under his feet and the smell of pine and damp earth. He'd brought a fire starter that would help deal with wet kindling. A chill penetrated his cotton shirt, and he wanted a fire to keep them warm as well as to cook their food. He'd elected to leave the stove in the truck.

He called back periodically to check on Olivia,

but she insisted she was fine, so he pressed on. They crossed a couple of shallow streams, using flat rocks as stepping stones. After about forty-five minutes of hiking he found the kind of spot he was looking for. The pine needle-covered area was perfect for pitching the tent, and enough loose rocks lay around that he could construct a small fire pit.

"This will do," he said.

"Oh, thank God." Olivia sank down on a large rock and gulped for air.

"Olivia? Are you okay?" Slipping off his pack, he hurried over to her.

"Just a little…winded."

"You should have said something." He eased the pack from her and dropped it to the ground. "I thought you were fine back there."

"Well, I was, at first." She put a hand to her chest. "And then I kept thinking we'd stop any minute, so I didn't want to call a halt and look like a wimp."

"Aw, Olivia." He felt like a louse. He'd known that she wasn't used to this, but he'd been so focused on getting away from the beaten path that he'd accepted her assurances without turning around to really look at her. If he had he would have known she was struggling. "I'm so sorry."

"Doesn't matter." She gazed up at him. "We're here in our own private little world now, right?"

"That's what I was going for, and yeah, I think we're pretty much alone up here."

"But we need to do stuff before it gets dark." She started to stand.

"I'll do stuff." He placed a restraining hand on her

shoulder. "You watch. In fact, I'll bring you a glass of wine to sip on while I set things up."

"But you were going to teach me how to camp. How can I learn if I sit and drink wine while you do all the work?"

"It's not that complicated. Once you observe how it's done you'll be able to handle it yourself, no problem." He returned to his pack and started pulling things out. Eventually he unearthed the wine box and a couple of plastic glasses.

She laughed. "You're just trying to make me feel better."

"No, I'm actually trying to get you relaxed and tipsy so I can have my way with you inside the tent."

"I don't think you'll have to work quite so hard to achieve that outcome."

"Good to know." But he tapped into the wine box anyway, filled one of the glasses from the plastic spigot and brought it over. Then he crouched down in front of her. "Your suggestion of camping was a lifesaver. I wasn't sure what I was going to do once Jack and I had our confrontation, but this...this really helps."

"I'm glad."

"You've been such a bright spot in this whole crazy episode, Olivia." He looked into her eyes. "No matter what happens, I—"

"If you're preparing me for the fact that you're going back to San Francisco never to return, I don't want to hear it. Besides, I don't believe it. You really like Jackson Hole and you're not that committed to staying in San Francisco. I say screw Jack Chance and make your own plans."

He smiled. "I like your spirit."

"Fortunately that's not all you like." She winked at him and took a long swallow of her wine. "Ah. I think I'll live."

"Excellent news. Sit there while I show off my expertise." He stood and walked over to his pack. "We camping technicians love doing that, you know."

"Then I'll stroke your ego until you let me stroke something more interesting."

His cock twitched and he turned back to her. "On second thought, maybe we should forget about the tent and just sleep under the stars."

"No, thanks. This camping virgin wants to feel safe and cozy inside a zipped-tight tent."

"Fair enough. So allow me to present our room for the night." He unrolled it with a flourish. "Lightweight, but capable of providing shelter for...whatever you have in mind."

"Hmm. You've admitted you spend more time in the woods than in your apartment, and I know for a fact that you like sex, so if this tent could talk, it—"

"—it would say it is brand-new this season, barely used."

Olivia's gaze challenged his. "So are you saying that this tent has never experienced passion?"

Wyatt couldn't help laughing. "Sadly, it has not." Last year's hadn't seen any action, either. He'd have to go back to the tent before that before he could claim one with a sexual past. Or sleeping bags with a sexual past, come to think of it. These had been new last summer.

"Good." She drank more wine. "I like that."

He hid a smile. If she liked the idea of being the first

lover he'd had in this tent, she might be getting possessive, which would be a good sign. It was a short trip from feeling possessive to serious pursuit.

"First we get the poles in place..." He assembled them quickly and fit them into the pockets in the nylon. "And presto, the tent is gloriously erect."

She spewed her wine but fortunately it only went into the dirt and pine needles at her feet. "You said it like that on purpose."

"Maybe." He watched as she licked stray drops of wine from her mouth and his cock twitched again.

"What's next?"

"A couple of self-inflating air mattresses." He pulled the bungee cords off each one and opened the valves before crouching down and allowing them to unroll on the tent floor. One thing about new denim—it didn't have much give to it when a guy had a hard-on. He stood, grimacing.

She gazed at his crotch. "Something else seems to be inflating."

"Nice of you to notice."

"I know nothing about camping but it seems to me that once you put the sleeping bags on those rapidly inflating air mattresses, which are übercool, by the way, you're in business."

"Well, the tent's ready, but I haven't constructed a fire pit or gathered wood or..." He had the good sense to stop listing chores as she drained the last of her wine, set down the glass and started untying her sneakers. He was even smart enough to grab the sleeping bags and unroll them on top of the air mattresses.

When he stood and turned back to her, he was

greeted by a sight that put the ultimate strain on the fly of his new jeans. She'd taken off both her T-shirt and her bra, and was in the process of unfastening her jeans.

He must have let out a little moan of need, because she glanced up. "Those jeans look uncomfortable," she said with a tiny smile. "Why don't you take them off?"

"Great suggestion." But before he did that he rummaged in his pack for the item he should have pulled out even before the wine. Tossing the box of condoms into the tent, he proceeded to get naked, but he was slower than Olivia. For someone who had never been camping, she sure did know how to occupy a tent in a hurry.

By the time he dropped to his knees to crawl in, she'd unzipped both sleeping bags and was nestled on the soft flannel interior like a centerfold.

He took a moment to admire her lying there. This tent would never look the same to him now. "I think you're getting the hang of this camping business," he murmured.

"I have a good teacher." Her gaze roamed over him in frank appreciation. "Coming in?"

"You know it."

"Don't forget to close that zipper thing. I like being close to nature, but I don't want nature to get too close, if you know what I mean."

"I hope that doesn't include me." He turned back once he was inside and zipped the flap.

"Actually, I was just thinking that I don't know you well enough."

"For what?" He glanced back at her, hoping to hell she wasn't about to shut down all his fantasies about having sex in this tent.

"I just think I need to get better acquainted with you if we're going to share a tent tonight."

"You want to talk...now?" He could barely contain his disappointment.

"I was imagining more of a hands-on learning experience."

"Oh." His disappointment evaporated in the heat of her gaze and his heart thudded heavily in anticipation of what she had in mind.

She patted the sleeping bag next to her. "Lie down on your back so I can get started."

He complied because only an idiot wouldn't follow directions like that. "Is this like when I used to play doctor with Mary Sue Jefferson in first grade?"

"Sort of." She cupped his face in one hand and feathered a kiss over his mouth. "Except I venture to say that I will do a better job than Mary Sue ever dreamed of doing."

As she began touching him, kissing him and generally rocking his world, he had to agree with that assessment. She became *very* well acquainted with all parts of his body, especially the part that had been standing at attention ever since she proposed this learning exercise. She licked and nibbled her way around that territory until he regretfully had to call a halt.

"But I have more to learn." She closed her mouth over the tip of his cock and sucked gently.

"Any second now you're going to learn that my control is shot." He gasped and clenched his jaw. "And then you'll learn how long it takes me to recover."

She lifted her head and met his gaze, but she kept her clever fingers wrapped around his johnson. "So I have to choose between making you come or allowing us both to come."

"That pretty well sums it up."

"Let me think about it." She ran her tongue over her lips as she slid her hand up and down in a motion guaranteed to produce results.

He grasped her wrist. "Much as I've loved this, and I have, I want to enjoy the entire experience, at least this time." He removed her hand from his cock and rolled to his side. "We can fool around with this program later, but…" rolling her to her back, he moved over her "…I want the whole enchilada, me and you, doing it the old-fashioned way."

Her blue eyes darkened and her breathing changed. "I could be talked into that."

"Good." Balancing on his forearm, he reached for the box of condoms. Dexterity proved valuable as he opened the box one-handed and pulled out a foil package.

"I'll take it from here." She plucked it from his grasp and ripped it open. "Now that I've mapped the territory."

"Just make it quick." He groaned at the brush of her fingers as she began the task. "I'm holding on by a thread." The snap of latex was music to his ears.

"That's it." She cupped his face and gazed up at him. "Bombs away."

That made him laugh, but it didn't stop him from burying himself up to the hilt. Laughing and thrusting made for an interesting combination, but soon the laughter faded as incredible friction claimed all his attention.

Holding his gaze, she arched upward, catching his rhythm and intensifying each stroke with movement of her own. Her lips parted and her breath came in tiny gasps, then whimpers, then cries of pleasure.

His breath hissed out as he felt her first spasm. "This is so good."

She moaned. "Yes."

He bore down, picked up the pace, felt his own climax hovering, reined it in. "I hope...we can...do it again...sometime."

She gulped for air. "Me, too. Oh, me, too!" She came then, his name a shout of joy on her lips.

Surrendering to the fierce pressure in his groin, he erupted with a groan of pure pleasure. As he lay there panting, careful not to collapse completely onto her, she sighed.

"Now the tent has known passion," she murmured.

"Yes." He drew a shaky breath. "It most certainly has."

WYATT DIDN'T GET THE FIRE built until after dark, but he was enough of a pro to accomplish it using a flashlight. Olivia was suitably impressed with his skills and told him so. This camping gig was turning out to be fun.

She'd felt quite daring when she'd exited the tent naked as a jaybird, as her father would say. She'd put her clothes back on, though, because once the sun had gone down the chill had set in. Knowing her hair was a mess after rolling around in the tent with Wyatt, she'd tied it back with the scrunchie she'd had the presence of mind to tuck in her pocket before leaving her purse in Wyatt's truck.

As they ate spaghetti and drank more wine, Olivia's thoughts went back to the reason they were here in the first place—Wyatt's problem with Jack. In some ways, it was none of her business. And yet, it was her business if the feud between the half brothers affected whether Wyatt would move his company to the Jackson Hole area or leave it in San Francisco.

If Wyatt moved to Shoshone, they had a future. If he stayed in California, they did not. She wasn't ready to commit to that future yet because she didn't want another failed engagement on her conscience. But she wouldn't mind having a fighting chance to create something lasting between them.

If she and Wyatt were ever going to be more than a fling, his attitude toward Jack had to be addressed before they returned to the ranch. She couldn't think of a better time than now, when they sat snuggled side by side on a ground cloth in front of the fire.

Wyatt had set their tin plates aside and wrapped his arm around her waist as they finished their wine. They'd made wonderful love an hour ago and she hoped they'd do it again soon.

But after another round of lovemaking she expected both of them to fall into an exhausted sleep. It had been an eventful couple of days. She'd sleep better knowing they'd talked this out.

Maybe he was already rethinking his stance. She hoped so, and she'd start from there. "Wyatt?"

He pulled her closer. "Ready for bed?" His voice was rich with promise.

"Not quite." She finished her wine and set her glass beside her. "I want to ask you something."

"Ask away."

"Now that some time has gone by, do you have any thoughts about Jack and the Last Chance?"

He tensed. "I'd rather not talk about Jack tonight, if you don't mind."

She gave a mental sigh. This wasn't going to be easy, after all. "I do mind. I...I have a stake in this now. I'd like you to move your business here, and I'm worried that after your fight with Jack you'll reconsider that."

He was quiet for a while, but he finally responded. "I won't lie to you, Olivia. Jack's behavior this afternoon makes me wonder if I'm just beating my head against a stone wall."

"I wouldn't look at it quite that way."

"No? I told you what he said."

"Yes, and you told me what you said." She chose her words carefully. "Obviously each of you has an ax to grind, but—"

"But what, Olivia? How can I expect to make progress with Jack when all he can think about is my connection to Diana, the woman he hates?"

"It's logical that he would. I'm sure he's still devastated that she abandoned him and chose to raise another family."

"But if only he could see that he got rid of a lousy mother and ended up with Sarah, who is wonderful. But no, he has the nerve to be upset with me, as if I had it better than he did because our mother stuck around while I was growing up."

Olivia was determined to hang on to her patience. "But if you could see it from his viewpoint, then maybe—"

"How about if he saw it from my viewpoint? If he had to spend even a week with Diana, he'd be a raving maniac. I guarantee it."

She said the words as gently as she knew how. "It's not a competition to prove who suffered more, Wyatt."

"I realize that, but her leaving him turned out to be for his own good." Wyatt's body had gone rigid with frustration. "Why can't he see that?"

She gazed into his angry eyes. "Does it really matter what he sees or doesn't see? Why not just acknowledge that he had a rough time and move on?"

"I wish it could be that simple, but I don't think it can. He couldn't even trust me to hold his kid, as if I'm permanently tainted because I'm Diana's son." His voice vibrated with pain.

"Give him another chance. I mean, when the stakes are this high, and you want to be part of this family—"

"Yeah, what a fantasy that was. To think I imagined blending into life on the ranch. I can kiss that idea goodbye."

"Maybe not. Wyatt, be the bigger man. Extend the olive branch to your brother."

"I've done that, and he slapped it out of my hand."

She stood up and faced him. "Could it be because you insisted on claiming that you were more damaged than he was?"

"Olivia, I made the trip from San Francisco. Twice. He wasn't particularly welcoming the first time, but I thought he'd get used to the idea, and I…I thought I'd finally found where I belonged."

"I know." She ached for him.

His jaw tightened. "But I can't keep laying everything on the line. It's time for Jack to step up."

"It's not a matter of stepping up." She began to wonder if she was wasting her breath. "It's a matter of wanting to heal this breach, of being willing to swallow your pride. Don't abandon the possibility of being part of that ranch community because you're too proud to try again."

He sighed and shook his head. "It's no use. I feel like the stray dog that keeps getting turned away. A man has to maintain some sense of dignity."

"But if you don't make peace with Jack then you and I have no future, because I'm here to stay. You do get that, right?"

He gazed at her, his expression unreadable. "Yes, and I'm sorry."

Which meant he wasn't going to try and work things out with Jack. As the reality of that sank in, a blanket of misery enveloped her. She'd watched him pull off one heroic deed after another, including spending time with her father and losing gracefully at chess.

She'd thought all he'd need was a nudge to be a hero in this instance, too. Instead he clung to his belief that he'd done all he could. He seemed willing to doom their relationship before it ever really blossomed.

16

ACCEPTING DEFEAT, OLIVIA helped Wyatt secure the camp for the night. They sacked the food and dishes together and used a rope to hang the bundle from a tree branch. Then they made sure the fire was totally out before they crawled into the tent, both of them fully dressed. Olivia put her shoes in the corner where she could find them easily.

"Let me get the flap." Wyatt started to zip it.

"That's okay. I might need to go out during the night."

"You're sure? I thought you were worried about critters."

"I'm more worried about desperately having to pee and not being able to find the tab on the zipper."

"Okay." He settled back on his sleeping bag.

They lay there in silence because there was nothing more to say. Although Olivia might have gotten some sleep, she felt as if she spent the whole night staring into the dark, waiting for the first light of dawn. She'd had such hopes for Wyatt, but if he put his pride ahead of all he had to gain by staying in Jackson Hole then he wasn't the man for her. Time to cut her losses and get away from him before he broke her heart permanently. It already felt slightly cracked.

After an eternity her surroundings became more visible. The sun wasn't up yet but it soon would be, and by then she wanted to be out of here. Wyatt slept soundly, his breathing rhythmic and undisturbed.

Her heart ached for him, and for Jack and their inability to see each other's point of view. But she'd given peacemaking a shot and Wyatt was more unwilling to bend than she'd realized. Maybe Sarah would be able to effect some change in the status quo, but Olivia wouldn't bet on it. Both men seemed as immovable as the granite rock marking the sacred site.

That rock was her destination now. Logic told her she wouldn't make it all the way back to the ranch before Wyatt woke up and missed her, even factoring in the time he'd take to break camp. She might not even have the stamina to walk all the way back. But she could make it to that rock and wait for him there.

Slipping out of the tent with her shoes, she shivered and zipped her hoodie. Then she sat down and put on her sneakers. Any distance she covered before Wyatt caught up with her would be that much less time she had to spend with him. After what they'd shared she couldn't bear the thought of packing up the camping supplies and enduring a hike with him back down the hillside.

But she needed to leave a note so he wouldn't panic. That was a challenge, but eventually she found a scrap of cardboard left over from the pasta box. A small piece of charred wood from the fire worked as a charcoal pencil.

"Headed down the trail. See you on the road or back at the ranch."

Moving as quietly as she could, she crept out of the camp and started down the trail. Every second she expected to hear Wyatt calling out to her, but he must have been really exhausted because the surrounding forest was silent in the gray light.

Once she was out of sight of the tent, she sighed and quickened her pace. She'd made it. Without a pack to weigh her down, she should reach the dirt road in no time. Her hair swung forward as she walked, and as she shoved it behind her ears, she realized that she'd lost the scrunchie sometime during the night. She sure as hell wasn't going back for it, though.

As she continued to walk the forest creatures began waking up. Birds chirped in the branches overhead and the underbrush rustled off to her left. A squirrel hopped out, bounded across the trail and scurried up a tree. Cute.

If Olivia were a heroine in a Disney movie she would break into song about now and the forest creatures would gather round and join in. Then Prince Charming would add his voice to the melody as he rode toward her on his gallant white horse. He'd scoop her into his arms and true love would be born.

Yeah, right. She could kiss that fairy tale goodbye. Apparently the guy who'd come to her rescue riding his gallant white truck hadn't read the script. It was all downhill from here. Ha.

She appreciated the ease of going down instead of up,

though. And when she caught a glimpse of three deer watching her through the trees, she stopped to admire them. The sight of the deer reminded her that there was a whole world out there that didn't revolve around her and her problems.

That made a very good case for getting out into nature on a regular basis, and she decided to do that. After all, she now lived in the middle of God's country. She could understand why Wyatt had chosen the profession he had, because seeing natural beauty on a constant basis could give a person perspective. Too bad he hadn't gained a little more of it.

Now that she'd challenged his assumptions he'd probably pack up his truck and leave the area for good. If she felt dismal knowing that would be the outcome, she'd have to get over it. Maybe she'd do that by taking more hikes. Obviously it wasn't that complicated, since she was doing fine all by herself this morning.

As she congratulated herself on her excellent plan to walk back to the road, showing some initiative and independence, she came to a fork in the trail. For one uneasy moment she stood there, undecided. The rocks and trees along each path looked about the same.

Finally she shrugged and chose the path on her left. Both of them headed downhill, and if she didn't come out right where the truck was parked, so what? All she needed to find was the road that would take her to the sacred site, and eventually, the ranch.

WYATT WOKE UP WITH A VAGUE feeling that something was wrong. He lay there with his eyes closed and quickly remembered why he'd feel that way. Olivia, who had seemed so supportive at first, had let him know last night she didn't approve of how he was handling things with Jack.

The tent was very quiet, so when he turned to find she wasn't lying next to him, he wasn't surprised. Her shoes were gone, but a neon-green bit of cloth lay on the sleeping bag and he picked it up. She'd put that in her hair last night after they'd had such great sex in here.

His gut twisted. He wished they'd had the kind of night he'd been hoping for, with a lot more sex and absolutely no discussion about Jack. And now...now he didn't know where they were. Nowhere, probably.

He didn't dare dwell on that thought too long or he'd discover just how into her he was. Technically they hadn't known each other long enough for him to be hooked on her. Then he thought about that kiss while they stood on the sacred site. He'd never had that kind of reaction to a woman before, where he'd had visions of a future with her flash before his eyes.

They should probably talk some more. He'd bet she could use a cup of coffee. Yeah, that was the way to go. Breakfast, coffee, the peaceful sounds of the forest first thing in the morning—that would bring them closer together.

Feeling more positive, he grabbed his hiking boots from the corner of the tent, stuck her hair doodad in his pocket and crawled out. A quick scan of the area as he sat down to put on his boots told him she wasn't there, but that didn't worry him. She'd probably found a private place to pee.

After he took care of that little matter himself, he walked back into camp expecting to see her. When she wasn't there, he called her name. No answer. He called again, louder this time. Still no answer.

For the first time since discovering she wasn't beside him in the tent, he became concerned. He searched the campsite more thoroughly and finally discovered the note she'd left on a scrap of cardboard. *Shit*. She had a head start but he was pretty damned fast when he needed to be.

Leaving everything except for his cell phone, he loped down the trail. A couple of times he paused to call out for her, but when there was no answer he wondered if she would even answer if she heard him. Maybe not. He kept going and made it to the truck in twenty minutes.

Still no sign of her. Her purse and cell phone were in the cab where she'd left them, but then they would be. She didn't have keys.

Fighting panic, he unlocked the truck and started it up. She wasn't in shape for a long walk, but adrenaline could make a difference. He drove back the way they'd come, constantly scanning the road for her.

When he reached the sacred site and still didn't see her, the cold sweat of anxiety trickled down his spine. This was not good. Not good at all.

And he wasn't going to waste any more time. He got out his cell and called the ranch, thinking he'd get either Mary Lou or Sarah. Instead he got—Murphy's Law—Jack.

He wasn't sure why Jack was answering the ranch phone early in the morning when he had his own house on the property where he lived with his wife and that baby he didn't want Wyatt touching. But no matter. This was an emergency and he had a feeling Jack was good at handling those, in spite of being stubborn as a mule.

"It's Wyatt," he said. "Is Olivia there?"

"Here? I thought she was with you."

"We had a...disagreement last night and I think she must have decided to walk back."

"I'll check." Jack was swearing as he got off the phone.

Sarah picked it up. "Wyatt? What's going on?"

"I think Olivia decided to walk back to the ranch."

"What on earth would have made her— Hold on. Jack's here." She came back in a second. "He says she's not in the house and her Cherokee is still parked where she left it. He's driving out there. Where should he meet you?"

"I'm at the sacred site, but I'm going back to the trailhead and make sure I didn't miss her somewhere between here and there. Tell Jack to keep going beyond the site about two miles and look for my truck. I'll stay there and wait for him."

"Got it. And, Wyatt?"

"Yeah?" He braced himself for whatever blame she might heap on his head.

"Don't worry, son. You two will find her."

"Thanks, Sarah." He wasn't used to quiet confidence in a mother figure. He was used to blame and panic. Rafe had done a disappearing act when they were about ten and Diana had been next to useless.

Yeah, he envied Jack having Sarah as a steadying influence most of his life, but Olivia's comments had stuck with him. He knew what total rejection felt like. He'd just experienced it from his half brother. How much worse would it be if it was your mother, and you were only two?

Turning the truck around, he started back down the road, going slower, checking the roadside in case she'd gone into the trees to rest or…no, he wouldn't start imagining all the terrible things that could happen to her alone out here. That wouldn't help.

No matter how thoroughly he searched both sides of the road as he crept back down the road, he saw nothing but rabbits, some quail, and back in the trees, a lone buck. What color had her blouse been? Oh, yeah, the same green as the scrunchie in his pocket. It was a color that could blend with the landscape, especially if she'd fallen down and… Once again he pulled his thoughts away from disaster.

Because the plain fact was he couldn't lose her. Not physically, and not emotionally either. She'd only tried to help last night, and he'd been a jerk who didn't realize what an incredible woman she was. She probably wanted to knock his and Jack's heads together, and he had to admit they deserved it.

But in order for her to do that, they had to find her. And by God, they would. He'd thought he never wanted to speak to Jack again, and here he was filled with relief and gratitude that his half brother was coming to the rescue.

OLIVIA HAD DONE SOME BONEHEAD things in her life, but this one had to be the worst. She'd hiked for well over an hour, although she couldn't be sure because she had no watch. And she had no idea where she was.

Instead of continuing down, the trail she'd chosen

ran along the side of the hillside. Once she realized her mistake, she'd turned around and started back only to find another fork she hadn't noticed before. Once again, she'd picked wrong.

She'd crossed a stream, thinking she was finally headed in the right direction because she remembered she and Wyatt had crossed two streams. The trail ended in a bluff that dropped thirty feet. She gazed out across the canopy of trees and searched in vain for the road. If it was there she couldn't see it from where she stood.

After wandering around on different trails, she'd finally had to admit that she was truly lost. And what did she, a girl from Pittsburgh, know about getting lost in the woods? Somewhere she'd read that you were supposed to signal searchers with something like a mirror or smoke.

She had no mirror and no matches. No doubt Wyatt had all that kind of stuff, but she'd elected, in her infinite wisdom, to set out on her own and leave her wilderness guide. But he was looking for her. She never doubted that for a second.

The only tool she had available was her voice, so she sat down on the bluff and started shouting for help. That lasted for about thirty seconds before her throat hurt. All she'd accomplished was putting a major scare into the little brown birds watching her from a nearby branch.

Besides, if Wyatt was searching, wouldn't he be calling for her? Therefore, if she couldn't hear him, he couldn't hear her. Then she remembered something else she'd heard about getting lost. Stay put and let the searchers come to you.

She could do that. She was dead tired, thirsty and hungry. If she sat here and listened for Wyatt calling her name, then she could respond when she heard him. Although she'd wanted to get as far away from him as possible this morning, she would be very glad to see him now.

She stretched out on the rock in the sunshine. With her head cradled on her arm, she closed her eyes. Just one short nap was all she needed. Then she'd be fresh and ready to respond to her rescuers. In seconds she dozed off.

WYATT PARKED THE TRUCK at the trailhead and got out. He wanted to start back up the trail to search some more, but he'd told Jack he'd wait for him. So he paced beside the truck and tried to estimate how long it would take Jack to get there.

No matter how long it took, waiting for Jack was the bright thing to do. Jack had grown up here and knew the trails, plus two searchers were better than one. If they didn't find her in the next couple of hours Wyatt was prepared to call in Search and Rescue.

But no need to get the authorities involved if it wasn't absolutely necessary. Wyatt knew instinctively that Jack would rather handle something like this internally if at all possible. Olivia hadn't been missing long…. *Missing.* What a stomach-turning, sweat-inducing concept. He wanted her back. In every sense of the word.

About two centuries went by before Wyatt saw a truck coming toward him. Because the road was still slightly muddy, the truck stirred up no dust. This time

Jack drove an ordinary ranch truck, which was a lot less imposing than the cherry-red semi.

When Jack parked the truck and climbed out, he looked every inch the cowboy in his Stetson, long-sleeved shirt and jeans. Every inch except for his feet. He had on deep-tread hiking boots.

Apparently he caught Wyatt staring. "You're not the only one allowed to wear them, you know."

"Yeah, but I didn't think—"

"That I'd tarnish my cowboy image?" Jack's dark eyes were neither hostile nor friendly. "My other boots are for riding and dancing, not for tramping through the forest." He walked around the front of the truck and opened the passenger door. "End of the line, pooch. Time to get to work."

No way. Wyatt came to the passenger side in time to watch Jack lift Rodney Dangerfield to the ground and snap a leash on the dog's collar. But the leash wasn't Rodney's only accessory. He was also wearing a bright orange life vest, a very snug life vest. The bottom of it scraped the ground.

"My God. He looks like…like…"

"A pig in a blanket? That's what I said, but Mom wanted him on the job and he has to wear his vest, even if it's a tad small, in case we hit water."

Rodney gazed up at Wyatt with his typical woebe-gone expression, which clearly said, "See what I have to put up with?" But his white-tipped tail wagged as if he'd accepted his lot.

Wyatt crouched down to scratch behind the dog's ears. "Thanks, Rod. Glad you're here."

"Now for the million-dollar question," Jack said. "Do you have anything of Olivia's we can give him to sniff?"

"Yeah, I do." Wyatt stood and fished in his pocket.

"I warn you, if you pull a pair of panties out of there I might have to deck you on general principles."

"You'd probably enjoy the excuse, but no such luck." He took out the green scrunchie. "She left this in the tent."

"Good. That should work. Got water? I forgot to bring any."

"Good thought. She'll be parched after hiking around all morning. Let me get my spare canteen." Wyatt sprinted back to his camper, grabbed the canteen and slung the strap over his shoulder.

"Okay, now let Rodney sniff that hair gizmo."

Wyatt hunkered down next to Rodney again. "Here you go, Rod. Find Olivia. Find her for us."

The basset made snuffling sounds as he inspected the scrunchie.

"That should do it," Jack said. "Okay, Rodney. Earn your keep."

17

WYATT STUFFED THE SCRUNCHIE back in his pocket in case they needed it later to refresh Rodney's memory. Nose to the ground, Rodney started toward the trail. That wasn't surprising. Olivia had walked that way yesterday afternoon.

As they started up the path, Wyatt decided to speak up. "I've never worked with a tracking dog before, but Olivia's scent could lead us to the camp because she walked up that way last night. But it will be a waste of time because she's not there now."

"I'm no expert, but I think he'll follow her old scent until he picks up something fresher." Jack allowed Rodney to lead the way. "At that stage we'll know we're tracking where she went more recently."

"Okay. That's logical." Concerns eased, Wyatt followed behind Jack. "Didn't expect you to answer the phone at the house this morning."

"That's because you don't know Sarah well enough yet."

"I don't get what you mean."

"Last night was supposed to be a party, and she

didn't want any more unpleasantness so she didn't deal with me then. I was called on the carpet first thing this morning, though."

Wyatt winced. "You know, Jack, I—"

"Save it. She's right. You're a guest in our home."

"Uninvited."

"Doesn't matter. Mom took you in, gave you a bed and showed you the best of Last Chance hospitality. I treated you like an intruder. I...had my reasons, all tied up with my kid and Diana, but...I regret how that all came down."

Wyatt could only imagine what it cost Jack to admit that he'd mishandled a situation. His chest tightened with empathy. "I regret the things I said, too, Jack. For the record, I got some similar behavior tips from Olivia. Thing is, I wasn't in a mood to hear them."

After another moment of silence, Jack blew out a breath. "When are we ever ready to hear shit like that?"

Wyatt smiled. "Good point. Speaking for myself, I can be a stubborn son of a bitch." He realized this kind of high-intensity conversation was best carried on exactly the way they were doing it, in the midst of a serious task, when they didn't have the opportunity to sit and look at each other.

"I've been called that a time or two," Jack said. They walked in silence for several minutes while Rodney kept his nose to the ground.

Wyatt wondered if that was the end of what they'd say on the subject. If so, that was okay. They'd made some progress.

But then Jack spoke again. "Sarah mentioned something this morning and I…" He took a deep breath. "I think she might be right about that, too."

"What's that?"

"She wondered if my rejection of you was payback, both to Diana, for rejecting me, and to you, because… because you didn't seem to understand how much…"

Wyatt wasn't going to make him say it. "I didn't," he said quietly. "But I do now. And it's partly because you rejected me, so in a way, you did me a favor there."

Jack's laugh was short. "Yeah, well, you won't get Sarah to agree with you."

"I might. Someday. That's assuming…" Now he was the one reluctant to say what he was thinking, in case he was wrong about where this exchange was heading.

"If you're wondering if you can hang around, the answer is yeah, I'd like that." Jack cleared his throat. "I'd like that a lot."

The tightness in Wyatt's chest loosened a little. Olivia was still out there and he wouldn't be able to relax until they found her, but knowing he and Jack were coming to an understanding gave him hope that they'd find Olivia, too. Between Wyatt's determination and Jack's knowledge of the area, they made a good team. Well, and Rodney, of course. Couldn't forget the basset hound and his excellent nose.

"Just one thing," Jack said.

"What's that?"

"Having you around—I'm okay with that. But having Diana show up is a whole other deal."

"Right." Wyatt felt the anxiety underlying Jack's statement.

"I'm doing my damnedest to separate you from her

in my mind," Jack continued. "I didn't do that very well last night, and when I saw you with Archie I had a sudden image of her holding him, and I...I really lost it."

Wyatt swallowed. "I understand. I won't let her become a problem." And he vowed that she wouldn't mess this up, for him, for Jack or for little Archie.

"Yeah? How are you going to keep her away?"

"Simple. Tell her she'll have to travel almost two hours' round-trip to get a decent latte. Issue handled."

Jack laughed. "Okay. That works."

It was the first time Wyatt had heard Jack laugh. He grinned to himself. Maybe he'd finally get to see the lighter side of Jack Chance.

OLIVIA WOKE TO LOUD BAYING of the kind she'd only heard in movies when they were tracking escaped convicts with bloodhounds. Rodney! Leaping up, she prayed that the baying was coming from the throat of a dog she knew and not from bloodhounds chasing an ax murderer through the woods.

She decided to take her chances. "I'm here!" She yelled as loud as she could, although her throat was dry from lack of water. "Over here!"

"Olivia!" Wyatt's voice had to be the sweetest sound in the universe.

"It's me!" She ran in the direction of the baying and Wyatt's voice. "You found me!"

Wyatt broke through the trees and they practically knocked each other down.

"Oh, my God." He held her tight, rocking her back and forth. "Oh, my God. You scared the crap out of me."

"I scared the crap out of myself." She hugged him

back just as hard. "But I knew you'd come. So I finally remembered if you're lost you're supposed to stay in one place, so I did." She heard Rodney yelping and whining, but she needed to keep holding on to Wyatt for just a little longer.

"Are you okay?" He pulled back to look at her. "Oh, I brought water." He lifted the strap over his head and unscrewed the cap.

"That's fabulous. I'm dying of thirst." She started to gulp it down.

"Go easy. Don't want you getting sick."

"Thanks." She made herself sip it.

"Sorry to interrupt, but this dog is going nuts trying to say hello."

That's when she finally realized Wyatt and Rodney weren't her only saviors. Jack Chance stood there holding a very taut leash. Rodney was ready to choke himself trying to reach her. And he was wearing…her hand went to her mouth to stifle a laugh. She shouldn't laugh at the dog who had so valiantly come to her rescue.

"Oh, Rodney." Handing the canteen to Wyatt, she went over to the dog and dropped to her knees so she could give him a proper hug. He slobbered all over her face and she didn't care. "You are the most handsome dog in the world, Rodney. When we get back I'm booking you an appointment for the works—shampoo, cut, blow-dry, nails, massage, you name it."

Rodney wiggled happily in her arms, whining as if to say he'd love that very much.

"It's his first official rescue," Jack said. "Guess I should give him the doggie treats I brought along."

"Definitely." Olivia stood and brushed off her jeans

as relief gave way to contrition. "Listen, you guys, I'm sorry to cause you all this trouble. Going off on my own like that was pretty dumb."

"Ah, it's just a rookie mistake." Wyatt sounded amazingly cheerful under the circumstances. "All's well that ends well."

"Yeah, it gave us a chance to test out the dog." Jack pulled two biscuits out of his pocket and tossed one to Rodney.

Rodney missed it, which both men seemed to find hilarious.

"Great tracker," Wyatt said. "But I wouldn't place any bets on him in a Frisbee tournament."

"You never know. With a little training…" Jack tossed the second biscuit in the air and Rodney missed that one, too.

Wyatt grinned at him. "The day you put Rodney in a Frisbee tournament is the day I dance *Swan Lake* in a tutu."

"You're on, twinkle toes. I already have it on good authority that you can shake your booty, so start practicing."

"Same to you, dog whisperer."

Olivia couldn't believe her ears. Somehow, some way, Jack and Wyatt had abandoned their hostility toward each other. Just like that. She didn't get it, but she wasn't going to question it either.

"Well, this has been fun," Jack said, "but some of us have work to do, so I'll be taking this Frisbee-champ-in-training back to my truck and heading for the ranch. Olivia, you can come with me or help our future ballerina pack up his gear. Up to you."

Olivia looked at Wyatt. "You left everything at the campsite?"

"Well, *yeah.*"

"Oh."

"You thought I'd take the time to break camp when I knew you were somewhere out here by yourself?"

She saw the depth of concern in his eyes and knew she hadn't given him nearly enough credit. "I really screwed up, Wyatt. I'm so sorry."

His expression softened. "It's okay. I understand why you wanted to head out. Listen, you're probably exhausted. Don't worry about the camping gear. I'll bring it back down."

"No, I'm going to help you."

"Really, you don't have to—"

"I'm going to help you, damn it! It's the least I can do for someone I scared the crap out of, don't you think?"

Jack laughed. "She wants to help you, man. Take it from a guy who wasn't always smart about these things. Stop arguing with the lady and go with the flow."

Wyatt looked as if he wanted to say something else, but then he scrubbed a hand over his face. "All right. I'll take that advice."

"Good. See you two back at the ranch, then. Oh, and I'll take care of calling Mom to let her know Olivia's safe and sound."

"Thanks, Jack." Wyatt held out his hand.

"You're welcome...bro." Jack clasped his hand and the two men exchanged a long look.

Olivia had thought this day might never come, and yet it all seemed so easy now. Funny how quickly things could change sometimes.

Jack and Rodney took off and Olivia stood gazing at Wyatt. "That's amazing," she said.

"Yeah." Wyatt gave her a wry smile. "All it took was a couple of smart women to straighten out a couple of dumb guys." He stepped closer but didn't touch her. "Thanks for talking turkey to me last night. It took some time for it to filter through my thick skull, but of course you were right, about everything."

"I don't care who's right and who's wrong. I'm just happy that you and your brother are going to be friends."

"Me too." He hesitated. "What about us? Are we going to be friends?"

"I think there's a very good chance we are."

He looked down at the ground for a couple of seconds and cleared his throat. When his gaze met hers, it was completely unguarded and filled with passion and longing. "That's not good enough," he said.

"No?" Her heart began to pound.

"No." He reached for her, drawing her into his arms. "I want to be your friend, but I want much more than that. I want to be your lover."

She looked into his eyes. "The job's yours. You're very good at—"

"But I want more than that."

"You want to clean my house? Wyatt, I don't know what to say. I've always dreamed of—"

"Smart-ass." He pulled her in close. "I want to be the guy."

"The guy?"

"Yeah. The one you count on. I want to be the one you come to when something terrible happens and you're overwhelmed with grief. I want to be the one you race to when something great happens and you're filled with joy. I want to be there for you, Olivia."

Happiness hummed through her as she wrapped her arms around him and hung on, loving the solid warmth of his body. "Sounds like you're getting serious."

"Yeah." He smiled. "I am. Think you could be getting serious, too?"

She nodded.

"That's good news."

"But about cleaning my house. I really could use someone to—"

"I'll clean your damned house." His mouth hovered over hers. "I'll do whatever it takes if you'll let me love you."

"I think that can be arranged if the agreement goes both ways."

"Meaning?" His mouth brushed hers.

"If I let you love me, you let me love you."

"Lady, you have a deal." His mouth found hers, and she could swear the woodland creatures began to sing, just like in a Disney movie.

Epilogue

"So there you have it." Sarah picked up her mug of coffee and took a sip. "Wyatt has to lead a few wilderness expeditions, but in his spare time he'll be taking the necessary steps to transfer his business to Shoshone."

Sitting across from her at the kitchen table, Mary Lou nodded. "I think that's great. And his mother still doesn't know about little Archie?"

"Wyatt's not planning to volunteer the information, but I feel guilty every time I think about it. I'm wondering if maybe I should contact her and—"

"Don't buy trouble, Sarah. She hasn't exactly inquired about whether her son married and had a child, now, has she?"

"No, she hasn't." Sarah cradled her coffee mug. "That's a valid point. And she may end up here even without me contacting her. I fully expect Wyatt and Olivia to get married before the summer's out. They're so in love. I can't imagine Wyatt marrying Olivia without his family here, can you?"

"No, I can't. But do you think Jack sees all that coming down the pike?"

Sarah nodded. "I think he knew from the first time Wyatt showed up that it was only a matter of time before he had to confront his mother."

"His biological mother. You're his real mother."

"I appreciate you saying that, Mary Lou, but…he'll never be totally free of her, so maybe it's better if he faces her and gets it over with. If Wyatt and Olivia get married soon, as I predict, it will force the issue. That could be intense, but a good thing in the end."

"Guess so." Mary Lou pushed back her chair. "More coffee?"

"No, I should get busy. Pete's coming by in an hour to go over last-minute details for when the teenagers arrive."

"About that."

Something in Mary Lou's voice alerted Sarah. "Are you having second thoughts? I hope not, because they'll show up in a week and a half."

"I know." Mary Lou fiddled with her mug. "The thing is, Watkins finally wore me down."

"Wore you down?" Then Sarah's eyes widened. "You're getting *married*?"

Mary Lou actually blushed. "Stupid, isn't it?"

"No! It's wonderful! But we don't have much time to plan with the kids coming, but don't worry about that. We'll figure something out. Mary Lou, I'm so excited for you!" She hurried over to give her friend a fierce hug.

"No planning needed," Mary Lou said. "We're going on a twenty-one-day cruise starting next week, and we'll have the captain marry us on board the ship. It seemed like an easy solution and wouldn't cause anybody any trouble."

Sarah looked at her old friend in shock. "A cruise? So how long have you been planning this?"

"Not long. You know Tyler still has connections, and she arranged it all." Mary Lou's brow furrowed. "You're not upset, are you?"

"Of course not! It's just a surprise, that's all. A good surprise, but still. And I feel horrible asking this, because your happiness is more important, but what are we going to do about the meals while you're gone?"

"Oh, that's covered. I've asked my niece from Nebraska to come and fill in. Her name's Aurelia Smith, and she's a whiz in the kitchen. She'll be great."

"I'm sure she will be." Sarah took a deep breath and walked back to her chair. "Maybe I'll have a little more coffee after all." This was shaping up to be a morning that required extra caffeine.

As she was taking her first sip, her son Gabe burst into the kitchen. "Houdini's broken out of his stall for the last time. I say we sell that worthless piece of horseflesh."

"Good morning, Gabe." Sarah smiled at her youngest son. "Won't you have some coffee?"

Gabe blew out a breath that ruffled his mustache, a bit of facial hair he loved and his wife, Morgan, was less fond of. "Sure. Sorry, Mom. I've just had it with that horse." He poured himself coffee and came to join them at the table. "I know he's valuable and could be a good stud for us, but he's such a pain in the rear."

"Pete was talking about a trainer who seems to have

a way with horses like Houdini. His name's Matthew Tredway. Ever hear of him?"

"Well, yeah, who hasn't? But he's hard to get. And expensive."

"Pete seems to think he could get him. And Pete's willing to pay the up-front costs because he's convinced Houdini will earn it back later. I just need to clear it with you and your brothers before I give Pete the okay."

"Hey, tell Pete to go for it, Mom. I don't see a downside. I can't imagine Jack or Nick will, either. That horse is getting on everyone's last nerve."

"All right, then." Sarah took another bracing sip of her coffee. People were always coming and going on the Last Chance, and she wouldn't have it any other way. It kept her young.

* * * * *

MILLS & BOON® Book Club
2 Free Books!

Get your free books now at
www.millsandboon.co.uk/freebookoffer

Or fill in the form below and post it back to us

THE MILLS & BOON® BOOK CLUB™—HERE'S HOW IT WORKS: Accepting your free books places you under no obligation to buy anything. You may keep the books and return the despatch note marked 'Cancel'. If we do not hear from you, about a month later we'll send you 4 brand-new stories from the Blaze® series, including a 2-in-1 book priced at £5.49 and two single books priced at £3.49* each. There is no extra charge for post and packaging. You may cancel at any time, otherwise we will send you 4 stories a month which you may purchase or return to us—the choice is yours. *Terms and prices subject to change without notice. Offer valid in UK only. Applicants must be 18 or over. Offer expires 31st January 2013. **For full terms and conditions, please go to www.millsandboon.co.uk/freebookoffer**

Mrs/Miss/Ms/Mr (please circle)

First Name

Surname

Address

Postcode

E-mail

Send this completed page to: Mills & Boon Book Club, Free Book Offer, FREEPOST NAT 10298, Richmond, Surrey, TW9 1BR

Find out more at
www.millsandboon.co.uk/freebookoffer

Visit us Online

0712/K2YEA

Special Offers

Every month we put together collections and longer reads written by your favourite authors.

Here are some of next month's highlights— and don't miss our fabulous discount online!

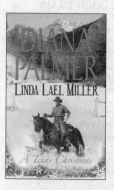

On sale 16th November   On sale 16th November   On sale 7th December

Save 20%
on all Special Releases

The World of Mills & Boon®

There's a Mills & Boon® series that's perfect for you. We publish ten series and, with new titles every month, you never have to wait long for your favourite to come along.

Blaze.
Scorching hot, sexy reads
4 new stories every month

By Request
Relive the romance with the best of the best
9 new stories every month

Cherish™
Romance to melt the heart every time
12 new stories every month

Desire™
Passionate and dramatic love stories
8 new stories every month